SUSAN GOURLEY

Medallion Press, Inc.
Printed in USA

The Keepers of Sulbreth

Susan Gourley

DEDICATION:

Evan Gourley, you're never forgotten.

Published 2010 by Medallion Press, Inc.

The MEDALLION PRESS LOGO
is a registered trademark of Medallion Press, Inc.

Typeset in Adobe Garamond Pro
Printed in the United States of America

ISBN: 978-160542065-3

10 9 8 7 6 5 4 3 2 1
First Edition

ACKNOWLEDGMENTS:

Love and thanks to my father and mother for always pushing me to do my best and for doing without during the lean years so I didn't have to. Thanks to my family for tolerance and patience so I had the time to write, especially Ron. I wouldn't have known where to start without Megan Hart and my friends at CPRW with all their wisdom.

PART ONE

Chapter One

"Not a drop of hot tea," Sir Nick Cassil growled.

Lord Edgar stifled his own grumble. "Perhaps we're both getting too old for this. Chasing about in the wild wood and making a cold camp is for young men with fire in their bellies and lightning in their swords."

Sir Nick squatted beside Edgar. His knees creaked a protest, and a grimace pulled his lips tight behind his beard. "I've still lots of thunder left to be your protector, my lord. Weren't so long ago none of this young bunch of swords could have stood with us."

The moldering leaves from seasons past leached their damp chill through the blanket Edgar used as his seat. Overhead, the heavy boughs of pine waved in a breeze that drew their scent amongst the men crouching in their shelter.

Not even that pleasant aroma chased away Edgar's longing for his own cozy hearth and a bit of warm wine.

Sir Nick rubbed his large hands together. Edgar noted there was still strength in the thick fingers made crooked by years of abuse. One did not wield a sword in battle without breaking a few bones. They'd been through much together. Had they grown soft in these years of peace? Edgar still wondered at his wisdom in hiring an outside sword for this battle.

In the way he had of knowing what Edgar thought, and why not after thirty years, Sir Nick spoke of the hiresword. "He's an odd one. Ice in that one's belly."

"He's done what none of our own hunters could do." The bastard was good, uncanny even, in the wood.

"Shame finding Finn that way," Sir Nick said.

"He must have gotten close for them to catch him."

"They'll pay for that," Sir Nick vowed.

Edgar's gut clenched as it had two days ago when the bastard hiresword led them to Finn's body. Wooden stakes had been driven through each shoulder. Thick ropes tied the stakes to the high branches of an old oak. The terror in the man's eyes told Edgar he'd been alive to feel the stakes tear through his flesh and the ripping agony as his own weight killed him.

"Aye, they'll pay. If they did him so to scare us, they kicked up the wrong fire," Edgar agreed.

Nothing warned them, but suddenly the bastard was there. Cage Stone sank down on his heels across from Edgar and Sir Nick.

Sir Nick cursed while Edgar hoped his old heart wouldn't explode in his chest. The bastard's quiet, unnatural ability to move about disturbed him on some level. The mere presence of the man wrought discomfort, though Edgar could put no word to the reason.

"How did you get by the sentries?" Sir Nick demanded. Was it anger or fear in his protector's growl?

"Your men are uninjured, only inattentive, Sir Nick," Stone answered in an even tone. He turned his cool gaze on Edgar then. The wood lay in thick shadow as the sun sought its rest in the west, but even in the deepening gloom, those dangerous gray eyes gave a man pause.

A shiver ran up Edgar's spine that had little to do with his damp seat. He sensed Sir Nick bristling beside him and held up a hand to forestall his protector's retort. "What did you find, Stone?"

If Sir Nick's anger touched Stone in any way, he gave no sign. Edgar suspected the young man was oblivious. More than his transcendent skills, frightening actually, the bastard's attitude made him a curiosity to others. Bastards occupied a lower rung in Futhark society, but this Cage Stone, though bearing the surname given to all the baseborn, acted as equal to any man. Nothing in his words or tone of voice confirmed Edgar's thoughts, but damn if the bastard didn't somehow hold himself above the rest of them. A quiet arrogance bolstered by rare and superior physical abilities.

"They've posted two watchers. One sits on top of the granite outcropping; one waits inside the tunnel."

"Tough to surprise them. There's too much open ground between here and that cursed tunnel. How did they find that hidden valley?" Sir Nick asked as they'd all wondered since Stone had led them to this spot.

Darkness settled quickly under the thick pines. Stone's light eyes glinted with the meager light as he looked at Sir Nick. "I'll take care of the sentries."

"Without giving us away?" Sir Nick grunted his disbelief.

Stone looked back to Edgar. The slight to Sir Nick was not even subtle. "There's a way along The Edge. They can't see the approach."

"Approach! Along The Edge?" Sir Nick leaned away from Stone.

Edgar sat up straighter and thought about saying a quick blessing to protect himself from the bastard's insanity. "What mean you?"

The bastard confirmed his flight from lucidity. He smiled. "The tunnel and the outlook post are only two long drays from The Edge. The watcher never looks that direction."

"Of course not," Sir Nick said. A long dray was only the length of a grain wagon with a four-horse hitch. "It protects their flank better than a wall forged of steel."

"It only protects from those of faint heart. The way isn't difficult."

Did Stone bait Sir Nick apurpose? "You intend to walk along The Edge?" Edgar asked, sure he comprehended wrongly.

"More of a climb," Stone said. A smug amusement curved his lips.

Even knowing the bastard laughed at their fear, Edgar couldn't find the lordly haughtiness to pull himself above the man. "You cannot."

"Anyone can walk there should the need be great enough," Stone said.

Edgar looked at his protector and saw his own instinctive fear reflected in Sir Nick's usually fierce eyes. All persons feared the boundary of Futhark. A sheer cliff where the land fell away to the sea far below, The Edge was its name. In some ancient time a powerful cataclysm had pushed the great nation of Futhark high to the heavens. The drop from land to sea was an unmeasured, unchallenged distance. Edgar had heard that great waves crashed against the base of Futhark, but no sound of the pounding water came to the ears of men. Too far. Too far and too steep for a man to even risk a look. Edgar had tried once in his youth, but such was the terror of being near The Edge that his legs gave way and would not carry him. He knew only rumors, and no man of his acquaintance had ever found the courage to go even half of a dray from The Edge.

"You mean to walk near . . . ?" Sir Nick didn't finish.

"I already did so earlier this evening. They didn't

see me even in daylight." Stone's amusement was gone. Instead he frowned at something beyond Sir Nick's shoulder. After a moment, Edgar heard the approach of one of his men.

"Lord Edgar, should the men bed down for the night?"

Edgar wondered at Stone's reaction to the young swordsman. The bastard's nostrils flared, and his eyes narrowed.

"Tell them to be still and sit as they are until Sir Nick tells them different." Edgar watched Stone as his man walked back to the rest of his men.

Stone glared at the shadows where the swordsmen waited.

"Is there a problem?" Edgar asked.

"Your men should bathe more often, my lord. I can smell them even when they're downwind."

"Watch your mouth, bastard," Sir Nick snarled.

Stone shrugged. "That one who spoke with Lord Edgar speaks to the others of taking your place, Sir Nick. He seeks the support of the others so he might demonstrate to Lord Edgar his greater qualities to lead."

"How do you know this?" Edgar asked, but it made sense to him. Burns often skipped over Sir Nick's position to speak directly with Edgar as he'd done just now.

"They speak as loudly as they smell. Now, to your bandits, my lord. We wait until the moon sets and the night is as dark as it can be under the stars."

"You take care of the sentries and we ride in without a

challenge?" Was it possible that the bastard would do in days what his own men hadn't achieved in a year's attempt? The frustration of suffering the attacks of the outlaws had eaten at Edgar for so long, he couldn't believe it could end in so simple a manner.

Again a small smile flickered across Stone's face. His very looks—lean body, sun-kissed skin, light eyes, and midnight hair—set him apart from the fairer people of the eastern provinces. The amusement itself seemed foreign on his features.

"How will we know if you're successful in taking the watchers?" Sir Nick asked.

"You may go with me if you wish."

Sir Nick glared, but he didn't volunteer.

"It seems too easy to have them cornered at last," Edgar mused.

"Not so simple or easy," Cage cautioned. "I read the signs of twenty horsemen through the wood. There may be even more who didn't go on the last raid."

"Finally we get back at those murderers," Sir Nick said.

Edgar smiled as he heard the battle eagerness in his protector's words. Even his old bones ached less at the thought of drawing his sword in vengeance.

"There'll be women and children in the camp," Stone warned, a touch of frost replacing his earlier amusement.

"Offspring of scum," Sir Nick muttered, "already in training to be killers and thieves. Bastards and whores, the lot of them."

"Bastards and whores, likely, but made so by the men you hunt. They've done you no harm, and you'll do them none based on what they might do in some unlived future." Stone bit off each word. An unspoken threat hung in the air for long moments. Night insects buzzed and vibrated to fill the silence.

"None of my men would purposely hurt a woman or child," Edgar conceded.

Stone fixed his cool stare on Edgar. Despite the dim moonlight slanting in through minuscule openings in the pines, he was sure the bastard could see him clearly. The bastard turned over his strange thoughts for a long, quiet moment, and then he stood.

"I trust the word of Lord Edgar, but let your men know I have great personal distaste for those who bring harm to the helpless, even if they are whores and bastards. Such persons have their uses to the more entitled; do they not?"

Edgar said nothing as there was no answer that wouldn't insult Stone.

"I'll be on watch if you wish to sleep, my lord." Stone dipped his head in a small nod. He took a few steps toward a great pine, its verdant green black in the night, then disappeared into the shadows.

"That arrogant slag threatened us," Sir Nick said.

"Aye." Lord Edgar wondered what he could do to intimidate a man who dared to walk The Edge. The Edge that filled others with terror and Cage Stone with amusement.

Edgar shook himself. He had hired the bastard to rid his holdings of the brigands. He wanted to get it done and return to his hall, which smelled of clean rushes and fresh bread. He wanted to sit on his cushioned chair that curved around his behind when he sank into it. "Let it alone. We'll use him for what we need done and then send him on his way with his gold. And whatever happens, you will see that none of the ladies or little ones are harmed even if they fight."

"Mistress Tamarin is delayed," Marshal Bachus said as he stalked along the limestone pathway toward Alvara.

"Delayed again?" Alvara groaned. She loved and respected Tamarin, but the aged Keeper tended to lose her focus. "What now?"

"I believe she extended her lesson for the middle students."

Tamarin could speak for days on demons, fell beasts, and teratology. No one knew more about monsters, and Tamarin dispensed her wisdom to the mids in a colorful fashion. Alvara remembered the enthrallment of hearing for the first time of the pestilence the Keepers battled.

"Nothing to do but wait, but we only have seven days left to prepare."

Bachus nodded, and his clear blue eyes sparkled. His stern posture didn't alter, but she knew him well enough to see her own excitement mirrored in him.

Seven days! They had trained for most of their adult lives for this. Alvara couldn't hold it back; she grinned at him.

"We're ready," he said, his own lips twitching in a rare smile.

After so many years together as Marshal and Keeper, Alvara found she and Bachus often thought the same thing at the same time. "Yes, we're ready."

Still, they would use every last moment to study and plan. Tamarin might think of one more thing to warn them of, and that one thing could be the difference between success and failure.

"Would you care for some tea while we wait, Mistress?"

"Only if you share it with me." Alvara didn't treat her Marshal as a servant or hired soldier as some of the Keepers did. She cared for him as her partner, her friend, closer than a husband or a lover. Only to him could she confess her fears, her doubts. To all others she showed only conviction and courage.

Bachus nodded and strode toward the kitchen. His boot heels clicked on the wide slate walk. The tall red maples marching beside the path striped it with shadows from their trunks. The days passed so quickly as they neared their departure time. Only a bit of daylight was left.

Alvara sank onto an oak bench and stared over the green lawn. She loved the peace of this back lot. As Bachus walked, a few maple leaves swirled lazily to the slate and scuttled from beneath his feet. Summer neared its end, and soon winter's cold darkness would conquer the mild fall. It would be even colder if she and Bachus failed.

As if he mirrored her thoughts again, Bachus slowed and then stopped. He turned but did not look at her. He stared over her head, his posture rigid. His sharp gaze locked on the towering pines that marked the Gate.

As Alvara turned her head to follow his gaze, a cold finger of dread brushed her senses. Her stomach tightened, and her knees weakened. She forced herself to stand and face the direction of Kingdom's Gate. The tall, thick fir trees hid the cavern from view, but she knew where it hunkered like the maw of hell.

The fine hairs on the back of her neck and along her arms stood on end. She turned in a slow half circle and searched for the source of the smothering terror rolling toward her. The shadows under the majestic oaks and leaf-laden maples no longer beckoned as a cool, inviting refuge. Wide gray trunks disappeared into the dark, impenetrable canopies, and a fog of dank, malicious promise crept beneath. As the formless evil rolled over it, the beautiful wood and lawn transformed from a guardian silva to an alien taiga.

Alvara stumbled back, her muscles weak and disobedient. *Run!* Her heart and mind shouted as primeval instincts sought to preserve her life. Instead she stood. Her years of training overruled her instincts. She mumbled a spell of protection, one she'd drilled over and over again. But why?

No fell creature could venture forth in the bright light of day, not even in this delicate and precarious time. Ten days remained until the full moon, but still her heart sent that deep visceral warning across her nerves.

She retreated a few steps. Something came. Behind her, Bachus bellowed in warning and challenge over the pounding of his boots. He wouldn't reach her in time.

A fast-moving cloud shadowed the sun for a moment. But no cloud could move so swiftly. She looked up and saw them coming right for her. She screamed.

"She's an infant, Father. She'll learn."

King Jerson shook his head at his son. When would the lad lose his endless optimism? A man couldn't rule a restless land like Futhark thinking everything would work out on its own. "Not even you can teach that bitch to hunt, Jonared."

"I can," Jonared insisted with a grin. He spurred his gelding after the recalcitrant hound.

"He'll manage it, Sire. He always does," Sir Frederick said as the prince called to the dog.

"He has a patience I never had. Not in my youth and not now in my maturity. He thinks he can fix the world."

"Not much to fix in this time of peace." Frederick frowned and glanced back over his shoulder. Dark, craggy peaks reached ominous thick fingers toward the sky. "Not if the Keepers do their duty."

Jerson's short burst of good spirits fell beneath the return of his dark mood. The heavy foreboding that had haunted his dreams for months now plagued his days as well. He'd hoped some time in the saddle under a bright sun might chase away the shadows pervading his thoughts.

Jerson shaded his eyes with his hand as he watched his son dismount and kneel beside the large wolfhound. The dog had run most of the distance back to the palace after retrieving the arrow Jonared had shot. Even at this great distance, the king could see the hound looking at her master with adoration. The animal loved the prince, as did all the people of the kingdom. Many young ladies of the court—and some of the matrons—looked at Jonared with the same worshipful hope as the pup.

"The prince must select a protector soon, your highness," Frederick said as they watched the dog romping about Jonared in play.

King Jerson smiled at Frederick, his own protector. His loyal swordsman had stood guard for him for almost forty years. He was not only bodyguard but friend, counselor, and a peer in age and experience though not in royal blood. Frederick knew the king like no other, but the swordsman never stepped over the boundary dividing liege and man-at-arms.

"I mentioned it to him not two days ago as you urged. Again. I would see him settled in marriage also."

Frederick snorted. "A protector is more important than a wife."

Jerson chuckled, and suddenly his grim humor seemed a silly foible. Frederick had never married, and though he had treated Queen Laverna with unfailing respect, he had never warmed to her. Truthfully, the marriage had been one of political convenience arranged by Jerson's father rather than one of love and passion. Still, she and Jerson had cared for each other and shared in the love and pride of their son. Frederick's sympathy at the queen's passing had been genuine even if he had thought of her as a necessary annoyance.

"The throne needs an heir and for that a wife for the prince. Fortunately, in these tranquil times, Jonared can pick his bride for suitability rather than to seal an alliance."

Jonared shot another arrow and sent the bitch after it.

Jerson sighed, thinking he should return to his duties soon. Exarch Lantana would join him later to report on final preparations.

A sudden chill brushed across Jerson's neck. The sunshine hadn't cheered him as he'd hoped. From whence came this dark cloud of despair that followed him?

"There's a chill of fall in the air today." Again the cold breeze, at odds with the bright sun, prickled his scalp like a sudden frost.

Frederick frowned and straightened in his saddle.

His horse sidestepped and tossed its head. Jerson's horse caught its herd-mate's mood and pranced nervously. The hound howled in an eerie combination of fear and warning.

Alarm punched Jerson low in his middle. His bowels tightened, and sweat broke out across his chest and back. Something came, something that confirmed his black thoughts, something real. He searched for his son and saw Jonared staring at something behind Jerson. At least Jonared was safe near the castle.

"There!" Frederick gasped.

Jerson forced his increasingly frantic mount to turn in the direction his man pointed. The menacing tors that marked Kingdom's Gate rose into the clear blue sky like the clawed fingers of a demon. A few crows raced toward them from the summit.

"I've never seen such large crows, or might they be vultures?" Jerson snagged the reins of his mount tighter.

Frederick pulled out the short sword he had strapped across his back.

"Frederick?"

"They're not birds, Sire."

Bachus sprinted, sword in hand, but the winged monster would reach Alvara before he did. His heart thumped in a violent, uneven rhythm so he couldn't take a deep breath. The path seemed a steep incline instead of the sedate, winding path he'd walked only a moment before.

Alvara screamed a spell and jabbed her fists toward the hellspawn spiraling down from the heavens. A white bolt of magical fire blinded Bachus for a moment.

The creature screeched, its heinous cry fouling the sacred grounds with its fell voice. The horrid sound spoke of hate and rage.

Bachus blinked away the lingering spots dancing in front of his eyes. The monster crashed to the ground almost at his feet as he skidded to a stop on the thin layer of brightly colored leaves. The reptile-like creature, almost as large as a horse, shook the earth on impact. It dug its finger-length talons into the green rug of the lawn as it struggled to rise. Its featherless, leathery wings ended in similar claws. It used them to drag itself toward Alvara.

Bachus worked his way around the fallen demon while staying well clear of its lethal weapons. He stopped at Alvara's side, his chest aching from his struggle to catch his breath again.

"What is it?" he panted. The small bit of running had little to do with his breathlessness. Pure terror did.

"It must be an accipitor," Alvara answered in a small voice that trembled with shock. "I've never used my magic in such a way."

"A fine first attempt then, Mistress." Bachus forced himself to calm. The first surprise and panic had passed. Now they needed answers and to get under cover.

"It should not be here. It cannot be here."

Her confused, weak voice worried him. "We must tell the Exarch. Let's go inside." He watched the wounded creature trying to rise on its short rear legs. Its determination to reach his mistress frightened him.

Alvara raised her glazed stare from the downed foe. Never had he seen such fear in her eyes.

"What?" His muscles tensed in response to her expression. His fingers hurt on the grip of his sword, but no amount of training could relax his taut nerves.

Alvara licked her lips and looked beyond him toward the hidden Gate. "Accipitors hunt in packs."

Bachus took her arm with his left hand. "Let us hurry."

She resisted. "They attack movement."

Too late. A high-pitched whistle pierced the clear morning air. The wounded one answered, startling them both as the shrill sound jangled their nerves. Another answered from their right. It took no understanding of the evil language to recognize the cries as a signal. Bachus looked at the short sword in his hand and swore.

They rose from the trees like a cloud of swarming mosquitoes. Bachus gave up counting them.

"Lost Guardians protect us," Alvara whispered. She raised her hands as the accipitors poured out of the blue. She unleashed her power and knocked one from the sky.

Bachus placed himself behind her, back to back. He wished for his crossbow or his longsword instead of the inadequate weapon he carried while on the fortress grounds.

The first accipitor came at him and almost tore his weapon from his hand as he slashed his blade across its long rear talons. The deadly claws grazed him and opened a long slice across the back of his hand.

Terrible screeches gave him hope that Alvara's shouted spells were taking a toll. He braced himself as another of the flying demons dove toward him. He swung his sword with both hands, fearing the blood gushing from his wound might compromise his grip. The accipitor veered right, and he missed its underbelly by a hair. The agility of the reptile surprised him as it flapped its wings to gain altitude.

Something hit him on the side of the head. Hard. Bachus cursed and stumbled. A trick, a clever feint by the first one so another could hit him.

Now two came at him as he fought for balance. He cut the first one and drew a spray of dark blood. The other hit him full in the chest. He grunted as the curved bayonets of its claws pierced him. Muscles tore in agonized defeat.

Cold yellow eyes stared into his as the accipitor bore him to the ground. Weakness inundated his body in wide ripples until numbness chased away the worst of the pain. It opened its beaked mouth, exposing rows of razor teeth. Its foul breath, reeking of carrion and swamp stench, made breathing unthinkable.

"Come closer, bastard," Bachus croaked despite the pressure on his chest. It blinked its merciless eyes and then dropped its head toward him as if it understood. Swift as his suffering body allowed, he rammed the entire length of his sword into its gaping orifice.

It gurgled and tumbled from on top of him. Its claws tore loose from his chest. Pain returned in a white-hot blaze.

Bachus rolled to his side, away from it, as the yellow gleam dulled in its soulless eyes. No thrill of victory sang in his heart.

Alvara stood a short distance from him, her green dress dark with sweat. He tried to shout a warning as an accipitor flew at her unprotected rear. Where he should have been standing. His damaged chest allowed only a small gasp to warn her.

He screamed, if only in his heart, but all he heard were the cries and screeches of the demons. A roaring filled his ears as somewhere in the far distance he heard a shout. Too late. He no longer fought the weakness of his limbs. He rolled to his back and stared at the innocent blue sky. Blackness crept in along the edge of his vision, and he gave into it.

He'd failed his mistress. It was only right that he should die also.

"Ride, your highness!" Frederick shouted at his king. His friend.

The horses needed no spur, only a loosened rein, to flee before the winged terrors. Frederick fought with his mount so to keep it behind the king's horse. He cursed himself for not reacting to the animals' instincts sooner.

The air about them seemed thick and difficult to breathe, as if some unnatural force carried fear in front of them. His very heart quailed as it never had in all his life with the sword. Strangling vines of terror squeezed his chest. He blinked away the sweat spilling over his brow to sting his eyes. He'd always expected to die protecting his king. It was his duty, his life's work. But he'd trained to face an assassin, not some monsters from the dark of hell.

Battle experience gained over the course of a lifetime warned Frederick they were losing the race. He dared a glance over his shoulder. His heart jumped into his throat. Three of the creatures glided only twenty paces behind them, little more than a horse's height above the grasses.

He fought his mount, using brute force to swing its head around so they could face the attackers. He lifted his sword and braced himself as best he could on his terrorized horse. Facing a human enemy he might have raised his voice in a cry of war. He couldn't even whisper a prayer.

The demons flapped their thin, featherless wings and rose high enough to pass over his head. He glimpsed yellow eyes and rows of sharp teeth in their beaklike mouths.

"No!" Frederick screamed, his voice returning at the enormity of his mistake. They were assassins after all.

He wheeled his steed and chased after them. His warhorse caught his urgency and found its own courage as it sped after the fell creatures and the king.

The lead demon hit Jerson in the back with its body and tumbled him to the ground. The king's horse galloped on toward the castle.

Two more of the hellspawn pounced on the downed king before Frederick reached him. He vaulted from his horse onto the back of one and then drove his sword deep into its body. Hot, oily blood washed over his sword hand as the creature bucked like an untamed colt.

The king screamed from beneath the other monster. Frederick cursed and cried, rage and desperation breaking his heart. He somehow pulled himself to his knees on the bony back of the demon and flung himself on top of the other.

Pain exploded across his back almost as soon as he landed. A dozen knives pierced his flesh. The sharp weapons sliced their way through his entire body and poked out between his ribs in front. A grunt escaped his clenched jaw as something jerked him into the air. It lifted him higher and then higher still.

Despite the horror of being impaled and the blinding agony, Frederick struggled to free himself. But his captor lifted him away. Away from his king.

King Jerson's cries and screams ended as more of the foul reptilian beasts joined the attack. Frederick wept and gave into the weakness. He hung limply, his body passing into a numbness he didn't welcome. He deserved the pain, the suffering.

As they reached a height equal to the castle's battlements, Frederick raised his head and looked toward the palace that had been his home all these years. Guards rushed from the rear gate onto the once-peaceful lawn. Prince Jonared rode toward his father at a dangerous speed. His hound led the way with brave devotion. Prince no longer, Frederick thought vaguely. King Jonared.

His chin dropped to his chest as the last of his strength left him. He watched his blood drip from his middle to splash like scarlet raindrops and stain the lovely green grass far below. He wanted to look at the blue sky once more, but his head was too heavy to lift.

The lethal spikes suddenly released him. Nothing could numb the agony. He screamed, a shriek torn from his soul. Frederick fell, eager to meet the ground and end it.

CHAPTER TWO

JONARED KNELT BEFORE EXARCH Lantana. The crown might have been made of lead instead of thin gold filigree. Her words of responsibility and duty rolled unheeded around the edge of his thoughts.

Concentrate! But how? Anger and grief searched for an outlet. His father, torn to pieces before his eyes, and except for the beast Sir Frederick had slain, the killers had escaped.

"Rise, King Jonared Otton," Lantana ordered, her voice firm and strong for one so frail in appearance.

Jonared stood and turned to the crowd gathered in the grand courtyard. His guard had begged to have the ceremony behind the castle walls. His nightmares encouraged the same, but the people of Sulbreth needed to witness his rise to sovereign. They needed to see his courage. Rumors abounded on the streets about his father's death. Jonared's public crowning would quiet the simmering fears of the common folk. Few of the nobility knew the details either. So it would remain.

A hearty cheer greeted him. He bowed his head in humble acknowledgment and provoked a greater roar. He didn't smile and hoped no one expected him to do so. His father was only three days dead.

"Enough, your highness," Exarch Lantana said. "Let's retire to your chambers. There's much to discuss."

Jonared lifted his hand and looked out one last time at his people. His people. He'd always carried a distracted affection for all the people of Futhark, but the weight of Lantana's earlier words suddenly fell on his shoulders. The cheering crowd in front of him had no idea of the danger lurking so nearby. Of the hell. He must keep it that way.

The men standing guard, almost the entire castle garrison, looked relieved as he followed the Exarch inside the gates. He wasn't too proud to admit to some comfort himself.

They proceeded through the halls he'd always known, though they were changed for him. The tapestries were of ancestors; some had won renown for courage and valor against usurpers; others had united the provinces under one crown and brought peace. Would he be the one who lost it all? The Otton forefathers looked down on him. He sensed their judgment and saw himself as they might.

A boy who played with his hounds all day and danced with women at night. He'd ignored his father's urging to learn the duties of a king and laughed at Jerson's pleas to take a bride, select a protector. What a spoiled boy he'd been.

"Jonared!"

Jonared slowed and closed his eyes for a moment. Not now.

"Cousin, we must speak."

"You will address the king by title," Exarch Lantana said as she turned and stopped.

Jonared stopped and turned also. He caught the displeasure on Duke Borak Rosmer's handsome face. Not so handsome actually, with his eyes narrowed and his mouth tightened into a thin line. But not even cousin Borak dared speak impudently to the Exarch.

"Your highness."

Jonared found his first smile in days, but it wasn't humor that curved his lips. How like Borak to corner him at this time of grief and crisis.

"What is it, Duke Borak?" Jonared wanted no familiarity of first names between him and this distant relative, a cousin many times removed from the royal line of Ottons.

Borak's nose flared at the curt question. "I thought that as your only surviving blood relation I would offer my personal condolences in private, your highness."

"Thank you." Jonared hoped he sounded as sincere as

27

the duke, which was not at all. His father had always treated Borak coolly. The reason was unknown to Jonared, but his father had had good instincts for men.

A few of the guardsmen shifted in the silence after Jonared's short answer.

Borak took a deep breath. "I can see you're still immersed in your grief. I shall give my respects another time."

Borak bowed, briefly and inadequately, before turning smartly and striding away.

"Is he staying in the castle, Sire?" Lantana asked.

Jonared sagged, his annoyance sputtering away and leaving fatigue. "I don't know. I've no idea how many of the nobility have been given rooms."

Lantana put a hand on his shoulder. "Someone must have seen to it for you. It's important politically who is invited to take rooms under your roof, but that's a lesson for another day. Come, before some other long-lost cousin jumps from behind the tapestries."

"More likely the duke came up from one of the drains," an older guardsman muttered.

Lantana took off at a brisk pace and held her silence until they were safely ensconced in Jonared's private salon.

"We must move quickly, my king," Lantana said. She signaled a servant, and he stepped forward to pour the thin wine favored for midday refreshment.

Jonared dismissed the man and sank into a stuffed chair. He need not act kingly in front of the Exarch. He looked around the rooms, once his father's, and sighed.

He wanted sleep, a deep slumber unhindered by grief or nightmares.

"Jonared," Lantana said with an impatient tone she would never use when others were about. "Have you seen to the details of the tournament?"

"Thirty days from now." An indecently short time after his father's passing. He sipped the wine to wash away the bitter taste of his plans. He looked more closely at the glass goblet etched with the Otton family crest. Crossed swords with crested doves resting upon each pommel, representing peace enforced with strength of arms. "Is something in this wine?"

A fair question. The Keepers were versed with all manners of herb lore. Such knowledge combined with their magical gifts gave pause even to one who trusted them unequivocally, as Jonared did.

"A measure of ginseng only, my king." Lantana smiled sadly. "I could never sneak your father a remedy either."

They both fell silent for a long time, enjoying the wine and the quiet.

"Has Mistress Cicely had any more visions?" Jonared asked when his thoughts threatened to turn to his father's brutal death once more.

"No. I hope for more when he draws near."

"And Sabelline?"

"Working hard. She's a bright lass."

"Can she do it?"

"She must. And she must have his help."

"You're sure he'll come?"

"You've put the manor up as prize?"

"I did. It has been leaderless since Durnhold died last spring."

"How can he resist?"

Jonared snorted. "How can any man resist? We'll have every second son and hiresword in Sulbreth stepping into that arena."

"I suppose."

"How will we even know him?"

Lantana rose and stretched. "We'll know. I'll take my leave, your highness. Take some rest. You did well today."

Jonared nodded, though not really in agreement. He trusted Lantana, but he was sure he heard doubts in her answer. Too much rested on Sabelline and this stranger spoken of in a foretelling. Too much.

"They're almost ready."

Cage nodded but didn't turn from the beauty below him. He heard Sir Berton take a few cautious steps forward.

"You're such a crazy bastard," Berton muttered without heat.

Cage smiled. "If you'd look at it just once, you'd be as drawn to it as me."

Berton snorted. "Not for all the gold rounds in the

king's treasury."

Cage lingered a moment longer. The white seabirds danced above the crashing waves far below. The sheer drop equaled the height of any thirty lord's manors. No one could scale the cliff side. No one dared try. None dared even look over the side. Cage wondered at the strangling fear that gripped men when they approached the natural boundary of Futhark. Though he sometimes questioned if there was anything natural about it. Some force clung to The Edge, an energy of sorts that worked on the hearts of men when they stepped too near. But it didn't work on Cage. He sensed the constraint, but it raised no fear in him.

"Step back now, lad. You test my poor old heart standing so close there."

Cage sighed. Something about the sea called to him. He'd heard that mountains surrounding the king's city of Sulbreth made The Edge inaccessible. It might be a long time until he could look upon the blue and green majesty of the sea again.

"We should be on our way."

"As you say," Cage agreed. He turned to Sir Berton, his friend and longtime mentor.

They walked together toward the tiny manor that had been their home for the past three years since Count Thrum had died.

The old coach and the hired driver sat before the front door. The housekeeper and stable master would stay behind to mind things while they were gone. They were the only two servants they could afford. The manor had no lands beyond a few pastures that fed only the horses. Sir Berton's name was on the rent agreement, though such an estate was far beyond the means of a common swordsman.

"What of Sulbreth, Berton? Can we afford a manor to rent while there?"

Berton shook his head as he stopped by his warhorse. He patted its muscular neck as the large animal stomped its feet in greeting. "It's been so many years, Cage. I doubt many will be available even if we could pay the price. The king's tournament will draw people from everywhere, if only for the spectacle."

Cage frowned. He'd never been to such a large city. "An inn then."

Berton nodded with his own frown. "I'll ask around. Surely there are some of good reputation. I wish we were arriving earlier. I fear the best rooms will be taken."

"You'll be at their side always."

"Yes, my lord."

Cage only shook his head at Berton's sarcasm. The two reasons for his recent sleepless nights stepped outside the manor. Berton hurried to assist them with the small valises each carried.

Cage followed with less enthusiasm. He'd rather the women stayed at home, but he'd lost that argument days ago.

"Sorry to make you wait," Anadalune said. She let

Berton take her hand as she swept down the wooden steps. She smiled up at the swordsman, and her expression hit Cage like a blow to the side of the head. When had that happened? Or had it always been? Berton's loyalty was as unwavering as his dutiful conduct.

"I'm so excited, Cage," Kristall said as she skipped down the steps.

Cage went to meet his sister before she came in reach of the warhorses. Bayard, Cage's mount, especially, didn't stand well for people flitting about him.

Kristall flung her arms around him. He savored it even as he despaired over her lack of propriety. A lady did not hug her bastard brother in public. He squeezed her tight and then set her back. "You must not . . ."

"Oh, hush, Cage. I'm not going to pretend you're my hiresword."

"I didn't ask you to." He wanted her hugs and her sisterly teasing, but the people of Sulbreth might not see it the same.

"Come now, Kristall," Anadalune called. "Don't torment your brother."

Kristall rolled her eyes but obeyed her mother. "I wish you two would make peace."

Cage wished it also. His apprehension about the trip burdened him enough without Anadalune's irritation with him. But though he wasn't raised at court, he had spent enough time amongst the nobility to know their standpoint on bastards. His association with Lady Anadalune and

Kristall cast a shade on their reputations. The stubborn ladies refused to give his concerns full credence.

Anadalune glared at Cage before stomping to the carriage and allowing Berton to assist her inside. Kristall practically hopped up the high step, giving Cage a bright grin over her shoulder. Within moments they were on their way.

Cage and Berton took turns at point and flanks. Two men weren't enough to guard such precious personages, but they had no coin for more. Cage's last hire with Lord Edgar had paid well, but the ladies needed proper attire for court and the upkeep of the small manor drained the coffers further. And what of Kristall's dowry? The pittance he and Anadalune had managed to put aside over the years provided more embarrassment than honor.

They passed through the village where they did most of their purchasing. The few people on the street nodded or waved. Cage acknowledged them. The simple folk treated his odd family with the respect usually given to a ruling lord, though he was nothing of the sort. Cage repaid them by keeping the surrounding countryside free of bandits and others of unsavory ilk. Though his earnings barely kept his family under roof, the villagers thought him rich. They were honored that Anadalune and Kristall graced their shops and spoke to them so kindly.

"Luck to you, Lord Stone," called the blacksmith who did all Cage's metal work, from horseshoes to swordsmithing.

Cage lifted his hand to Samuel Hugo. If luck blessed him and he won the king's prize, Cage would bring the man to his new manor. Hugo was skilled and wasted his talents on plowshares and iron candlesticks.

And most of all, the man saw no conflict in the name he called to Cage. Stone was the family name given to all those who were bastard born and unrecognized by their fathers. Lord Stone, indeed. What would the titled folk of the king's court think of that?

After they passed the last cottage on the village's one lane, nothing but small scattered crofter huts and trees greeted them. Not that Cage minded. Large oaks towered overhead, softly humming a tune of seasons come and gone. The humans riding beneath them meant nothing to the trees. Sun, water, and a life of never-ending growth provided contentment for the sturdy giants.

Cage shook himself. Listening to the foliage again, he chided himself. He swore Bayard laughed at him. He had hidden his odd quirks as best he could ever since he was old enough to realize not everyone experienced the world as he did. It was fairly easy here in the country among simple people who worried more about their own struggle to survive than the business of others. But how would he fare in the king's civilized city?

"That's all I know," Cicely said.

Exarch Lantana took a deep breath and reminded herself to stay calm. "His name? His look?"

Despite her assurances to King Jonared, she wasn't nearly so confident they would recognize him.

"He's a warrior," Cicely said.

"We already know that," Lantana snapped. "Why else would the king be having the tournament? Think, Cicely."

Harmon frowned and shook his head. He stood behind Keeper Cicely, his thick arms crossed over his muscular chest. "You've been very helpful so far, Mistress. Is there any other little thing to help us?"

Cicely closed her eyes. Lantana waited, knowing the woman was attempting to recall her visions. Cicely alone possessed the gift of foretelling. The flashes of the future came to her in random, vague scenes, or sometimes little more than a sense of impending doom or disaster.

"He's young," Cicely said, her eyes still closed. "He's highly skilled. And he's alone."

"Alone?" A strange thing to sense. "No family?"

Cicely shook her head. "Alone as in different. He thinks of himself as odd, set apart."

Lantana sighed in relief. He had to be the one. "And he's coming to us?"

"For the tournament," Harmon agreed softly.

Cicely's eyes popped open. "I only know for sure that I'll meet him soon."

Lantana smiled, regretful of her impatience with the

young woman. Cicely understood though. So much was at stake.

"Thank you, dear. Go have your morning tea. Tell no one, as before."

The Exarch waited until Keeper Cicely closed the door on her way out before letting her full excitement show. Harmon retained the same stoic expression.

"You're confident, Mistress?" he asked.

Lantana admitted to herself that it was a worry. Cicely's visions were so vague. They knew only that he had great skill with the sword. And he would come to them in time.

"We'll set a watch for those who come to the tournament. I'll greet each one if I must." Where would she find time for that?

"If he's such a swordmaster, perhaps you need only meet the winners of the first day."

"I'd rather see them all." She didn't trust the luck of the arena. Few knew what Lantana's own gift allowed. Her ability to see the minds and hearts of those around her frightened people. She couldn't actually read their thoughts, but she could sense their intentions, spot a lie, and judge the nature of a man. Hence her confidence in the young king. "If he's the one we need, I'll know him."

"Do you think he'll really be of their blood?" Harmon's skepticism matched her own in that regard. "Would he not look different?"

"We would have heard rumors of someone who looked like them. He must appear human." Such thoughts were only conjecture. A waste of time. "We shall see. The king's notice went out ten days ago. Seven days should see the first arrivals."

Harmon frowned. Having all those swordsmen in Sulbreth, many of them mercenaries, made the Marshal tense. It was for him to worry over.

She rose from behind her desk. Her heart lightened with the first real hope she'd felt since Alvara's death. There was still much to do in the wake of that horror.

"Let's check on Sabelline. The poor child carries a burden beyond the rest of us combined. Then we'll visit King Jonared and see how he fares."

Lantana paused and stared at the painting hanging over her fireplace. The work was as old as the Keeper's fortress. The beings in it had made the Gate according to the histories. Then they gave the responsibility of guarding it to women with the gift. Those women became the first Keepers of the Gate.

As head Keeper, Exarch Lantana intended to live up to that sacred duty. She needed this mysterious swordsman. And she would have him.

"Don't be so hard on yourself, Sabelline," Mistress Tamarin said.

Sabelline blinked back tears as she stared at the lump

of hematite in front of her. It was melted into the slate table-top. The odor of molten metal stung her nostrils, but that wasn't the cause of the tears.

"You did better today," Tamarin lied. "I think it looks a bit like a pouncing cat. That was what you intended; was it not?"

Sabell smiled. Tamarin's infinite optimism kept her going at it each day.

"Now, Sabelline, you listen to me." Tamarin sat beside her and took Sabelline's hand between her own two gnarled ones. "You're trying too hard. You work the hematite like it's bread dough. I could never make it as malleable as you do."

"What good is that if I can't form it into what I need?" Sabelline berated herself for whining. She lifted her blouse away from her chest where sweat beaded uncomfortably. Molding the metal was hot work beyond the effort she put forth.

"You will, child."

"But there's no time, Tamarin."

Tamarin smiled and squeezed Sabell's hand. "Trust yourself. The world turns with its own purpose. Stop worrying about all the things you can't control."

"Like that silly tournament."

"Exactly. Let it take care of itself. You have no control over it, but you do have control over your gift. You could make a fine cup from this lump if you concentrated." Tamarin frowned and looked at the blob of hematite. "Of course, it would be a damn heavy cup."

Sabell laughed. "I shall try."

Hours later she'd shaped a lopsided bowl, but it was the closest thing to actually forming something she'd achieved in her entire training. It had taken years to be able to soften the metal; now she needed to learn to shape it with only a little more than a month's training.

When she finally left Tamarin's workroom, three Marshals surrounded her. They escorted her everywhere. Their presence gave her comfort, but she missed the freedom of insignificance. The men were kind and as unobtrusive as large armed swordsmen could be, but how did one gossip with a friend with the stern warriors standing nearby?

The worst was when Marshal Bachus guarded her. The poor man still looked thin and pale from his injuries, but the real wound was in his eyes. To look into his blue eyes was to peer at a dead soul. Only the dutiful body remained of the proud man. Sometimes Sabell found his living more sorrowful than Alvara's death. She thought Bachus felt the same if he felt anything at all.

"Sabelline!"

Sabell stopped and waited for her best friend, Reseda, to catch up. They'd joined the Keepers the same year and possessed the same gift. Until Sabell had been selected to study with Tamarin, they'd shared a room and each other's secrets.

"How did it go today?" Reseda asked. She was the

40

only one Sabell trusted with her self-doubts.

"Better. I think I finally made some progress."

For a moment Sabell thought Reseda looked disappointed, but her friend quickly smiled and the glimpse was gone. Sabell understood Reseda's conflict. Reseda had hoped for the honor of being chosen, but only one was taken into training. Her friend hid her disappointment as best she could and never once showed jealousy.

"Well then, we should celebrate." Reseda linked her arm through Sabell's. "What say you we sneak down to the king's courtyard and goggle at the brave, strapping swordsmen signing up for the tournament?"

Sabell glanced at the Marshals. One shook his head at her. Concerns for her safety made her a prisoner of the grounds.

"I think I'll celebrate with a quiet cup of tea in my room without reading a single text or historical tome. Then a long, hot bath." Sabell read the protest in Reseda's dark eyes. "But you come by later and tell me all about them."

Reseda seemed mollified by that. She chatted on about the handsome contender she'd seen earlier in the day until they came to Sabell's room.

"I shall see you after dark then," Reseda said as she hurried toward the stair. She batted her eyes at one of the younger Marshals as she passed.

Sabell smiled, wishing she was more easy with the men. Her childhood spent under the protection of her vigilant father had left her ill prepared for flirtation or even polite discourse. No wonder the life of a Keeper appealed so to her. At least her sister, Leesa, had escaped such an upbringing. Sabell's choice to become a Keeper had devastated her father, but it had made him rethink his child-rearing methods.

One of the Marshals entered her rooms and checked it before she was allowed to step through the door. Even her bedroom and bath were inspected. She hated it. The cot inside the door drew her attention as she waited for permission to enter into her own quarters. Soon she wouldn't even have privacy when she slept. Soon a man, a complete stranger, would spend his every moment with her.

Her belly clenched. She fought against the apprehension and tried to take Tamarin's advice. She had no control over such things. Whoever was appointed her Marshal, she would deal with him when she must. She would learn to sleep with a large armed man in the room. She must, for all their sakes.

"Splattering blood and stomach contents everywhere," Borak continued with a bray of amusement at his own story.

Jonared took a gulp of wine and wondered if he was drinking too much of the stuff. But how else was he to get through the duke's need to bloviate on his prowess in battle?

"So you see how it takes a strong arm to rule the North Highlands."

More bravado or a subtle threat? Was Borak that cunning?

"Sounds like you've had more than your share of miscreants, Duke." Jonared still stubbornly refused to converse on a first name basis with Borak. He'd put this meeting off for ten days and finally run out of excuses. Duke Rosmer was one of the highest-ranking nobles in Futhark.

"I apologize for going on so about myself, Sire, but I know you've yet to form your table of advisors."

Jonared's head started to pound.

"Your father's table served in name only. Everyone knew Jerson relied only on his own opinion and those of the witches across the lawn."

"Witches?"

"Don't pretend, Jonared, they're nothing but."

The slip in the address mattered little compared to the disrespect to the Keepers.

"Take care, Duke Rosmer."

"I only seek to open your eyes, your highness. I hoped to find your young mind more open to the modern world. Force of arms is needed, a standing army, to combat the demons that killed your father."

"Duke Rosmer, you don't know . . ."

"I do know. Those women have conjured the dangers that threaten us. How else would they justify their existence and the support of the crown?"

Jonared pinched his nose. Could he have a duke thrown from his chambers?

"You must repudiate them, Jonared. They've leeched the wealth of this kingdom for too many years. Your father would not listen to me until . . ."

Jonared lifted his head. "Until what?"

"I visited you father three months ago. I again begged him to remove their heels from his neck."

Jonared bristled. No one put their heels on his father's neck.

"I believe for the first time he was ready to listen to me. I know the subject of the Keepers brought some deep worry to the surface. I knew your father that well."

"My father had many pressing matters on his mind this past year."

"Such as?"

"Business of the monarchy. And now I have to be about it also." Jonared stood, forcing Borak to do the same.

"I fear you father did believe me, your highness. I think that may be why they killed him."

"They?" Gruesome memories of his father's death tightened his voice.

Borak stepped back from him, some hesitation finally in his manner. "The witches, Sire. They called those demons with their evil magic because they knew your father's mind. He was about to take action against them."

"He was planning no such thing," Jonared snapped. Borak stepped closer to him. Now Jonared saw the light of fanaticism in his eyes. They burned with scorching passion.

"You're deluded, Duke Rosmer," Jonared said in what he thought was a reasonable, calm tone.

His words sparked more intensity in Borak's stare. He dared to shake his finger in Jonared's face. Two guards stepped away from the wall, hands on sword hilts. The duke didn't even glance sideways.

"If you continue on the same cursed path as your father, the witches will destroy you also."

"To what end? If they benefit from my support, they will protect me, not harm me."

"I didn't say they would harm you. Supporting them will bring you down, King Jonared. Patriots of Futhark will demand a true monarch who rules for the good of his people, not the puppet of tricksters and charlatans."

"Are you threatening your king, Duke Rosmer?" Jonared leaned toward him and glared down from his greater height.

To his dismay, Borak held his ground. "I warn you, dear cousin. Think carefully on your alliance with the Keepers."

CHAPTER THREE

"TWO ROOMS AT THE END OF THE hall." Sir Berton sighed as he slid onto the bench beside Cage.

"Did you inspect them?" Cage asked. His sharp gaze swept the common room again before settling on Berton.

Berton lifted his mug of ale and took a long, deep drink. Kristall ducked her head and hid her smile.

Cage scowled at the older man, a storm building in his smoke gray eyes. Kristall wished Sir Berton wouldn't tease Cage so, but her brother brought it on himself.

"I'm sure the rooms are fine, son," Kristall's mother assured Cage. The two had made a fragile peace on their journey, but only because they'd had few chances to test Cage's rules. His frown grew darker.

Kristall reached for the mug of ale the enthusiastic

tavern lass had set in front of her.

Quick as a thought, Cage's hand shot out and grasped her wrist. "You're too young to drink that. I'll have them bring you some water."

"Seventeen is old enough to get married and have children. I think I can have an ale now and then. Of course, I'll never meet a man with you around."

Cage answered her with his sunny smile, all the more charming because it was so rare, especially for the past eleven days when they had been traveling. He'd been like a rooster with a sore toe.

"Only a man brave enough to get by me will be strong enough to deal with you."

Kristall stuck her tongue out at him.

"Children," Anadalune admonished. "We're in the city now. Try to overcome your rustic upbringing."

"The rooms are adequate," Sir Berton said. "We've had better and less fine. The price is thievery, though."

"Too bad the rain slowed us down." Cage waved the serving girl over and asked her for mugs of water. He never touched ale, for reasons he kept to himself. Kristall had managed a few sips at the inn they had stopped at two nights past. She didn't really care for the taste anyway. She thought she should learn though, now that she was seventeen.

The girl hastened back with the water and then lingered to fuss over Cage. As did all the young women they met, as well as many of the older ones. It mystified Kristall.

"If we'd arrived two days ago, we might have found better rooms." Cage looked about the room constantly, as alert as if they were camped along the trail.

"Doubt we could have afforded it," Sir Berton said.

Kristall's enjoyment of the sights and sounds of the tavern shriveled. Though her mother and Sir Berton seldom spoke of wealth, or rather their lack thereof, Kristall knew they counted every silver and gold round. Cage's earnings as a hired sword were most of their income. Sir Berton brought in a few copper and brass rounds now and then on small jobs that kept him close to home.

The innkeeper, a thin harried man with sweat-soaked hair and a jolly nature, brought them a fragrant loaf of warm bread and a small block of hard white cheese.

Their hunger held them quiet while they munched on the yeasty loaf. It was tasty fare, especially compared to what they had had when they camped along the trail.

"This tavern had a different name and a slovenly owner when last I was in Sulbreth," Sir Berton observed. He took out one of the knives he carried on his belt to slice the cheese. "I'd heard the king brought prosperity and order to the city."

"The dead king?" Kristall asked.

"Kristall! Use some manners," Anadalune whispered. She looked about as if they might be thrown out for rude words.

"Yes, the dead one," Berton said with a twinkle in his blue eyes. "His son has yet to prove he's of the same

48

metal as his father."

Anadalune leaned forward. "I've been out of society for almost twenty years, but even I know it's unseemly to hold a tournament so soon after his father's death."

Cage frowned but said little. He exchanged a look with Kristall and then shrugged. The ways of nobility meant little to him except as it affected her and her mother. At least he gave that impression.

"There has to be more to the whole thing," Berton said. "An entire manor and its lands as a prize?"

"Perhaps the king wants a strong ally living close to his city. The man who wins that will carry an obligation to his sovereign for the great reward." Cage frowned at his own speculation.

"So it's close to the city?" Kristall hadn't heard that.

"Only a long day's ride," Berton confirmed.

"So we can do our marketing in the city?" Kristall tried to imagine what the dress shops might be like. They ordered all their dresses from the local seamstress back home, and her mother sewed Cage's and Berton's clothing herself.

"Don't be moving into the manor yet, lass," Berton cautioned.

"Cage will win. You tell us all the time he's the best."

Cage twitched an eyebrow.

Sir Berton cleared his throat and almost looked embarrassed. "I only tell you that so you and your mother don't worry overmuch when he's gone."

Anadalune reached across and put her hand on top of Cage's. He started to pull away, but she tightened her grip. "Cage, you know I've had reservations about this from the first rumor we heard. I'd rather turn around and go back home than have you get caught up in some trickery."

"The king would be involved in trickery?" Kristall always thought of the king as some distant figure who touched their life very little out in the provinces. Surely, though, he was a noble figure above reproach.

"He's advised by the Keepers. I've heard they have a finger in all the dealings of the crown," her mother explained.

"Shush," Berton said. "We're in the king's city now. We can't say what we would about the hearth at home, my lady."

They ate the rest of the bread in silence and finished the cheese. The serving girl tried to press more ale on them at the same time she pressed her full bosom against Cage's shoulder. He declined both offers and herded Kristall and her mother toward the stairs.

The odor of cooking, ale, and smoke hung at the top of the wooden steps, but Berton quickly led them down the hall. A high, small window was propped open at the end of the hall and alleviated the worst of the stale air as they neared their rooms.

"You will win, won't you, Cage?" Kristall asked as Berton opened the door to the last room and looked about inside.

One medium-sized bed stood in the middle of the room, and someone had stowed their bags on the single chest. A stand held a large pitcher of water and a wooden bowl. None of the furniture matched, and the floor was bare but clean.

Cage gave her one of his grins, his white teeth flashing in the dark room. Berton turned up the single bedside oil lamp.

"I didn't come all this way to enjoy the sights and scents of the city," Cage said.

Kristall laughed. She knew Cage was sensitive to odors and found many things offensive she couldn't even smell.

"Don't be over-sure of yourself, lad. Many a swordsman defeated himself that way," Berton warned.

"When have you ever known me to be so, Berton?"

"I think we should all get some rest," Anadalune said. "Come here, Cage."

Cage obeyed, though he gave Kristall a wary glance.

Her mother stood on tiptoe and gave Cage a kiss on the cheek. She wrapped her thin arms around him. After a brief hesitation he returned the hug with the gentle desperation her mother inspired in him.

Anadalune stepped back and blinked her shining eyes a few times. "I know you won't allow me to do that before you step into the arena. I want you to remember that you are my son. I will never say otherwise, no matter what you wish."

She held her hand up when Cage started to say

51

something. "You've been a son to me since I first took your hand in mine. I won't deny it, not to the court, not to the king. A family can be joined by more than blood."

Kristall held her breath. Cage and her mother had argued about this from the moment they'd planned the trip.

Cage shook his head. "Please don't leave the room without Sir Berton in attendance. I have to go early in the morning to put my name on the list."

Sir Berton nodded his own good eve and then followed Cage out, closing the door behind him.

The two women undressed in silence. The excitement of staying in an inn had passed for Kristall on the second night of their journey when she found bugs in the sheets. She and her mother checked the bed together and found it clean and fresh smelling.

"Sit here," her mother ordered. Kristall settled on the foot of the bed, and her mother sat cross-legged behind her. Anadalune took out their precious brass-handled brush with stiff boar bristles and worked it through Kristall's long hair. It had been a gift to them both from Cage years ago.

Kristall closed her eyes and enjoyed the attention. It was a nightly ritual for the two of them. Nothing relaxed her quite as much as having her mother's firm strokes smoothing her hair into long silken waves. Her mother finished by twisting it into a neat braid.

Then they switched positions. Kristall had always

loved her mother's hair. She remembered her first attempts to twist the blonde mass into a braid. How many nights had her mother slept with one of the horrific tangles Kristall had been so proud to produce? Her mother had fussed and exclaimed over her efforts and acted as if the queen's hair mistress herself had done it.

When he was younger, Cage had sometimes done the braiding for them both. He had a natural talent for weaving and working the silken strands. Some woman would be very lucky to take him to husband someday. More than once, he'd fixed her mother's hair in an intricate weave she wore about their manor. That was before Kristall's father died and Cage started fighting to support them.

"Mother, do you think Cage is happy?"

"I think he is, in his own way."

"His own way?"

Her mother shrugged instead of answering.

Kristall pressed on, wishing for answers her mother never gave her. "Sometimes, I think Cage doesn't know we love him."

"Let's hang up our gowns, Kristall, and give the wrinkles a chance to work out."

Kristall sighed and put the brush aside. She tied a thin blue ribbon around her mother's braid and slid off the bed.

Hanging the new gowns on the hooks above the chest

didn't cheer her as it should have. They were the nicest clothes she'd ever owned. Even the traveling gown she'd worn earlier was new. But at what cost? How much blood had Cage lost to purchase such fine apparel? And all the while, he and Sir Berton wore their homemade shirts and pants. Their boots were worn and old. She set her two new pairs of slippers beneath the gowns.

She thought about her earlier insistence to him that he win the king's prize. Did her brother think she wanted him only for the gold he provided? And if he did, was her greediness what put that belief in his convoluted thoughts?

Cage marveled at the crush of humanity at this early hour. He'd carried his sword to many towns and defended many manors, but all of them together didn't rival the magnitude of Sulbreth.

Wagons rattled by on the packed dirt streets as he walked out of the inn. The owner nodded, his eyes still heavy with sleep. A few merchants were about, readying their wares in small booths squeezed between the motley collection of inns and taverns. He paused to take in the merry chaos as noise bounced off the tall buildings and cascaded onto the wooden walkway.

After a quick look into the stable behind the inn to

check on the horses, Cage merged into the crowds. He'd rather ride Bayard, but the warhorse attracted too much attention. The animal wasn't used to the smell or the teeming throngs of people. Much like himself.

Even without the warhorse, Cage sensed the stares as he walked along the street. He avoided making eye contact; otherwise some curious soul would ask him of his birthplace. His foreign appearance always drew the notice of strangers. Why would Sulbreth be any different?

The lane widened and rose gently as he walked toward the sprawling stone castle of the king. Strangely, the wider the lane, the thinner the crowd. The buildings grew in size, and soon the wood walkway met with a stone one. The buildings towered high enough to block the morning sun, so the lane was shaded as if the dawn had yet to arrive. Apparently the rich of Sulbreth woke later in the day than the common folk.

Here the morning mists still hugged the ground and floated eerily on unseen breezes at eye level. Even in this street of immaculate homes and gated lawns, the stench of human waste and rotting food assaulted him. He ignored it as best he could.

Most of the buildings this near the castle appeared to be private residences, but a few places of business stood dark and unwelcoming. Why open early as a merchant if your customers slept late? One of the shops had a large window with a dress of shimmering silver hanging behind it. Cage paused and stared at the fancy gown. How would his sister or mother look in such a fantastical creation?

He walked on, shaking his head at such thoughts. It took all his skill and effort to pay for their tiny manor and clothe his family in the most simple of attire. That was why this tournament was so important.

If he could win the manor, they would no longer pay rent. He would continue to hire his sword so they might have real coin income. But at least if something happened to him, Kristall and Anadalune would be secure. Berton would watch over them as he always had. Cage must win.

The lane widened even further so twenty horses might ride abreast. After he passed a few more extravagant houses, it opened into a large, grassy courtyard. Yellow bricked paths circled and crossed the open area in a pattern that pleased Cage on some level.

He lifted his gaze to look around and froze as the black cliffs looming over the castle caught his stare. His chest muscles clutched so he had trouble drawing a breath. His hand dropped to his sword hilt, and only willpower kept it sheathed.

As clear as the sunshine touching his shoulder, Cage smelled the decay and malicious will of the mountain. It drew him and repelled at the same time.

"You there," a curt voice called. "What's your business here?"

Cage jerked his gaze off the threatening crags and took another step forward. A single guard stood by a small iron gate. He eyed Cage as he admitted two well-dressed men through the entrance. A large double-door gate of oak graced the center of the two-story wall surrounding the castle.

Directly across from Cage a small wooden table stood near the wall. Two guards flanked the table, their fierce glares fixed on Cage. They wore hip-length red coats and black pants tucked into shining black boots. A rotund man sat on one of two chairs at the table. He had asked the question.

Cage started on a bricked path that would take him to the table. He moved his hand away from his sword hilt as he moved into the shadow of the walls. Once the mountain was out of sight it was easier to ignore.

A flicker of movement to his left caught his attention. A large man ducked through another, well-disguised iron gate. He wore no red uniform, but he looked like a soldier. A short-sleeved green shirt revealed thick forearms decorated in curving tattoos. They circled around his arms and even trailed up to his fingers. A black squiggle of art ran across his forehead also. Though he looked well past his prime, Cage suspected the man was more dangerous than all the king's guards in the courtyard combined.

The curving path to the table took him back to an angle where he could see the black tors again. They glared at him still. If this tournament wasn't so important to Kristall's and Anadalune's future, he would have heeded the warnings in his heart.

Before he reached the table, a tiny woman hurried out

of the gate held open by the tattooed man. She trotted with the energy of a child to the second seat at the table and then smiled at Cage with a sparkle of joy in her eyes. She was easily as old as the tattooed man, who strode over and stood behind her with his arms crossed over his massive chest.

Cage stared into her eyes and saw power there. The malicious shadows cast in his thoughts by the mountain diminished.

"Name?" the man with the curt voice demanded. His fine simple dress marked him as a cleric of some sort. He looked at Cage, a bored, impatient glare in his pale eyes. Did he represent some religious sect, the king's chosen perhaps? Cage avoided such men when possible. Every province had its own version of history and salvation.

"Name?" the cleric asked again, his voice raised as if he could threaten Cage by power of position alone. Some things were the same in the city as the provinces.

Cage kept his own voice neutral. "Cage Stone."

"Stone!" the cleric snorted. He shook his head. "The law allows no bastard unrecognized by his father to own lands. You know the law. Now be gone."

Cage had faced such prejudices all his life. He had never learned to back down before it. "The king's invitation made no such limitations."

"All rules of the kingdom apply. Now go back to the whorehouse that whelped you."

Cage took a step forward. "You pick up your plume,

58

you little mongrel, and put my name on that list, or I'll do it myself."

An empty threat since Cage had never mastered the most simple of writing or reading. He wasn't even angry. The snide little worm wasn't worth the effort.

"I know of you," one of the king's guards said.

Cage looked at the guard and out of the corner of his eye caught the old woman staring at him with a rather unnerving intensity.

The guard sported an embroidered silver stripe on the shoulder of his jacket that likely denoted some type of officer rank. He extended his hand toward Cage. "We've heard of your swordwork even here in Sulbreth, Cage. I'm High Sergeant William Stone."

Cage took the man's hand, appreciating the calluses and strength of a fellow warrior. The gesture was well-done. William spoke the "Stone" name without shame or apology. His professional conduct reprimanded Cage. The odious mountain had him out of sorts, as did the city.

"I'm aware I can't own land, priest. If I win the tournament, the reward would be titled to my family."

"Family?"

"My sister is the legitimate offspring of a count, and her mother is his widowed lady wife."

The cleric frowned, and then his eyes widened. "You're the bastard get of Count Thrum?"

"Yes," Cage ground out. Even at the age of twenty-five, any reminder of his benighted sire chafed at him.

"A woman cannot own land without a husband to manage it for her," the weasel lectured.

Cage wanted to shake the sanctimony out of him. Anadalune had run Kulback Holding for years while her husband, Cage's father, gambled and whored away the profits. In his many hired ventures, Cage had encountered many women who ruled the manors despite the presence of their husbands. What did this little book man know of what it took to manage an estate?

"Didn't the count's younger brother inherit the title and lands? It's his responsibility to provide for his brother's wife and child. She has no need of her own lands." The rotound little peacock waved his soft hand in dismissal.

"The Lady Anadalune has no desire to live under the roof of the new count." Or to reside in the snake's bed. Only the presence of Sir Berton and the threat of Cage's inevitable revenge had prevented Thrum from taking Anadalune to mistress, willing or not. Recourse for a widow was limited. Cage needed to win this tournament.

"What is your interest in your father's widow?" A sly look gleamed in the man's pale eyes. "I understand she's still attractive and not that much older than yourself."

Cage's temper ignited. He rarely experienced real anger, but when he did it burned with a cold fire that numbed all his other emotions. He knew some whispered about him and Anadalune, but it was a brave or stupid man who did it to his face.

"She's a mother to him."

The woman's voice sliced through his chill rage. He'd forgotten her presence for a moment. He finally dared to really look at her.

Though many fine lines bracketed the woman's eyes and mouth, her skin was as clear and unblemished as a girl's. Her gray hair shone with vitality as it hung loosely around her shoulders.

"Put his name on the list," she ordered. She stood up and walked around the table until she was in front of Cage. She tilted her head back and looked into his eyes. "You're very tall."

"I didn't try to be, Mistress."

She smiled, but her gaze was sharp as she looked into his eyes. After a long moment of scrutiny, she nodded.

"I should consult with the king on this departure from the law, Exarch," the cleric said in a timid voice.

The woman started walking away. "Do as you wish, but his name stays on the list. Good day to you."

"You're not staying, Exarch? You've supervised the lists each day."

"I see now you can handle it, good sir," she called over her shoulder. The large tattooed man followed her toward the iron gate. He opened it for her and then paused before passing through himself. He gave Cage a quick once-over with a measuring gaze and then ducked after his mistress.

Whatever was an Exarch? He'd have to ask Berton and Anadalune.

"Put your mark here, Stone," the cleric ordered, his tone more sour than before.

Cage didn't care what the man thought. He was on the list. He carefully drew the lines that stood for his name. His family had worked with him endlessly on the reading and writing thing, but the squiggly lines made little sense to him.

He bade William farewell and started back to the inn. The morning mists were all burned away by now, and even some of the rich folks were about. The sun shone with bright promise.

He was on the list. It had been no small worry. He and Berton had discussed the possibility he wouldn't be permitted, though they said nothing to the women of the concern. On the list! Now he only had to win.

"What think you of him, Harmon?" Lantana asked her Marshal as they sat together for their midday meal. She took the chair behind the large paper-strewn desk that had served many Exarchs before her.

Harmon carefully set aside some of the scattered papers to make room for the wooden tray holding cups of vegetable broth and meat pies for each of them.

He waited until she picked up her cup and only then

settled himself in his usual chair. "He carries himself like a swordsman and keeps his pride in hand most of the time."

Lantana laughed softly. "Over forty years together and still you answer so carefully."

"I've asked about and spoken with that young sergeant. He's known as a dangerous man despite his youth. They say he foresees his enemies' plans and anticipates their moves in combat. Some accuse him of sorcery."

"He has no magic, Harmon." She sipped the warm broth. "His ancestors were said to have superior hearing and sight as well as the quickness of a cat. His natural intelligence accounts for his success in anticipating his opponents' strategy."

"You're sure he's a descendant of that mythical race?"

"It's not a myth. He's not of pure blood, but I see the traits in him."

"He did have an odd look about him."

"Yes, his tall, slim build. Yet I believe if you tested him, you would find strength in him as if he were a larger man." She gestured toward one of the paintings on the wall. "His gray eyes were common among his breed as well as his fair appearance and dark hair."

"Many men have such characteristics."

"Did you notice the way his attention was drawn to the Gate?"

"I did, but many strangers to Sulbreth stare at those

mountains. None like them are seen elsewhere in the kingdom."

"It was more than curiosity. He felt them, their danger."

"I can't doubt you on that point, Mistress. You would know what he felt."

"I want him for Sabelline."

"His reputation marks him as already skilled, but he might not agree to it. He has chosen to sell his sword rather than take a position of honor in the service of a lord. That's the normal life for a well-born bastard."

"Yet I sense honor in him. See what you can learn of this odd family he seems to have. Surely his father's widow should despise her husband's bastard, yet he fights to gain her a manor? I think we'll learn whatever we need to know about the man if we solve that mystery."

"As you wish." Harmon ducked his head in respect before he left. Though he was more assistant than protector these days, he still used the proper manners of a Marshal.

Lantana stared at the closed door without seeing it long after he'd gone. Despite her excitement at finding Cage so easily, she knew the situation was still desperate. She was tempted to visit Cicely again, but the girl's gift was sporadic at best.

She comforted herself with knowing he'd come as foretold. Events would turn now on his decisions. They must have him. One of Cicely's earliest senses of him was the necessity of him helping the Keepers.

Lantana put a hand to her head as if she could hold

64

back the coming ache. She would have his cooperation. If she'd learned anything as Exarch, it was how to
manipulate people.

Cage Stone had a family of sorts. If he cared about them
at all then they could be used to bring him about to her plans.

CHAPTER FOUR

"GENTLE NOW. A MAN'S SKIN IS SOFTER and thinner than this cowhide." Mistress Pinxter put her hand on top of Sabelline's and guided her to demonstrate the amount of pressure needed to push the needle through the leather.

Sabelline's stomach lurched, and a cold sweat beaded on her brow.

"You're doing fine, dear," Pinxter assured her.

Sabelline grimaced and tried again. The needle skidded across the surface of the softened hide. She threw it across the table. "I can't do this."

"Don't be silly. You must, as must all Keepers."

"I can't even stab this . . . this dead animal." Her stomach quivered some more. "I'll sick up if I have to poke this needle into a living person."

"You can. Many people are depending on you.

Your Marshal will need all the help you can give him." Pinxter beckoned Sabelline over to a small, round table covered with a bright orange plaid cloth. "Have a bit of cinnamon tea with me. It calms the nerves."

Sabelline sank into a spindly chair. She didn't think the strongest cinnamon in Sulbreth could calm her enough to use that cursed needle. Brandy perhaps.

Mistress Pinxter bustled about, lifting a steaming kettle from its iron stand near the blazing fireplace. She pulled a blue-speckled cloth bag from the shelves bracketing the mantle and took a few pinches of auburn powder from it. She added it to the kettle of tea. The ambrosial scent of cinnamon spread like a gentle wave across the room.

Sabelline relaxed despite her doubts of the rapprochement benefits of the tea. She looked around Mistress Pinxter's small atelier.

Two long, narrow tables covered by white cloths took up most of the room. The tables stood side by side with a tall cart in between them. The instruments on that cart were the cause of her disquietude. Needles of various widths and lengths soaked in a pan of triple-distilled alcohol. Small, clear bottles of ink, from dark to almost clear hues, sat in neat rows. All the necessary tools of a tattoo artist.

"Here now," Pinx said. She carried two mugs of the fragrant tea to the table and joined Sabell. "Have a sip of this. I buy my spices from a trader that deals with the

Yorkian tribes."

The tea wasn't as hot as Sabell liked, but she appreciated the gesture.

"Don't worry so much, Sabelline. Others have trouble at first too. When the time comes, you'll be able to do it."

"I don't think so. I wish I didn't need a Marshal at all."

"You know your mission is too important for you to be unprotected. You'll be grateful to have him before you're done. After this latest catastrophe, your Marshal will need to have all the enhancements you can give him. If you fail at this, you fail him and fail to give yourself the best chance to not only succeed but to survive."

Sabell sighed and sipped her lukewarm tea. All this she knew. The violent death of Mistress Alvara had brought this staggering responsibility to her before her time. She should have had years to study and prepare. Some days the urgency and burden of her duties threatened to overwhelm her. Especially sessions with Mistress Pinxter.

"I will be right here to help you, dear. We all will."

Her teachers were all so kind and patient. Sometimes they even made her believe she might be up to the task before her. She thanked Pinxter and took her leave. She wound her way through the various classrooms and study areas on this floor of the castle. She had some time to herself until her next lesson with Mistress Tamarin.

She climbed the north steps to the third floor, her guards pacing her in front and back. She still didn't feel at home in her new larger quarters and missed living on the higher floors with the other young Keepers. She missed the tinkles of laughter and camaraderie that came with training mishaps and successes.

She entered her room after it was checked and paused at the alcove to the right of the entrance. Someone had fixed the cot with fresh linens. A sparkling new wash-stand held a blue pottery pitcher and washbowl. The braided rug, though not new, smelled of fresh air. Everything was prepared for her Marshal except her.

She moved listlessly past the entrance into the sitting room that separated her Marshal's space from her bed-room. The room held little welcome. The mantle held only a small charcoal sketch of her family home. A silver vase graced the middle of the small table. Its lonely glory added to the cold unwelcome of the room. Her sister, Leesa, had given her the print so she might remember their home. The cold metal vase had also been a gift. From her father. She never put flowers in it. Seeing it barren fitted the spirit in which it had been given.

She passed from the algid room into her bedroom. The cushioned window seat was the one thing she loved in her new quarters. The sun had warmed it, and now it drew her. Her window overlooked the lawn known as the Marshal's Courtyard.

She studied the men practicing with short swords. None of these men was to be hers. The king's great tour-nament would select a Marshal for her and a protector for the throne.

Her mind turned to the ignorant fools eager to sign the lists for the lavish contest. The rare value of the prize, should a man win, drew scores of men to Sulbreth each day. In less than a week, the combative games would begin. The poor dupes would fight for the grand reward.

It was a paradox, and the contestants were ignorant of the truth. The winner would be her Marshal, and that would make him the ultimate loser.

"Only the purest honey from Kervonian hives was used in these sweet breads, your highness." The plump baker waved his hand over his display of dripping rolls and glistening cakes.

Jonared nodded and tried to appear interested as the eager man described the succulent ingredients in his various confections.

"Send a sample of each to the castle chef," Jonared interrupted, more to end the man's babbling than because he cared to taste the sweets. His stomach tolerated little of rich foods these days.

He continued his meandering path through the colorful market booths in the street fair. People moved out of his path with respectful nods and small bows. The unmistakable pleasure on their sun-beaten faces gave Jonared strength and courage. These good folks, so grateful for his attention, reprimanded him for the spoiled child he had been.

He stopped for a moment in front of a display of intricately carved wooden statuettes. None were bigger than his fist, but the elaborate detail bespoke a talented hand. He lifted a figure of a hunting hound.

"Take it, your highness. I hear you have a love of hounds." A skeletal old man grinned at Jonared, displaying large wooden teeth. Each tooth had a small picture of a flower bud engraved on it.

"I do love my dogs," Jonared answered with a smile. "But such a work of art is too valuable to be given without recompense."

One of the guardsmen following on Jonared's heels hurried forward. He took a purse from behind his belt and pulled two silver rounds from it.

The merchant beamed and stowed the coin in his own ragged purse. He wrapped the carving in a bit of soft cloth. Another guard tucked it into a sack with the other items Jonared had purchased.

"Will you be returning now, Sire?"

"Not yet." Jonared regretted his tone, but the sergeant had already asked the same question three times. He needed to be out among the people. Rumors of his father's gruesome death and Jonared's own narrow escape flew about the streets like snowflakes swirling in a winter gale. Did he look hale and hearty to these people? Did they see the fear in his heart, the unabated grief for his father, his doubts for the future?

Jonared strode with more purpose to the next cluster of displays. Two finely dressed women and their armed escorts studied the wares at a clothing merchant. The sight of such ladies in this setting gave Jonared pause. He shopped at these provincial street fairs because he must, but few other of the nobility cared for the merchandise found in the open-air markets.

He studied the ladies, not recognizing either of them from his court. They must be from the countryside, come to Sulbreth for the tournament. One of the men, though older, was still a soldier in his prime. The other man had his back to Jonared and stood a step back from the women.

Jonared's curiosity drew him closer. He took one more step, and the one with his back to him spun and dropped his hand to his sword with the quickness of a striking snake.

Jonared's heart leaped even as one of his guards shouldered his way in front of him.

The tall stranger glared, his gray eyes flashing. He was young, his face handsome and unscarred. His clothing marked him as a soldier, in the service of the ladies' father no doubt.

The two women turned also. Sisters. The older one put her hand on the young soldier's arm and spoke a low word to him. His glare turned to a frown, and his hand dropped from his sword.

The woman stepped in front of the soldier and bent her knees in a shallow old-fashioned curtsy. "Your highness, forgive my son. We're from the outer provinces, and he didn't recognize you."

The young man turned his frown on the woman. "I can speak for myself, Lady Anadalune."

Jonared lifted his chin and waited, giving the soldier his own best glare.

"I beg pardon, your highness. It is as the lady said. I did not know your face."

Had anyone ever begged his pardon with less conviction?

"We didn't expect to meet you here, your highness," Lady Anadalune said quickly.

Jonared turned his attention to her and bit back his smile as her slender elbow stabbed the arrogant son in his side. He wasn't in the mood to chastise young lords who were likely as pampered as he'd been not many days ago. If the man was here for the tournament, he would be humbled soon enough.

"I visit the street fairs often. I also didn't expect to meet such lovely company."

"But isn't it a wonder, your highness?" the younger girl asked. She brushed past the young man. "We've nothing so grand near our home. You must love marketing here."

One of Jonared's guards snickered softly behind him. Not softly enough. The girl blushed and ducked her head.

Jonared looked over his shoulder. The guard grimaced

and lowered his head also.

The young man's glare returned and even looked a smidgen dangerous.

Jonared smoothed his own expression as he spoke to the young, so-innocent lass. "I've had a fascination with the markets since my own father first showed them to me."

The older woman gave him a grateful smile, but her son's expression eased not at all. "We should start back to our lodgings, Lady Anadalune."

"Your names, good ladies," Jonared ordered. The large brown eyes of the girl watched him with an admiration tinged with curiosity. The lively sparkle in them lifted the dark cloud hanging always in his thoughts since his father's death.

"I'm Lady Anadalune Thrum, and this is my daughter, Lady Kristall Thrum."

Daughter? The matching long yellow hair of the two women and their soft brown eyes made them seem more twins than parent and child.

The lady continued, gesturing toward the older man. "This is Sir Berton Wall, who serves as our protector, and my stepson, Cage Stone."

Stone, a bastard title. A lady traveling with her husband's illegitimate get? "You're in Sulbreth for my tournament?"

"We are," Stone answered, and after a moment added, "your highness."

Jonared couldn't help but give the Lady Kristall a

long look. She was beautiful. But he had no time for such personal distractions.

So much depended on the winner of the tournament, at least according to Lantana. His kingdom. The lives of his people. The next assassins could come for him at any time. The dark dread returned to his mind and his spirit.

"Good luck in the lists, Stone," Jonared said without even an attempt at sincerity.

He led his entourage back toward the castle. Despite the return of his bleak mood, the image of the fair Lady Kristall intruded and distracted his thoughts. Not only her beauty but her genuine delight at the simple pleasures of the street fair. An unspoiled country lass whose very presence lightened his spirits.

Perhaps he should take a lover. Though obviously of noble birth, the Thrums appeared to be of meager means. The women wore fine dresses, though the style might not be the latest. The clothing of the two men gave it away. Stone and Wall wore old, low-quality shirts and pants. A liaison with a king, no matter how brief, could benefit the family in many ways. Perhaps he could even offer the bastard half brother an assignment in the royal guard after he lost in the tournament.

Something about Cage Stone bothered him, though. A fierce pride sat on his brow, and his eyes gleamed with a strength of will normally beaten out of unwanted bastards at an early age. Something in his features gave him an odd appearance, though it wasn't one particular thing.

Rather the combination of gray eyes, clear golden skin, and lean, graceful build combined with his attitude separated him from the crowd.

"Sergeant."

"Your highness?"

"Find what you can about the Thrum party. Where they're staying and their circumstances."

"I will take care of it personally, Sire."

"Good. Report only to me."

"My father will join us after he speaks with the king," Leesa said. She pointed at a troupe of trained dogs and giggled at their antics.

Kristall smiled at the older girl's endless enthusiasm and constant rambling discourse. She'd learned much from Leesa since they'd met two days ago at the king's parade of tournament contenders.

"The king's father and my father were good friends at one time. We visited the palace often when I was little." Leesa giggled again. "I was so smitten with Prince Jonared."

"You haven't visited lately?" Lady Anadalune asked. She sat behind the two girls in a carved wooden chair. Leesa had kindly invited them to join her and her father in their private pavilion.

Kristall turned and looked at her mother. More

than simple curiosity was behind the question.

Leesa's sparkling green eyes dimmed, and her mouth turned down as she too twisted to look at Kristall's mother. "We stopped after my older sister took the pledges to be a Keeper."

"Keeper? What does that mean?"

"You really don't know, Kristall?" Leesa shook her head. "You really are from far in the country. Don't you know anything about the king's city?"

Kristall turned back toward the front. The grass-covered tournament field stretched before her. The pavilion belonging to Lord Merlin Shelton, Leesa's father, had been erected close to the king's in a place reserved for those favored by the regent. None of the fighters had taken the field yet, but jugglers, tumblers, and trained animals entertained the waiting crowd.

"I'm sorry, Kristall," Leesa said. "Sometimes my busy mouth runs ahead of my thoughts."

Kristall forced a smile. Leesa didn't mean to poke fun at her. "Just add the Keepers to the list of things I'm ignorant about."

Leesa took Kristall's hand and patted it. "Not knowing about the workings of the city and the court doesn't make you ignorant. It makes you lucky. Especially if you don't know the Keepers. It was because they took my sister that my father no longer came to Sulbreth. I think he and the old king argued about it."

"Your sister is a sorceress then?" Anadalune asked.

Kristall looked at her mother in surprise.

Leesa nodded and looked even sadder. "She's six years older than me. More like a mother to me as we grew up. Our mother passed on when I was only eight."

Kristall took Leesa's hand and squeezed in sympathy. She couldn't imagine not having her mother.

"My sister, Sabelline, hid her talents from us. One day, shortly after she turned eighteen, we came to visit King Jerson." Leesa's eyes misted over, and she blinked a few times. "Sabell walked out of the palace and into their squat, ugly castle."

Leesa pointed to the imposing red and black stone building across the field. It didn't appear a squat anything to Kristall. The square towers and tiny windows scattered about the tall structure resembled a fortress to her. Though it stood only half the height of the king's glorious residence, it looked more solid. A buttress against the mightiest of storms, built to withstand a powerful foe.

"Your father disapproved?" Anadalune asked.

The sun ducked behind a cloud for an instant, causing a dark shadow to pass briefly over the Keeper's fortress. Kristall shivered and turned back to her friend. If Leesa and her kind father despised the Keepers, then Kristall would also. Who wouldn't think evil of someone who took away a loved one?

"My father wanted her to make a good marriage. She and Prince Jonared were the best of friends. She might be queen now."

"Is she happy in her life?" Anadalune asked in the gentle way she had when she wanted Kristall to figure something out for herself.

Leesa shrugged and swiped at her eyes. "Father doesn't let me visit. I've managed to send a letter or two to her through friends, but I've heard from her only a few times. I believe my father tosses out anything she might send to us."

Kristall put her arm around Leesa. The girl seemed so fortunate, but her life of apparent privilege had been filled with unhappy events.

"This is the first time my father has returned to Sulbreth since Sabell abandoned us."

"Why did he return now?" Kristall asked. How lucky she was to have her loving mother and brother. And Sir Berton was as a father to her, more so than her real one had ever been.

"He received a missive from the new king right after we heard the horrid rumors of Jerson's death. My father was sad to learn of the old king's passing."

"Perhaps this return to Sulbreth will help your father go forward and leave the past," Anadalune said.

"I asked him if we might see Sabelline while we were here, though it took all my courage to speak of it. He looked so sad and shook his head. I hadn't the heart to press him."

Lord Merlin left the king's pavilion and started back

toward them. Kristall noticed the king looking their way. Toward her. He was so handsome. And noble. And kind. Why did he stare at her so?

A guilty heat warmed her face hotter than the noontime sun. The attention of any man so fine thrilled her, but to have the gaze of the king fall upon her lifted her heart to her throat.

Her mother touched her shoulder. "Don't stare at the king, dear."

"Mother?"

Sir Berton turned from his post standing at the corner of their pavilion. His brow furrowed into a frown.

Anadalune leaned close and whispered, "Remember, he may be king, but he's a man first. Stay away from him."

Sabell winced as another fighter cried out. She wished only to return to the cool sanctuary of her quarters. Even the bareness of those rooms seemed blessed compared to the primeval spectacle in front of her.

"Look at that one," Reseda said.

Sabell didn't want to look anymore, but she had convinced Mistress Pinxter to shorten her lesson earlier so she could attend the tournament. Anything to escape the needlework.

Reseda gestured at the same tall warrior she'd pointed

out earlier.

Sabell fought down her distaste at the entire debacle and watched the man with as much dispassion as she could muster. Like all Keepers, she practiced with the short sword and knew something of the art of defense and attack. This man glided about his short, thicker opponent like a dance master.

Sabell glanced around the loud chaos of the tournament field. This first day of the fighting had started hours ago with sixteen circles of sixteen men each. An officer of the royal guard was in charge of each group. The fighters drew lots and then took turns moving into the middle of their given circle and meeting their selected opponent. The winners of the first round then fought in the next round. Now, an hour before sunset, all the circles had only four or perhaps even the last two warriors still standing.

The warrior Reseda so admired handled each opponent in an efficient manner that made his foes look like fresh boys.

Reseda gasped and tugged on Sabell's arm as her favorite feigned a stab at his opponent's middle. The over matched man swung his own wooden tournament sword to block the coming thrust. Except the tall man glided aside and slammed the flat of his sword against the side of the unfortunate man's head.

Sabell found herself mesmerized for a brief moment by the near beauty of the man's style. Seeing the loser crumple like a broken toy chased away her admiration. Only a man experienced in the games of war could be so skilled. Dismay and dread filled her. What if such a battle-hardened man became her Marshal?

"Isn't he something?" Reseda crowed.

Yes. A killer.

"I wonder who he is. Perhaps we could arrange to meet him after the tournament."

Sabell looked at the man who once again stood on the edge of the circle and watched the next two men fight. He would win against his last opponent. Neither man in the circle had even a modicum of his skill.

His short hair lifted in the light breeze. The wind barely stirred her thick hair, but it blew his about as if it were made of down feathers. His light-colored eyes followed the fighting in the center with a studied gravity and intelligence she didn't expect in a man wed to his sword.

"He looks like he must be from an outland province," Reseda said.

He had high cheekbones and smoothly tanned skin, not a common look for men of Sulbreth. Many of those in the far provinces seldom came to the city.

Reseda's attention turned to another man. She gushed over his muscular arms until Sabell thought her head would split. Perhaps spending the afternoon with Pinxter would have been better.

"Isn't that your family banner, Sabell?" Reseda pointed across the fighting arena toward the king's pavilion.

Sabell stood and stared at the red banner with five silver stars scattered on it. It flew almost beside the king's seats.

Any curiosity about the fighters fell away beneath the wave of trepidation and desperate hope rising in her breast. Had her father forgiven her then? She strained to see him and her sister, Leesa, beneath the white awning. Four figures sat in the box, but it was too far to even tell if they were male or female.

For the first time since Alvara's death, something other than her duty filled her every thought. She'd believed her heart hardened and healed. She'd accepted her separation from her family as permanent.

She hurried down the steps of the Keepers' pavilion and admitted her own self-delusion. She had to get closer. She had to see her father's and sister's faces one more time before she entered the hell of Kingdom's Gate.

CHAPTER FIVE

"DOES THIS ONE HURT?" BERTON pressed on a spot on Cage's upper arm.

Cage knocked his hand away. "No."

"Humph. You asked for it if it does. How did one of those flappers get his weapon past your guard?"

Cage rose from the fireside bench and moved out of Berton's reach. His best shirt hung on a peg by the bed.

"Do we really have to go to this banquet?" he asked as he slipped the light blue shirt over his head. Maybe Berton would stop his lecture on Cage's fighting style if he couldn't see the bruises.

"You don't ignore an invitation from the king, you country oaf, especially if you're hoping to win his tournament."

Cage ran his fingers through his short, damp hair.

The lingering scent from the sweet soap provided by the inn assaulted him. "I don't like pretty parties such as this."

"What are you wrinkling your nose at now?"

"I wish I could have had a fresh bath." He would smell the soap the rest of the night. Along with the various perfumes everyone else would wear.

"You mean one of those ice baths you prefer in some little stream? Don't know how you've survived all these years without catching a lung fever. And don't say you don't like pretty parties. You've never been to one, at least not one as grand as the king's."

"Have you been to one of the king's feasts?"

"Not the likes of me, but I've heard tell of the rich foods and endless entertainment."

Cage tucked his shirt into his newest black pants, though they were quite worn also. He'd spent all the coin they could spare on clothing for his sister and Anadalune. Who would have guessed he might need to dress in the fancy also?

"You've grown soft, old man, spending these last few years sitting by the fire in the manor. All you think about is food." Cage shrugged into his black vest and laced the front.

"I've never loved sleeping under the stars like you do. Give me a soft bed and a roof to keep out the rain. But don't accuse me of taking the easy way. It was your idea that I stay at home and keep away the wolves that would come after your womenfolk."

"And a good job you did." Cage picked up the cloth he'd used for bathing and began working on his only boots. They were covered with the dust from the tournament field. Even the dry scent of the gritty dust and crushed grass was better than the soap. How could he ever explain the sense of renewal that came with the rain or the invigoration of the morning dew on his bare feet? He had given up trying long ago.

"We're going to look like paupers next to the ladies tonight," Berton muttered as he changed into his own well-used garments.

"We are paupers, Berton."

Cage walked to the narrow window and looked out at the shadows. Despite the tall buildings blocking the rising moon, he knew it peeked above the mountains. Less than an hour until they were expected at the king's table and the expense of a coach to take them there.

The stench of the city rose to offend his nose. Men, horses, and rotting food all added their fetid scents to the mix. He'd managed to ignore it the first few days, but his tolerance decreased as he stayed longer in the city. And over it all hung the greater pall of the black mountains.

"Shall we see if the ladies are ready?" Berton asked. He took a last swipe at his own boots.

One thing Cage liked about the idea of going to the king's castle, or at least the tournament grounds beside it, the air smelled cleaner. It might even be beautiful if not for the looming crags beyond it.

86

"Now mind your manners when we're at the castle," Berton said as they belted on their swords. "I know Lady Anadalune taught you some in the dim past. You bordered on disrespect when we met the king at the market. A more prideful monarch might have had your head for it."

"Did you ever wonder at the order of things, Berton, when a man demands respect because of who his father was rather than because he's earned it?"

Berton shook his head. "How does your mind work, lad? The ideas you come up with frighten me at times. Don't ask anyone at the palace such a question. They'll accuse you of inciting rebellion."

"Perhaps I was rude, Berton, but what gives any man, regardless of title, the right to look at my sister as he did?"

Berton turned and poked Cage in the chest with a blunt, strong finger. "Many men are going to look at Lady Kristall and her mother that way. There are many men of privilege attending the king, and honor doesn't always come with it. We must protect them without getting ourselves up on a gibbet. You put your mind to the tournament, and I'll keep the ladies safe, as I have until now."

Berton would give his life to do so. Cage trusted him completely on that, but would it matter if his royal majesty set his greed on Kristall? The royal brat might find out exactly how far past rude Cage could be.

Sabell paced as she waited for her audience with the Exarch. The private study outside the head Keeper's office only allowed eleven angry steps before she had to turn. She glared at Marshal Harmon each time she passed him.

The burly gray-haired man ignored her as he stood at ease near the closed office door. He'd intercepted Sabell earlier, before she reached her father's pavilion. He'd brought her here with no explanation other than the Exarch wished to see her.

None of her pleading or reasoning moved the Marshal to alter his intentions. She should have tested him to see if he would have resorted to brute force.

Now she fumed and paced. Why was she being prevented from seeing her family? Other Keepers were visited by their parents and siblings whenever they wished. Sabell's throat tightened, but she refused to give in to tears. Tears of anger surely, not further heartbreak.

The office door opened without warning. Elderly Mistress Tamarin shuffled out and nodded to Sabell. She continued to the outer door and left without a word.

"The Exarch will see you now," Marshal Harmon said.

Sabell threw her most venomous glare his way as she marched past him and into the Exarch's sanctum.

Not even her righteous ire could overcome her respect

for the head Keeper and her authority. Her stomach burned around the hot words trapped inside.

Lantana frowned at Sabell, but it didn't frighten her as it once had. She motioned for Sabell to take the chair in front of her desk.

The large expanse of oak should have dwarfed the petite woman, but something about Lantana gave her a stature that suited the size of the antique furniture.

"Sorry to make you wait, Sabelline, but I had to arrange your final training needs with Tamarin. Such a duty should never have befallen her. She deserves to have some ease in her end days."

Sabell nodded, but she refused to let the reminder of her grim duty deflect her anger. She could hold it in no longer. "Why was I not permitted to see my family, Exarch?"

Lantana pressed her lips together and folded her hands in front of her. She stared at them for a moment before answering. "I thought it best if I spoke to your father first. I wasn't aware until today that he had accepted the king's invitation."

"Why must you speak with him? He's come to Sulbreth. Surely it means he's forgiven me."

"Forgiven? That stubborn man?" Lantana rose and walked around the desk to sit beside Sabelline. "I asked the king to summon your father. You know Jonared's father was much pained by the rift that kept his friend away. Your father let Jerson know he would only return by a royal decree."

Sabell rubbed her chest. All her hope for nothing. Only the king's command had brought her family to Sulbreth.

"You're soon to perform a task for the kingdom that is beyond all other services one can undertake. I wanted you to make peace with your father before you go. For the sake of you both."

"I've no wish to see him if it takes the king's sword to force him here." Bitterness filled her mouth, the taste of her own words.

"Sabelline, I insist you see him. He will see reason once I speak past his pride. Only great love could cause him this unforgiving grief."

"I don't think I could find anything to say to him."

Lantana squeezed Sabell's hand. "You don't have to see him immediately. I'll be speaking to him before the banquet tonight in the presence of the king. Jonared has always been your friend, Sabelline, since you were children. If the words of an old lady will not convince your father to redeem himself to you, then the anger of the king will. Perhaps tomorrow a meeting can be arranged."

"I must attend the tournament tomorrow." Even that display of chaos and the fury of fools seemed a welcome escape from such a dreaded confrontation.

Exarch Lantana smiled with a hint of naughtiness in her eyes. "I have a surprise planned for the banquet tonight. There will be no tournament needed tomorrow.

The winner will step forward tonight."

"If I may, your highness?" Count Witbier Thrum asked as he added a short bow.

Jonared nodded and gestured toward a chair to his left. His man had discovered some interesting information since their encounter with the lovely Lady Kristall Thrum. Apparently, the widow of the late count and her daughter refused to live under the roof of this new Count Thrum. Was this uncle an ally to his cause? Legally, this man should have responsibility for his brother's widow and his niece.

"A fine spread, your highness. It speaks of the prosperity your father brought to the kingdom." Thrum's thin lips turned up in a bright smile. "My compliments to your baker on the extraordinary sweet breads."

Jonared smiled back and wondered how the count and others of the nobility would feel about the pastries if they knew they came from a street market. "You've traveled a fair distance to attend my tournament, Count Thrum. I'm surprised you bothered."

Thrum shifted in his seat. His beefy face darkened, and his false cheer melted from his face. "Actually, another matter brought me to Sulbreth."

The count glanced away for a moment. Jonared followed his gaze. Kristall Thrum sat between her mother and Leesa Shelton. All three women stared back at him. Damn, what was this?

"You see, King Jonared, with the untimely passing of your father, I resisted bringing such a small matter to your attention. I assure you, your father was prepared to resolve it for me when last I spoke to him."

Jonared settled back in his chair and folded his hands across his middle. He didn't remember Thrum visiting his father anytime in the past year. Still, the count wasn't the first noble to bring a dispute before him hoping to gain something from the young king they couldn't have won from his more experienced father.

"My elder brother passed on after an unfortunate accident a few years ago."

Jonared recalled it was a drunken fall from his horse while riding home from a house of ill-reputed women.

Thrum plowed on with his explanation. "Since he sired only a daughter, I inherited Kulbach Holding and took as my duty his widow and child."

Jonared said nothing. The law said such things were done in this way. Unless a man had sons, his widow and daughters were left nothing but the largesse of relatives on his death.

"I found the estates in dire circumstances." Thrum leaned closer, a hint of flowery perfume coming with him. "Not to speak ill of my brother, but he had more love for the gambling halls and other wild pursuits than for farming, your highness."

"And you've done well, I've heard, Thrum. What is the problem?"

"I doubt you would know or care about this here in Sulbreth, but Thrum bred himself a bastard."

"Cage Stone. He's in my tournament."

Thrum's mouth dropped open and then snapped shut.

"I make it a point to be knowledgeable of my kingdom, Count, and the people in it." Jonared looked toward the ladies again. Kristall frowned at him and for the first time resembled her bastard half brother. Not that they shared similar features, rather the arrogance of her expression. Frown at the king, indeed.

"You can't know the character of all your subjects, your highness. This man sullies your court with his presence. His mother was thought to be an outlaw witch who seduced my brother with her exotic beauty and devilish spells."

"I've heard only that he's an exceptional swordsman who hires out to hunt outlaws and highwaymen." With great success, according to Jonared's sergeant. Apparently, many men of the king's guard had heard of this fellow, Stone.

Thrum gestured toward the table where all the tournament survivors sat together. It wasn't difficult to find Stone. He glared back at Jonared.

"Has Stone tried to claim Kulbach Holding for his own?"

"No, but he . . ."

"I see no reason for you to have dealings with him then."

"But, your highness, he's interfered with my other rights."

"Other rights?"

"My brother's widow, Lady Anadalune, and her daughter should have remained at Kulbach Holding under my care. Instead, Stone and a rogue guardsman, Sir Berton Wall, spirited the ladies off and hid them in some deep forest."

Jonared sat up. "They were taken away against their will? Kidnapped?"

"Just so. You know that unwed ladies must be under the direction of a man. They're not capable of making important decisions."

"You mean they went with him by choice and not by force?" The word games played by the lords surrounding him day by day tired Jonared. "Speak plain, man. What is your grievance?"

"Even though the Lady Anadalune has completely soiled her reputation by taking up with her bastard step-son, I'm willing to take her under my care and find a place for her among polite society. I searched out a number of good matches for Lady Kristall already. I hoped you would assist me in acquiring what is mine by right, your highness."

"It seems the lady has no wish of returning to you, Count." Jonared's stomach turned at the greed in the count's eyes. The society position for Lady Anadalune would likely be as this man's mistress. How many years had he coveted his brother's wife? "She's turned to her husband's bastard to escape you. What am I to think

94

of that?"

"She's a flighty woman, your highness. She needs guidance."

The Anadalune he'd met in the market seemed poised and quite well spoken. "Have you spoken with her, Count Thrum?"

A vile emotion flashed in Thrum's eyes. "As I said, she's been hidden from me, and that bastard won't let me near her."

"He's one man, Thrum."

Thrum flushed. "He's a known killer, your highness."

"I shall think on your request, Thrum." Jonared nodded his dismissal, which the count had no choice but to obey.

Other lords approached to curry favor or beg an audience for another day. Jonared dealt with each as patiently as he could. Lantana had explained the political importance of having the support of the nobility. After his confrontation with dear cousin Borak, he realized it wasn't a game.

Once he saw Count Thrum making his way toward Lady Anadalune, but Lord Shelton intercepted him, bless him. Leesa Shelton seemed to have attached herself to the Thrum women. They made an attractive trio seated together as they were. His bored mind imagined what type of melee might have erupted if not for Shelton's actions. He had no doubt the bastard Stone would have taken exception to Thrum accosting his lady folk.

Jonared caught Kristall looking his way once more. He nodded to her, and she bowed her head in return. She didn't give him another of her bright smiles.

Damn, but the girl was beautiful. He hadn't forgotten his thoughts of taking her as a lover, but after hearing Count Thrum's plans for Anadalune . . .

Jonared had no wish to behave like Thrum. And to complicate things more, Kristall's very protective brother was a finalist in his tournament. If he fought with the same skill he'd shown today, Stone might actually win.

Not even the king was more important than the outcome of the tournament, according to Lantana. Jonared berated himself for thinking of his personal pleasure at such a time. He smiled grimly. What if Stone came in second? That swordsman would be offered the position of king's protector. If Jonared took Kristall as lover the knife at his throat would likely be that of his own guard.

A server filled his wine goblet. When had he emptied it? The Thrum women were counting on Stone to win, no doubt. The legal conundrum of the odd family coming into the estate would have to be settled. Why would the bastard and the widow of his father be together? Was it as sordid as Count Thrum implied? Was the stepson actually Anadalune's lover?

Jonared sipped more wine, giving a brief thought to how much he'd consumed already. His disgust with Thrum mellowed along with his mood and brought his thoughts full circle.

Lady Kristall should be honored to share his bed. Her other choice would be a marriage arranged by her uncle. Count Thrum would likely arrange something that would most benefit himself. An aging lord, perhaps, who would pass and give Thrum control of his lands.

She couldn't hide in the forest all her life, and Stone couldn't legally keep her from the count. Surely a vital young woman would prefer the glamour and excitement of his court. She would wield a certain amount of power as his lover. At least until he married. He drained his cup of wine and plotted to have it so.

"I'm so worried about Father," Leesa said.

Kristall pulled her gaze from that of the king and her mind away from her own worries. She looked across the wide table to where Lord Shelton sat. The poor man appeared to have aged ten years in an afternoon. His broad shoulders slumped, and his hands shook as he lifted his mug of ale.

"What has happened?" Kristall whispered, though she doubted Lord Shelton could hear her above the bedlam of the great hall. Leesa's father had not only welcomed them into his pavilion but had guided Lord Thrum away from them twice already this evening.

"He was summoned to a meeting with the Exarch

right before we arrived tonight. I'm afraid he's received some terrible news about my sister. He tells me not to worry, but . . ."

Kristall squeezed Leesa's hand. The girl was usually very cheerful, so her despair, especially at such a grand celebration, pained Kristall's own heart. "What is an Exarch?"

"I keep forgetting you know nothing of Sulbreth. The Exarch is the leader of the Keepers. Some say she's more powerful than the king and is his chief advisor." Leesa lowered her voice even more and leaned closer to Kristall. "Some say she uses witchcraft to bespell the king. She's sitting to the king's right."

"Do you believe that?" Only a tiny elderly woman sat where Leesa indicated. She looked like a kindly grandmother.

Leesa shrugged. "Father said I might be able to visit Sabelline tomorrow."

"Isn't that what you want, Leesa?"

"More than anything. But what if she tells me something awful? Why is father so sad?"

Kristall put her arm around her friend when tears filled Leesa's eyes. "You're worrying over nothing. Probably the Exarch gave your father a stern lecture on shunning his daughter. He's feeling guilty; that's all. What terrible thing could be wrong?"

Leesa smiled, albeit a bit tearily. "Thank you, Kristall. You always look for the best outcome for everything. You have the right of it. It's not like there's a war or anything. My sister's few letters spoke of days and days filled with studies. The worst that could happen to her is boredom."

They giggled together. Anadalune turned from her conversation with the lady seated next to her and frowned at them. That made them giggle more.

All serious conversation ended then as they gossiped over the court fashions. It amused Kristall to see the men dressed as prettily as the women.

Except the men sitting at the tournament fighters' table. Those hardened men wore neutral colors of more conservative cut than the lords decorating the other tables. Kristall couldn't help notice that Cage and Sir Berton appeared a bit shabby even in that company. Her enjoyment of her own best golden dress shriveled.

"Your brother is so handsome," Leesa said.

"Most women find him so." How might he look if he had a new leather tunic and a red woolen shirt? Many of the lords wore red. Perhaps it was the fashion of the season for them.

"If he weren't a bastard, the women would be begging for his attention," Leesa said in such a straightforward tone, Kristall couldn't take insult. It was the truth.

"My mother says he resembles his mother as I do mine. I believe my father had weak blood and passed none of himself to Cage or me. At least, I hope it's so."

"Do you know the swordsman beside Cage?"

Kristall shook her head. "Cage won't talk about the fighting. He says it's not a fit topic for a young lady."

They giggled again at Kristall's imitation of Cage. The swordsman seated beside her brother looked at them and smiled. His clear blue eyes sparkled as he gave them a charming nod. He leaned toward Cage and said something. Cage looked over and frowned at them.

The girls couldn't help themselves. They giggled even more.

The many side doors suddenly opened, and servants bustled through carrying large trays. Kristall's mouth watered as pastries dripping with warm honey were placed in front of everyone. Each delicacy was as large as both her hands put together. She carefully cut a piece with her eating knife and lifted it toward her mouth. She feared the dripping sweet might soil her costly dress. The feeling of being watched stilled her with her hand halfway to her mouth.

She lifted her gaze and found the king staring at her. A heat much warmer than the honey filled his dark eyes.

Kristall wanted to look away and obey her mother's admonition. Cage had offered his own lecture on the ride to the palace. But King Jonared's stare trapped her as surely as a hare in a wire snare, and the king was the hunter.

100

"They're a couple of pretty ones," said Sir Maton Reves. "You'll be hard-pressed to protect that sister of yours from the vultures of this court."

Cage sighed. Every man in the room stared at his sister, not the least of whom was the king. Cage knew he could frighten off any lord or other minor noble lusting after his sister, but what of his liege?

"Have you heard what type of contest they have planned for the second round tomorrow, Sir Maton?" Berton asked. He sat to Cage's right while Maton occupied the seat to his left.

"It's a well-kept secret," Maton answered. "It matters not to me. I'm expert at all manners of combat."

Cage liked Maton. Berton opined the young fighter would be Cage's closest adversary in the tournament. "Expert always loses to experience."

Maton laughed. "We shall see on the morrow."

The servants finally served the final course to the fighters' table. Cage had no liking for the overly sweet pastries, but Sir Berton loved such things and gladly took two onto his own plate.

Cage had grown accustomed to the stares of the curious as the evening progressed, but now someone directed more hostile attention his way. He sensed the malicious gaze with an instinct he neither questioned nor understood. It was just there. It didn't take him long to find the source.

Count Witbier Thrum and his son, Berlin, glared at

Cage from their place near the end of the king's table.

He didn't hate the two as they hated him. He only wanted to keep the weasels from getting what they wanted: Anadalune and Kristall.

The Thrums towered over most men as had Cage's father. Though Cage was equal in height to his uncle, his cousin stood half a hand taller. Both men were thick through the chest and layered with muscles. They frightened Anadalune and Kristall as they might any woman unlucky enough to catch their interest.

"Don't worry, boy. I'm keeping a watch on them. They've been asking around, trying to find out where we're staying. That earlier supplication to the king was about our ladies, you can bet."

"You stay close to their sides tomorrow."

Berton nodded. "I hate leaving you alone. You're the only fighter without a man to do for you. They didn't arrive until after the matches today, but I'm sure they'll try to get to the ladies tomorrow. Lord Shelton is a good man, but he can't handle them himself."

"Be careful. The king might not look kindly on the killing of one of his counts. Maybe the women should stay at the inn."

Berton guffawed. "You try to convince them of that one."

Cage muttered a curse. "If the king sides with the count, we'll be in a spot."

"Keep your mind on your fighting, Cage. We'll take

on the other if we have to."

Cage knew Berton was right, but it wasn't so easy to put aside his worry. He'd come to Sulbreth to win a holding and therefore security for his sister and the woman who had raised him. He feared he'd brought them into a viper pit instead.

CHAPTER SIX

"WE'RE READY, EXARCH," MARSHAL Harmon whispered.

Harmon was better at sneaking up on her each year. She should have sensed him entering the hall, but her abilities weakened a bit more with each passing day.

Lantana took a deep, bracing breath and leaned toward the young king. She'd first joined the Keepers when Jonared's grandfather ruled Sulbreth. She'd served Jerson for all her years as Exarch until now. Fear of failing this new ruler kept her awake at night and squelched her appetite to nothing. Jonared had the inner strength and moral compass to be a just and kind monarch of long renown. If he could survive this first colossal task. "It's time, your highness."

Jonared looked at her, his brow crinkled with concerns

he'd broached with her earlier. "Are you sure this is the best way to find our winner? I thought to have a mounted competition on the morrow."

Lantana understood poor Jonared. He'd seen his father's grotesque death not so many days ago. The contest would reawaken those horrifying memories.

"Horses can't be taken through Kingdom's Gate, my king. Such an exercise won't select the best swordsman for our needs."

Her heart filled with pity at the grief in Jonared's dark eyes. "I'm sorry, your highness. I wish you didn't have to be there, but the contest is named as yours."

Jonared's expression hardened into angry resolve. "I have no problem attending. I think I can face anything now."

Lantana hadn't the heart to tell the brave, but ignorant, king that there were many things beyond the Gate that were worse than the monsters that had killed his father.

The king rose and the hall fell silent. Lantana watched Cage Stone, curious to see his reaction.

"My good friends, thank you for attending this celebratory feast. The evening will continue for most of you with more entertainment." Jonared gestured toward the musicians setting up their tools in the far corner of the hall. "However, our remaining contenders will now retire to the rear lawns for the next round of my tournament."

A loud buzz rolled away from the king and filled the hall as the ladies and lords reacted to the surprise.

Cage Stone's only reaction was to shift his gaze from Jonared to Lantana. The piercing quality of his stare startled her. Though she knew he wasn't capable, he seemed to look into her mind.

Jonared's guards moved in between the head table and the fighters so Lantana could no longer see him. Excitement lifted her hopes. So the bastard had proven great skill in the weapons arena. Now they would test his bravery and intelligence.

Cage watched the wily old woman as she smiled at the king. She looked very self-satisfied when he made his announcement.

"Stay here," Cage said to Berton.

"It's not like I have a choice."

The king's guards herded the other contestants toward one of the side doors. No one else was being permitted to follow.

A seed of apprehension, a feeling he trusted, settled in Cage's middle. "I trust our ladies to you."

Berton put a strong hand on Cage's shoulder. "Knock them down, lad."

Cage fell into line while avoiding so much as a glance at Anadalune and Kristall.

A guard led them through a dim hallway to a narrow

stair. No one spoke as they began their descent.

Cage listened to the various sounds made by the other men's boots. The sharp click of fancy boot heels mixed with the soft footfalls from boots made to cushion and comfort feet weary from a day of toil. His boots were the only pair he owned. The thick leather soles would last longer still despite their outward appearance. How might their footgear affect combat on the damp grass outside? He would use every advantage against the others.

Cage touched the smooth, dry stones of the walls, the strength of the old, strong, earth bones slowing his building anticipation of battle. These boulders had been carved from a far mountain and brought to this place ages ago. The cares of man meant nothing to them as they sat in their patient rigidity.

"What are you doing?" Maton whispered.

Cage lowered his hand from the wall. How could one describe the flight of an eagle to a child born blind? The beauty of the stone was no less.

"Where are we going?" Cage asked. Maton had visited the king's residence many times in the past with his family.

"I think we're heading to the king's private lawns. They stretch almost from the castle to the mountains."

They filed down another long flight of steps. Cage listened as the stones gave a vague comfort in their stoic ancient existence. They almost distracted him from worry over this odd turn. Rumor said the king held the tournament to raise his spirits and those of his subjects after the recent death of the old king. Yet now King Jonared robbed the masses of their entertainment by moving the contests to his private lawns?

The stairs ended, and they entered a long, wide hallway. Cage caught the scent of hounds, grass, and dirt. The fresh air brushed his face as they rounded a corner and found an open door. More guards waited there. A heavy dew lent its moisture to the night scents and sparkled on the grass illuminated by the torchlight.

Maton muttered a curse as they stepped outside. Tall, thick stakes held torches high above the ground, marking off a rectangular area the size of a fighting arena.

Somewhere in the dark beyond the torches, leather armor creaked, cloth whispered against cloth and men sweated. Women hid there also. The subtle scent of female hung in the damp air.

Cage stepped away from the torch right outside the door. Once out of its bright glare, he could see the shapes of women and heavily armed men beyond the flickering torches. An ambush? He sensed no malice from them, but an uneasiness touched his mind.

"Welcome to my playground, my good men."

Cage and the others turned back toward the castle when King Jonared spoke. He stood on a balcony two stories up with the tiny old lady beside him.

The seed of trepidation blossomed into a tense anticipation of danger. The menace was like a whiff of an old animal carcass. He concentrated on placing the source, and then he knew. The black crags stood behind him, in the gloom beyond the inadequate light. It took all his willpower to face the king and listen to his words rather than turn to face the oncoming threat.

"All of you have proved your prowess in force of arms, but tonight you must show your other qualities. Witness to your performance will be my close advisor, Exarch Lantana, and other selected Keepers and Marshals."

The tattooed man who seemed to be a protector for the old lady stared down on them from her side. His stern scrutiny touched Cage like the poke of a stiff finger.

Four bright torches flamed on the king's balcony, but Cage stepped closer so he might see even better. The Exarch's small face tightened with displeasure or . . . something else.

Goose bumps ran up Cage's arms and down his back as something flowed down from the balcony and across him. He spun to look after it and reached for his sword.

Lantana muttered the last word that would trigger the illusion spell she'd set earlier. Other Keepers helped power the spell to give it more vivid life. Beyond the last torch, the spell sparked into being. Three yellow gor-dragons rose from the grass and bellowed their rage.

A Keeper screamed, and Marshals shouted warnings.

Lantana patted the king's hand as their plan unfurled. Her people acted their part well and gave the illusion added reality.

"Now we shall see who has the courage to stand," Lantana said to Jonared and Harmon.

The conjured demons resembled over-large oxen in size, but there was nothing bovine about them otherwise. Scaly armor covered their muscular bodies, and their feet were claws rather than hooves. Their red eyes glowed in the torchlight above their dragon-like snouts, giving them their name.

Lantana watched the fighters below her rather than her creations. Some of them had run for the castle doorway already. Cage Stone showed no panic. He stared at the oncoming illusion. She'd noticed him turn to face the threat even before she finished the spell. Another young man pulled his sword and moved up to stand side by side with Stone in front of the others. Interesting.

The gordragons paused as planned and turned to face the torches. Lantana smiled as Sabell, right on schedule, ran into the middle of the field. She stopped and stared at the illusions until Lantana turned them toward her. When they'd fixed their red glares on the young woman, she turned and ran toward Cage and the others.

To a man, the fighters fled before the oncoming beasts. Except for two. Cage Stone and the man beside him held their ground.

Uneasiness touched the edge of Lantana's concentration

as she sent the creatures after Sabell. She struggled to hold the illusion. She needed to see what steel might be in the two men left on the field.

Sabell reached Stone. He shoved her into the other man's arms and charged toward the gordragons.

Lantana started to laugh, but her heart suddenly seized in her chest. Stone ran straight through her creations and toward the end of the lighted area. Lantana lost control of her spell, and the gordragons winked out of existence. At least her three did. At the edge of the torchlight, two more of the monsters rumbled onto the lawn. The ground shook beneath their gargantuan weight. Their very real jaws stretched open as they roared their unholy challenge.

Sabell grunted as she bounced against the hard chest of the blond man. He swore in the most colorful, rude fashion before he pushed her behind him.

"Run to the castle, my lady," he ordered. He pulled a short sword from his back harness to match the long sword already in hand.

Sabell ignored him and sidestepped him. She wanted to see what the other fighter was about. Instead of battling the Exarch's illusions—they were gone—the man sprinted away toward the end of the lawn. Shouts of alarm rose from the Marshals and Keepers still in shadow beyond the torches. It sounded so real.

"Son of a demon lord!" the man beside Sabell said. "Where did the first three go? How did Cage run right through them?"

Sabell said nothing. It wasn't her place to explain the test. She strained to see beyond the torches. Marshals ran toward the end of the lawn and joined the man who had flung her aside.

Alarm swept over her and sent her heart to pounding. Keepers joined the charge away from the castle. The growing mayhem crashed about Sabell as the king's guard poured out of the door behind her.

"You there." Marshal Harmon's shout penetrated the chaotic noise. The blond man beside her looked up at the balcony behind them. "Get Keeper Sabelline inside and block the door. They're after her."

The young man acted without hesitation. He took Sabell's arm and pulled her toward the castle. Sabell stared up at the Exarch. Her leader's face shone pale and stark in the torchlight. Guards surrounded the king and pushed him away from the railing.

Sabell tried to tug her arm from the fighter, but he was too strong. Before she ducked inside, she saw the dark-haired man meeting the charge of a real gordragon with nothing but his sword.

Cage raced to meet the real demon, the first he'd ever seen in person. He passed through the misty fabrications that had chased the young woman and wondered at her pretend fear. What purpose? The Exarch had somehow created the illusions, but was she also responsible for these real demons?

It made no sense to him. Not that it mattered at the moment.

The creatures' stench assailed his sensitive nose as he neared. Rotted meat and damp mold. The monsters glistened with layers of lizardlike scales instead of animal hide. Not something his sword could hope to pierce.

When the lead creature rumbled a mere step from him, Cage leaped to the side as high as he could. He slashed across the creature's eyes with his sword as he flew a whisker's distance out of the reach of its lethal teeth.

His ears rang as the demon bellowed. Cage landed lightly on his feet and swung his sword again, this time at the underbelly of the lumbering hellspawn. He swore as his blade slid across the thick scales doing little damage.

The monster stopped with much tearing of grass and dirt. It swung its massive head toward Cage. It gave him small satisfaction to see the red glow had gone from its eyes. He'd taken its sight, but what other senses might

113

such a magical beast possess?

A loud clap akin to thunder shook the lawn. Cage fell backward as a wave of thick air slapped his chest. He couldn't pull any breath into his lungs. Still, he rolled away from the invisible force and came to his feet with his sword ready.

Another loud clap reverberated through the cool night air. A bright flash stole his vision for a moment. Cage stumbled back from the battle. Who was attacking what?

The demon he'd blinded sank to its knees and screamed in vicious protest.

As his vision cleared, he saw the other beast fall to its side. A number of men and women approached the downed monsters with slow, cautious steps. Cage stood his ground with sword drawn. Shards of agony shot from the center of his chest as he tried to draw in a full breath.

"Are they dead?" the little lady, the Exarch, asked as she strode into the light.

"This one is, and the other is dying," one of the women answered.

The Exarch stared at the monsters for a long time with narrowed eyes and a tight mouth. Then she lifted her gaze to Cage. "Are you injured?"

Cage lowered his sword. He knew there were no more demons abroad, but he wasn't entirely sure all danger had passed. Damn, his chest hurt. He could barely see the tiny lady across the carcass of the beast. "The demon didn't injure me."

The Exarch raised a fine eyebrow, but Cage didn't care what she thought of his tone. He hurt, and this little lady had started this dangerous havoc.

"Come with me," she ordered Cage.

He held his ground for a moment. What had all this to do with the king's tournament? Had this been the final contest, against such fearsome creatures? He took a step and gasped as it jarred his chest.

The Exarch paused and looked back at him. He followed, fighting back a wave of dizziness.

Somewhere behind him lurked a dark menace. It felt more distant and less focused than it had been right before the demons appeared, but it was real. And before him marched a little lady filled with secrets and capable of deception. And magic.

Cage rubbed his chest and followed her. The fear he hadn't felt at the appearance of the hellspawn filled him now.

He wished he could pack up his womenfolk and flee Sulbreth, but the instincts that never failed him warned him he was ensnared in a trap from which he could not escape.

PART TWO

CHAPTER SEVEN

THE TATTOOED MAN, MARSHAL Harmon, led Cage and Maton Reves to a large study. The furnishings were of the finest quality, but Cage didn't care. While Maton lingered beside the fireplace, a dark frown on his usually jovial face, Cage watched his captors.

The Marshal and the Exarch whispered together near the door, and not even Cage's exceptional hearing could pick up their words. After much discussion, the Exarch nodded at the Marshal and turned to leave.

Cage hastened after her, but the large man stepped in his way. "You're to stay put, lad."

"You've no authority to keep me here," Cage answered. He didn't even know what a Marshal was, but the man seemed a body protector of some type. "I've broken no laws."

The Exarch paused outside the door. Her eyes glinted with temper when she looked at Cage. "You're not a prisoner, but you will await my return."

"I have family waiting for me."

"They can wait," she said. "I must speak with the king, and then I'll be back. The king himself may wish to talk with you."

"I'll give your man the name of the inn I'm staying at, and you can send a message when you wish to speak with me." Cage had no intention of remaining at the inn. They would be on the road as soon as he could ready the horses and hire a coach. Surely Sir Berton had taken the ladies back to their lodgings. They couldn't be quit of this demon-cursed city soon enough.

"You will stay in this room until I return, young man."

Cage had faced desperate cornered outlaws. This tiny lady didn't intimidate him. He took another step. The big guard shifted to keep himself between Cage and the Exarch.

Cage matched the Marshal's glare. "Then you do think to make me a prisoner?"

Maton stepped closer, but he said nothing.

"Think?" the Marshal asked with a humorless smile. "Boy, if we wanted to hog-tie you and keep you here until the next snowfall, we could. I'm tempted to give you a lesson in manners."

Cage didn't respond to the challenge. He stared at

the Exarch. The Marshal was only her muscle, not the real authority.

She narrowed her sharp eyes at him but spoke to her guard. "No need to threaten, Marshal Harmon. He's not of Sulbreth and knows little of the Keepers or our powers. He'll learn."

The threat in her words carried more potency than Harmon's. Still, Cage held his ground.

The Exarch took two clipped steps back into the room and shook her finger at Cage. "You stay in this room until I return. I'll post twenty guards outside this door if I must. If that's not enough, I'll give you a taste of my power that will make that blow you took earlier feel like a lover's caress. Now sit you down. I have many things to do and no time to bandy words with you."

She turned for the door again, but Cage dared to follow. He believed her threats, but his sister and mother needed him. "My lady, please give me a moment."

With a mighty sigh for one so tiny, the Exarch turned back to him again. "What is so dire?"

Cage hated to speak of it in front of Harmon and Maton. "I fear for the safety of my sister and her mother."

"What?"

"They have only one man to act as protector, and he'll be no proof against the attentions of the ladies' enemies. I must see to them."

The Exarch huffed and spun back to the door. She called back over her shoulder, "I'll see to it. Stay here."

The door slammed shut behind her. In the quiet following her departure, the crackling fire seemed loud.

Cage prowled the room, his worry unabated and growing. Did the Exarch have the power in the king's court to keep Count Thrum from Anadalune and Kristall? And who would keep the king at bay?

Cage stopped at the single window. Though the heavy drapes were closed, he knew he faced west; he sensed the stars and moon outside. If only he and his family were camped underneath them somewhere.

The door opened to admit a servant carrying a tray laden with decanters of strong spirits and a small plate filled with sweet cakes.

Maton poured himself a drink and raised an eyebrow at Cage. Cage shook his head. Even one drink of spirits muddled his thoughts and tripped his tongue and legs. Sir Berton took great delight in Cage's intolerance of ales and wines.

"Why do you think they're holding us, Cage?" Maton asked, his voice low enough to escape the Marshal's attention. "And what the hell were those things? Was that part of the damn tournament?"

All good questions, but Cage had no answers. The Marshal stood in front of the door with his massive arms crossed.

"How did you know they were there?" Maton asked.

Cage shrugged and looked around the plush room. A prison despite the trappings of wealth. He'd give the Exarch until the moon crossed over its apex, and then . . . then he was leaving this place.

Kristall turned away another young lordling's invitation to dance. How could she dance when they'd taken Cage away? She remembered him helping her learn the swirling steps under her mother's instruction so she might not be ignorant should the need arise. She couldn't dance now when each dip and swing would remind her of her brother.

Her mother fidgeted beside her. Though Anadalune kept her expression serene, her eyes betrayed her own fears. For Kristall, the entire adventure to Sulbreth had taken on a sinister air. There was something too secretive, a hidden plan beyond what they were being told.

"They've been gone a long time," Leesa said.

"It only seems so," Kristall said, more to reassure herself than Leesa. Her friend worried on her behalf as a good ally should. Kristall stared at without seeing the dancers, no longer intrigued by the glitter of the ladies' gems or the softness of her own wonderful dress. Once again the enormity of Cage's sacrifices for her and her mother made her feel small and greedy.

"Cage can take care of himself," her mother said.

Kristall pretended to agree with her mother, though

Anadalune's tone wasn't very convincing. She searched the hall for a sight of Sir Berton. His steady presence would reassure her. His faith in Cage's abilities never wavered. The crowd applauded in drunken appreciation as a troupe of acrobats leaped and flipped onto the floor.

Kristall turned from the garish display and found Sir Berton standing along the wall not far from them. She tried to read Berton's stoic expression, but his frown told her little.

"Does this mean we won't see more of the tournament tomorrow?" Leesa asked.

"Might your father know what the king has planned?"

Lord Merlin' sat across from them, isolated by the noise. He slumped in his chair and stared into his mug of ale, his expression slack with too much drink and a stark sadness in his eyes.

A flurry of movement drew Kristall's gaze before Leesa answered. A large burly man threw a slow, inebriated punch at Berton, who dodged it with ease. Berton pushed past the sot and walked with brisk purpose toward their table.

Something in Berton's eyes alarmed Kristall. What had happened? Then a heavy hand fell on her shoulder.

Kristall jumped and turned in her seat. Berlin Thrum slid his hand off her shoulder and up toward her neck. His clammy skin sliding over her nape sent shivers down her back. Her stomach clenched and roiled with a sudden nausea made worse by the stagnant odor of old pipe smoke clinging to him.

"You're looking lovely tonight, cousin." Berlin's smile revolted as much as his touch. He stared at her with the hungry greed seen in a starving mongrel.

"Get your hand off my daughter," Anadalune said, her voice low and tight.

"Who is this person?" Leesa asked.

Berlin pressed on Kristall's shoulder when she tried to rise. She wanted to run or at least crawl under the table. Anything to escape his noxious touch.

Anadalune shot to her feet. Kristall saw Leesa's father stand also, though he swayed a bit.

"I tell you again, unhand my daughter." Her mother raised her voice, and many heads turned their way.

"No need to make a scene, my lady aunt."

Kristall glared up at her towering cousin. She hated and feared Berlin. Her memories of him during their childhood were filled with his many small acts of cruelties toward her and especially Cage.

A purulent smile curled his thin lips, and his fingers tightened on her bare skin.

"Step away from her, Thrum," Berton growled as he moved in between Anadalune and Berlin.

"Go away, old man. You have no authority over these women, and you certainly can't order me about." Her cousin didn't even look at the swordsman.

Berton cursed under his breath. Fear grew in

Kristall, for herself and Berton. Attacking the son of a count while at the king's banquet could be disaster for Sir Berton. He could end up in the dungeon or worse.

"I see you've grown into the same kind of uncouth lout as your uncle and father, Berlin." Her mother's voice shook with anger. "And like the coward you are, you wait until my stepson leaves before accosting us."

Berlin's face darkened and his lascivious smile slid from his face, but his fingers tightened even more. Kristall knew she would wear bruises. Cage would kill his cousin for this.

"What are you about, Thrum?" Lord Merlin demanded.

Kristall realized everyone near them had fallen silent. Humiliation joined her fear and disgust.

"You misunderstand your position, Aunt Anadalune," Berlin said, his voice no longer coated with slimy honey. "My father has petitioned the king for wardship over you and Kristall. You'll be living under my roof now."

Lantana hurried through the corridors leading to the king's castle. Few knew of the deep tunnels that connected the Keepers' fortress with the royal residence. She nodded at the king's guards as she strode past them, but her thoughts were elsewhere.

Real gordragons! Her heart still raced with remembered fear and the heady rush of danger. So close to the castle, to Sabelline and Jonared! She still waited for the report from Kingdom's Gate. What of her Keepers and her Marshals standing watch? Their fates weighed heavy on her heart.

Despite her grave worries, a part of her sang with hope and relief. The bastard half-breed had performed beyond her expectations. Somehow he had recognized her illusions and sensed the real danger before the rest of them. How? She longed to speak with him, pick his mind, explore the depths of his abilities.

But first, the king waited. She turned into the narrow servants' hall that would lead her around the banquet hall and to the king's private chambers.

"Damn." She changed course toward the noisy door leading into the banquet. She had seen into Cage Stone's heart when he pleaded with her to go to his sister. He feared greatly for them, and she must keep her promise.

She entered the noisy hall and muttered another soft curse as she looked at the teeming colorful confusion. The king had pointed out the young woman earlier, but how was she to find her and her mother in this crowd? A small altercation drew her attention toward one table. A rather shabbily dressed man-at-arms shoved at a much larger man. Despite their size differences, the larger man stumbled back a step. When he moved, Lantana glimpsed the gold gown and bright hair of the Thrum girl. So Cage Stone's worries were valid.

"Men and their damn passions." Lantana stalked forward as two of the king's guards closed in on the disturbance. Many of the gathered nobility turned their attention to the spectacle they found more interesting than the paid entertainers.

"Get your hands off me, you country oaf," the tall man said. Whined, rather. "I'll have you whipped if you dare touch me again."

The guards looked relieved to see Lantana hurrying forward. Reprimanding the nobility was always a tricky thing.

"Gentlemen," Lantana said, her temper still short from dealing with Cage earlier. Seeing his fears confirmed didn't soothe her. "You will cease this."

The tall lord turned his petulant glare on her, but his expression changed quickly when he recognized her.

Lantana ignored the whelp and looked beyond him. The beautiful young girl stared at Lantana with a swirling mixture of anger and fear in her large brown eyes. She was the type of woman men would fight over. And Jonared had noticed her. The woman beside her looked young to be the mother.

"Would you two ladies be relatives of Cage Stone?"

"We would," the mother answered.

Lantana dredged up a smile, though her patience stretched beyond bearing. "I wish to extend the invitation of the king. He has made rooms ready for you here at the castle."

Lantana expected bright smiles and gratitude.

"I'm not sure," the mother said. She glanced at her protector, her pretty brow furrowed with some concern.

Must Stone's family be as difficult as him? Lantana didn't have time for this, so she bullied as she had with Stone. "The king does not make a request. Send your man for your possessions. He can sleep outside your door if you desire."

Lantana turned from their stunned expressions to the pair of king's men. "See that no one further disturbs the ladies. Escort them to the guest quarters yourselves."

Lantana turned away but then remembered something else. She addressed the protector. "When you collect the ladies' possessions, bring along Cage Stone's as well. He'll be staying here for some long while."

Jonared took the proffered wine from a servant and then dismissed the man with a nod. He set the cup, untasted, on the ornate table beside his chair. A few drops splashed out, betraying the tremors in his hand.

He rose and paced about his small private salon. He took deep breaths to steady himself, but still his heart raced. More monsters! Had they come for him as they had for his father?

He hated the fear wrapping his chest so tight his

breath shortened and his heart thumped in a frantic uncontrolled thunder. Gordragons. Thinking the name made his steps falter. What might have happened if the Keepers and Marshals had not been there? If he had been taking his hounds for a run? He stopped midstride as he recalled the heroic charge of the bastard, Cage Stone.

What kind of man ran toward such terrors? Jonared had tried to reach his father the day of his assassination, but it was his beloved sire. Stone ran to meet the gordragons for no apparent reason. Was it courage or supreme arrogance?

A guard opened the door and looked inside. The poor man wore the same haunted look as all the palace swordsmen. The monsters they'd seen of late were not the enemies they expected to meet in the service of their king. "The Exarch, your highness."

"Show her in. After I finish here, have my captains report to me."

Lantana pushed her way by the guard, her face in a dark scowl. "Also send for strong tea, but allow no other interruptions."

The good man looked to Jonared for his nod before bowing out of the room to follow the Exarch's orders. On another day Jonared might have taken the Exarch to task for ordering his men about but not tonight. Tonight he needed this woman's guidance, her advice, and most of all, her reassurance.

Lantana sighed as they settled into adjacent chairs.

She bade Jonared wait while a young kitchen lass scurried in with a tray of tea. The young girl dared only one frightened glance at the Exarch and none at all at her king before she ducked out of the room.

The Exarch took a long sip of the hot, dark liquid. Jonared eyed his wine but resisted the temptation. Tea would curdle in his stomach, so he waited with little patience for Lantana to speak.

"What happened?" Jonared could stand it no longer. He tried to keep his voice strong, but to himself he sounded like a bewildered child.

Lantana set her cup back on the tray, her hands steady. "I've not kept you waiting on purpose, my king. I knew you would want some answers. The gordragons came through the Gate, of course. I only now heard they injured my two Marshals posted at guard, one severely. Actually, the creatures ran over them."

"And were these demons sent as assassins for me? Or perhaps for Sabelline?"

Lantana hesitated.

Jonared's fear rose a small notch as he saw her unsure in a way she seldom was about anything. "Am I marked for death as my father was?"

"I can't say for sure. The gordragons were stopped before their intent was clear."

"What other reason could there be for their attack, then? At that moment, when we were all in the open? How can they know such things?"

"I must do more research and speak with my fellows, but I've read of a possible reason in some of the histories. When the seals on the Gate are weakened enough, use of large amounts of magic on this side seems to draw the creatures through."

A spark of anger flickered in his chest, welcome as it burned away some of his fear. "You mean your illusion show brought them here?"

Lantana raised an eyebrow. "It's one theory. But if it's true, the seals are much weaker than they should be."

Jonared sprang from his chair and stomped to the little table where his wine sat. He gulped it down in a few swallows. His anger cooled as his relief grew. He hadn't been the prey. His family and the Keepers were allied in their duty to guard Kingdom's Gate. It gained them nothing to place blame.

"It happened, but it's over," Lantana said. "Now, let's talk about the good thing that occurred tonight."

Jonared set his empty wine goblet down and took his seat again. "You mean the bastard, Stone?"

Lantana's face remained serious and tired, but her eyes sparkled. "He performed beyond my expectations. He saw past my tricks and sensed the presence of the true monsters."

He didn't share her enthusiasm. "You attribute this to some magical power he has?"

"No, no." The Exarch settled back in her chair. Did he imagine that she was smaller and frailer than just hours ago? "I'm more sure than ever of his ancestry. Their sense of the spiritual and physical worlds is much more developed than that of humans."

"Humans? He's not even a man?"

Lantana narrowed her eyes at him. "He's a brave man who may hold our hopes in his half-human hands, Jonared. You'd best hope he's human enough to want to help us. I've spoken with him, and he's not the type we can force to accept this task."

Jonared looked away. Were his pride and prejudices going to impede his rule? Did not the kingdom come first? What mattered if this bastard showed minimal respect for the crown?

"By the by, I've arranged rooms in your guest quarters for the Thrum widow and her daughter," Lantana said, her voice again that of a tired old woman.

Despite the fear still gnawing on his middle, Jonared's heart took a small exultant leap. "You surprise me, Exarch. I didn't know you cared so much for my personal comforts."

Lantana rose slowly, her glare as hot as the steam from the clay teapot. "You will keep your lustful thoughts and lecherous touch from the girl. How do you expect us to gain the boy's cooperation if you make a casual whore of his sister?"

Jonared reminded himself that he was the monarch, not this tiny woman managing to loom over him. He knew her power and knew it would never be turned on him. Or would it? A roll in the blankets was not reason enough to test her.

"Then why did you bring her here?" He strove for commanding rather than a whine.

"Because her cousin accosted her in your very own banquet hall. Cage Stone refused to stay unless I saw to her safety. And that means from you also."

"Cage Stone refused to stay? Who the hell does he think he is?"

Lantana wagged her finger at Jonared. "Get beyond whatever sets you off about the boy. We need him. You need him. As far as who he is, I'm going to speak with him right now. Perhaps he knows things about his mother and her people that we've only guessed about them. He may have knowledge that could open secrets buried for generations."

"Why wouldn't he have come forward with such?"

"Why would he? He's been raised as a bastard unwelcomed by his father. He's struggled to survive. What opportunity would he have to know the value of his blood? And perhaps he knows nothing. We shall see."

Jonared stared at the door after Lantana left. Her chastisement, though deserved, blackened his morose mood even further. At least the foul humor pushed aside his remaining fright. Still, the king shouldn't be made to feel a spoiled child, reprimanded for selfish behavior.

He rose to look for more wine and then stopped himself. He drank too much of the calming beverage. He vowed to drink less, especially not for comfort. Indeed, he must work side by side with the Keepers as ever his family had done and hold vigil on Kingdom's Gate. He would not be the king to fail in his sacred duty and let the great evil escape.

CHAPTER EIGHT

"YOU'RE TO GO RIGHT IN, MISTRESS Sabelline."

She didn't know the young Marshal guarding the Exarch's door and wondered where Harmon was. Sabelline took a deep breath and tried to calm her racing heart. Her mind leaped from disaster to disaster as she tried to turn her thoughts from one dreadful thing to another. The worry of seeing her father on the morrow nagged under and over everything else. The anticipation of the Exarch's contest had kept her nerves on edge and then the actual horror of the real gordragons. Was it any wonder she tumbled over the edge of reason and control?

She wanted only to curl up with a cup of hot cinnamon tea or strong wine and rid herself of the tremors that would not leave her.

The Marshal opened the door for her, concern on his serious face.

Sabelline entered the large room that served as the Exarch's office. Rather than waiting behind her daunting desk, Lantana waited in one of the two large cushioned chairs flanking the fireplace.

"Come in, dear." Lantana gave a small smile and motioned to the other chair.

Sabelline drew some comfort from the Exarch's calm. Many of the Keepers and Marshals hastened about their duties with nervous glances and edgy energy.

Sabelline settled in the offered seat. She looked into the Exarch's kind eyes and hoped cowardly fears didn't shine in her own.

"It will be all right, Sabelline, but we have much to do."

Sabelline nodded. Was there excitement in her leader's tone? "What happened tonight? What went wrong?" She would never have questioned the Exarch so only a few months ago. But now everything directly affected her. She deserved the answers.

Lantana's expression tightened, and her smile changed to a brittle appearance. "We'll discuss that in more detail later. I've yet to consult with the others. We should talk about the wonderful thing that we witnessed, however."

Wonderful? Unable to think of anything even remotely resembling such a description, Sabelline stared at the Exarch.

"Did you see the way he went after those gordragons? He recognized them before any of us. He even stopped one entirely on his own. I believe he would have killed it if we hadn't been there."

The Exarch's bubbling enthusiasm stunned her. How could Lantana speak so joyfully after the appearance of those monsters? "He? Who?"

"Cage Stone, of course!" The Exarch rose and paced as if her excitement pricked her too much to sit. "He might be more than we hoped for. What an advantage for you if he can sense the fell beasts before they appear."

Sabelline's overworked nerves made her head spin in confusion. The Exarch's exuberance baffled her. Had her leader lost her hold on sanity? Sabelline's stomach clenched. She wanted her bed and the forgetfulness of sleep to put this day of disasters behind her.

"He will be an excellent Marshal for your journey."

Sabelline's scattered thoughts slammed to a stop. She pulled her chaotic nerves under control. That had been the purpose of tonight's debacle. To select her Marshal. Despite the gordragons, Lantana apparently counted the evening a great success.

"I . . . I missed most of what happened," Sabelline managed. She gripped one trembling hand with the other as she thought back to the events on the king's lawns. The one man had pulled her inside the castle just as she saw the real gordragons. She had heard the tale from many Keepers, but each woman told her own version.

Lantana sat down once more and leaned toward Sabelline. "He was magnificent. His speed, his agility, and his skill with the sword, all beyond our hopes. Only think what you and Mistress Pinxter can do for him!"

"The stories are not exaggerated?" Sabelline couldn't believe everything reported of this night. A man blinding a gordragon?

Lantana smiled her inappropriate grin and patted Sabell's hand. "You shall see for yourself soon enough. But for now, your new Marshal has unfortunately taken a bit of a bruising."

"He's injured?" She hadn't heard that.

"He was standing too close when we used a concussion spell to kill the gordragons. Not badly, but more than he's showing us. I want you to go to him and heal him."

"Tonight? Now?" The relationship between Keeper and her Marshal was very close and very personal. This man would spend more time by her side than most married couples spent together. What if they didn't like each other?

Lantana gave her a kind, patient smile. "From what we know, his ancestors were known for their physical beauty. This young man, though not full-blooded, is quite fair to look upon."

"That doesn't matter to me, Exarch."

"Feel no shame at such thoughts, Sabelline. You're a handsome young woman yourself. Despite our powers, Keepers possess the same sensibilities and desires as other women. I've seen this man's heart, and it is good. Combine that with his physical skills that might save your life, and he's everything you could want in your Marshal."

"Of course, Exarch."

"Come now. I've heard more joy from a dog getting a bath. Why the dread I see in your eyes, dear?"

Sabelline shrugged. "I feel like I'm going to meet my groom in an arranged marriage for the first time, and the wedding is tomorrow."

Lantana didn't laugh at her. Instead her expression sobered. "I'm so sorry you've been rushed into this, child. You should have a chance to see if you and your Marshal suit each other. But there's no choice and no time. You must go, and he's your best chance to succeed. If he's really good, you might even survive."

Cage never paced, but tonight he understood why some men did. He stared into the low flames and stood quietly. Inside though, his thoughts raced and every turn they took brought him back to his fears. His fears pushed his temper closer to the surface. As the moon slid closer to its highest point in the sky, he hardened his resolve to leave this cursed city as soon as he found his family.

The man named Harmon stood watch inside the door. Cage's hearing told him two more men bracketed the outside as well. Escape from this room was possible, but could he find Anadalune and Kristall? Had they returned to the inn? What had the Exarch lady meant by saying she would take care of it?

A new sound outside the door pulled his gaze from the fire. A female voice spoke to the outside guards.

Cage turned to face the entrance and folded his arms across his sore chest. He would have his answers from the Exarch this time.

Maton Reves stood up from his slumped position on the settee. He had dozed off and on for most of the last few hours. He rubbed a hand through his tousled blond hair and yawned. "Someone coming? Do you think they're going to let us out of here soon? I could use a real bed."

Cage didn't answer. Truthfully, the answers they both wanted worried him. Maton didn't seem too concerned except with his own comfort. Cage didn't trust these Keepers at all.

Someone knocked softly on the door. Harmon opened it and stepped aside with a respectful nod. The young woman who had run before the gordragon illusions earlier in the evening stepped into the room. Her green eyes were large in her face as she met his stare across the room. She carried a small basket in her arms.

"I thought you might be asleep."

Cage wanted to rail at her, demand answers and his freedom. But there was a hesitation in her steps and a reluctance in her voice that stopped him.

Maton walked to meet her. He took her hand and led her toward the fire. "Your hands are like the ice on a mountain lake, my lady. Warm yourself."

Cage wanted to throttle the man. Maton was an incorrigible flirt, and women seemed to fall mindlessly for his charming smile.

"Have you brought us more sweets in that little basket?" A grin accompanied Maton's smooth words.

The woman shook her head and pulled her hand free. She glanced at Cage over Maton's shoulder. "I'm here to see to his injuries. I am Mistress Sabelline."

The disquiet in her eyes increased. Cage thought she wanted to be in this room as much as he did. "Who sent you?"

She raised an eyebrow, and her mouth turned down with a frown. "Your ribs were injured by the gordragons?"

"No," Cage snapped back. To Hades with her innocent manner. She was one of them. "My chest was injured by your friends when they finally arrived and attacked the gordragons. That was after they called the demons upon us."

Maton stepped back, amusement dancing in his eyes. Cage heard Harmon growling a curse and taking a step in their direction.

"The Keepers didn't call the gordragons," the lady said. Her jade eyes snapped with irritation, all timidity gone. "Perhaps if you hadn't charged the monsters like a silly boy playing at war, you wouldn't have gotten in the way."

"I got in the way?" His temper found a target. "I behaved like a silly child? More so than you with your playacting? More so than the silly phantoms your Exarch created? Was that not a call for the real demons to charge?"

"Enough!" Harmon snarled. The other two guards stood inside the door behind their leader. "I've tolerated your rude manners the night long, you young whelp. Allow Mistress Sabelline to help you. Or I'll have you roped like a wild dog, and we'll do it that way."

Cage glared first at Harmon and then at Mistress Sabelline. She leveled an equally frosty stare at him.

"I need none of your treatments," Cage said, stowing his temper away. "I want only to leave this room, this building, and this blighted city."

"I am to heal you," Mistress Sabelline insisted. She set her basket on a small table near the hearth with the careful touch one used when trying not to slam a door in anger.

Maton coughed behind his hand. He didn't even try to contain his grin when Cage frowned at him.

The lady lifted some small glass bottles from her basket and held them to the light. She selected one and pulled the cork from it. After tipping a few drops of clear oil into her hands, she set it aside and rubbed her hands together. The soothing scent of lavender rushed from her hands and slammed into Cage's senses. She stepped toward him.

Cage took a quick step back as the soft aroma filled his nostrils.

The lady raised an eyebrow and took another step. "Take your shirt off so I can minister to your injuries."

Cage retreated again as her disapproving gaze flicked over him from head to toe. She stalked after him, her mouth firm in her determination.

"I need no healing," Cage insisted. The muscles in his legs quaked with growing weakness as she neared him.

Harmon mumbled an order for the other guards to assist.

Cage backed toward the wall, aware of Maton's puzzled stare.

"Let the girl help you, Cage," Maton said in the reasonable tone usually used for a spooked horse. "What can it hurt?"

Cage shook his head, his throat getting tighter even as his muscles loosened.

"Take your shirt off, lad," Harmon ordered as he signaled his men to cut off Cage's slow retreat. "It's only going to cause you more pain if we have to do it for you."

Cage knew he stood no chance against the three muscular men confronting him. "You have no right to force this upon me."

Harmon smiled, showing a lot of teeth. "You're under the king's roof. You're his subject."

"This is a decree from the king? That I should submit

142

to this?" Cage scoffed.

"Same as," Harmon answered with a shrug. "Now make your choice, hard or easy."

Cage glanced away from Harmon to the lady, but her glare was as unbending as Harmon's words. The other men moved closer.

"I don't always respond well to certain herbs used in healing," Cage stalled.

Harmon closed in at his side.

Cage started to unlace his shirt and over vest while his heart pounded heavily in his chest. He'd learned to avoid the healers as a child. Lady Anadalune and Sir Berton knew how to treat his wounds and injuries, though mostly he healed quickly without assistance. Only a few medicinal plants were safe for him. Lavender wasn't one of them.

"I don't intend to use herbs alone to heal you," Mistress Sabelline answered.

Cage pulled his shirt and vest over his head, refusing to flinch at the stabbing pain that shot through his ribs as he lifted his arms. He held his shirt at his side and noticed the lady's gaze didn't skim so quickly over him as before.

"You have some impressive scarring there, lad," Harmon said in a less combative tone. "Either you've fought a lot of battles or you're not too good at getting out of the way."

Cage didn't answer. He watched the lady.

Mistress Sabelline moved within touching distance. "This won't hurt."

She lifted her hands toward his chest, her palms gleaming with oil.

"Please don't touch me," Cage said. His head spun as the thick, sweet smell of the lavender inundated him.

The hard certainty in Sabelline's eyes wavered for a moment. Cage turned his head. He took a short, shallow breath, desperate for a mouthful of fresh air to clear his head so he might escape.

Sabell wondered at the humble plea from the hard man standing in front of her. Another swordsman in his position, shirtless and surrounded, might have appeared helpless. But not this odd man.

She understood Reseda's admiration of the man as she stood so close to him. His gray eyes were beautiful even when filled with suspicion and distrust. His face was all lines and leanness put together in handsome order. His skin, despite the scars on his torso, glowed with golden health. When he'd removed his shirt, the flow and ripple of taut muscles as he moved had left her momentarily speechless. Not a smidgen of fat or softness lurked anywhere on what she could see of him.

She shook the admiration from her thoughts. Her

orders were to heal him. She rubbed her hands together, the comforting scent of the lavender oil stilling her nerves. He turned his attention back to her. He had looked away for a moment after his odd plea.

He stared at her and took another step back. He bumped into one of the Marshals.

Sabell wondered at his odd behavior as she put her hands on his warm injured chest.

"Don't," he groaned. He gripped her fingers with his rough swordsman's hands. His touch was gentle as he tugged at her hands.

Beneath her palms, his heart beat strong and slow. Very slow. And slower. She lifted her gaze from his chest, the cracked ribs and bruised muscles, and looked into his eyes. The gray intensity glazed over as his hands dropped back to his sides. He leaned toward her, his weight pressing against her hands.

"I think you should sit," Sabell said. His heart slowed even more. Worry quickly blossomed into fear.

"Please," her soon-to-be Marshal rasped. His eyes rolled back, and his knees buckled.

Harmon stepped in and caught him as Sabell stumbled back. The Marshal cursed and shouted at his men to help.

The other man who'd led her to the fireplace earlier rushed to her side. "What did you do to him, damn you? You make us prisoner here and then work your sorcery on Cage. Is that to be his reward for saving so many from the demons?"

Harmon and another Marshal carefully deposited the unconscious man on the large settee. The third Marshal ran from the room.

Sabell ignored the outraged friend of her Marshal and cautiously approached the settee. Had she missed a more serious injury than the broken ribs? She had healed such many times. The Marshals often suffered all types of bruising in their daily training.

Sabell knelt on the floor near, what was his name, Cage's head. She reached for him, but Harmon stopped her.

"It might be best if you didn't touch him, Mistress," he warned. His gruff voice was not unkind, but his words hurt anyway.

Sabell jerked her hand back. Had she killed her Marshal with some gross mistake? Gooseflesh ran up her arms and across her back. She hugged herself and sat back on her heels.

Silence fell on the room except for occasional soft, but imaginative, curses from the other man. Harmon kept the angry swordsman away from the settee.

Sabell stared on her patient, or victim. Long dark eyelashes lay against his sun-kissed skin. His short black hair lay in disarray across his forehead. Was it as fine and silky as it looked? She refocused on his slow, deep breaths and watched the rise and fall of his muscular chest.

A light, cold sweat born of foreboding dampened Sabell's skin beneath her dress. The sound of quick footsteps outside the door startled her from a deepening gloom. Though worried this newest disaster might be her fault, Sabell only felt relief that help had arrived.

The Exarch bustled into the room with two Marshals tight on her heels.

"What is this?" Lantana demanded as she swept forward and knelt beside Sabell.

Sabell spilled the story out in a rush, her words stumbling into each other and sounding confused and panicked even to herself. Marshal Harmon added details of the swordsman's reluctance and his own role in demanding his compliance.

Lantana frowned at both of them. "You should not have forced him to accept the healing. It is not our way."

"The boy has been so stubborn about everything, Mistress," Harmon said. "I thought he was protesting to be obstinate."

Sabell offered no excuses. Her nerves had interfered with her good judgment and her compassion. The poor man had fought real gordragons. He had placed himself between the monsters and herself though he knew her not a whit.

"We'll discuss this later." Lantana leaned over the man and listened. "He breathes as if in a deep sleep. I wonder if you can hear me, Cage Stone?"

Sabell rubbed her hands together, wishing she had cleaned the slippery lavender oil off before Lantana arrived.

The Exarch turned a hard stare Sabell's way. "Is that

lavender I smell?"

Sabell froze. "Yes."

Lavender was the preferred method to relax a reluctant patient. She'd learned that as a first year student in a basic herblore lesson. A gifted healer could relax a patient even to sleep. Sabell's fuzzy thoughts cleared for the first time since the young man had fainted beneath her hand.

"Go wash that from your hands," Lantana snapped. "Harmon, have someone show Sir Reeves to a bed in the barracks for tonight. See the king gets a message that our meeting must wait until the morning."

Marshal Harmon snapped out orders. Reeves started to protest, but the Exarch glared him into compliance. Sabell rubbed the oil from her hands with a rough cloth she carried in her herb basket. She didn't stop until her skin stung and turned red.

She rejoined Lantana, kneeling beside the older woman.

Lantana smoothed one of her wrinkled hands along the unconscious man's cheek and then trailed it down his chest. She felt along his ribs on both sides and shook her head. "You're a tough one, Cage Stone. Strutted around here like you were going to take on my Marshals with these cracked ribs."

Sabell let the name roll about in her thoughts. How long until it no longer belonged to a stranger? She could imagine no intimacy of companionship or friendship with the dangerous man lying before her.

Harmon closed the door after the other Marshals had retreated to the hall once more. Lantana stared at Cage Stone for a long moment, her brow creased and her mouth turned down in a frown.

"We must tread carefully with his treatment, Sabelline." Lantana gave her a quick, grim smile. "I don't blame you for this, but myself. I know what he is, and still I make mistakes. Why would I assume the known remedies would be the same for him?"

"What he is?" Sabell wondered if the Exarch was overtired. Cage Stone was a man as any other, though obviously gifted in weapons work.

Lantana patted Sabell's hand in an absent manner. "We'll figure him out as best as we can. I wish we had time to study him."

Study him?

"He'll make you an exceptional Marshal, Sabelline," Lantana continued as if her words made perfect sense.

Sabell glanced at Marshal Harmon to judge his reaction to his mistress's odd words. The stoic guardian stared without emotion at the man on the settee.

Lantana placed both her hands on Cage's ribs. Magic brushed its cool touch on Sabell's senses. Cage Stone groaned as quiet as a whisper and tossed his head. Lantana finished it quickly and lifted her hands away. He sank back into deep sleep.

They both watched his chest rise and fall. Though

he sprawled shirtless and helpless, Sabell despaired that she could form a close bond with such a man. His earlier antagonistic attitude and blatant arrogance characterized everything she despised in a man. She was accustomed to respect and even reverence as a Keeper. He had looked at her with no hint of either. The vague figure of her future Marshal she'd built in her imagination was nothing like this man. He was too young also, perhaps not even of her own age.

"Get some rest, child," Lantana said. "I've put the both of you through enough this endless night."

Her bed! What a temptation! Duty stayed her. "If he's to be mine, Exarch, I should take the responsibility. I'll stay with him."

Lantana smiled, true and kind. "Every day I grow more confident in you, my dear. Tomorrow will be soon enough for you to take this rascal in hand. If your young man holds true to his nature, he's going to be steaming hot when he wakes. Better he turns it on me."

Guardians save her, she hadn't thought about things from his side. The first time they met, she'd been part of a plan to trick him with the gordragon illusions. Now she'd poisoned him and used force to do it. He would despise her more than she did him. If the success of her mission depended on them working together, things were bleak indeed.

"I'll sleep here tonight." Sir Berton gestured toward the maid's cot half-hidden behind a screen in the sitting room.

Kristall ran her hand over the polished oak mantle. The suite of rooms given to them was only a bit smaller than the manor they'd lived in the past few years. The sitting room held twin settees and a round table with four heavy padded chairs. More soft chairs flanked the fireplace. A servant worked at lighting the kindling as they entered. Another arrived behind them with a tray of tea and sweet breads.

"Will Cage join us soon?" Kristall asked. The opulent surroundings did little to distract her. Sir Berton had returned quickly with all their possessions as ordered by the Exarch lady, arriving even as their new quarters were prepared. No one answered her question. She noticed her mother and Berton exchange a look.

"Why don't you get ready for sleep, dear," her mother said. "It's been a long day, and the beds look so fine."

Two large bedrooms and a separate bathing chamber completed their suite. One of the bedrooms had thick drapes and bedcoverings of pink and white, the other in varying shades of blue. It was a girl's dream come true but not on this day. Not for her. She waited until the servants hurried out and closed the door behind them.

"I'm not a child, Mother. Tell me what's going on. Why are we prisoners, and where is my brother?"

Anadalune sighed and sank onto one of the settees. Her shoulders sagged. She gripped her hands together in her lap. Hands that shook. "I don't know any more than you."

Kristall looked at Sir Berton. He turned and stared into the fire but not before she saw the haggard concern on his rugged features.

She hurried over to her mother, sitting beside her. She berated herself for being so childish and selfish. Her mother and Berton loved Cage as much as she. She wrapped her mother in a hug. "Don't worry, Mother. You know Cage. He's always all right."

"Of course he is," Anadalune agreed, but her words hitched with a small catch.

Kristall steeled herself. Her faith in Cage was based on years of adoration for her older brother. He could do anything. He was protector, provider, and teacher. All these years he'd looked out for her, from her first steps until this very day.

"We have to do something," Kristall said. She sat back and took her mother's hands in her own. All these years they had depended on Cage; perhaps it was time they helped him. "We must insist they tell us where he is and let us see he's safe for ourselves."

Berton shook his head. The despair on his face

weakened her resolve.

A knock on the door forestalled whatever bleak thoughts Berton had been about to share. Anadalune stiffened and rose. Kristall stood beside her so they could face their visitor. Berton opened the door, his face hard.

A stern young man stepped into the room. His bare forearms drew her attention. Tattoos swirled on his skin, highlighting the lines of his muscles. More ornate artwork encircled his wrists and the backs of his hands. His cool gaze swept the room before it settled on her mother. He nodded respectfully.

"My pardon at the lateness, my lady. I'm Marshal Mezzin. I've come to see you're settled and secure. I will stand watch outside your door this night."

"Why?" Sir Berton demanded.

Mezzin's gaze and demeanor remained calm. "I've been ordered by the Exarch."

"Why?" Sir Berton insisted, his scowl as dark as his tone. "We are prisoners then?"

The Marshal's cool facade slipped a bit as surprise flashed across his face. "Not at all. I'm here to protect you."

"Protect us from what?" her mother asked.

Mezzin looked more confused. "I only know no one is to enter without your invitation. I heard the bastard, Cage Stone, requested protection for you and your daughter."

Kristall's breath rushed from her as a great wave of relief flooded her. Surely this meant Cage was fine.

Then again, he always thought of them first. "Where is my brother?"

Mezzin frowned before answering. His words sounded guarded. "I'm not exactly sure, but he is under the care of the Exarch."

"Under the care?" Anadalune stepped toward the man. "He was injured? In the tournament?"

Kristall's relief fled. Her heart leaped against her ribs.

"He was injured in the attack," Mezzin answered. Again he looked puzzled, as if they should know of what he spoke.

"Attack?" Anadalune's voice rose. "Someone attacked my son?"

Mezzin, big and muscled as he was, retreated a step as Anadalune stalked toward him. "I'm sorry, my lady. I didn't know you were unaware. We were attacked on the back lawn tonight before we finished the tournament."

"By whom?" Sir Berton asked, joining Anadalune in the inquisition. "By brigands? And what mean you by 'we' were attacked?"

Mezzin snapped his mouth closed and glared at Berton. He softened his look when he turned back to her mother. "I fear I've spoken out of turn, my lady. I thought you were apprised of the events. Someone of greater standing than I must explain all this to you. I can assure you that Cage Stone suffered no dreadful injuries. Indeed, I saw him walk from the field myself."

"I want to see him," Anadalune said.

"I'm afraid I cannot make that happen, my lady. I have a man waiting outside to take Stone's possessions to him. I understand your man here went to fetch them."

Anadalune stared down her nose at the Marshal for a long moment. He met her glare with calm determination. Finally, she nodded to Berton. He stomped to the chair holding Cage's one bundle of extra clothing along with two sheathed swords and three knives of various lengths.

"This is all of it?" Mezzin asked.

Kristall's face heated with shame as she touched the full skirt of her expensive gown. She was sure Cage owned not more than three changes of clothing, each more threadbare than the last.

Mezzin frowned and carried the pack out into the hall. Kristall heard the rumble of men's voices, and then the Marshal returned.

"I'll be in the hall if you have need of me," Mezzin said.

"Wait," Kristall said as the man started away. "Please, can you not tell us something of my brother? What has become of him?"

Mezzin shook his head. "I've told you all I can. You're all under the king's protection as requested by your . . . brother. As to Stone, I assure you no harm is meant to him."

"Is the tournament to continue tomorrow since there's been this mysterious attack?" Sir Berton asked.

Mezzin smiled for the first time. The curving of his

lips chilled Kristall rather than comforting her, though it wasn't a cruel expression. There was something of bitterness or grim irony in it, not amusement. "The tournament is over. Cage Stone finished it quite nicely. He won. Congratulations to you."

Lantana hesitated before scrubbing the lavender oil from Cage's chest. When else might she have a chance to study his features? He was such a restless young man. Even though he often stood as still as one of the king's marble statues, an invisible energy hummed about him. What inner forces and strengths illuminated him in such a way?

Muscles roped Cage's bare torso beneath his golden skin. Various old scars and newer bruises marred his natural beauty. It was more damage than a young man should have suffered. He should have been protected and treasured, raised to . . . No, it was as it must be. The brutal, unforgiving, mercenary life forged men into the type of weapon Sabelline needed.

Lantana pulled her own basket of herbs and remedies to her side before she let herself sink into remorse and guilt. She would use Sabelline and Cage as she must. She searched through the things she'd gathered so frantically when called to Cage's side.

She found her small bottle of allspice and jiggled

out the cork stopper. She rubbed it lightly on the visible bruising on Cage's chest and then moved to the areas injured deep inside him. She'd detected the inner damage with her earlier use of magical probing. Over forty years ago she'd learned the basic healing skills any woman of magic could be trained to employ. The allspice had healing qualities of its own so she only needed to add a small flow of magic to increase its natural properties.

Working slowly and with a sharp eye on Cage's breathing, she directed the mending of cracked ribs and torn muscles. She feared he might react unusually to the allspice as he had to the lavender, and perhaps he did. His body mended so quickly she wondered if she even did it or if another power had a hand on him.

When she was sure she'd done all she could, she wiped all traces of allspice from her hands. She searched her basket for another small bottle. After pulling the cork from this one, the gentle soothing scent of cucumber rose first, along with the harsher odor of lye. Only a small portion of lye was mixed in with the thick cucumber cream, but it would clean most anything. The cucumber prevented irritation of the skin.

Again Lantana proceeded cautiously as she used a soft cloth to clean Cage's skin with the concoction. Before she finished wiping the last of the cream off, he stirred and his eyelids fluttered. She took a last swipe and watched with growing amazement as he thrashed his legs and rolled his head side to side.

"He's waking? Just like that?" Harmon asked, the same wonder in his voice that Lantana felt.

Cage stilled, a statue, but an aura of energy sizzled about him, if only in her imagination or detected with her magical senses. His motionlessness reminded her of a cat preparing to pounce.

Lantana jumped back in startlement when Cage's eyes snapped open. Though the fog of sleep clouded his gray eyes still, his glare pierced her anyway.

He said nothing and didn't move. Lantana allowed herself a wry smile. He deserved an explanation, and he knew it.

"My apologies, Cage Stone," Lantana said. "Mistress Sabelline meant only to help."

Cage sat up. He rubbed his hand across his chest and frowned. "I suppose you worked your healing wiles on me while I was unable to bid you cease?"

Taken aback by his accusation when she'd expected gratitude, Lantana stared at him. Harmon growled a curse. She burst into laughter. Why had she thought he would react as another might? This fierce, prideful man was nothing like she had pictured him when she learned of his existence.

"I'm glad I amuse you, Mistress Exarch," Cage grumbled. He stood, completely steady, and picked his shirt up from the floor. After he pulled it on, he glanced around the room. "Am I free to go now?"

Lantana trusted that Harmon had kept some guards

outside the door. She wasn't sure the two of them could keep Cage here if he wished to leave. Not without injury to someone. "I wish you would stay here tonight."

He raised a dark eyebrow. "Now it's an invitation?"

Lantana sighed. He made every conversation a confrontation. "I prefer you stay of your free will."

"But you will keep me regardless."

"Yes."

Cage looked around. "I'm to sleep in here?"

"I can give you something to ease your rest if you wish," Lantana said, surprising herself with the spiteful tone in her voice. But she leaned toward him in an intimidating fashion. Even the king quelled before her in her present mood. Damn, but Stone brought out her worst side.

Cage narrowed his gray eyes. All traces of the lavender's effects were gone from the frigid stare he bent upon her. "Keep your witch's potions away from me."

Lantana shook her head. The day had lasted forever, and she was no longer a youngster. She hadn't the time or strength to fence with this one. There was no surrender in him.

Lantana recorked her bottles and stowed them back in her basket. "Someone is fetching your belongings. I'll have water brought to you at sunrise."

"The sun rises now," Cage interrupted.

Lantana paused. How had he known that? There were no windows in this room, and he'd been in a deep sleep for some time. She took up her basket, too tired to ponder one more oddity.

"Then you'd best get cleaned up, Cage Stone. As the winner of the tournament, you have a meeting with the king as soon as you break your fast."

CHAPTER NINE

JONARED WAITED UNTIL THE DOOR closed behind the last server before taking his seat. Sir Maton Reeves and Exarch Lantana flanked Cage Stone. The three of them sat down facing Jonared after he waved his approval. Marshal Harmon put his back to the door. No one would disturb them in this most private of the king's chambers. Perhaps Harmon meant to prevent Stone from fleeing. Lantana had warned him the man cared not for hospitality.

Cage Stone glared at him. Jonared was good and sick of the impudent bastard. Only Lantana's insistence they needed the fellow prevented Jonared from ordering him whipped and put in chains.

"Shall we begin, your highness?" Lantana asked.

Jonared sighed, glad no one could read his childish

thoughts. Stone's arrogance was beneath his notice. He started with the easy part. "Sir Maton Reeves, you've earned second honors in my tournament. You've demonstrated great skill in the combative games and true valor when faced with a terrible enemy."

Sir Maton ducked his head respectfully. "My gratitude for the opportunity, my king."

Jonared's mood lightened. Here was a man who valued his king. "Though the prize for second was not announced, Sir Maton, there is a reward. I offer you the station of protector to the king."

Reeves slid from his chair and dropped to his knees with his head bowed. "I'm deeply honored, your highness. I offer my life before yours against all enemies."

Jonared's heart swelled at the feverent vow. Still, he must warn the young man. "Even enemies such as you faced last night, Sir Maton?"

Maton raised his head and met Jonared's gaze. "All enemies, my king, of this world and any other. If they can die by blade or human hand, I shall slay them. This I vow."

Jonared nodded. "You'll be shown to your new quarters as soon as we complete this meeting. The royal seamstress will fit you for overtunics and my personal armorer will see to your weaponry."

"As you say, Sire."

"The times are such that your fine skills and grand courage will be needed."

"I shall not falter or fail you, your highness." Reeves

eyes glistened with excitement.

Jonared's mood plunged and soured as Maton returned to his seat. Now to deal with Stone. The gray-eyed warrior stared at him with only cold emotions in his eyes. Damn his insolence. The desire to have at him with the lash surfaced again.

"Your actions of last night earned you first place in my tournament, Stone." Jonared kept his voice even, but his heart raced at even speaking of the events. Was he so much a coward or did the two men in front of him hide their fears better? "And so shall you have the promised reward. However, law does not permit a bastard to own land such as Durnhold."

He wasn't sure, but Jonared thought he might have detected a small flinch of emotion in the cool distance of the bastard.

"Your law, King Jonared," Stone said, his voice tight.

Jonared lifted an eyebrow. Perhaps Stone was a superior swordsman, but he obviously lacked in intelligence. "A law that has been in place hundreds of years and served this land well."

"I doubt you even know the origin of the law," Stone scoffed and added after a brief hesitation, "your highness."

Jonared didn't know. His brief feeling of superiority fled. "And you do?"

This time Cage Stone lifted an eyebrow. "I'm not the one quoting it or enforcing it. The passage of time does not make a wrong into a right."

"It matters not," Lantana put in before Jonared could answer. Not that he had an answer. "We're not here to discuss philosophies, your majesty."

Jonared turned his glare on Lantana. She should know better than to reprimand him here, in front of others. He would speak to her of it later. He looked back to Stone. "Your family, such as it is, will receive the title to Durnhold Manor and its lands."

Stone's expression was still, but he nodded.

"However, that raises another problem. Durnhold backs up to the northern Edge. It has long been a watch-tower to protect the flank of Sulbreth."

"It has sat empty for many months, your highness," Stone said.

Jonared sighed over the suspicion in Stone's eyes. "My father neglected to name a master to the estate. The road has become unsafe with brigands and the like. I need a warrior in place there. Your family consists of your sister and widowed mother. By rights, Lord Witbier Thrum will control the estate until the girl marries."

"Another law of long custom, your highness?" Stone all but sneered.

Jonared leaned forward. "I have no more wish to turn the ladies over to Thrum than you do, Stone."

Stone eyed him warily. "I shall protect them from him."

"You have no legal means to keep him from them. He can use the law to gain what he wants, and you shall have no say in it," Jonared said. He frowned as he comprehended his own words. Was he agreeing with Stone that the laws might be inadequate?

"I know of a way to protect the ladies if you let me speak with them, your highness."

There was no hesitation before his title this time. Jonared nodded his agreement. Stone relaxed, his entire posture appearing less antagonistic.

"Now that we've settled that, might we get to the true purpose of this meeting?" Lantana snapped.

"Please, Exarch, begin." Jonared endured her glare at his sarcasm, but he'd had enough of her pushiness.

Lantana's reproachful expression promised a lecture for later, but she started her explanation. "Let me give our two swordsmen a short lesson, history of the isle of Futhark as we know and understand it. Much is conjecture."

Jonared watched the men, interested in their reactions. Few outside the monarch's family and the Keepers had ever heard of the things Lantana would tell them.

"More than ten centuries ago, Futhark was not as we know it. Another people lived among us. They were a people of exceptional grace and beauty. They walked and lived in tune with nature and the land. They understood the world in ways our race cannot. They helped us waken the magic in our own beings. Indeed, they trained the first Keepers."

Maton hung on Lantana's words, much like a child hearing an exciting bedtime tale. Stone watched the Exarch with his usual wary look.

"These early allies of our ancestors were people of peace. We believe that the first of our kind may have come from another land and slowly spread over the entire kingdom."

"Our kind, you say," Maton interrupted. "These others were not of our kind, not human?"

Jonared watched Cage Stone. This time he was sure. He saw a flinch in the man's stoic expression.

Lantana frowned at Maton but answered him. "Not as you and I. Little is known about them, though we have some drawings and a few written volumes that describe them. You've probably seen their image in old tapestries and paintings. Some name them the elvish folk."

"Elves?" Maton laughed. He sobered abruptly when he glanced at Jonared and then back at Lantana's stern face. "My apologies, Exarch, but I find such speculations just this side of ludicrous."

"And you are so well-read you know of everything, Sir Maton?" Lantana sighed and shook her head. "If you have trouble believing this, perhaps you are not the man to protect your king. Ask your friend if he believes in the elvish folk."

They all looked at Stone.

He glared at Lantana. "They exist. I don't see why we need this lesson, Exarch."

"I don't understand either," Maton said. "How does this history help me protect the king, and why does Cage need to know at all?"

"You will understand if you let me continue. The elvish folk were a peaceful race and helped the early settlers learn to survive in their new land. But not all our ancestors were dedicated to peace and honesty. Small disputes and petty crimes increased along with the population. Men rose in power and named themselves lords. Some ruled with cruel force. The elves withdrew from our everyday life and began to keep to themselves, presumably dismayed by man's natural tendency to violence. It was only a matter of time until some greedy fool accused our benefactors of being the root of the growing troubles."

Lantana sighed and shook her head. "It was a shameful time in our history. Greedy men attacked unwary elves. They thought the elves possessed hordes of hidden treasures. Some lords harassed the elves to steal their lands. But throughout it all, the elvish race maintained their friendship with those who were true to them."

"The Keepers?" Maton asked.

Cage Stone no longer looked at Lantana. He stared at the wall beyond her.

"The women of magic and a few honorable lords protected the elves as best as they could," Lantana said. Her eyes bore the sadness they always did when she spoke of the end of that time. "Though the elvish folk could easily have defeated those who did them violence, they clung to their peaceful ways and took up no arms in defense. Then the demons came."

Jonared's chest spasmed with remembered fear and

sorrow. He must have shown some outward reaction, because Cage Stone swung his attention to stare at Jonared.

Jonared looked away. Being in the presence of two men who had faced the gordragons so bravely made him feel craven.

"Accipitors, cave boas, gordragons. All manners of monsters. The elves told the Keepers of that time that these horrid beasts were lured from their dark world to the world of men when they sensed the growing evil in men's souls. The demons ravaged the lands, killing and destroying human and elf alike. It was a chaos of terror. The elvish folks had had enough of us."

"They left?" Maton asked.

"They disappeared entirely from Futhark. But before they went, they created a powerful magic to imprison the demons. To the Keepers, they entrusted the knowledge necessary to renew the spell and keep the prison sealed. Hence our title. To protect the Keepers, they raised one honorable lord to the station of King. His line has served to defend and assist the Keepers in their sacred duty since that time."

Jonared wondered if any king, aside from the first one, had been so burdened by his duty. As far as he knew, his father was the only one of his line to be assassinated.

"Where is this prison? How could the elves have disappeared?" Maton asked, his tone less skeptical. "Are you saying the gordragons of last night were demons that escaped this prison?"

"The seals weaken over time and must be renewed with a powerful magical working. Only a few Keepers are born with the ability to work it. One of those most special Keepers and her Marshal make the dangerous journey to strengthen the seals. The appearance of the gordragons and other happenings are proof that the seals have weakened to their most dangerous level since they were first put in place."

"Still there is no way off Futhark," Maton challenged. "The elves could not have left."

Lantana looked at Stone when she answered. "Nobody knows how they left or where they went. It was foretold in a prophecy given to a Keeper gifted in such a way that one of the elvish race would return. I believe one did so and, as foretold, she gave birth to a half-breed child. This child was to grow to maturity in time to help us with the greatest challenge Futhark has ever faced."

"This is true? Such a person exists?" Sir Maton asked, his tone once more of total disbelief.

Lantana said nothing. She stared at Stone.

Jonared held his breath. Lantana believed their success depended on Stone's agreeing to help them. Was the bastard even aware of his heritage? Jonared had only become convinced of it when Stone charged the gordragons. No normal human would do that and almost kill one.

Stone rose gracefully from his chair. He surprised Jonared by giving him a respectful bob of his head before speaking to Maton.

"She speaks of me, Maton. I have the rare privilege not only of being bastard born but of being only half human as well. My mother was an elf."

Cage sank back into his chair. How had the Exarch known? The king showed no surprise either. What other knowledge was held in the hall of the Keepers? Could he learn more of his mother's people? Could he perhaps find out why she abandoned him? Why she left him with the cruel Lord Thrum? Had she found his mixed blood so hateful that she couldn't bear the sight of her own son?

"You, Cage?" Maton asked. "This is so much to take in, your highness."

"It is, Sir Maton, but if you're to be my protector, you must believe it all."

"How do legends and tales of the past and of great magic affect my ability to serve you, Sire?"

Lantana answered for the king as a spasm of pain crossed Jonared's face. Cage watched his liege as the Exarch spoke to Maton.

"You know that King Jerson died not long ago. What few have been told is that he was attacked by demons. Demons that should not, could not, have been here. He was targeted for assassination, Sir Maton. The monsters came with the intent to kill the king. Only the quick actions of some palace guards saved the prince from death that same day. Jerson's protector died in his valiant but vain attempt to save his king. Are you prepared to sacrifice the same way? You've given your answer already, but might you not change your mind now that you know the malicious powers we face? Are you able to show your courage even before monsters worse than what you've seen? For your king? For Futhark?"

Cage saw the fear and horror lurking in the depths of the king's eyes. Despite his mistrust of the monarch's intentions toward Kristall, Cage felt a surge of sympathy for the young ruler.

"I will put my life before the king no matter the enemy, Exarch. Must I say it again?" Sir Maton answered.

Lantana nodded. "We judged you correctly then."

Cage wondered why he was privy to this meeting. He wanted to make arrangements to take his family to their new estates. It was a dream beyond any he'd entertained. Their own lands, a permanent home for Kristall and Anadalune. He would be their captain, protecting them and their people. Why was he here? Did the Exarch think he had knowledge of his mother's people? The Keeper likely knew more than he about the elves. None of his memories of his mother involved any demons or magic.

"Now to you, Cage Stone," the Exarch said as if she

read his thoughts. "We have great need of your service also. You are named in the foretellings as the one who can help us."

Cage shook his head. "I'm sorry to disappoint you, Mistress, but I know nothing of the mystical powers of the elves. I've lived my life as a human."

Her smile was grim. "Yes. A human who has learned to fight, as none of your mother's people were ever able to do, but still with their unique abilities. Your life has been one challenge after another. It has trained you to be a tough, uncompromising warrior."

Cage didn't answer. Foreboding filled his chest so that he couldn't breathe.

"How did you sense the real gordragons? From where did you get the speed and strength needed to blind one of them? How do you know the place of the sun and the moon even when enclosed in a windowless room?"

Cage held his silence. He knew his abilities in many things surpassed those of other men. Better eyesight, keener hearing, and his sense of smell was sharp enough to often cause discomfort. He healed rapidly and was never ill. He could move faster than a striking snake. These things he never spoke of to anyone, and he would not satisfy the curiosity of these people. His family knew somewhat of his uniqueness, but they guarded his secrets well.

The Exarch let the silence stretch to an uncomfortable length before she sighed and continued. "As I explained, about every twenty years, a specially trained

172

Keeper and the Marshal who guards her must journey to renew the seals that keep the demons from Futhark. This is the year, and the seals are obviously weaker than ever before. A few days before our Keeper was to begin her journey, she was killed. Murdered on the same day as the king by the same demons."

"Sent to disrupt the strengthening of the seals?" Maton asked. "How would they know?"

"Can you imagine the chaos the kingdom would have fallen into if my father and I were both slain on the same day? Any number of ambitious lords would have tried to take the throne," King Jonared said, his tone dark and bleakness in his eyes.

Cage's respect for the king grew. He wasn't the spoiled rich child he'd thought. Jonared was a man carrying a great responsibility which most people would never know about. Unless the Keepers failed.

"If that had happened, the Keepers might have been pulled into the conflict," Lantana said, again as if reading Cage's thoughts. "With our trained Keeper dead, and us involved in civil strife, the seals would have time to fail completely."

"You have no one to replace this Keeper?" Maton asked.

Cage was glad Maton asked. Questions burned in his own mind, but he would not ask them. He wasn't involved in this disturbing series of events.

"Another Keeper had already started her training to be the next restorer of the seals. But she should have had another twenty years to perfect the complicated spells and gain confidence in her abilities. Now her education has been expedited so she might make the journey before the onset of winter."

"Journey?" Maton asked.

"Through the Kingdom's Gate."

Cage had never heard of it. He stared at the tapestry on the wall directly in front of him. It depicted a group of peasants happily harvesting wheat under a golden sun. He didn't believe he'd ever seen such joy on the sweaty faces of real farmers as they labored at the dirty, dusty job.

"Everything will be well then? After she restores the seals?" Maton asked.

Cage listened despite himself.

"Not quite, Sir Maton," Lantana said. "It's not that easy. She must renew the seals soon, or it won't matter. We'll all be slaughtered by the demons escaping into our world or ruled by whatever malicious power orders them. Every day she waits means the journey will be more dangerous and difficult. There isn't time to fully prepare her or her Marshal."

"Marshal? Such as Harmon?"

Cage wished Maton would be quiet. The king had given out his prizes. Cage wanted to leave before he learned more of demons and the Keeper witches. The sooner he took his family from Sulbreth and the king's court, the safer they would be.

"Each Keeper, when she's ready, is assigned or

permitted to select a man-at-arms to guard her. That man is specially trained to protect her from the evil entities she might face. Harmon has been my Marshal for more years than you've lived in this world, young man. Every time a Keeper is selected to renew the seals, great care is given to the selection of her Marshal. It must be a man with exceptional warrior skills and intelligence. He must possess great courage, as the path to the seals is long and dangerous. Little is known about it, and this unprecedented time with demons boldly striking into our world adds more mystery to the journey."

Cage struggled to appear uninterested. A man politely waiting for the king to end this audience.

"The Marshal needed for this mission must begin training immediately. There's much for him to learn."

The stares of the others in the room pricked Cage like a lady's lacquered nails. He ignored it as he had the unwanted attention of many a lady.

King Jonared broke the silence. "Most Marshals are men of valor and honor who step forward and volunteer for this most important service to Futhark."

"And why would a man wish to do so?" Cage asked. He could hold his silence no longer. "Is he then separated from his family? Is his duty for a lifetime? Does it pay well, or does the king expect a man to sacrifice out of patriotism for a land that has treated said man, a bastard, with little respect or honor?"

Cage glared at the king, but Jonared regarded him

with little anger at the blatant challenge. "Yes, they do it for Futhark. If not for patriotism, then so they might know their families are safe from the hellspawn that might otherwise slay them in their fields or their homes." Jonared smiled wryly. "Some even do so because their king asks it of them."

Cage pressed his lips together. Let them say it outright. Let them ask. They had set a clever snare for him. A long-buried memory of his mother surfaced. She had given him a name, an elvish name. She told him it meant "demon slayer." He would never share this with these people.

"Stop being stubborn and pretending obtuseness, Cage Stone," the Exarch said. She stood and shook her finger in his face. "You admit what you are. Do you want me to say it plainly? We need you to escort our Keeper to the seals. You already have abilities beyond most men and the courage to match. You love your sister and her mother. I see it in your heart. Would you gift them with their new manor only to have them barricade their doors and windows to keep out the terrors?"

Cage glared back at the tiny woman. "You have other Marshals. Did they not keep me prisoner last night? Send one who is already trained."

"No." Lantana folded her arms across her chest. "You were named in the foretelling as our only chance of success."

Cage heard Maton's sharp intake of breath, but

he wasn't impressed with such superstition. "You base your work on the interpretation of prophecies, Mistress Exarch? I've met women who practice such art at town fairs. They have colorful tents and tell me I'll marry well and have many fine sons."

The Exarch surprised him by smiling and appearing a kindly grandmother again. "You're a tough one, Cage Stone. Does nothing rattle you? Is there no authority in this land you bow to?"

"I sell my sword to the lord who's willing to pay for it, Mistress. Beyond that, I make my own way." Cage didn't look at the king, whom he imagined seethed with the slight to his sovereignty over all people.

"Then I have a solution," Jonared said.

Cage looked to the king in surprise and sensed Lantana's also.

"Since your loyalty and service is only given for gold, Stone," the king continued, "I offer one thousand rounds of gold to buy your service as a Marshal. I'm sure your odd little family will need the wealth to bring Durnhold to prosperity again. What say you, Sir Mercenary?"

Cage ignored the sarcastic title. A thousand rounds of gold was a fortune. He could hire out his sword for eighty years and never earn so much. He had expected they would live in genteel poverty, surviving on the small purses he earned hunting outlaws for other lords. With the king's offer, Kristall and Anadalune could live the pampered lives they'd been denied.

Cage looked to the Exarch. She frowned at the king. "The king has bought you a Marshal, Mistress. When shall I start my training?"

CHAPTER TEN

"THERE ARE SOME CONDITIONS," Stone said.

"Such as?" Lantana sounded as if she were choking.

Jonared knew the Exarch was angry at him and Stone. But he understood Cage a little better perhaps than Lantana, even though the Keeper could see into men's minds. Stone was like a wary animal. He wouldn't be tamed easily, but he might be bribed and find himself trapped. Jonared had provided the bait, and the bastard had snapped it up like a hungry wolf. What more did the arrogant man want?

"The king must stay away from my sister."

Anger surged through Jonared. He sprang from his chair and faced a cold and calm Cage Stone. The bastard didn't even flinch before his kingly wrath. "Don't think you can tell the throne how to conduct itself, Stone. You're not so valuable you can't be lashed the same as any miscreant."

"Of course, your majesty." Stone put as much sarcasm into the king's title as Jonared had earlier with his naming. "I merely say I won't cooperate with the Keepers if you lay one hand on my sister. Controlling your royal lust seems little to ask."

"Your sister will be safe," Lantana said. "I give you my word."

Sir Maton looked from Jonared to Stone and back. The new protector looked confused and unsure what to do. Well, Maton would soon find he was privy to all the king's secrets.

Jonared took a deep breath and regained control of his temper and his dignity. He wouldn't argue with the bastard like a common soldier in a tavern. "Why are you so concerned with this, Stone? If I did have interest in your sister, it would only increase her social standing among her peers."

Stone's glare became impossibly colder. "You think being your tart increases her worth? I know you think me arrogant, your highness, but nothing I've ever said or done compares to that belief. My sister will be no man's whore, not even yours. She will birth no bastards."

Jonared stared at Stone. The damn man made a good argument. Would not Jonared see things the same way if he stood where Stone did? His attitude toward his sister was admirable. He didn't want to think well of Stone, but his respect for him grew.

"I give my word, Marshal Stone, that I will give your sister no attention that is not honorable."

Stone stared at him with a suspicious, wary look in his eyes as he mulled that over. Then he nodded and turned to the Exarch. "I am yours, Mistress."

Lantana gestured to Harmon. "Show him to the trainee barracks for now, Harmon. Get him settled and fed. Introduce him to his instructors and have them get started before the sun reaches its high mark."

After the two men left, Lantana looked back to Jonared and gave her own nod of respect. "You handled that in a truly royal manner, Sire."

Jonared inwardly cringed at the boyish pleasure Lantana's praise gave him. He was king and need no one's approval. Still, the Exarch so often lectured and instructed him, and her words did hold meaning for him.

"You'll keep me informed of his progress, Exarch?"

"Certainly. We can only hope he learns quickly. Sabelline will need all the help she can get."

"And you've been well?"

Sabelline nodded at her father's stiff inquiry. Sir Merlin had ever been a stern man. He appeared as pained by this meeting as Sabell, though he alone bore the fault of their estrangement.

Leesa stood behind their father, her eyes bright and damp. A wide, emotional chasm separated Sabell from her sister and father, and she saw no bridge. Until Leesa moved.

Leesa ducked around their father and flung herself against Sabell. Then they were clinging and crying, laughing and hugging until their arms ached.

Only after a long time did Sabell step back. She held Leesa's hands and smiled at her. "I've missed you so much."

"And I you," Leesa answered in a voice rough with tears. She looked at Sir Merlin. "We both have."

Sabell stared at her father. A volatile mixture of anger, hurt, and joy roiled about in her chest. She wanted to hug him and rail at the rejection that had kept them apart since she had joined the Keepers.

Her father looked away and let the silence grow. Finally he looked back at her, a heartrending sadness in his eyes. "I've missed you. You're my little girl. Forgive an old man's stubbornness. It was only the fear and anger of a father who felt he'd failed to protect his daughter."

His voice caught, and tears welled in his eyes. "Now they tell me of your duties, and I know I've failed."

"Oh, Father." Sabell held back no longer. She went to him and let his warm, strong arms enclose her in an embrace that promised safety and love. Kingdom's Gate and demons seemed very far away as she clung to this pillar of strength and steadiness remembered from her childhood.

Three bittersweet hours later, Sabelline regretfully bid her father and sister farewell. The Exarch had arranged their meeting in a private salon near the king's rooms. Her father let her go with great reluctance and vowed to visit her as often as permitted before her mission.

Sabell floated on a cloud of high spirits as she strolled along the paths of the Keepers' private gardens. She must thank Lantana for arranging the reunion. She stopped and plucked a few black-eyed Susans and a delicate, lacy, white carnation. Many of the flowers were past their blooming time as fall deepened. These would be perfect in the vase sitting so empty and cold in her quarters.

"Sabell." Reseda hurried down the path that led from the solarium. "Mistress Pinxter sent me to find you. You're late for your lesson."

The day wilted around Sabell. She had forgotten, perhaps on purpose. She hated the tattooing lessons. Even now her stomach clenched as she thought of the tiny sharp needles.

Reseda hustled to stand in front of Sabell and bent a stern glare at her. "I'm to tell you to get your behind there immediately. You've only a few days to master the first pattern."

"I don't think I can do it." Sabell heard the whine in her own words. She pictured the golden skin of Cage

Stone and winced at the idea of desecrating such beauty.

"Then perhaps you shouldn't be the one going," Reseda snapped without mercy. "If you don't have the fortitude to do this, how will you meet the dangers you must face on your journey?"

Surprise jolted Sabelline from her self-pity. Venom dripped off of Reseda's words. Two years ago, they had both been contenders for the coveted honor. But only one could be selected, and the Exarch had marked Sabell. Still, Reseda had remained Sabell's close friend.

"All of Futhark is counting on you, and you avoid your training for fear of a few needles?"

Stung further by the sharp words, Sabelline couldn't speak to defend herself. She had never told Reseda how she thought the magic involved in the tattoo spells more repellant than the actual use of the needles.

"Stop acting the spoiled child and do your duty." Reseda stomped off, back the way she'd come, kicking at any unfortunate blossom that hung over the pebbled walkway.

Sabell stared at her friend's back until the solarium door closed behind her. She started toward Mistress Pinxter's workshop. Even her dismay at Reseda's anger was pushed aside by her dread of the lesson.

Again the image of smooth golden skin, forever scarred by spells, rose to sicken her. Some of the tattoo spells would actually change his thoughts and feelings, making him a different person.

She paused outside the workshop and stowed away her conscience. The survival of Futhark was more important than one man. Becoming a Marshal was a voluntary act. No one forced him. Somehow she would find the resolve and courage to set the spells upon his person.

"I don't know all the details," Sir Merlin said. Leesa's father smoothed the thick stack of documents out on the table. "The king asked me to represent him to you."

Kristall and Anadalune stared at the stack of papers and then looked at each other.

"These are the deeds to Durnhold?" Anadalune asked.

Sir Merlin gestured to one thick stack of papers. "These are signed with the king's own hand, giving you and your descendants direct inheritance of all title to the lands. If your line ends, the holding reverts back to the royal family. The papers name the extent of your lands and which citizens are bound to you and for how long. It also explains the taxes and obligations to the crown."

Kristall knew little about such things, but her mother nodded soberly. Sir Berton stood a short distance behind the women, his stern presence a comfort. They had been summoned to this small library by one of the king's liveried servants even before they broke their fast. Not that they were hungry. The food and drink delivered to them the night before sat untouched in their rooms.

"Do you wish to look them over or have me read them to you, Lady Anadalune?" Sir Merlin asked. "I assure you on our daughters' friendship, that all is fair and as the standard."

Kristall pressed her lips together. Her mother had warned her to be quiet and make no demands.

"I believe you, Sir Merlin. This is the promised reward for the winner of the tournament?" Anadalune asked in a much cooler manner than Kristall could have managed.

The night had passed slowly with none of them sleeping much. Worry about Cage's whereabouts and their own situation had kept them awake except for small fits of restless dozing.

Sir Merlin nodded. "It is."

"Then where is my stepson that we might celebrate with him?" Anadalune sat straight and stiff, her tone the intimidating manner of a fine lady.

Sir Merlin shifted his gaze to the table and straightened papers that didn't need it. "From what I understand, he's volunteered to take up the sword for the Keepers. As of sunrise this morning, he took the title of Marshal."

"No!" Kristall could contain herself no longer. "He wouldn't! We made plans. We're going to go to this manor and make a home where we can live as a family and answer to none."

Sir Berton's strong hand fell on Kristall's shoulder. "Peace, my lady."

Kristall fell silent. She dared not look at her mother, not without giving in to the mass of tears choking the back of her throat.

"My lady speaks true, Sir Merlin," Berton said. "We've not seen Cage Stone since last evening. We wish some answers and will not be distracted."

Sir Merlin smiled, though there was sadness in his eyes. "I wouldn't call Durnhold a mere distraction."

"You refuse to give us answers?" Anadalune asked, a hint of despair beneath her cool voice.

Sir Merlin shook his head. "I can't answer your questions, dear lady. I know only of this contract I bring to you and nothing of the making of it. But come, look upon this particular document. It is freshly prepared by the king's own treasurer."

Kristall felt no curiosity. Instead, she wondered where she might start searching for Cage. If she was not a prisoner, she should have freedom to explore. Surely her brother would have come to them himself unless he was held against his will.

Anadalune gasped. She looked up at Sir Berton standing behind her and showed him the paper. "I don't understand."

Sir Berton leaned forward to read the paper and whistled softly.

Kristall's frantic planning halted. What now?

Sir Merlin smiled in his sad way again. "The king has awarded you one thousand gold rounds to help you get Durnhold running and prosperous. You need never worry about funds again."

Anadalune sprang to her feet and paced to the window and then spun to face Sir Merlin. "You tell the king he can't buy my son from me. I insist on seeing Cage before the day is done."

Kristall joined her mother, giving her silent support.

Sir Merlin sighed. "I shall pass on your wishes, my lady, but you may not make demands of the king. Take what he has given you. I too have lost a child to the service of the Keepers. I'll do what I can to make sure you don't suffer for years as I have."

"Years?" Kristall whispered. Why had they ever come to this cursed city?

"I'm sorry," Sir Merlin said. "I'm afraid both of our families have been pulled by fate into something so large our wishes are irrelevant. You must try to accept that Cage Stone is lost to you forever."

CHAPTER ELEVEN

CAGE WAITED AS PATIENTLY AS HE could outside the Exarch's office. He disdained the stuffed chairs pushed against the wall in this small outer room. His muscles and every other part of his body ached so much he might never get back up if he sat down.

His last two days had been visits to hell. As a lad he'd trained hard with Sir Berton, sparring against men older and stronger than himself. Working with the Marshals was different. They were hard men, skilled and ruthless as they battled against him. They came at him one after the other or sometimes two or three at once. And they were quick, too damn quick to believe, and strong.

It had taken Cage almost the entire first day to discover the source of their incredible abilities, though he had no understanding or proof of his beliefs. Magic of some form.

The other Marshals weren't unfriendly, but neither did they welcome him with warmth. That was fine. His sword had been bought with the king's gold. He wasn't here to join a brotherhood.

One of the older Marshals came out of the Exarch's office. He paused when he saw Cage. "I'm Bachus. I'm to work with you after the noon meal."

Cage nodded. He knew little about the muscular red-haired Marshal. Though Bachus often watched the training, he'd never taken part with Cage. Bachus had cold blue eyes, windows into a soul devoid of emotion. He stared at Cage for a long moment, his gaze searching for something. Then without a nod or another word, the dour man turned and strode out the door.

The fortress of the Keepers was a strange place filled with odd people. Cage walked to the wall and pushed aside a colorful wool hanging. He placed his palm against one of the large stone blocks and sought the heart of the ancient earth bone. Long ago it had been carved and shaped to build this mighty construct. Shaped by the loving careful hands of the elves. The stones recalled gentle hands brushing aside the dirt that hid their inner beauty and waking them from the deep sleep. The gray rocks mourned the loss of the fair voices that once sang in these halls. All this he learned from the stones, though he couldn't explain how. The earth bones welcomed him, welcomed him home to this gray fortress now infested by the Keepers.

"What are you doing?"

Cage pulled back from the contact with the wall. When had he leaned against it and closed his eyes? For a few moments, he'd not been alone. He straightened to stand erect and turned to the Exarch. He must not let himself be so distracted or sink into such comfort. Not when surrounded by these witches.

"What were you doing?" she repeated.

"Admiring the architecture."

She frowned at him and shook her head. "Come in. We have to talk."

Cage followed her into her private sanctum. The furniture in here was old and exotic compared to the sturdy furnishings in the barracks and dining hall. Intricate carvings climbed the legs and arms of the chairs. Fantastical creatures and exotic birdlike figures danced along the sides of her desk, and more were on the bookshelves. Though he'd never seen such beings he knew them for real.

"Examining the woodwork now?" the Exarch asked with gentle sarcasm.

Cage shrugged. He wouldn't humor their curiosity. He lived with the constant speculation in the eyes of the Marshals in the training yards. Even in the baths, the stares of the other Marshals followed him. No one questioned him directly, but they searched for his oddities.

Word of his elvish heritage had spread like spilled

milk. So he hid himself even more, trying to appear human. They had bought his sword, not his secrets. Not even his family knew all his quirks. More disturbing were the new abilities that came to him since he'd moved into this fortress. Some essence of his mother's people lingered here, and it woke that part of him.

The Exarch took her seat behind her desk. She gestured for him to sit opposite herself.

Cage clamped his jaw to prevent a wince as he sat down. Sir Berton would roll on the floor laughing if he saw all the bruises marking Cage's body.

"I hear your training is going well," the Exarch said with a tight smile.

Cage said nothing. He wasn't going to make small talk.

Her smile turned wry. "Do you intend to be as difficult as possible?"

"I'll abide by my contract with the king."

"I'm sure you will," she said in a tired voice.

She stared at him, but it seemed she looked through him. A tiny brush of the Exarch's thoughts stroked against his mind. The light touch became a more insistent pressure. Magic! Trying to see inside his mind?

Fury rolled through him in a great wave. The Exarch gasped and flopped back in her chair. Cage staggered to his feet, his limbs as weak as if he'd fought a battle. He stood behind his chair, gripping the back with his trembling hands.

"What right have you?" he snarled. How could he

trust these people?

The Exarch took a couple of deep breaths. Her face was pale enough that some of Cage's anger abated. She looked like she might faint.

"I apologize, Marshal Stone." She sounded breathless. "I had no right."

Cage cautiously took his seat again. His nerves hummed in readiness for another attack.

The Exarch sat up straighter, and her expression hardened. "I made a mistake, but my intentions were not harmful. I wished only to determine your commitment to our endeavor."

"I've given my word." He emphasized each word, making his tone as hard as hers. But in truth, this magic of hers frightened him. What else might these Keepers be able to do?

"Are you frightened, Cage Stone?"

Her question increased his fear. How many times had it seemed the Exarch read his thoughts? Did she do so now without him knowing? "I am."

"And I'm afraid of you, Marshal." She got up and turned her back to him so that she looked out the tall, narrow window behind her desk. "You don't understand what you are or what you're capable of. I wish to study you and learn how best to use you, but there is no time. I fear your stubbornness, your temper, and your tenuous commitment to our cause."

"How are we to work together with this distrust

between us?" He had no intention of giving her reassuring words.

She spun and gave him a grim smile. "Trust? There are few I trust these days, Marshal Stone. You're a long way from being one of them. Unless you drop your resistance to my probe and let me see inside your thoughts."

"I've nothing sinister to hide, Mistress, but I've no wish to suffer such a violation either."

"Then I shall know when you trust me. As soon as you're satisfied in your heart that my need is just, you'll let me see inside you. Unless, of course, you are not true to your own word."

Cage said nothing.

The Exarch took her seat again. "I've another reason to speak with you. Two reasons, actually. Each Marshal is assigned to a Keeper when his training is advanced enough. You already know we have a special Keeper for you to guard."

"The Keeper trained to renew the seals?"

"Yes. You met her already when she attempted to heal you."

Cage couldn't help his grimace.

Lantana smiled but didn't mention the disaster. "Bachus will be the Marshal who will help the two of you learn to work together. He'll instruct you in the duties of a Marshal."

The Exarch folded her hands together, and her expression was stern. "I know you and Mistress Sabelline got off to a bad start, but she is a fine young woman. She should have had years more to train and practice, but like you, she is being rushed forward in her education."

Cage nodded because she waited for some response from him. Did she think he was going to feel sorry for one of her fellow witches?

"Some of your lessons will be together, some separate. After your next session today, I want you both to come back here together so I can explain more things to the both of you."

Cage took his leave, wondering what further surprises the Keepers had in store for him. He fought exhaustion of mind and body. He was surrounded by people he didn't trust and maintained a high level of alertness all the time. He feared to even sleep deeply, and it was beginning to wear on him.

He ran his hand along the bare walls as he wound his way along the passages leading to the Marshals' dining hall. The stones comforted him with their quiet undemanding spirit. Still, his mind would not rest.

Were Anadalune and Kristall safe? He feared Sir Berton would endanger himself trying to protect them. The Exarch had promised he might visit them as least once before he went with the Keeper to renew the seals. One chance to say good-bye. The longer he worked with the Keepers and the Marshals, the more convinced he was that the mission would be one of no return.

Sabell approached the training yard with more than a little trepidation. Though she was competent with the short wooden sword she carried she had no love of the martial arts as some Keepers did. She accepted the necessity of the training, but she couldn't enjoy it.

She tugged on the bottom of her hip-length tunic. The snug thick cotton blouse fit over a pair of equally tight cotton pants. She always felt exposed in such garments, although the Marshals were too well mannered to give so much as an offensive glance at her legs. It wasn't as if her body was the thin, petite form preferred by men anyway. She was overtall and cursed with generous breasts and well-rounded hips.

Two men stood in the middle of one of the sandy training pits with their backs to her. She recognized Bachus from his distinctive hair color. Her heart spasmed with sorrow and fear at the sight of him. Losing Alvara had destroyed the poor man. The fear was for herself.

The other man turned and fixed his cool gaze on her, though she was sure she had made no sound to draw his attention. Sabell wanted to groan. Cage Stone surely resented her for the lavender incident. He'd begged her to cease, and she'd ignored his plea.

Inserted into her discomfort over their first encounter was her last private conversation with the Exarch.

Lantana had told Sabelline of Cage's mixed parentage. She wasn't sure how to act around him. How different was he from other men? She was half in awe of his relationship to those who had constructed the seals, and half dismayed that she must find common ground with someone unlike anyone else in all of Futhark.

"Join us, Mistress Sabelline," Bachus called.

Sabell strode toward them, hoping her steps appeared confident. She'd heard enough about Cage's prowess in combat to be intimidated by that alone. She needed to establish her authority in their new relationship.

"Good day, sirs." Sabell nodded to Bachus and only then looked at Cage. There was no welcome in his light gray eyes. As before she was struck by the perfection of his features and flawlessness of his skin. The tilt of his head was somehow graceful and completely arrogant. "I've been told you are to be my Marshal, Cage Stone."

"I've been so instructed, Mistress." His even tone gave no hint of what was in his mind. If he resented her for the earlier encounter, he gave no clue. If he felt honor in his new position, it was well hidden.

"Let's start," Bachus said. "Stone, you're a gifted swordsman and fight well with your hands, but battling a demon in tandem with your Keeper is a special way to fight. You must learn to stay out of each other's way."

For two hours, Bachus took them through the dance of teamwork developed over generations of Marshals and Keepers fighting together. Cage learned quicker than

Sabelline, demonstrating a natural instinct for guarding her back and anticipating her moves. After the first hour, two more Marshals joined them and played the foe.

Bachus was a stern instructor but gave praise when due. Cage impressed Sabell as he listened intently and followed the advice of the older man. In a short time, she and Cage were disarming their opponents with smooth ease. She wasn't even sure Cage needed her to do so, but Marshals were not demons. Cage would need her magic when they confronted the terrors lurking beyond the Gate.

"You two work well together," Bachus pronounced as he leaned on the long wooden staff he had used to try to penetrate Cage's defense.

Sabell's arms ached with fatigue. She had missed most of her weapons training since Alvara died so that she might spend more time with other lessons.

"We'll do this every day at this time until your departure," Bachus said. "Tomorrow we'll bring in the hounds."

Sabell gaped. The large wolfhounds were quicker than men and massive in both height and muscle. Only the best of the Marshals ever trained with the dogs. How were they to fight them? The thought of their long fangs sent a shiver of fear up her spine.

If the plan for tomorrow worried Cage, he made no remark. He walked toward one of the benches overlooking the pit. He sat when he reached it and lifted a clay bottle to his mouth. As he drank from it a few drops of water escaped and crept slowly down his chin and then hastened down his neck.

Sabell shook herself. Why did she stare so? She thanked Bachus and the others and stomped toward Cage. "Care to share that?"

She knew she sounded rude, but a gentleman would have offered it to her first. Her clothing was damp with sweat against her skin, but Cage looked like he had done little more than sit and watch. That switched her temper up a notch.

Did he forget he was her Marshal? Her welfare came first. Most Marshals treated their Keeper with the reverence of a common soldier to a fine lady. Surely a bastard-born male like Cage Stone understood such social divisions.

He lowered the jar and gave her a wary look. He slowly extended the water to her, keeping his gaze locked on hers.

She took the water and lifted it to her lips. It was cool and satisfying after her exertions. She let her eyes drift close to savor the reviving nectar as it rolled down her throat.

"Don't drink it all."

Her eyes snapped open. The nerve! She stopped drinking and considered dumping the rest on his head. "Apparently you're ignorant of the Keeper-Marshal relationship, Cage Stone."

He reached out and took the water from her. He took another drink but kept his considering gaze on her while he did. When he lowered the jar, he offered it back to her as he spoke. "I understand I'm to protect you, Mistress. Is there more?"

"Is there more?" she sputtered, ignoring the offered water. "You're not just my guard."

He set the jar on the bench with care and stood up. He strapped on the shoulder baldric that held his real sword and then slipped a long vicious knife into the leather holster affixed to his belt. When he looked at her again—and by this time her temper was in high boil— his eyes held a grave curiosity.

"I am only a guard, Mistress. That is how my duties were explained to me."

Sabell almost snapped at him, but something in his wary look gave her pause. He wasn't being disrespectful. "You've seen the other Keepers and Marshals interact."

He shook his head. "Only the Exarch and her shadow, Harmon. I can't say I understand their relationship. They almost act married with her as queen and him as her consort."

He thought the Exarch and Harmon acted married? She didn't laugh. He looked so serious. Then she realized what else he said. "You've never seen a Keeper and a Marshal together besides the Exarch and Harmon?"

"From a distance. I'm in the Marshals' barracks. I never heard of Keepers and Marshals until a few days ago, Mistress."

Staggered by his ignorance, Sabell's temper took her again. She directed it at a different target. "Excuse me, Marshal. I must go see the Exarch." His puzzled expression only made her angrier at Lantana.

"I'll go with you," Cage said. He picked up the water and took another quick swallow before offering it to her again.

Sabell hesitated enough that he started to pull it back. She quickly reached out and took it, mumbling her thanks. Their hands brushed momentarily and sent a shiver up her arm. His skin was warm, almost hot.

Sabell almost didn't recognize the dim emotion of physical desire that rose in her. How long had it been since she'd felt it? Reseda may have gushed over Cage's physical beauty, but Sabell only admired it in the way she would a stunning sunset. She never engaged in affairs with the Marshals or the king's guards as did other Keepers. There were no rules against it; she simply wasn't attracted to fighting men.

Was her self-discipline weakened by the stress and fear, her constant companions of late? Had seeing her family destroyed the emotional barriers she had used to stave away the loneliness? Or was it Cage's overwhelming masculinity that shook her so?

She steeled herself and finished the water. "Thank you."

"You're welcome, Mistress. Shall we see the Exarch together? She told me this morning she wished to speak with both of us after our training."

Sabell hadn't wanted to speak with the Exarch in front of Cage, but she would if she had to. "Let's go."

Cage looked down at himself. "Perhaps I should bathe first."

He looked fine to her, but her own tunic was damp in spots. She wondered if she smelled as slimy as she felt. "I'll meet you in the Marshal's study. It won't take me long."

Cage nodded and followed her toward the manor. Once she stumbled over a clump of grass. His strong hand caught her under the elbow and steadied her.

When she turned to thank him, he was close. Close enough to see how clear his gray eyes were, how black his eyebrows, and how smooth his cheeks. He was tall enough she had to bend her neck back to look at him. Her breath hitched and she pulled away. She walked briskly and with care after that. If her heart pounded it was only in anticipation of her meeting with the Exarch. She wasn't attracted to the violent man behind her.

Chapter Twelve

CAGE DIDN'T TRUST HER, BUT HER scent titillated his senses. Mistress Sabelline walked beside him as they made their way to the Exarch's office. She was taller than many women, with the top of her head coming to his nose. A good fit in bed, though it would never happen. Despite her womanly form and arousing aroma, he would never put himself in such a position. Lust blinded a man, made him lose control and awareness of his surroundings. He'd never feel safe enough with a Keeper to risk that.

Still, his body responded to her. Traveling with Anadalune and Kristall had hindered his freedom with women. Many days had passed since he enjoyed the sweet embrace of an eager female. Plenty had offered on their journey to Sulbreth.

As they entered the small salon outside the Exarch's office, Cage wondered grimly if he'd ever be with a woman in such a way again. Did these people really believe a single man and woman could fight off demonic beasts like the gordragons alone? The duty was a death sentence.

"Please let me speak first, Marshal Cage," Mistress Sabelline said before she knocked on the door.

At her imperious tone Cage's attention slammed back to the matter at hand. What exactly was the expected association between Keeper and Marshal? Was the Marshal expected to be servile? He should have asked more questions.

Harmon opened the door and closed it behind them as soon as they entered. The Exarch invited them to take seats.

Cage studied Harmon as he walked by him. The old Marshal had more tattoos than most of the others, including some around his eyes and on his forearms and hands. The markings worried Cage. He'd known swordsmen who wore them as symbols of their lords or accomplishments. Some thought them attractive or perhaps frightening to opponents. Cage found them distasteful and unnatural. But the inking on the Marshals disturbed on another level.

"I've been expecting you," the Exarch said in her grandmotherly tone. "How did your training session go?"

The wily old woman probably already had a full report.

"It was fine," Sabelline answered. "I have some

questions for you, Exarch, if I may ask."

"Ask me anything, Sabelline."

"As I spoke to Marshal Cage today, I realized he knows nothing about us. Until a few days ago, he'd never met a Marshal or a Keeper."

"I'm aware of that."

"Then how do you expect us to work together?" Sabelline's voice rose in volume. "He doesn't know his . . ."

"His what, Sabelline?" the Exarch asked kindly.

Cage looked at Sabelline. What didn't he know? His duties? She glanced at him and quickly looked away. Her face darkened, and Cage's curiosity spiraled upward. What bothered her so?

"He doesn't know his place."

Her answer stunned Cage. He never forgot the stigma of his bastard birth, but few had the nerve to speak of it in front of him. He'd thought Sabelline a bit of a snob earlier over the water incident, but she hadn't acted as if working with a bastard was beneath her. Was he to bow before her noble, legitimate blood? How surprising she could bring herself to drink from the same jug as filth such as him.

The Exarch looked more shocked than Cage as she stared at Sabelline.

Disgust and anger filled Cage. He'd actually felt lust for this woman?

"I'm afraid you'll have to give me specifics, Sabelline," the Exarch said. No grandmothering now.

Sabelline frowned and hesitated for a long moment. "He thinks he's only my guard."

"He is," the Exarch said, her own frown turning puzzled.

Sabelline gestured toward Harmon. "I've observed Keepers and their Marshals together for years, Exarch. They've more than that between them. They're more like lady and protector."

Cage's anger sputtered. What the hell was she talking about?

The Exarch relaxed and smiled. "You're correct, but Harmon and I have been together for many years. Such a relationship takes time to develop."

"But we don't have the time. How can we learn to work with each other the way you two do? I think it would be better if a more experienced Marshal such as Bachus went with me. He has already had all the training."

Cage certainly didn't want to go on this desperate journey, but his pride stung at her words. At least she didn't want him because of his experience and not because of the circumstances of his birth.

Exarch Lantana shook her head. "You know why he must go. You'll adjust and learn to deal with each other. Every Keeper and Marshal have a unique relationship, some closer than others. I'm having Marshal Cage's things moved to your quarters as we speak."

Cage tensed. His things? Her rooms? What was this?

Before he could form a question, the Exarch spoke

again.

"Tell me, Sabell, how did your Marshal perform today against Marshal Bachus?"

"He defeated Bachus." Sabelline looked at Cage. "He beat them all."

"Let's have no further discussion. Cage Stone has agreed to be your Marshal, and you will have him. Despite his exceptional performance today against men, he must be even better. You might meet all manner of fell beasts behind Kingdom's Gate. Some we know of; others might be of a kind we've never seen."

"Exactly how long do I have to prepare, Mistress?" Cage asked. He tired of them speaking as if he had no piece of this. All this training they planned—hadn't he proven his mettle with the sword? None of the Marshals could defeat him in fair combat.

"Until the next new moon," the Exarch answered. "Twenty days."

"A question nags at me, Mistress." Cage wondered if he could believe anything these women said. They had so many secrets. The Exarch hid more than Sabelline. "Why are only the two of us going? I've gathered we're going through this Kingdom's Gate, but why not send numerous Keepers and an army of Marshals?"

"A fair question. Traveling to the iron seals requires stealth rather than brute force. If we tried to fight our way through, especially using magic, we would draw every imaginable monster to us. We'd never make it.

On top of that, we might bring the cavern down on top of ourselves."

"Cavern? Draw the demons to you?"

"When we designed our little test for you on the king's lawn, I fear my magic drew forth the real gordragons from Kingdom's Gate. We're usually careful not to use our gifts too near the entrance to the cavern. That they came when we were so far away is very disturbing. And yes, Kingdom's Gate is the opening to a great cavern, dangerous and mostly unexplored."

Cage put aside his questions about the cavern. "Do you mean you carelessly used a plan that endangered all those you strive to protect? You speak as if with expertise, Mistress Exarch, but the only time I've witnessed your magic it led to disaster."

Harmon growled a curse behind Cage.

The Exarch narrowed her eyes. "You're quite impudent for such a young man."

"Perhaps I seem so, but I'm not a young man when it comes to fighting or planning a battle."

"No, you're not. It's one of the things that makes you so valuable to us. That and, of course, your heritage."

Her words sent Cage's thoughts tumbling to the things that were coming to him since he'd acknowledged his ancestry. He'd closed so much of himself off for years, trying to be human, and now every day his senses sharpened and his agility improved, among other things. Sometimes he was frightened by his increasing selfishness.

"Another thing keeps us from sending more Marshals and Keepers with you," the Exarch said, oblivious to his disquiet. "If Sabelline successfully resets the seals, all the demons and monsters that have already drifted through will be trapped on this side. They'll find their way to Kingdom's Gate, and we'll deal with them. I fear we'll have more on this side than ever before in our recorded history. Never have gordragons been seen on the outside, and accipitors attacking in daylight is even more troubling."

Cage detected no lies in her words, but he wondered how knowledgeable and competent the Keepers really were.

"And if Mistress Sabelline doesn't succeed?" Cage asked. "Is another young woman training to be the sacrifice?"

"Mistress Reseda has started her lessons," the Exarch said. "Enough. I'm sure you have thousands of questions. Many will be answered in your lessons. It's time to speak of the next phase of your training."

The Exarch nodded at Harmon. The stoic Marshal strode over to stand beside her desk. He loosened the ties on his shirt and pulled it over his head.

Cage's heart thumped hard against his ribs. Intricate patterns of tattoos ran across Harmon's chest and down his arms. A wolf's head snarled from one piece of artwork, but most of it resembled interlocking chains. One of the chains appeared to entirely circle the man's neck. Some of the links continued to the edge of the waistband of Harmon's pants.

A shiver crawled across Cage's skin. He sensed the enchantments in the inking much as he had the illusionary gordragons of the Exarch.

"Did you notice during your training how quick our Marshals are, Cage Stone?" the Exarch asked.

"They're challenging opponents." Cage realized he was leaning away from Harmon as if the witchery might spill over onto him. He tried to relax, but he couldn't even look away from the tattoos.

"A Keeper assists her Marshal in many ways. Sabelline can fight at your back with a sword as she showed you today."

Cage nodded, though he stared at Harmon still. Yes, Mistress Sabelline was quite competent.

"But a Keeper can do even more. Using a small touch of magic, she can power strong spells that will enhance her Marshal's physical skills, strength, and stamina."

Cage waited. He knew little of magic, hadn't really believed in it until he came to this cursed city.

"Once these spells are drawn on the body of a Marshal, the latent magic bound into these grounds powers the spells to a certain extent. The men you've been training against have not been assisted by their Keepers, only by the fortress itself. We believe your ancestors left the trace of wizardry behind to assist us. I think you've felt it yourself."

Cage held his secrets but probed hers. "So your

Marshals are capable of greater skill than I've seen?"

"Yes, though I understand you've accounted quite well for yourself."

"Why not send one of them then, if they've greater skill than I?"

"They only have greater skill if their Keeper gives to them of her magic. Only the Keeper who initiates the spell on a Marshal can then power it. But even the best of them are limited by their human forms."

The shiver on Cage's skin settled into a cold ball of fear in his middle.

"You hold your own against them as no other man could. You start at a level of ability beyond their enhanced states. Think of the warrior you could become if Sabelline assists you with her magic."

The cold ball of fear spread into nausea. Cage swallowed back the bile rising in him as he stared at Harmon's disfigurement. "No."

Lantana didn't look surprised when he made himself glance her way. "I won't try to talk you into this. We could force it upon you, but I'd rather you do it with a willing heart. Instead, I'll show you something to convince you."

Cage's steps faltered. The tall trees at the end of the

long lawn hid this thing they called "Kingdom's Gate" from his sight. But he felt it.

The aspens and maples behind him whispered a warning as they begged him to stay and walk among them. He turned and looked at their delicate leaves waving in the breeze. Many had turned yellow or red and floated to the grass. But the soil beneath the verdant lawn held the dark essence of blood spilled. A woman had died in terror, her life taken by violent, unfeeling malevolence. And almost overwhelming the warm scent of her blood was the lingering stench of cold reptilian death. The demons that died here had hated until their last breaths.

"Are you coming?" Exarch Lantana asked. She, Harmon, Sabelline, and five other Keepers and their Marshals waited a few paces farther along the path, where the maples and delicate aspens gave way to towering oaks.

"Yes, Mistress." Cage hurried to catch up, appreciating their reticence. Their expressions were questioning, but they didn't ask why he'd stopped.

The oaks were old compared to the lesser trees. Their ancestors had been set here to watch over the Gate, many generations of oaks ago . . . Cage shut the trees' memories from his mind.

Sabell, he liked her shortened name, dropped back to walk beside Cage. They followed a slowly curving path into the deep shadows of the trees. The dark mountain rose in front of them, but Cage realized not all the gloom was from hill and thick canopy. Slimy fingers of dread feathered across his senses. His instincts screamed for him to turn back.

Their little procession slowed. Did they all feel the baleful emanations directed at them? Sabell walked closer and closer until every step caused her arm to lightly bump against his. He heard the increase in her breathing, shallow breaths, smelled her fear, and knew she also sensed the forbidding presence before them.

They stepped from under the trees into an open area. No grass or bush grew between the last oak and the mountainside. It towered before them, its rocks smooth and darker than the deepest night. It climbed to thrice the height of the king's vainglorious castle. The sun was well behind it, though hours remained until actual sunset, so that its sinister shadow fell over them.

"Welcome, Exarch."

The woman's voice pulled Cage's attention from the mountain. Black gravel, the dust of centuries of weather damage on the slopes, covered the half-moon-shaped clearing. Four Keepers and their Marshals stood about the barren yard. Though a large area, the clearing appeared small before the sheer slopes. The Keepers and Marshals were as ants before the peaks.

"We weren't sure if you were coming, Exarch," one of the Keepers said.

"Yes, well, never underestimate the stubbornness of

this one."

Cage studied the guards as the men and women stared at him. They wore the stern alert looks of warriors expecting an attack at any time. And he saw the fear, fear that they would be overrun, though they kept watch anyway.

Despite his concern the Keepers were bungling along in ignorance, Cage respected the courage it took to stand before the mountain. And he couldn't forget they had attacked the gordragons as he had. He'd heard those who had guarded the Gate were still not recovered from that terrible night.

"We've a need to show our newest Marshal what we face." The Exarch waved at Cage to follow her.

Cage itched to reach for the sword hanging behind his shoulder. He followed the Exarch and Harmon closer to the base of the mountain. Sabell stuck by him, no longer bumping into him, but her breath whispered against his shoulder.

They walked another twenty paces or so before Cage's breath froze. He stopped so suddenly, Sabell walked into him.

"Stop," Cage whispered, but he knew it was too late to be quiet. Harmon and the Exarch heard him. "Get behind me."

Sabell took a step to obey. The Exarch opened her mouth to speak, but Harmon pushed her behind him as he moved to stand shoulder to shoulder with Cage.

"What is it?" Harmon whispered, so quiet his words might have been the breeze.

Cage carefully drew his sword. He heard other swords sliding free behind him. He stared into the deep shadows in front of them. Large boulders littered the foot of the steep slopes. Something hid among them. It watched, unblinkingly, mercilessly. Hungrily.

"Back away," Cage said. His throat was tight, making his whisper rough. The ground beneath his feet didn't speak to him; the rocks did not waken to him. It was all dead. Except the thing that watched and now moved. He heard a sliding sound on the loose gravel.

Cage heard others running to join them. They should run. But not toward him and the demon coming for . . . Sabelline.

Their group of four shuffled back. Magic brushed against him, but it was directed toward Harmon. The Exarch fed her Marshal's spells. Cage shivered despite the danger approaching.

"Can you tell what it is?" the Exarch demanded.

Cage urged them back farther. Sabell had a grip on his shirt and tugged as if to hurry him. Her fingers trembled. He feared if they turned and ran it would attack.

"Do you see anything, Harmon?"

"No, Exarch." Tension made the Marshal's answer curt. He stayed even with Cage, his sword poised and ready.

"I hear it," Cage said. "It's coming."

They backed up a few more steps. Other Marshals lined

up on either side of them, all touched by Keepers' magic.

"I hear it, too," Harmon said. "It sounds big."

The stench of rotton meat and moldy vegetation rolled over them in a wave as thick as warm, rancid butter. The sound of its grating approach grew louder.

"The women should run," Cage said.

"The women can fight it better than us, boy," Harmon said.

It came around a large boulder. Men and women gasped, either from fear or wonder. He didn't. His breath was too frozen to even curse as the vision from hell stared directly at him.

CHAPTER THIRTEEN

SABELL OPENED HER MOUTH TO scream but found her throat paralyzed by terror. For a long moment everything and everyone froze, stunned into statues.

Cage broke the spell with a string of vile words, many of them incomprehensible. The Exarch gripped Sabell's arm in a painful grasp. Sabell panted, her chest tight with fear.

The snakelike creature slithered toward them. On and on it came, seeming to have no end to its long, ropey body. Its height was taller than a man, and it kept its head raised off the ground to twice that height. Black empty eyes stared at them, at her.

"It's a cave boa," the Exarch shouted over the harsh grinding sound it made as its heavy body slid over the gravel. "Never has one passed outside the Gate."

Cage pushed Sabell back farther with Harmon shoulder to shoulder with him. Beside her, the Exarch chanted a spell.

The cave boa paused. Its long black split tongue shot from its mouth and flicked around. Eyes dark as tar stared at her. She was sure. The soulless eyes looked at her.

"Run, Sabell," Cage shouted. "It's come for you."

"He's right," the Exarch agreed. "You must go."

A brief flash of memory, of Alvara's mangled body, gave her impetus. Sabell turned and ran. Guilt almost made her stop as she passed the other Keepers. They stood so resolute behind their Marshals.

The ground shook with the force of whatever magic the Keepers released. The women assigned to guard the Gate were skilled in the use of concussion spells. Somehow they compacted the invisible air into a fist as heavy as a boulder. They'd killed the gordragons with it.

Shouts of pain and dismay behind her slowed her dash for safety. She couldn't leave them to face what came for her.

Sabell turned. Bodies sprawled on each side of the demon snake. In the deepening twilight she couldn't tell individuals apart. Did her Marshal lie among the fallen? The Exarch?

She had little control over the power of the air, but the hard elements of the earth were her strength. The boa slunk forward, ignoring a Marshal hacking ineffectively at its scaled side.

She took a deep breath to calm herself—useless—and then flicked her hands as if rolling up a ball of clay. Except the ball she made was thousands of pieces of gravel from the barren field. It swirled and tightened until it formed a boulder the size of a wagon. Her concentration wavered as the snake neared. Its scales rattled as it moved its armored body across the ground. Sweat beaded on her brow as she held on to her control. The soft hiss of its breath told her it was close enough. She flung her hands and threw the constructed boulder at it with all the strength of her will behind it.

The boa lifted its head even farther off the ground just as she threw her weapon at it. Instead of hitting it between the eyes as planned, it struck the demon on its broad snout. The boa reared up higher, its low hiss rising to an ear-piercing squeal. It continued to lift its body until the fearsome head was as high as the great oaks.

Sabell stumbled back, her physical body weak and exhausted by the amount of magic she'd expended. The demon seemed only angry, not even slightly injured. She hadn't the energy left to toss a pebble at it. Sweat, born of fear and exhaustion, dripped into her eyes and joined her tears.

The great head darted down. Its jaws opened wide and exposed its dark maw. Fangs longer than a great sword dripped with saliva. Sabell tried to run, but her knees buckled. She fell to the ground. She scampered backward, pulling herself along with her hands. She refused to lie still and die.

A dark shape jumped in front of her as the shadow of the descending head fell upon her. She couldn't see his face, but only Cage Stone moved so gracefully. A flash marked the swing of his sword. She closed her eyes, not brave enough to watch his death and hers.

She might have screamed, but the screech of the boa drowned out everything. Something struck her, and she thought it was the dreadful fangs at first. But it was warm and heavy. Cage's body?

Complete darkness surrounded them. Then the air filled with a fetid odor of fruit gone bad. She waited for the fangs to slice through them both.

Cage's arms, already weary from his useless attempts to slice through the snake's armored hide, shook with fatigue as he braced his sword over his head. He straddled Sabell, worried she might be injured but unable to do anything about it. He'd seen her valiant attempt to face the demon alone as he raced to her aid. The other Marshals and Keepers might be dead. The initial blast of magic the Keepers cast at the monster had barely slowed it. It plowed over the men and women in its path as it sought the true prey.

The foul breath of the boa flowed over him as its terrible head descended. Cage looked up into the throat of hell and adjusted the angle of his sword. A great jolt traveled down his arms and knocked him over. As he fell on top of Sabell, he twisted his sword before it wrenched out of his grip. Hot liquid poured down the sword as he reached blindly and regained his weapon. He thrust upward as the head continued its powerful descent.

Sabell struggled beneath him, but he couldn't move off her. They were enclosed within the open bleeding mouth as if in a dark, deadly tomb.

One last great hiss followed by a great gust of hot, sour breath and the cave boa became silent and still.

Cage didn't want to even breathe, but his body screamed for air. He took in a mouthful of air. It was as bad as he expected. His hands gripped his sword so tightly he had to unlock his fingers one at a time to release it. When he pulled his hands away, the sword stayed in place, deep in the roof of the demon's mouth.

"Are we dead?" Sabell asked.

"No." Cage tried to straighten a leg but encountered a lower jaw. He turned his head. The meager light made seeing difficult even for him. One of the sharp fangs had missed impaling them both by a margin as narrow as the edge of a sword. He looked away—better not to contemplate that—and saw the lower fangs were driven into the ground.

"Is everyone else dead?" Sabell asked. She lay quietly

beneath him, but her voice trembled.

"I don't think so." Cage had seen Harmon going to the aid of the Exarch.

"I can't breathe."

Cage shifted some of his weight off of her, but there was little room.

"Better. I wish I could see."

Cage looked at the blood dripping from his sword and splattering on their legs. Was it black? "No, you don't."

Cage quieted, straining to hear. The crunch of gravel and voices neared somewhere outside their morbid prison.

"We've failed. They're dead." Despite being muffled, Cage could discern the despair and defeat in the Exarch's voice.

"We're here," Sabell called. Her voice trembled only slightly.

Cage said nothing. He had no strength left to shout. He and Sabell sat in their cramped awkward trap and listened to their rescuers working outside.

For a moment Cage wondered how they would lift the massive body off, and then he decided he didn't care. He was too tired. He let his head drop back onto something soft. Sabell's breast? If she minded, she didn't say. He thought she had to be as spent as he was. What was a little improper touching after battling a cave boa?

Cage sensed the sun setting in the west, and still they were trapped. Sabell sighed a few times and squirmed her hips and legs about. Her hands fluttered around and finally settled on his shoulders. They stayed in that position for another hour before the carcass shifted. Magic swirled, and the snake's head slowly rose off the ground.

Strong hands reached in and pulled them out into brilliant torchlight. They were barely clear when the heavy head smashed back into the ground.

Cage let Harmon lift him to his feet. His legs were cramped and stiff. The faces illuminated by the torches were grim and relieved at the same time. The two Keepers supporting Sabell managed shaky smiles.

The Exarch took Sabell's hand. "Are you well?"

Sabell looked over the old woman's shoulder to Cage. "I think I am. The others?"

"Some injuries, but all will heal. It wanted you."

Cage wiped his hands on the front of his shirt only to find it covered in drying, sticky blood also. He'd learned to block off his sense of smell at times, but this was too much. He pulled the shirt over his head, searching for a spot clean enough to wipe his hands. He lifted his gaze when silence fell upon the group. They all stared at him.

"I didn't show you what I wanted you to see, Cage Stone," the Exarch said.

"Another of your plans gone awry, Mistress?" Cage flung the useless shirt to the ground. "I need a bath."

"You killed a cave boa," one of the Keepers said.

The Exarch shushed the woman. "Harmon, arrange the duty for tonight. Triple it and set guards among the oaks also. Mistress Pinxter, bring me a report on the injured as soon as they all are treated. Mistress Reseda and Marshal Bachus, the two of you escort Mistress Sabelline and Marshal Cage back to their quarters. Both of you stand guard outside their door for the remainder of the night."

"I'm without a sword," Cage said.

Everyone fell silent again and stared at him. Many of them looked at the demon and then back at him. One of the Marshals guffawed behind his hand and then another. More joined in, and even Exarch Lantana smiled. Very odd people.

"We'll get you another on the morrow," Harmon said. He smiled at Cage for the first time in their brief acquaintance.

Cage didn't understand their amusement. "I need another one now. It's a long walk back to the fortress."

Everyone sobered. Harmon pulled his own sword and offered the hilt to Cage. "Take this one. We'll find you a new one at the armorer tomorrow."

Cage nodded his thanks and took the Marshal's heavy sword. Its balance felt odd in his hand, but he could use it if he must. He would prefer his own blade back instead of a new one if they could retrieve it from the demon body.

"I want both of you in my office at first light," the Exarch said. Though the little woman snapped out her commands in a brisk voice, the finger she shook at them trembled. She wasn't the rock she attempted to emulate.

Cage took the rear guard position as they started through the oaks. No one argued when he insisted on watching their backs. He considered the Marshals and how they had met the attack of the cave boa. The Keepers had fed the enchantments spelled out in the tattoos worn by the men. Their speed and grace impressed Cage. He'd never seen a man move in such a fashion. They were almost as fast as him, and they were absolutely stronger. Of course, none of that had mattered against the cave boa. Its thick hide had even shattered some of their swords.

The fortress was a welcome sight as they walked out from under the shadows of the oaks. The aspens and maples pulled away from the scent of death on them, but as they neared the ancient gray building, Cage sensed its strength. It offered sanctuary from the sleepless malice of the Gate. At least for this night.

Before going indoors, Cage took one last look at the dark peaks beyond the trees. The maliciousness there sought to encroach on the city of Sulbreth. How many other demons lurked behind the Gate? How would an innocent citizen of Sulbreth fare against such an attacker? He jerked his mind away from thoughts of Anadalune or Kristall facing such hellspawn.

He turned and followed Sabell inside and up the stairs that led to the Keepers' quarters. What had the Exarch intended to show him? Whatever it was, it couldn't have been more convincing than the cave boa. It had come for Sabelline. Sabelline was the hope of Futhark. She was also his responsibility. He must do whatever it took to protect her.

Sabell's knees shook as she climbed the last flight of stairs. Bachus walked in front of her. More than once she was tempted to lock her fingers around his belt and let him pull her along. Reseda walked behind her, but her friend's presence gave her no comfort. Were they friends anymore? They seldom had time together. Was Reseda still angry from their last encounter? Cage brought up the rear, but his footfalls made no sound. Twice she turned to make sure he still followed.

Lights blazed throughout the entire fortress. Keepers and Marshals hurried about, the newest crisis having put everyone on alert. Many stared at her little party, but no one asked questions of them.

She noticed most of the Keepers stared at her bloodied, shirtless Marshal. Did they stare at his manly form, or was the word already about that he'd slain a cave boa by himself? She understood Cage shedding his shirt. The same reptilian blood stained her skirt. She dragged up the last step hoping only for a hot bath, clean clothes, and her own familiar bed.

Mistress Tamarin waited in front of Sabell's door,

her ink-stained hands folded tightly in front of her. She shook her head when she saw Sabell. "My poor dear. I have a bath ready, all nice and hot."

Sabell wanted to hug her. She let herself be led into her own room. She stumbled to a stop inside the door. The unused cot sitting in the alcove was made up with a dark green quilt and two large pillows. A few nondescript garments hung from the hooks on the wall. A pitcher and washbasin sat on the small table near the foot of the narrow bed along with a steaming mug. She'd quite forgotten this was to be Cage's first night as her guardian.

Something made her turn. Cage stared at his sleeping area also. He lifted his gaze to meet hers. As usual, his thoughts were hidden from her.

"You don't know me yet, Marshal Cage." Tamarin said, "I'm Keeper Tamarin. You'll be starting lessons with me tomorrow, though I think I might learn a few things from you. I've ordered a bath for you in my own chambers down the hall. Would you show him the way, Reseda?"

"My pleasure," Reseda answered, a small smile curving her lips.

Cage grabbed a pair of pants off the wall hooks and followed Reseda out of the room without another glance or a word to Sabell. Reseda looked back over her shoulder at Sabell, an oddly triumphant expression on her pretty face.

Sabell hadn't the might to wonder. She tottered to her own bathing chamber. With Bachus guarding the door and the fortress around her, Sabell finally felt safe. She undressed slowly, aches screaming in her joints and muscles. Her rear hurt too. And her ribs where Cage had fallen on her.

She sank into the blessedly hot water and relaxed. Her tired thoughts turned sluggishly to Reseda. Was Reseda jealous? Jealous that Sabell was going on a death mission? The cave boa had convinced Sabell more than ever that she and Cage would not survive. Could they even reach the seals? Reseda had to see that.

Sabell ducked her head under and scrubbed her hair. It took three attempts to get the grit and bits of sticky blood out. Tamarin came in with a kettle of hot water and poured it into the tub. "Want some help, Sabelline?"

"I'm fine. This is what I needed."

"I'll go help with the others then. A busy night for an old lady." Tamarin gathered up Sabell's discarded clothing, likely ruined, and quietly closed the door on her way out.

The peace turned her thoughts to Reseda again. They'd been friends since they were first years together. Reseda always had a free and easy way with men. She made no secret of her many affairs with Marshals and even some of the young lords who spent time with the king. Was this about lusting over Cage? Or was Reseda determined to take him to her bed because she really was jealous of Sabell's duty? Either choice saddened Sabell.

Sabell sighed and leaned her head back on the edge of her brass tub. Did she care if Cage accepted Reseda's offer? She might. Cage belonged to her. In a way. But Marshals were men as any other. She didn't know him at all, but tonight he had saved her life. Didn't he deserve any chance he could get at pleasure before they walked through the Gate?

Sabell stood up out of the cooling water and wrapped a towel around her hair before drying off with another. Was Reseda helping Cage dry off even now?

Cage pulled his boots off. Damn, they would need to be cleaned. He had only the one pair, but splatters of dried blood stained them. Later. He went to work on the laces of his pants.

"Need any assistance?" Mistress Reseda still stood in the bathing room doorway.

Cage paused. He wanted her to leave. The demon stench clinging to him sickened him. "No, thank you, Mistress. I've been bathing on my own for a long time."

She walked farther into the room. Mistress Tamarin's bathing area carried a light remembrance of wild rose, but the woman approaching him drowned it out with the hot scent of female arousal.

Cage really looked at her for the first time. Her thin

blouse clung to her round breasts. Her skirt rode across her trim hips, hips that swung side to side as she sauntered toward him. She stopped, not quite touching him, her warm breath stroking his bare chest.

"I can wash your back." Her husky whisper made his gut clench.

Cage said nothing as she took over the laces on his pants. She tugged them loose and pushed them down over his hips. He wore nothing but his own arousal underneath. Cage had fought in enough battles to know the thrill of swordplay often led to such excitement. Knowing it didn't mean he could stop his reaction or that he wanted to stop it.

"I need a bath." He added a curse when her hand brushed across his erection. He jerked away from her and stepped into the steaming tub. The blessedly clean water cleared his head. He sank under the water and scrubbed at his sweat-stiffened hair.

When he came up for air, Reseda leaned over the side of the tub. She held up a small cloth. "Let me do your back."

Cage leaned forward to give her access. His back burned from being thrown aside by the snake when he first attacked it. He had slid across the gravel on his back before regaining his feet. The water stung as Mistress Reseda rubbed the cloth across his shoulders.

"You're injured. You have a thousand little scrapes and cuts on your back." She gentled her touch. "I can

230

heal you."

Cage jerked away from her touch. Not more healing. "It's a minor thing."

"And it will take minor effort on my part. Relax. Let's finish your bath first."

When had his bath become a project for both of them? But her soft hands were good. His aches melted into the warm water. Tension seeped from his body.

Cage let himself drift into mindless contentment for the first time since entering the city of Sulbreth. The warm water, the woman's touch—he sank into a dreamy pleasant place. Her hands wandered from his back. His body yearned for the oblivious release she could give him. And why not?

One of her hands stroked his neck. He turned his head when her warm breath fluttered across his ear. She waited for him, her lips hot and moist as they kissed.

She knew how to kiss. Good.

He heard the footsteps in the outer room only a moment before the door swung open. He broke away from Reseda.

Sabell stood in the open doorway, her scowl hotter than his bath water. "Helping my Marshal with his bath, Reseda?"

Reseda rose slowly to face Sabell. She dragged her hand across Cage's back in a provocative manner as she did.

Cage turned from the women and searched under

the water for the cloth Reseda had used. He found it on the bottom near his thigh. He scrubbed his chest and arms as if the Keepers' conversation had nothing to do with him.

"He needs a little tender care, Sabell. I know how reluctant you are to offer the more feminine gifts to men. If you even know how. I'll return him to you when we're finished."

Cage scrubbed harder.

"I'm perfectly capable of taking care of my Marshal. Thank you for your assistance. Please go."

Cage thought the ice in Sabell's voice might freeze his bathwater. He had nothing left to scrub.

"The Exarch ordered me to guard both of you tonight. I'll keep an eye on Cage. I'm sure Bachus will watch over you."

Cage looked around for a drying cloth but saw none. His clean pants were out of reach also. No escape.

"I don't understand, Reseda. Where has this come from?"

Cage heard something in Sabell's voice. A loneliness to match his own. He realized the confrontation wasn't about him. He was only in the middle of something going on between the two women.

Reseda sniffed. "If you weren't so busy being the savior of Futhark, perhaps you'd be more a part of the world you live in now."

Any attraction Cage had felt for Reseda wilted at her

cruel words. He spotted a folded white cloth on a small bench behind Reseda.

Reseda reached out and rubbed her hand on Cage's shoulder. The image of an icy claw rose in his mind.

"Why don't we ask Cage?" Reseda fluttered her hand through his wet hair. "Shall I help you finish your bath? I think I missed a spot."

Cage looked from one to the other. Reseda had promise in her dark eyes. Only a few moments ago, he would have taken her offer with no remorse.

Sabell glared at him, but what had he heard in her voice? Beneath the green fire of her eyes lurked a hurt, a silent pain. Damn the two women for putting him in the middle of their dispute.

"I'm finished with my bath and wish only to seek my bed. To sleep," Cage clarified. Neither woman moved and the water was cooling rapidly.

He stood up and reached past Reseda for the cloth. Reseda giggled, and Sabell's eyes opened wide. He stepped out of the tub and dried himself. He started with his hair. The ladies remained quiet as he did a thorough job. So much for embarrassing them into leaving. He draped the cloth over the bench and pulled on his clean pants.

"Thank you, Mistress Reseda." Cage edged past her. She shifted so their bodies brushed together. "We should get some sleep, Mistress Sabelline. Remember our meeting with the Exarch in a few hours."

He didn't wait for either of them to say anything. Sabell moved out of his way as he strode through the door. Bachus waited in the outer room. He gave Cage a cool look.

Fatigue rolled over Cage. He needed less sleep than most men, but the last few days challenged even his stamina.

Sabell's room was four doors away from Mistress Tamarin's. How many Keepers were there? The fortress was massive. Once he went in Sabell's room and saw his bed, such mundane thoughts fled. He dropped face-first on top of the soft quilt. It smelled of the outdoors and soap. He turned his face to the wall and sighed. His muscles relaxed, so he sank into the warm embrace of the bed.

He heard Sabell come in and hoped she'd go straight to bed herself. She closed the door and walked over to him. He kept his eyes shut.

"Cage, I'm sorry. Your personal life is none of my affair. If you want to be with Reseda tonight, I understand." She didn't sound like she understood.

"Get some sleep, Mistress."

She touched his bare back. She ran her fingertips over the scrapes and bruises, her touch as light as a summer breeze. His sleepy inclinations weakened.

"You were magnificent today, Marshal Stone." She spoke quietly, as if to herself. Her voice caught. "I was so scared."

Cage turned over. Her hand fell away from his

back. He wished her touch back as soon as it was gone. "Everyone was frightened, Mistress. You stood and faced it. I saw you fling the boulder at it. Only bad luck prevented you from stopping it."

The lamps were turned low, but he had no trouble seeing her small, rueful smile. "I'd call it more than bad luck. I've never used my magic to fight before. Inexperience and pure panic is a better description."

"You slowed it down and gave me enough time to get there. We killed it together."

Sabell put her hand on his shoulder. "Don't coddle me, Marshal Cage, and don't try to raise my confidence. Now turn over so I can heal your back."

Cage didn't move. Her green eyes sparkled with ironic humor. The scent of hyacinth clung to her damp hair. She wasn't offering the comfort Reseda had, but his body responded to her closeness. He now understood what she meant earlier about him not knowing his place as Marshal. Were Marshals and Keepers permitted to be lovers? Was Reseda's flirtation the usual or against the rules?

"My scratches need no attention, Mistress." He recognized the passionate thoughts coursing through him as remnants of battle lust. Still, why tempt her touch?

Sabell urged him to his stomach. He gave in, unable to give a good reason to refuse.

"I need to practice my healing skills on you. You're

different from other men. Remember the last time?"

As if he would forget. Had it only been a few days ago he'd fallen beneath her ministrations?

She again touched him lightly with her fingertips. A pleasant tingling moved beneath his skin, and his muscles relaxed again. She mumbled something, but his exceptional hearing failed him. He struggled to renew his distrust of her, but an odd peace settled over him. He was too damned tired to be alarmed by it or fight it.

Cage's taut muscles softened slightly beneath her hand. Asleep as quickly as putting out a candle. Exhaustion? He should be tired. She wished she felt safe enough to rest so easily.

Or had her magic done this to him? No, she hadn't used any lavender.

Sabell stroked her hand lightly over his back until every tiny scratch was healed. Even after she finished the healing, she continued to slide her hands over his smooth golden skin. His muscles were firm and well defined in his shoulders and back. His waist was narrow to the point of being thin, but she remembered how heavy he felt when he fell on top of her. Solid. Cage Stone was a solid man in many ways.

She stopped touching him. It was an intrusion on

his person. She stared at him. He was beautiful. Oddly, the more time she was with him, the more appealing his appearance became. His features were unusual with his high cheekbones, his light gray eyes, and the perfect symmetry of his bones. But it wasn't only those things. He was stubborn, proud, and distrustful. Something about him, something deep and fine, made up for those faults. Was it his blind courage, his unfailing confidence, or, more likely, his chivalrous tendency to throw his body between her and death?

That thought led to a vivid recollection of the snake rising above her, ready to finish her. A small shudder ran through her body. Would she have been swallowed whole and suffocated while being digested? Or would the vicious fangs have impaled her and ended it quickly?

She looked at Cage. He might not know many things about being a Marshal, but he knew the most important. He'd saved her. Tomorrow she would put the first tattoo on him. She'd dreaded it from the first, but a new determination filled her. She'd been willing to do it for the sake of her mission, but now she would do it for him. Today he had demonstrated he would do anything to save her. She must do her part to help him.

Sabell yawned, her jaws popping. Now was not the time to contemplate tomorrow or her relationship with Cage Stone. Marshals and Keepers were often close. She hadn't expected to feel for him so quickly. After the incident with Reseda, she admitted to herself he was a very desirable man. And he was hers. She didn't want to share him.

She was overtired. That explained her disquietude. She put out the lamps as she went through the sitting room. Tamarin had left one burning beside her bed also. Her bed was turned down. Wonderful! She put out the last lamp and dropped her robe to the floor. She stretched out and pulled the blankets around her shoulders. The warmth from her bath lingered in her muscles, and despite the chaos in her thoughts, her body relaxed into the mattress. The shadows in the corners of her room didn't seem as friendly as usual, but her heavy lids refused her wish to remain alert. Once she closed her eyes, they wouldn't open again.

She knew she was sleeping. Dreaming. But her fear was real. The giant snake raced toward her. It was going to bowl her over, but then it stopped at the last moment. Terror squeezed her chest so that she couldn't scream. She tried to call her magic, but it wasn't there. Where was everyone else? Cage?

The snake stared at her with cruel, black eyes. Its thick forked tongue flicked out, almost touching her chest. She couldn't move back; a great boulder pressed into her spine. Trapped. The demon lifted its upper body high above her head. To her horror, its exposed belly wasn't covered with scales but rather a double row of tiny white arms. Each arm ended in a three-fingered hand. Long curved nails sprouted from each fat finger.

They reached for her. She found her voice and screamed. And screamed.

Hands grabbed her shoulders, but instead of pulling her forward, they shook her. Someone called her name. Help was coming, but the hands shook her harder.

Sabell opened her eyes and saw a shadow leaning over her. She pulled in a deep breath to scream again.

"Mistress Sabelline, wake up!"

Her strength left her. She was sitting up in bed, but now she sagged against Cage's bare chest. His arms wrapped around her.

"I had a dream," she croaked. Her raw throat told her the screams were real enough.

"It was a day to cause nightmares," Cage said. He held her securely, his voice vibrating in his chest beneath her ear.

Sabell nodded against his warm skin. His calm, steady voice soothed her.

"Everything all right?" Bachus asked from her bedroom door.

Sabell's face heated. Bachus and Reseda guarded her room. They would have heard.

"She's fine," Cage answered.

Sabell stayed in Cage's arms until she heard Bachus close her bedroom door. She felt a brief satisfaction that Reseda would have seen her in Cage's arms. Then she realized no lamps were lit. Reseda couldn't have seen a thing.

With a reluctant sigh, Sabell disengaged herself. Cage let go and leaned back. She missed his warmth immediately. Waking had not dispelled all the terror. It waited for her to close her eyes again.

"Thank you. I'm all right now," she lied. He needed his rest.

"Why don't I stay with you until you fall asleep?"

Sabell lifted her legs over the side of the bed and fumbled for the thick wooden matches. Cage pushed her hands aside and soon had the bedside lamp glowing.

"I'll leave the lamp burning." She didn't intend to close her eyes at all.

Cage went to the fireplace and stirred the embers. He fed some kindling until he had a small blaze. When he was satisfied, he sat in one of the upholstered chairs beside the hearth. "I'll sit here awhile, Mistress. No demons will visit your dreams again this night. I've had enough sleep."

He did look well rested. Why was she arguing when she wanted him to stay?

She lay down again and curled onto her side so she could see him. He stared into the flames, giving her his profile. Sleep surprised her as it took her with ease. Her dreams were of virgin forests and stones that sang slow sad songs.

CHAPTER FOURTEEN

JONARED NOTICED THAT THE BASTARD, Cage Stone, hesitated when he saw his king present for this early meeting.

"Come in, Marshal Cage," Lantana said. "We've been waiting for you and Sabelline."

Sabelline nodded her head respectfully at Jonared, and he smiled in return. They'd been friends since childhood, though they had grown apart since she'd joined the Keepers. They might have married if things had gone differently. Sabell might be queen now. Instead, she would be something more important. If she survived.

"I'm glad to see you in good health, Sabell," Jonared said. He rose and took her hand. As he led her to the table himself, he noted she looked some the worse for this latest misadventure. Dark circles underlined her eyes, and shadows haunted the green depths. His heart rebelled against what they asked of her, a sweet, kind lady. Why must such as she face these horrors? How much guilt could he carry for asking it of her?

Sabell smiled. "I'm unhurt, your majesty. The Marshal you found for me has proven his worth."

Jonared returned to his seat at the head of the table. Even though this dining room belonged to the Exarch, the commanding spot was his. As the others took their seats also, Jonared noted the cool stare of Cage Stone on him. Damn the arrogant man. And bless him.

Marshal Harmon and the Exarch looked as they should after being up all night and killing a dreadful demon. Jonared's own eyes were scratchy and heavy. Sir Maton had woken him from a restless sleep with the news from the Keepers. Sir Maton stood by the dining room's door, his expression still as grim and tense as during the dark hours.

Only the bastard appeared untouched by the strain. His eyes were clear; his posture alert, ready to battle afresh. Everything about the man irked Jonared, but the Exarch's report only reinforced their need for Stone.

"It was another assassin beast," the Exarch said with her usual tendency to get to the point.

"How could it have known Sabell would be there?" Jonared asked.

"It was waiting for her," Stone said.

"What do you mean?" Jonared noticed Harmon

and Lantana stared at Stone with the same surprise he felt himself.

Stone shrugged and reached for the goblet of water sitting in front of him. The servants milled in the halls with trays of food and waited only for the king's signal to begin. Otherwise, the table was readied for the morning meal. Cage drank his water and made no attempt to explain.

"You must explain, Marshal," the Exarch said. She used a gentle tone where Jonared wanted to bellow at the arrogant pup.

"I can't, Mistress Exarch." Stone looked at Lantana and then the king. "I only know it had been waiting for her for quite some time. Its only purpose was to kill Mistress Sabelline."

Jonared believed him. Why? He wasn't sure. "So it was an assassin as before."

He was sorry he had spoken when Sabell's face went as pale as the white napkins folded beside each plate. He felt a bit light-headed himself.

"Are you sure it was the only demon?" Sir Maton asked. The swordsman dropped his hand to his sword hilt as if the threat might walk in the door at any moment.

The bastard gave another nonchalant shrug. "How can I know?"

"You knew this one was there before anyone else," Maton said. A dark scowl matched the anger in his voice. "Wouldn't you feel the presence of others?"

Cage Stone glared at Maton. "I said I don't know, Reves. Perhaps I only sense them when they're very close or about to attack. Conduct yourself as if there's hell-spawn around each corner."

Silence fell across the room. Jonared wondered how they would survive. Stone was right, but how to live and function under such enduring stress?

"I think we all agree with Marshal Cage. We must be on our guard. Another will come. We can only assume that Sabelline and King Jonared will be the prey for such. I'd like to assign a Keeper and her Marshal to be with you at all times, your majesty. I'm already doing the same for Sabelline." Lantana's calm words pushed back the fear a bit.

Jonared agreed, somewhat relieved. He doubted Sir Maton, no matter the man's skill with a sword, could stop a demon by himself. The magical assistance of a Keeper would be welcome. Perhaps he could even sleep the night through without a nightmare or waking at each small sound. His castle groaned and creaked so much in the still of the night, he often wondered if the stones were speaking to one another.

"I'm not sure that's a good idea," Cage Stone said.

Jonared knew the bastard didn't like him, but did he wish his king dead?

"Why not?" Lantana asked.

Jonared tired of the polite way she dealt with the bastard. "Yes, why the hell not?"

Stone turned that damned cool gaze of his on Jonared. "I wonder how the demons know that Mistress Sabelline is the one who will close their prison door. If I have the tale correct, how did the first assassins know the king and his son would be riding in the fields that day? And how did they find this Mistress Alvara?"

"You say we have a traitor, a spy, among the Keepers?" Harmon asked.

"Or the Marshals," Cage said.

"I thought of it after the first attack," the Exarch admitted. "But I find no clues pointing to anyone. I can't even imagine one of our people doing such a despicable thing."

"Do you have proof, Marshal?" Jonared asked. It made terrible sense.

"I have only the suspicious nature developed hunting outlaws, your highness," Stone answered. "I think erring with abundant caution would serve you on this."

"Am I to fear the Keepers and Marshals now?" Jonared asked. Was nothing safe? No one dependable?

"I wouldn't, but I also advise you not to have them as your guards," Cage said. "I don't think this spy will attack you directly."

"There must be a way to make my king safe," Sir Maton said.

The damn shrug again, but this time Stone answered. "Vary every day's routine. Keep the king's plans secret from everyone, especially the Keepers and Marshals. Be vigilant always, especially outside. And watch. If there's a traitor, he or she could give him- or herself away by trying to learn the king's whereabouts."

"If only I could sense these abominations like you can," Sir Maton said to Stone.

Jonared wished it also, but Sabelline needed a guardian with special skills more. Besides, Jonared thought he'd probably order the arrogant bastard put to the rack for insolence if they had to spend much time together.

"I've heard the king loves his hounds," Stone said.

Jonared raised an eyebrow at Stone's strange turn in the discussion. Everyone knew his truest pleasure was training and hunting with his hounds. "I have the best in Sulbreth and probably all of Futhark."

"Then use them, your majesty. Sleep with them, eat with them, walk and ride with them. Go nowhere without them, not even to this fortress. Animals sense things men do not. They might give you the warning that will save you."

Jonared remembered the day his father died. The hound had acted strangely, and the horses had danced with nerves as if a storm approached. "I shall. Thank you, Marshal Cage."

Stone actually ducked his head in acknowledgment. "At your service, your majesty. Can we eat now?"

Harmon guffawed, and the women smiled.

Jonared's gratitude soured. The bastard had the others charmed but not him. Damn the man.

"We set this lesson to convince you of the necessity of the tattoos and their magic," the Exarch said.

"Is it to be as convincing as what you showed me last evening, Mistress Exarch?" Cage asked. The small windowless room they were in reminded him of an animal trap. They were two floors underground, but even here the stones hummed with remembrance. "If I recall, last night was to sway me."

"It didn't turn out quite as I planned."

"Does anything?"

Harmon growled a curse under his breath, and the other three Marshals in the trap glared at him. He didn't care.

"The test with the gordragons was not as you planned. The first healing Mistress Sabelline tried on me was not as planned. What exactly did you intend last evening? What plan went awry?"

The Exarch held her hand up to stop Harmon as he took a step toward Cage. "We deserve your doubt, Marshal Cage. Disaster is rushing at us so quickly, we've been caught unaware too many times. Twice now you've saved us from calamity."

Did she think to flatter him to ease his misgivings? "Mistress, I have to wonder if your preparations and strategy for Sabell's journey will also go awry."

The Exarch didn't answer with anger. Instead, she

looked more tired and worried. "What would you have me say, Cage Stone? Shall I confess we're half blind with ignorance? Do you want to hear that so many unprecedented incidents have occurred that we're afraid to face each new day? But that we fear the loss of the sun even more? Must I speak of this? Surely you've figured out that we're desperate for your help. Your ancestors taught us the tattooing magic so we might better protect ourselves from the evil of this world. If one elfin magicker was here, she might teach us a better way to deal with this approaching catastrophe. But it's just us, and now you. Will you stop fighting and questioning us at every turn?"

The Exarch paused as if to calm herself. Cage seldom felt guilt, but the wizened lady in front of him attempted to introduce him to the emotion.

"I know you sense and feel things we do not. You know things you don't share with us," the Exarch said in a quiet voice. "Last night, I wanted you to feel the great evil near Kingdom's Gate. I've seen the way you look at the mountain, glancing over your shoulder like it watches you. I thought if you actually went close to it, you would accept the great danger we battle."

He was cooperating, wasn't he? Cage took a look inside himself. He did harbor resentment toward the king and these Keepers for taking control of his life, taking his freedom. He didn't trust them. He believed they struggled against a malicious enemy but had no faith in their methods. Their apparent willingness to sacrifice

Sabelline and himself appalled him. What kind of battle plan was that?

The Exarch wasn't done. "I know you love your sister and her mother. Can you not see that you do this for Futhark and not for the Keepers? Do you understand that the closest manor to the city is Durnhold? If we don't stop these demons, the entire city of Sulbreth will fall to their insatiable appetite for killing. Where do you think they'll go next?"

The Exarch finished and waited. Small sounds were discernible in the relative quiet. Cage heard the Marshals breathing. The Exarch's dry skin rubbed against itself as she twisted her hands in an impatient knot. Someone walked across the floor two stories above their heads. Cage stared at the lamp smoking slightly over the Exarch's shoulder. How to answer? "I don't doubt your sincerity in wanting to stop the demons."

"No, you doubt our competence to do so," the Exarch said.

Again the lady read his thoughts.

The Exarch sighed and shook her head. "We need your help, Cage Stone, you stubborn, knot-headed man. All of you, not the bare minimum you give us."

"Did last night not show you I'm willing to give everything to protect Mistress Sabelline?"

The Exarch's face softened, and she smiled. "It did."

"And I did what none of your tattooed magicked Marshals could, Mistress Exarch. So how is this newest lesson going to convince me to allow this desecration of my body?"

"Your battle sense and experience gives you an advantage over my Marshals. It's part of your value. Few of our Marshals have taken part in real battles as you have."

"So I'm quicker, smarter, and deadlier than your Marshals? Again, why would I submit to these tattoos?"

"To make you more lethal than you are now. There are worse things to face in the days ahead."

"It isn't necessary."

"Are you ready for the lesson then?" Harmon asked.

Cage heard the goading challenge in the old Marshal's voice, but he couldn't resist. He tired of being treated like an unblooded youth.

"Then I'll leave the teaching and learning to you, gentlemen. I must warn you, Cage Stone, that all the Marshals present will be fully empowered by their Keepers' magic." The Exarch left and closed the door behind her.

Harmon put out the lamps one by one as the other three Marshals spread out across the room. None of them had weapons, so it would be a test of speed and strength. And cleverness.

Harmon looked at Cage with a bit of a smirk before putting out the last lamp.

Cage closed his eyes and listened. The Marshals moved in near silence in a planned, coordinated attack. He opened his eyes and discerned their dark, faceless forms. As they came toward him, he realized they could also see him.

Could they also hear him? He glided from his spot, and they followed. Cage dropped and rolled toward the Marshal on his right. Never let the enemy force you to follow his plan; make your own, attack first. So had Sir Berton taught him.

They were good. The Marshal he went for leaped into the air to avoid Cage. But Cage had survived on the field of battle since his early teen years. He stabbed up with his fist, the blow directed at the man's groin. The Marshal's reaction was not so quiet.

Two more rushed at Cage, but he had never stopped moving. One landed a glancing blow across Cage's shoulder, but he'd suffered many worse injuries without faltering. He kicked toward the midsection of one, and a rib cracked beneath his foot.

Harmon approached from behind, his steps stealthy but not quiet enough. The other uninjured Marshal dove at Cage. Cage knew how to leap also. He jumped, tucked, and turned a complete roll in the air as he flew over the head of the diving Marshal.

He heard the two men crash into each other as he landed lightly on his feet. Harmon cursed the other Marshal.

Cage used the cover of the noise to glide to a corner. He quieted his breathing and leaned tight against the wall. He froze like a mouse under the shadow of a hawk on the wing.

The Marshals swung their heads from side to side, searching, listening. They didn't see him. Harmon gestured toward one wall. The two men separated, and each started making his way along the perimeter of the room. They would see Cage if he tried to move to the middle.

Cage held fast. Any twitch might catch their eye. Still, he noted that even their enhanced vision was inferior to his own. Harmon stopped a few steps away from Cage. He stared right at him.

"Is my lesson over yet, Marshal Harmon? One of your men needs the attention of a healer, and the other needs a cloth to dry his tears."

Harmon swore, but he turned away to light one of the lamps.

Cage squinted against the sudden illumination.

The door slammed open. The Exarch and three Keepers rushed into the room. They looked around and then turned hot glares on Cage.

The Exarch's thin shoulders slumped. "I see another plan has failed. As you expected, Marshal Cage. I'm not sure how else to convince you to take the tattoos."

Cage looked at the destruction he'd wrought. Harmon helped the man with the broken rib to stand. The Marshal who had taken the cruel blow to his privates sat with his knees pulled to his chest. His Keeper knelt beside him with her arm around his shoulders.

"May I speak with you alone, Mistress Exarch?"

Cage asked.

"Follow me." She led him to a small room across the hall. Harmon came in behind him and closed the door. This room also appeared to be a windowless cell.

"Say what you will," the Exarch snapped.

Cage didn't blame her. She probably expected more snide remarks concerning her competence. Anadalune would be ashamed of his conduct since he came to this place. He hadn't treated Lantana with the respect due an elder. His battle prowess gave him a freedom of manner with others. Who dared call him to task for his pride or stubborn ways? Not many. Could he trust Lantana enough to be honest?

The Marshals had impressed him with their abilities. He believed the tattoos could improve his skills. But still he feared them. "I confess to the true reasons for my reticence, Mistress."

"What do you mean?"

Cage wished Harmon wasn't in attendance, but he knew the old man wouldn't leave. "I'm afraid of them."

The Exarch's mouth dropped open, almost comical in her shock. "In what way, Cage?"

She took his hand as if he were a child fearful of the dark. He let her hold it.

"They're not painful, and I'm confident they'll work on you the same as they have for other men. We'll start out slow and careful to be sure, but it's similar to our healing magic and that works on you."

"It's not that." Cage gestured toward Harmon. "I assume the designs and placement on the body directs the spells?"

"That's correct. I didn't take you for a vain man. Is it the change in your appearance you dread?"

"No." Cage glanced at Harmon. Could he get an honest answer? Not from a Marshal and he trusted no Keepers. "I must wonder if the spells change a man. Change who he is."

The Exarch didn't deny it as he expected. She nodded, her eyes thoughtful. "A valid fear. You worry we can control your free will and perhaps your very thoughts with the spells?"

Cage shrugged. "Who is there for me to ask? A Marshal already under the spells?"

The Exarch walked over to Harmon and touched him above the collar of his shirt. A tattoo in the design of a thin elegant chain encircled his entire neck. "There is only one spell we want you to take that could affect you in that way. This tattoo is one you must have if you're to go with Sabelline. I won't let you go without it."

"What does it do?" A cold shiver worked its way up Cage's spine.

"It prevents another entity from stealing your loyalty. It ensures you'll stay with your Keeper and serve none but her. Some of the demons you might encounter will have magical abilities. We have in our histories accounts of magic the creatures use to bespell the mind of a man.

This particular spell protects a Marshal from such evil intent."

Cage swallowed. His fear remained, though he sensed she spoke the truth as she believed it. The well of ignorance he found among the Keepers didn't lend much comfort in that. "I wish to see my family before the tattooing."

The Exarch's wise eyes filled with an understanding he didn't wish for. "I can arrange a visit on the morrow, but Sabelline already waits to begin the enhancements. I'll ask that she start with the less obvious ones. Yet I must know. You defeated our best fighters; why do you agree now?"

Cage thought of Kristall and Anadalune living in a remote manor. Even surrounded by hired swords, how would they fare against demons? "The Marshals fought well, better than any men I've faced before. Anything I can do to increase Mistress Sabelline's chance of succeeding, I will do."

Chapter Fifteen

Kristall picked at the sweet tender ham on her plate. Eating in the presence of the king further depleted her sparse appetite.

"Your cook is surely the envy of your entire court, your majesty," Anadalune said.

Kristall appreciated her mother in a way she never had before. Anadalune spoke and acted with a measure of assurance as if they dined with the king every day.

"My father stole him away from Lord Henri a number of years ago," King Jonared said. "I fear your daughter isn't as impressed with the fare."

Kristall's face heated. "Not at all, your highness. It's delicious, much finer than I'm accustomed to eating."

She thought she sounded like a child, but the handsome king nodded and turned again to her mother.

Jonared sat at the head of the long table with Kristall on his left and her mother on his right. The servant who had led them here informed them it was the king's informal dining hall he used for entertaining small gatherings. The three of them seated at one end of the lengthy table made the hall seem cavernous. The oak furniture gleamed almost white, it was so finely polished. Pink linen covered the table, the fork she used was heavy gold, and the plates were hand painted.

"I asked that you dine with me that I might inquire of your plans. Are you intending to move to Durnhold soon? I hope you understand that you're welcome to abide here for as long as you wish." Jonared glanced at Kristall as he spoke to her mother. She dropped her gaze from his.

"Thank you, your majesty. My man, Sir Berton Wall, is in the city arranging for craftsmen and servants to precede us to Durnhold and make sure it's habitable. I understand it has stood empty for a time and was ill kept before."

"Sadly true. You're right to be concerned. The manor sits close to The Edge. Vicious storms and endless winds blow in from the sea."

"I love the sea air, your highness," Anadalune said in a voice sweeter than the sugar-cured ham. "Only one thing could make me happier in my fortunes."

Kristall lifted her gaze and watched the king for his reaction. She thought him the most handsome man she'd ever seen, and he'd been very kind to her and her mother. He carried himself with an air of nobility that reminded her oddly of her brother. But shadows lurked in his brown eyes. She wanted to look for truth when he answered to her mother.

"I already know what you would ask, Lady Anadalune." Jonared's lips twisted into a wry smile. "Cage Stone has passed from under my rule. As a Marshal, his life is in the hands of the Keepers."

"You are the king. All fall under your sovereignty," her mother said in a stern tone.

Jonared lifted an eyebrow in surprise. Kristall doubted few dared speak to the king in such a way. "Not in this matter."

Kristall swallowed around the lump in her throat. She would be as strong as her mother. "You mean I'll never see my brother again?"

Jonared covered her hands with his. His eyes were warm with compassion. "Not at all. Tomorrow you shall see him and know he's committed to the course he has chosen."

"Chosen, or forced to take, your majesty?" Kristall dared to ask. Warm eyes and strong hands would not deflect her from helping her brother. "I can't believe Cage would agree to be separated from us."

Jonared pulled back and gave her a puzzled smile. "I always wished to have a brother or sister, but it wasn't to be. This closeness you share with Stone intrigues me.

Few form such attachments to bastard siblings. And you, Lady Anadalune, you treat him as one born of your womb rather than as your late husband's by-blow."

Kristall heard the king's antagonism for Cage in his words. Why did the two men so despise each other?

"I raised Cage as my own from the time he was four years old," Anadalune said in a tight voice. "He is my son."

"Did your husband insist you accept the child?"

Anadalune laughed, but it was scornful. "Not quite, my king. My unlamented husband hated Cage and refused to have him in his presence. I used threats and tricks to keep Cage at my side. Only the fear of losing my father's financial support kept the count from throwing his son into the gutter."

"But why would you trouble yourself for a child of no consequence to you?"

"Trouble?" Anadalune's laugh was real this time. "Cage? Trouble? Your majesty, I swear Cage has taken care of us since he came into our lives. He never asked me for anything, not even attention. He was eight years old when Kristall was born. From the first time he set eyes on her, he was her protector, her champion."

From Kristall's earliest memories, Cage had been there to pick her up when she fell. He taught her to ride and to stand up to her father's nasty temper and hide from his violent drunken rampages.

"Cage took care of us, your majesty," Anadalune said, glaring at the king. "I would give my life to protect him."

"I understand loyalty to kin," the king said, "but your family is so odd."

"Surely, your majesty, you've spoken with my brother," Kristall said. "How could we not be odd with him in our family?"

Kristall clamped her hand over her mouth as she realized what she'd said. Jonared's eyes widened, and then he laughed. Her mother joined him. Kristall smiled, thinking the king looked even more handsome when he was happy.

"This won't hurt much at all," Mistress Pinxter said in her motherly tone.

Cage said nothing, but his glance strayed to the little table holding inks and needles. Sabell couldn't bring herself to look at the instruments.

Despite her earlier determination, her skin was clammy under her light cotton dress. Cage's sudden decision to cooperate had surprised her. Now she must do her part.

"What will you do first?" Cage asked. He sounded calm, but there was wariness in his posture. He looked like a bird about to take flight. Not any bird, but a proud eagle such as sometimes flew near The Edge. Seldom seen up close, the eagles were mysterious and elusive.

Mistress Pinxter nodded at Sabell, encouraging her to answer. "The Exarch told me you want to start with less obvious spells. I thought we might start with your sight enhancements. We use a light ink around your eyes, so it's barely noticeable."

"Why don't you use such inks for all the spells?"

Mistress Pinxter answered. "The darker the inkings, the more power in the spell."

Cage sighed. "Fine. Let's get started."

"Please lie on your back on this table, Marshal," Pinxter said. "The eyes are a delicate area to work around, and it's vitally important that you don't twitch or blink."

Pinxter pushed a thick pillow under Cage's neck so his head tilted back. "To protect you and get the spell perfect, we have to use a light sleeping spell. We'll wake you as soon as we finish."

Cage looked at Sabell, a question in his eyes. She nodded, surprised and pleased he sought her assurance. Perhaps it was the beginning of trust.

"Mistress Sabelline can tell you that not all your treatments affect me the same as they do most men," Cage said. He watched Mistress Pinxter as she lifted a pinch of white powder from a shallow bowl.

"This is true," Sabell said. "A small bit of lavender oil sent him into a deep sleep."

"I heard of this," Mistress Pinxter said with a frown at them both. "Is your sense of smell superior to most men, Marshal?"

"It is."

His ready answer surprised Sabell. They knew so little of Cage, and he volunteered nothing. She knew the Exarch and others of the Keepers wanted nothing so much as years to study him.

Mistress Pinxter held up her fingers. A tiny bit of powder remained on her one finger and her thumb. "The powers of the poppy are strong even in tiny portions. Let's be overly cautious."

She held her hand over Cage's face and rubbed her fingers together while chanting a spell that sounded much like a child's lullaby. Very few grains of the poppy powder floated toward Cage. But his eyelids fluttered and then slid closed. It couldn't happen so quickly! Sabell almost believed he faked his slumber.

"Interesting," Pinxter muttered. She put her hand on his chest and counted his slow breaths. "He's fast asleep. Gather your needles, Sabelline."

Sabell pulled the small table closer to Cage's head. The long bench he slept on was higher than the table so she could work without bending and straining her back.

"What do you think?" Pinxter held two different jars of ink against Cage's cheeks. "He's so evenly colored it seems not to be the work of the sun but some other touch of nature. Which ink best matches his skin shade?"

Sabell stared at the bottles, but neither matched perfectly. "Too light will be as noticeable as too dark."

Pinxter clicked her tongue and selected more of the tiny bottles. None were better and most were further from matching.

"He has the most beautiful long lashes," Pinxter said as she frowned over her ink stores. "They're so dark; perhaps we should match them rather than his skin. It might only make his lashes appear thicker. And the spell is stronger with the darker ink."

Sabell stared at Cage's relaxed face, trying to imagine. Already his light gray eyes surrounded by his long dark lashes bordered on pretty. What would he think if she made him . . . prettier?

"We need to decide, Sabell, before the poppy wears off."

"Use the dark. By the time we finish with him, he'll see in the dark as if the sun shines."

They bent their heads over their work. After all her weeks of frustrating training, Sabell surprised herself. She worked the needles in a sure, deliberate fashion. Perhaps her nerves were steadied by her determination to mold her Marshal into a more lethal weapon than he already was for both their sakes. Her possessive emotions of the previous night had grown and twined with other feelings.

The women each worked on an eye, making their needle pricks around the very edge of his eyelids. But when the time came to make the last few pricks to connect the circle spell, Sabell completed both eyes. She spoke the words to set the spell and tie it to her own abilities and the residual power of the fortress.

Mistress Pinxter performed a light healing spell to relieve the redness and soreness from the needle sticks.

When all was done, they sat back and admired their work. Startled, they stared at Cage, at each other, and then back at him. The tattoos did as they expected, making his lashes appear thicker and larger. He was beautiful. He also looked exactly like the ancient paintings of his pure-blooded ancestors and less like a human male.

Cage turned on his side and stared at the wall. Though all the lamps in Sabell's quarters were extinguished for the night, he saw everything as if the sun sat high in the sky. His entire world had changed since he woke in the tattooing room. He'd struggled his whole life to act like other men, and now he must adjust again.

His bed was four paces from the wall, but he could see the intricate layering of the world in the multicolored stone. Had he thought the earth bones gray in color? Blues, violets, oranges and reds meandered through the rock. He could stare at it all night.

The training session in the fighting pits had tested his concentration. He'd ignored the dust motes floating like snow around them. He'd refrained from examining the complex crystal formations of the sand. But as he lay by himself, he let his new abilities loose. The weave of the blanket drew his attention. The slight thickness of one thread over another, the variance of the dye from one section to another.

He closed his eyes, seeking control over the reckless desire to explore the world opened to him. Such wonders and now he had no time. He must remember why he'd accepted these spells upon his body.

Tomorrow he would see Anadalune, Kristall, and Berton. Would it be the last time? He hoped not, but who knew with the secrecy these Keepers wrapped around themselves?

His family had given him reason to live and fight for so long; how could he say his farewells? The manor and gold would allow them a good life. They needed him no longer.

He pictured his sister and mother in fine dresses, maids attending them, suitors . . . Who would protect his sister from the rakes drawn by her beauty and impressive dowry? And wouldn't such men also be drawn to Anadalune? Though she was as a mother to Cage, she was still a young, desirable woman. And what of the Thrums? Might they use the arcane laws of Futhark to take the ladies under their control?

Sleep eluded him as he pondered the morrow. Was he strong enough to let go of the only three people he loved in the world?

Cage opened his eyes and stared at the bright, unlit room. He already had let them go. Until he agreed to the tattooing, he'd secretly harbored hope to escape his role as Marshal despite the promises. As of today, he belonged to Mistress Sabelline. A woman he wasn't prepared to trust. After the meeting with his family, she would put the mark of loyalty on him. There would be no other life for him. No going back to what was.

PART THREE

Chapter Sixteen

KRISTALL CAUGHT HER BREATH WHEN Cage walked into the library. The Exarch had led them here herself, telling them Cage would join them in a short while.

Anadalune rose from the silk-covered settee and threw herself against Cage's chest. He wrapped his arms around their mother and lifted his gaze to Kristall.

She heard herself gasp out loud. Only a few strides separated her from her brother, but the changes in him made the distance more. She'd known Cage was handsome and special, but now his appearance was beyond that of a man. His gray eyes were clearer, lighter, his lashes darker and longer, his face more chiseled.

"Kristall?" His voice was the same.

Kristall hurried to him and joined her mother in a

tearful welcome. It was long moments before she could let him go. Sir Berton smiled and offered his hand to Cage when Kristall and her mother finally gave him room.

They settled on the two facing settees. A low table in between the two divans held a tray with sweet rolls and a steaming pot of tea. They ignored it.

"Tell me how the king treats you," Cage demanded after they sat down.

Kristall smiled, her heart lighter than it had been since the terrible night of the banquet. He was still her wonderful, overprotective brother.

"He's given us a spacious suite of rooms," Anadalune answered.

"Do you see him often?"

"Only once since the night they took you." Anadalune frowned at Cage. "They told us you won the tournament and then agreed to join the service of the Keepers as a Marshal. A large amount of gold came to us also. I've been away from the intrigues of the courts for a long time, but I know tangled tales when I hear them."

Cage smiled, a quick flash of sunshine, and then shook his head. "I knew you wouldn't believe so easily. The king and the Exarch offered me the role of Marshal in such a way I couldn't refuse."

"I knew they forced you," Kristall cried. She took Cage's hand and squeezed it tight. He squeezed back, his calluses scraping her soft skin. "We'll get you free, won't we, Mother?"

Anadalune and Sir Berton shared the other settee. They both stared at Cage, but their expressions were pained instead of hopeful.

"Kristall," Cage said, pulling her attention back to him. "It can't be undone. I've given my word."

"Why? Why would you do that? The manor means nothing if you can't share it with us! We were going to live together as a family. Our own place. You wouldn't have to go off and fight bandits anymore. We'll raise horses and crops of wheat and oats to feed them and us."

Kristall pulled her hand free of his and swiped at her eyes. Her heart hurt as it thumped against her ribs.

"It's more complicated than you know." Cage's expression was stark, his eyes sad.

"Tell us why." A terrible thought came to Kristall. "Did they threaten you? Are we hostages to make you do this?"

Cage shook his head. "No. It's not like that. I agreed willingly. If there was any under-dealing done, it was by me. I demanded the king give you gold on top of the manor as the prize."

"Why?" How could Cage leave them so easily? But why not? They were a burden to him. All his hard-earned money, gold given for risking his life, went to their needs. Could he not have purchased a small holding of his own long before if he hadn't needed to care for them?

"They needed a master swordsman to act as Marshal to a very special Keeper. The king held the tournament to find the best fighter in Futhark." Cage folded his hands in together and leaned his elbows on his knees. "The man who came in second has been named the king's protector."

Cage stopped as if his words explained things. It didn't to Kristall.

"Why would you agree to this, Cage, knowing we would be separated?"

Sir Berton answered, "It was because they needed you. You and no one else. This tournament was to bring you to them."

Cage stared at Berton for a long moment before sighing and nodding. "There's no reason to keep it from the three of you. You're the only people in Futhark I trust with my secrets. Yes. They needed me, someone of elven heritage."

Kristall watched the blood drain from her mother's face. Her own head spun for a brief moment. A myth brought to life in her beloved brother? Sir Berton had suspected? Surely, Cage was different than other men, but of a different race? The painting on the wall beyond her mother caught Kristall's gaze. It depicted a sunlit forest glen where a group of tall, lean people mixed with the animals of the wood. People with dark hair, perfect skin, beautiful in a wild, foreign way. People who looked like Cage.

"How did they know?" Anadalune asked in a weak voice. "How did they know you existed? Why do they need you that the king would give a fortune to have you?"

Cage studied the tea set, not looking at any of them as he answered. His words had a careful hesitancy to them. "There is a great danger facing Futhark. Few people are aware of it. The Keepers and their Marshals, even the king, seek to thwart this menace. They think, and have convinced me, that success is more likely with my assistance. I can't turn my back on their need, not even for my own family."

"Or for your own life?" Sir Berton asked, a bitter bite to his words.

Cage looked up at the man who had been part of their lives for as long as Kristall could remember. "More lives than mine are at stake, Berton. If the Keepers are unsuccessful, all of Futhark will eventually fall."

"What is this great foe you face?" Anadalune asked.

"I can't tell you more. You must ask the king or the Exarch. I would that you never know the greater details." Cage took a deep breath. "There are things I must ask of all of you. Sir Berton, would you bring Bayard here to the Keepers' stables? I would see him settled before you travel to Durnhold."

"I'll bring that hellion you call a warhorse if he'll let me. Do they have a stable master that can handle him? He's full of himself. I check him each day, but penned up as he's been, I don't know how he'll settle anywhere."

"I'll speak to him about his behavior."

Cage's simple words about speaking with his horse

sent a shiver through Kristall. She'd never thought of his facile ways with animals being odd. Being elven.

"Have you nothing to ask of me?" Kristall forced her mind from such disturbing images.

"I do," Cage said with a brilliant smile that broke her heart rather than cheering her. "I would ask that you look upon the king with all the suspicion I've tried to teach you these years as your brother."

Kristall frowned, but Cage only smiled back and continued. "The king carries huge burdens, and I fear he may seek comfort where he can find it without due consideration. You're a woman grown, and I must trust you to take care. Hold the man to his honor when he would forget it."

Kristall nodded around the lump closing her throat. She heard the farewell in Cage's words. He was saying he would no longer be there to watch out for her. No more lectures. No more intimidating glares at possible suitors. She rocked back and forth to subdue the sobs struggling to be born.

"I have something great to ask of you," Cage said to Anadalune.

"You know I would do anything for you. You are my son."

Cage didn't smile at her. "When you took me in, you set aside proprieties and treated me as your own. Though a child, I heard the whispers among the servants and visitors. But you ignored their cruelty and made a life for me. Now I ask that you do so again. Do it this time for yourself, your happiness."

Anadalune stared at him with a perplexed look. Kristall was distracted from her own distress as she wondered at Cage's meaning.

"The vultures will descend on Durnhold once you take residence. The rumor of your new wealth will already have spread. You'll be besieged by suitors and thieves alike. You need a strong man to keep them at bay. I ask of you that you take to husband one that you love already and make him Lord of Durnhold."

They all looked as one to Sir Berton. The kind, gruff soldier had been as a father to Kristall and Cage. Always he stood at her mother's back through hard times, always loyal and respectful.

The look of love that passed between Berton and her mother made Kristall feel like a selfish child. Cage had seen, had known. Sir Berton was a fine-looking man, still in his prime, a fit husband for her mother. Why else would the soldier have stayed with them except for love?

"It is an easy think you ask of me," Anadalune said with a watery smile. "It is the most secret wish of my heart."

Sir Berton's face darkened to the color of the fine cherry wood of the table. "It wouldn't be proper. I've not a drop of noble blood in all my line."

Cage snorted. "One thing I've learned in my life as bastard born, Berton, is that nobility has little to do with the seed of the father. Do this as a comfort to me and a just end to your faithfulness."

"We'll speak of this in private, Berton," Anadalune said in a tone that meant it was settled. "Now tell us how you live, Cage. Where do you sleep? Are you well fed? Are those new clothes you're wearing? Do all Marshals dress in such plain . . . black?"

Cage gave them few particulars as he spoke of days filled with training and study. He avoided questions about his lessons. His vague answers, probably meant to keep them from worry, only frightened Kristall more. What terrible danger did he face?

"When will we see you again?" Anadalune asked when Cage said he must go.

"If you plan a quick wedding, I will make sure to be there," Cage said as he rose.

"Quick?" Anadalune asked.

"Within days," Cage clarified.

Her mother blinked, her eyes wide with the same dismay Kristall felt. Days until what? Until Cage faced this horrible enemy? Days until he died?

Kristall's stomach churned. Her breath hitched, stuttered, and burst forth in a short sob of sound. Cage didn't look at her.

"We shall marry quickly then," Anadalune said, her voice soft and trembling.

Cage nodded, his own lips pressed tight together. He tried to shake hands once more with Berton, but the older man pulled him into a hug. Anadalune couldn't let him go once she had her arms around him. Tears rolled silently down her cheeks.

When he finally turned to Kristall, her sobs spilled out in an uneven torrent. He held her as he had when they were children. When her first pony passed and her heart was broken. Always he made it better, but this time he was the cause.

He backed away, sliding from her arms, from her life. He caught one of her tears on the tip of his finger and put it to the corner of his eye where his own tears glistened.

He opened his mouth but could not speak. He walked backward to the door, his gaze terrible with love and despair. Then he was gone.

"Enough," Bachus barked.

Sabell had never seen the icy Marshal angry before. It distracted her from Cage for a moment. Only a moment.

Her Marshal stood at her side, his foot on the neck of Marshal Regon. The burly Regon was the latest victim of Cage's frightening rampage. Sabell hadn't used her sword even once during their training session. They had started late because Cage's meeting with his family had extended beyond the planned time.

She wondered what had happened in the encounter that made her Marshal into this unbeatable warrior. The other Marshals couldn't touch him. He battered them mercilessly, efficiently, and worst of all to them, effortlessly.

Regon staggered to his feet, growling curses at Cage. Sabelline avoided Marshal Regon when she could. She found him coarse, and his gaze made her uncomfortable. He never treated her with disrespect, but he looked at her with a hunger in his eyes she didn't welcome.

"Either you're possessed today, Stone, or you've been holding back," Bachus said.

Cage offered no explanation. He stared back at Bachus with a light in his eyes every bit as cold as the other Marshal's.

"Marshal Mezzin, bring the hounds," Bachus called over his shoulder.

Sabell's shoulders sagged. She hadn't slept well again. She was too tired to face the hounds. Their previous lesson with them had been canceled because of the attack by the cave boa. She was afraid of the large attack dogs. They were trained not to bite the Marshals and Keepers, but her mind couldn't seem to get beyond the size of their teeth to accept that.

Cage stood, silent as he'd been since the start of the session. Had his family treated him coldly as her father had when she first joined the Keepers? She wished she could talk to him, offer comfort. But they were still strangers. The arrival of the hounds forestalled her speculations.

There were four of the large dogs. Even as quick as Cage was, he wouldn't be able to fight them all at once. Mezzin and another Marshal assisted Cage and Sabell in wrapping the thick leather armor around their forearms. The hounds would go for their arms.

Cage pushed Sabell behind his back as the Marshals backed away. Bachus gave the order to release the dogs.

Sabell braced herself for the charge. The hounds crouched down and then sprang forward all at once. A scream welled in Sabell's throat, and she thought she heard Bachus cry out in alarm.

The dogs closed the distance in four leaps, a wild baying pouring from their gaping jaws. They leaped upon Cage as he dropped his wooden sword to the sand.

Her heart stopped, but then the hounds did too. They danced up on their hind legs and then dropped to all fours as they frolicked before Cage. They pushed their long noses into his hands and thighs, begging his attention.

Her Marshal knelt to receive their adoration. The hounds yipped like joyful puppies reunited with a litter-mate. Cage fondled their great heads, patted their backs, and then ordered them to sit.

The hounds sat. Their eyes shone as they watched him. Their tails thumped against the ground and each other.

"No one has ever had any luck setting the dogs on me, Marshal Bachus," Cage said.

Sabell only now looked at the other Marshals. Their

expressions were comical on such stern men. Disbelief battled with amusement and no small amount of amazement.

Bachus shook his head. "I don't know what to do with you anymore, Stone."

Cage kicked at his wooden sword. "I was promised a new sword, but I still carry a borrowed one. Help me find a good weapon."

"Mezzin, take the dogs for a run before you return them to their kennel," Bachus snapped out. "Meet me here tomorrow, Stone. Instead of training, we'll visit the armory."

The dogs left only after Cage commanded them to obey Mezzin. Sabell wondered what would be next.

"After you, Mistress," Cage said.

"What?"

"I have a lesson with Mistress Tamarin," Cage said. "But I can't let you stay here on the lawn without me."

"Oh." Since the cave boa, Cage insisted she stay in the fortress when not with him. She needed little urging to obey.

Cage followed her inside and then took his leave. She watched him stride down the hall leading to Tamarin's study. She had thought they might be developing a working relationship, at the least but today Cage was distant from her. She'd noticed a touch of resentment in his eyes and a deep anger.

She went on her way, comforting herself that she was noticing emotions in those gray eyes she'd previously believed were filled only with cool indifference.

"This harmless-looking plant is called a night daisy," Mistress Tamarin said as she flipped the page of the large text to reveal the next colorful illustration.

Cage studied the picture of the white-petaled flower with a bloodred center. Cup-shaped leaves lined its thick stem. "It sucks blood with its leaves."

Tamarin's wrinkles deepened when she smiled. "You realize I must tell the Exarch that you recognize these denizens of Kingdom's Gate. None of them exist on this side, yet you know of them."

Cage stared at the book rather than look into the kind, but piercing, eyes of the elder Keeper. Sabell had told him Tamarin's history. The lady deserved honor and respect. Twenty years ago, Mistress Tamarin and her Marshal had passed through Kingdom's Gate and renewed the hematite seals. Only the Keeper returned from the dark, but their mission was completed successfully. Did only Cage see the deep sorrow beneath her sweet airs? Was it for the Marshal who had died protecting her? He saw more also. This old lady with her grandmotherly appearance was steel.

"I'm to be the teacher here, yet sometimes I think you could instruct me, Marshal." Tamarin made her gentle statement a soft probe for information. She'd spent the last twenty years serving by training those who would follow her, but Alvara was dead. Sabelline's training was not half done, and neither was his.

"Memories come to me when I see the pictures, Mistress. I think my mother may have given me instruction." Cage shrugged. What mother would have spoken of such things to a small child? Perhaps one who cruelly abandoned that same child to a hateful father.

"What an odd childhood that would make," Tamarin commented without inflection. "Well, perhaps I can still teach you some new things."

They spent some time poring over the pictures while Tamarin told Cage everything she knew about the various demons. She often added small personal accounts from her journey beyond Kingdom's Gate. Again Cage noted the strength of the tiny, frail woman beside him. Her courage in the face of terror and hardship dwarfed the exploits of anyone he knew.

"We hid from a pack of these lizards for half a day at least." Tamarin pointed to the dark gray, cat-size lizard depicted on the last page. "They make no sound that we know of. That's how they got my Jules."

Tamarin looked up at him, moisture pooling in her eyes. "We were almost home when they found us. He stood between them and me, taking several wounds from their vicious little teeth. I killed a number of them and finally drove the rest away, but it was too late. Their saliva carries a venom that slowly paralyzes its victims. I tried . . ."

Cage took her tiny hand as her words stumbled to a stop.

Tamarin swiped at her eyes with her other hand. "I used every healing spell I could. He begged me to leave him, but I could not. Finally the poison spread so he couldn't talk. I held him until it froze his breath and his heart." Her voice hardened. "Then I burned him to ashes so that none of the hellspawn in that place could touch him again."

"He died knowing he'd succeeded. The seals were renewed, and you were safe."

Mistress Tamarin took a deep, ragged breath and squared her thin shoulders. "I know you mean to comfort me, son, but never a day goes by that I don't think I might have been quicker or more alert. I might have saved him. He was my life match, and it's lonely without him. Sometimes I wish I'd died also. Only my duty to the other Keepers brought me back here. I'll teach you all I know, and Sabelline too, so that my pain is not relived in either of you."

Cage could say nothing. He and Sabelline didn't have the bond of love between them that Tamarin had shared with her Marshal.

"Now," Tamarin said with more strength in her voice, "let's take a look at the maps and see what I can tell you that might help. This isn't the time to bring up old hurts or fear new ones."

They went to another wide table. Cage helped her unroll the first map. As they studied the first section of the tunnel, Cage wondered how he and Sabell were to survive if Tamarin almost failed despite twenty years of study. How would either of them learn enough in time?

As if to confirm his fears, Tamarin pointed at a rough decline on the map. "This is like a set of wide stairs. Every pair that ever went into the Gate and returned safely, reported that no demons accosted them before this point." She shook her gray head and poked his chest with a gnarled finger. "Don't trust that. With the terrible goings-on around here, I'm afraid things might be entirely different for you. The fell beasts might wait for you on the very threshold. How can we prepare you for that?"

Cage stretched out on the tall table as he had the day before. Yesterday, he'd been nervous and wary. Today the tattooing frightened him.

Sabell and Mistress Pinxter discussed which inks to use as they took their seats on each side of him.

"We'll need your shirt off, Marshal," Mistress Pinxter said. "And roll over. We'll start on the back of your neck and work around. I'm glad you wear your hair short."

Cage sat up and unlaced the top of his shirt. He pulled it off and handed it to Sabell. He caught her staring at his chest. Feeling exposed and defenseless, Cage lay down on his stomach.

Mistress Pinxter folded a small cloth and put it under his forehead so he could be facedown.

Sabell touched him lightly on his shoulder; he knew her touch, and his muscles tensed though he worked hard to relax them. She stroked his skin in a casual caress while Mistress Pinxter gave her additional instructions.

Despite his distrust of the spell-setting and the Keepers, Sabell's touch soothed him. He chided himself for calming as if a hound beneath its master's hand even as his muscles slackened.

"Now, Marshal Cage, this is one spell I can't help Sabelline draw. Your mistress must do it herself to ensure all your loyalty is to her. So take a nap if you wish. It will take her quite a while."

Sabell tinkered with her instruments, making small clinking noises as she selected her tools. Cage braced his nerves, his muscles tensing again, when her hand touched the back of his neck.

"Did I tell you I have a younger sister, Cage?" Sabell pricked his neck with the first needle. "I understand she and your sister have become friends."

Cage frowned into the table. He didn't know of this. Sabell rambled about her childhood home, the passing of her mother and the raising of her sister, Leesa.

She spoke softly of her father's angry reaction to her decision to become a Keeper.

Sabell moved to Cage's other side, and the needle pricks resumed as she described her reunion with her family. He smiled with her when she gave a shaky laugh at the joy of hugging her dear father and sister.

"Roll over," Sabell said as she again switched sides of the table.

"You're finished already?" Cage rolled over. So far he felt no different, only surprised that time passed so quickly.

Sabell gave him an abashed smile. "Mistress Pinxter suggested I talk to you to calm us both."

Cage stretched out on his back. He glanced at the older woman puttering around the little jars stacked on narrow shelves against the back wall. Even such personal conversations were nothing more than part of some Keeper plan.

Sabell continued her work in silence as Cage considered their conversation. It has seemed so friendly, between comrades who would shortly go into battle together. Sabell's family meeting sounded much like a farewell, as his own had been. When she shared the experience with him, they seemed less like strangers. Instead of two lonely individuals, he felt a kindred experience. But she'd only been distracting him, distracting herself?

"You're getting tense," Sabell whispered. She was so close as she worked the inking onto his neck that Cage could see each individual eyelash. A few strands of her light brown hair drifted free of the knot she always wore it in on the back of her head. He noted the swirls of gold as the light played on the shiny mass. The touch of her fingers was as light as the puffs of breath that feathered on his neck. His awareness of her rocked from confusion to a purely male physical reaction.

The temperature in the room rose as his breath snagged in his chest. He closed his eyes to block the sight of her smooth perfect skin. With his eyes closed, her touch only impacted him more.

"Man of mine, be true to me," Sabelline mumbled.

Something tightened around Cage's throat. His ill-advised lust wilted as panic bloomed.

"Through fires of hell and demon kiss, be my shield and resolute champion." Sabell worked her inked needles while she spoke the words to ignite the magic.

Cage fought a growing sense of being smothered, but his limbs were frozen. He panted against the constriction on his soul.

"And let this bind me as steadfast to him, as he is my guard so shall I be his. Hold him and me as one thought, true to our bond before pledges to all others."

Her words of troth to him broke through Cage's panic. He relaxed. The spell spread through him like a cool breeze. It embraced his body and soul.

He was hers. She was his.

Chapter Seventeen

SABELL FELT CAGE'S RESISTANCE BREAK as she finished speaking. Her magic tingled down her arm, through the last needle, and into his body. Sweet release swept through her senses. Her muscles softened with satiated pleasure and left her breathless.

She pulled the needle from his skin and dropped it clumsily on her tray while her nerves tumbled in joyous chaos.

Cage's chest rose and fell in a rapid rhythm similar to her own pounding heart. His hand shot out and grasped hers. "Is it supposed to be like that?"

Sabell looked from their hands, his fingers hot as they touched her own heated skin, and then lifted her gaze to his gray eyes. A wild fey look lurked in the light-colored depths. If she had known nothing else about him, she would have recognized the nonhuman quality behind his sharp gaze. It didn't frighten her. A thrill of lust entangled itself with her pleasure.

"Is something wrong?" Mistress Pinxter asked as she waddled over to them.

Cage dropped Sabell's hand and sat up. He reached for his shirt, but Pinxter stayed his hand.

"Let me see that it's done." Pinxter had Cage lean forward so she could examine the entire spell. "Looks perfect."

Sabell thanked her for the praise, but she already knew it was perfect.

"This is the most powerful spell you'll need," Mistress Pinxter said to both of them. "I think that's enough for today, but you must plan on more time tomorrow. We have much to do, and it takes practice to use the enhancements."

Cage put on his shirt while Sabell stored away her instruments and cleaned her needles. He waited patiently until she'd finished, though something restless danced in his eyes. He walked beside her out into the hall.

Sabell wished she could read the thoughts churning inside his mind. Around the next corner Bachus and Reseda would be waiting for them at the top of the stairs, so she stopped. Cage also stopped and turned to her. The questions in his eyes matched her own confusion, but he remained silent.

Sabell knew something needed to be said. What had happened when she ignited the spell was too powerful, too incredible to ignore, but the strange intimacy of it held her tongue. She reached out and lightly touched the inking on his neck.

She squeaked as Cage roughly pulled her to him. Her body slammed into his solid chest and thighs. He wrapped his arms tight around her, and she melted against him.

His warm breath heated her scalp though her hair. Indeed, the entire length of him warmed her. His strong hands caressed her back in a slow manner, either warily or thoughtfully. She wrapped her arms around his waist and stood with him, neither saying a word for long moments.

Cage released her and stepped back. "I'm not sure why I did that. I'm sorry."

Cool air filled the space between. Sabell wanted his arms back, their warmth and strength around her. "I needed to hold you too. I guess it's the spell. We'll become accustomed to it in time."

Cage's mouth curled in a wry smile. "Time? The time we don't have."

Sabell grimaced. Only seven days until the full moon. The plan was to pass through the Gate the morning before the full moon. Ready or not.

"I have a final lesson in working with the hematite before you join me for our map lesson," Sabell said. Her odd need to touch Cage cooled as she thought of the chores ahead.

"I have an appointment with Bachus to visit the armory." Cage's expression cleared of his earlier bemused look.

They walked together to the stairway. Cage's hand occasionally brushed her back in a protective gesture that carried a hint of intimacy. He'd never acted in such a way before and seemed unaware of it now. She really needed to speak with another Keeper about the loyalty spell.

Reseda glared at them as they approached. Bachus only looked as cold and empty of emotion as ever. Sabell's spirits plummeted. Before the wretched tournament, Reseda had been her best friend. Now Sabell dreaded being anywhere near her. Before, she might have shared her wonder of the spell with Reseda. No longer.

"I'll see you for our next lesson," Sabell said to Cage.

"Yes, Mistress." Cage and Bachus strode down the hall toward the back stairs that would take them to the Marshal's training grounds and the path to the armory.

Sabell took the stairs that led up to the next floor, where Mistress Tamarin had her library with its volumes of tomes and rolled maps. She didn't speak to Reseda but could hear the Keeper padding up the steps behind her. An itch started between her shoulder blades, but Sabell refused to acknowledge it.

Reseda spoke as they crested the top step and started down the hallway. "What happened in Pinxter's work-room? You and Cage both looked spooked afterward."

Though tempted to ignore the impertinent question, Sabell chided herself. She need not be obnoxious in response. "I don't know what you mean. We did the tattooing as planned under Pinxter's instruction."

Reseda sniffed but didn't press for more. Sabell didn't like lying to her former friend, but Reseda had lost her right to know Sabell's secrets. It hurt to lose a friend.

At least she had her family back, if only for a short while. And she had Cage. They were strangers still, but they were connected now. Their hold on each other was more than that of lovers or spouses. Nothing could break their magical attachment except death itself.

Jonared nodded at his cousin to sit. Duke Borak Rosmer lowered his squat, muscular body onto the cushioned chair to the king's right. Irritation added to Jonared's discomfort. Even more than Cage Stone, Borak's posture was arrogant and aggressive.

"I've heard more rumors, Jonared."

"Of what?" Jonared snapped. He tired of the political niceties. He might fear demons from Kingdom's Gate, but such as the duke didn't intimidate him.

Borak smiled but not in friendship. Jonared's temper bristled at the condescending expression.

"Why don't you send your man for a walk so we might speak plainly?" Borak gave Maton a dismissive glance.

"Sir Maton goes with me everywhere. Speak your mind, or stop wasting my time." Jonared had heard that Borak moved about the castle having quiet conversations with other powerful landholders. Lord Merlin had advised Jonared to have this meeting.

Borak controlled most of the northern highlands, and the minor nobles of the region gave their loyalty to him. Jonared's father had warned him once that the duke might bring trouble when the prince took the crown. Did Borak really dare to contrive an uprising against the king to gain the throne for himself?

"You know few things can be hidden in Sulbreth. People whisper that these witches you take as advisors consort with demons of the most deadly kind. I've even heard the vile tale that they killed your father by calling one down upon him."

"To what purpose?" Jonared asked through clenched teeth. He didn't doubt Borak had started the rumors, if they even existed.

"To put you on the throne. A young untried man, terrorized by his father's gruesome death, that they could manipulate through his fear. And is that not what is happening?"

"You speak of things you haven't the faintest inkling about. Put your mind at ease and return to your home. Your holdings have been long without their lord."

"I fear I must put the whole of Futhark first." Borak clasped his hands together and leaned toward Jonared. "These witches should be stripped of their place as your advisors. They've enthralled and blinded you to their evil ways."

"What evil have they done?" Now he might find out how much Borak knew and if he had spies in the castle.

"Is not killing your father enough for you, Jonared?" Borak leaned back and smirked. "Perhaps you were too young to remember your mother's death."

Jonared's heart leaped in his chest. What was this?

"I've found witnesses who believe the witches poisoned her and then seduced your father king with some exotic creature not of this world. And now they've brought the result of your father's mounting of the creature back into Sulbreth. They call him Cage Stone. The human part of him is your brother. But what is the other half?"

Cage leaned on the heavy wooden sword. His chest ached with his efforts to breathe. His arms had long since passed from ache into outright pain. His opponents showed little sign of fatigue, and the bruises he'd managed to inflict on them hindered their attack very little.

"Enough," Bachus ordered the three Marshals. Bachus had surprised Cage with this training session, or was it a punishment session?

Cage had thought they were taking a day off to go to the armory and select his new sword.

Bachus motioned the Marshals and the Keepers away from Cage and spoke quietly to them. The Keepers had powered the tattooed spells for their Marshals for the entire time. With the magic, their quickness and strength had amazed Cage. Unlike the unarmed combat in the dark room, the weapons made them more than his match. He'd only lasted as long as he had against them through experience and pure unwillingness to accept defeat. If their plan had been to humble him, they'd succeeded.

Cage straightened his shoulders and stood upright when the little meeting broke apart. He wasn't sure he could go another bout, but hell if he would say so. But the Marshals nodded to Cage and took their leave. He didn't even know their names. Except for Bachus, most days different Marshals challenged his skills. Between his lessons and protecting Sabelline, he had no time for socialization. Then again, why make friends when he'd be gone soon?

"You did well," Bachus said in his gruff way. "When Mistress Sabelline draws your spells, I would guess you'll be the most dangerous man to ever walk these lands."

Cage picked up his shirt, wincing when he bent down. He hesitated to put it on until his sweat dried. "I have a question, Bachus, and there's no one I can ask but you."

Bachus raised an eyebrow, a great show of emotion for him.

"It's personal," Cage clarified.

"I'll answer anything that might help you succeed in

294

your journey, but I don't think I can help with anything personal."

"It's about the journey and being a Marshal. You've been training for years for this duty. Why can't Sabell take control of your enhancements or draw over them so she can power your spells? You're already prepared, and I'll never have time to learn all you know."

Bachus looked away. Cage regretted the flash of pain in the older man's eyes. But when Bachus turned back to him, his expression was as hard as ever.

"When you've been connected to a Keeper for as long as I was, you become linked in ways no one quite understands. When the link is severed, the remaining member is . . . injured. My enhancements can't be re-done. Once linked to a Keeper, you can never be joined to another."

Cage pulled his shirt on over his head as he sought the words for his next question.

"Come along," Bachus said. "Let's visit the armory. You need more than a new sword. Ask what questions you must."

Cage set his wooden sword in the rack with the dozen others. The Marshals' training yard and the lawns beyond were empty except for the two of them. A sense of home startled Cage. He shook it off. He knew few people here except in passing. Now that he slept in Sabell's room, he didn't even see the other Marshals in the evenings. They took their meals in a large dining hall where he sat with

Sabelline or by himself. This wasn't his home.

Bachus led him toward an outbuilding connected to the outer wall of the fortress. Cage had noticed the building before, especially the comings and goings of Marshals to the nondescript structure. Though the stone matched the rest of the fortress, Cage knew as soon as he touched it that humans had built this. Not his ancestors. The stones still slept, though they stirred sleepily beneath his hand.

Bachus waved him into the dimly lit interior.

"Hello, Marshal Bachus," a gray-bearded elderly man greeted as they entered the shop. Actually it was more of a smith's workhouse. A forge, cool and unused, took up one entire side of the long room. The other side displayed the finest-looking collection of weaponry Cage had ever seen. Swords of every width, length, and style hung in long rows against one wall. Knives, bows, and axes cluttered benches and racks against the back wall. "I see you finally brought the young lad I've heard so much about. Want him fitted up?"

"Master Renald Lang, meet Marshal Cage Stone."

The old man limped forward and took Cage's hand in a firm grasp that belied his aged appearance. Cage noted the massive forearms and shoulders, testament to a life working the metals.

"So you're the one what has the other lads all abuzz?" Lang looked Cage up and down. "You don't look strong as an ox and quicker than a flea."

Cage smiled, comfortable with the rough-mannered man as he hadn't been with anyone since coming to the Keepers' fortress.

Bachus sighed. "He's to take the evening meal with the Exarch, Master. Do you have naught to suit him?"

Lang gave Cage another canny once-over before he limped over to his treasure trove of swords. "Perhaps."

"My sword served me well," Cage said. It was the one thing he'd spent his hard-earned gold on for himself. A man needed a good weapon if he intended to make his life with it. He'd survived many battles with the precious blade.

"I saw the notches on your sword, Stone," Bachus said. "Find another and select a short sword and some knives. Some places beyond the Gate are too narrow for use of a long blade."

Cage moved to the wall of weapons, fascinated despite his lingering loyalty to his old blade. How would he choose from such a banquet?

"Try this one," Master Lang suggested. He pulled a long, wicked sword from its hook on the wall.

Cage looked at it and couldn't look away. The pommel was unadorned except for a small delicate etching of a flowerless vine. He took it in hand. As his fingers closed around it he knew he would look no further.

An open area near the forge gave him room to swing the sword and test its balance. Perfect. It was as if the sword had been designed exactly for him.

Cage smiled at Lang, and the old smith smiled back with an almost fond expression.

"What?" Cage asked.

"The Exarch knew."

Some of Cage's sudden ardor for the weapon deflated under a wave of cool foreboding. "What do you mean?"

"I didn't make that sword, lad. The Exarch brought it to me years ago and instructed me to offer it to every Marshal that came to me. She said one day a man would come that could wield it."

"When did she bring it, old man?" Bachus growled, his expression clouded with confusion to match Cage's.

Lang gestured for Cage to give the sword to Bachus. A sudden fierce possessiveness surprised him. He hesitated, wondering if the older Marshal could claim it for his own.

"Give it to him, lad." Lang grinned. "I guarantee he'll give it back."

Cage offered it hilt-first to Bachus, putting aside his fanciful feeling.

The older man frowned as he lifted the blade. He took Cage's place in the open area and moved the sword through a few sweeping arcs.

"You need to work on this one, Master Lang. It's the most unbalanced weapon I've ever toted. How many young Marshals did you try to foist it on?"

Lang's grin stretched even further. "Every one of them for the last ten years. I always offer it first."

Bachus returned it to Cage. "Select another, Stone. Don't let this old horsethief trick you into this one. Some beginner smith smelted it."

Cage hefted the sword. Perfection. He shook his head at Bachus while his mind searched for an explanation. This was his sword. "Where did the Exarch get this, Master Lang?"

Lang's grin slipped. "She never said, and such as me don't question the orders of the Exarch. I can tell you the metal is different than the steel I work with. I'm thinking it's some type of antique, found in a distant province and come to her somehow. You'll have to ask her your questions, lad."

Cage stowed away his questions for later, though the uneasiness lurked beneath his thoughts. He selected two short swords and numerous knives of varying sizes from Lang's store. Many of the longbows were magnificent weapons, but they would be of little use in close quarters. Lang suggested a small crossbow that could be hung from a belt. The tiny bolts were sharp tipped and might be used against small beasts or even be useful to blind a larger attacker.

"I suppose you're proficient with that too," Bachus grumbled as Cage added the crossbow to his take.

Cage shrugged as he searched through the soft leather harnesses. Master Lang helped him fit a dark baldric for his new sword and leather wrist guards that could hold some of the smaller knives. A belt held the short swords and more of the knives.

After everything looked to Cage's satisfaction, Lang took them all back. "I'll have all these honed to a fine edge for you, Marshal Cage, and deliver them to your quarters by nightfall. Take the sword now, though. Its blade carries a sharper edge than I can make."

After giving thanks to the crusty old man, Cage and Bachus started back across the expansive lawns. Cage studied the leaf pattern on the hilt of his sword. The delicate design reminded him of his mother. She'd worn a barrette in her hair that was similar or exactly the same, a memory that only now returned to him. He knew where the sword must have come from, but how did the Exarch come to possess it? He was sure it had been designed specifically for him. His mother must have known he would deal death as a grown man. And still she left him behind.

"I noticed you took the loyalty spell today," Bachus said.

The statement startled Cage back from his brooding thoughts. Too often his mind turned to his memories of his mother and the mystery of her abandonment. This fortress did it, reminding him of his heritage constantly. Even now, he heard a faint song from the sword. Cage stopped and stared at Bachus. The stone-faced man seldom spoke except to give orders, though he answered questions readily.

"I did." Cage paused, searching again for the words he couldn't find earlier. He feared the chaotic emotional event resulted from his unique heritage and hesitated to speak of it. He tired of people studying his every move. He tired of being apart from them all.

Bachus looked away and stared at the dark mountains that shadowed their lives. "There's no rule against a Marshal taking a wife and having a family. At one time, I thought I would do so. Few Marshals ever do. Because of the loyalty spell. It creates a connection between Keeper and Marshal like no other, not even marriage vows. Loyalty is not a thing of the mind but the heart. A mind can be changed but not a heart given totally to another. The longer you're with your Keeper, the deeper the spell burrows into your being. How can a Marshal ask a woman to wife when he's already given all that he is to his Keeper?"

The haunted tone in Bachus's words sent a shiver up Cage's spine. Something about Bachus frightened Cage. Was it because he feared he might become such a broken man himself should he fail?

"The spell makes the Marshal fall in love with the Keeper?"

Bachus still stared at the mountain, though he didn't seem to see it. "It's more than love. Other than love. I think some Keepers and Marshals do fall in love. Many share a bed for no other reason than it is too difficult to be with another. What is greater than love?"

Cage didn't answer. He loved Kristall, Anadalune, and Berton. He knew nothing of love of any other kind.

"Already you feel the need to be at her side, don't you?"

Cage nodded slowly. He should be angry, but the spell was necessary. Was that acceptance proof the spell was already deeply embedded? How could he not be upset at the manipulation of his emotions?

"That is why I can't be attached to another Keeper." Bachus finally looked at Cage. The stark pain in the hard man's eyes made Cage look away. "My heart is frozen into a rock. I can't give my soul to another Keeper. It died on that blood-soaked lawn with Alvara. I wish I had died also."

Cage still had his questions, but Bachus's pain stopped him.

"Go ahead and ask, Stone. My memories hurt no less because I don't speak of them. I'll tell you anything that might help you succeed in your mission or ease your way. It's my way of honoring Mistress Alvara. Nothing is too personal."

Cage looked into the cold eyes of the older man. "Did you love her? Were you lovers?"

Bachus's mouth twisted, not a frown, not quite a bitter smile. "We loved each other, but as warriors love their fellows. We were lovers only once."

Bachus lifted his hand and traced the loyalty tattoo on his neck. Before he realized what he was doing, Cage did the same thing. This time Bachus's lips did curve in a bitter smile.

"The day she put this spell upon me, we went back to

our quarters and acted on the astonishing intimacy created by the magic." Bachus looked away again. "It was the most intense experience I ever had with a woman. Something that could never be repeated. Without the initial urges brought on by igniting the spell, Alvara and I weren't attracted to each other in that way. And though I've been with other women since, no encounter matched that one time. I believe it was the same for Alvara. I advise you to resist, Cage. I scheduled the training session today so you might work off some energy. The appointment with Master Lang was also to give you more time to resist and let the longings dissipate somewhat. If you and your mistress are to become lovers, better it happens under less artificial circumstances."

Cage understood and appreciated Bachus as he never had before. Cage's body still raged with hot lust for Sabelline, though the physical exertion of the training yard had dulled the intensity somewhat. The mystery of the sword further distracted him.

Women had always come easily to Cage despite his bastard parentage. Some wanted to sample the hand of a dangerous swordsman or were intrigued by his different appearance. The fear of fathering a bastard held him from young inexperienced girls. He had avoided many beds that might welcome him. He could control himself and would this time also.

"I think I'll see how my horse fares in his new stable," Cage said. "Thank you, Bachus."

303

"You can thank me by resetting the seals and living to brag on it. I would go with you if the Exarch would allow it."

"Why don't they send more than two?"

Bachus shrugged. "They've been doing it the same way for centuries. Stealth above force. I agree with them this time. You must avoid the demons. An army of Marshals couldn't fight their way through what we suspect prowls the tunnel. If you succeed, our task on this side might be more than we can handle as it is."

"Will the demons trapped on this side of the seals come out in a rush, then?"

Again Bachus shrugged. "I was new to the Marshals the last time the seals were renewed. One gordragon and a small cave boa came out together. A lone accipitor a bit later. We know some beasts live in the cavern at all times, such as the little beasts that killed Jules."

"So likely no one living has ever experienced such attacks as we've seen?"

Bachus snorted. "We didn't even know cave boas grew so huge."

"What do they feed on in the tunnel? Do they devour people when they attack or only kill them?"

Bachus' mouth curved in a bitter smile again. "Questions for the Exarch, Stone. If the Keepers know that answer, it's never been shared with the Marshals."

They walked past the training yard, kicking up red and gold leaves as they went.

"Why don't I go with you to the stables?" Bachus said. "I've been hearing things about this murderous warhorse of yours."

Cage smiled, glad to put aside the subject of demons and magic. "He's like a child's pony. What say we give him some exercise?"

CHAPTER EIGHTEEN

JONARED KEPT THE TWO HOUNDS close. They acted as dogs will when offered an open field after spending most of their time indoors for many days. Only his firm command of their animal faithfulness prevented them from frolicking in the sunshine.

The bright sun of late afternoon warmed the grass beneath his feet while a long, dark shadow crept slowly toward them from the west. He wished the lovely fall day would warm his heart. He didn't truly believe Borak about the Keepers, but his father had taken a lover after his mother died. Such information was well-known. Had there been a bastard child? Not Stone, surely? Stone, whom Lantana praised and treated with undue care. No, Borak lied. The Keepers hadn't called the demons upon his father. Had his mother been poisoned?

He stared at the mountain. The black crags of Kingdom's Gate rose in defiance of light and life against the cloudless blue sky. Jonared shivered, his gloomy thoughts giving the mountain more power to depress his spirits.

He shook himself. He would enjoy this grand day outdoors and put his mind to rest later. He would confront the Exarch and know the truth.

Sir Maton stood only a few steps away, his body tense and alert. The young swordsman had proven himself a good companion. His youthful, carefree personality had sobered since taking the position of protector. He seemed more dangerous with his ready frown and lethal air. Maton tended to intimidate some of the lords who presented themselves to Jonared. Futhark had been peaceful for so long, few men were familiar with men-at-arms who looked ready to battle at any moment. Jonared found he trusted Maton as he'd never thought to trust another man.

"Let's take them for a run," Jonared said. He mounted his waiting horse while Maton did the same. The tall , muscular hunting hounds whined and spun in tight circles as they sensed the start of a hunt.

"To the east, your highness?"

"Definitely."

He gave the dogs the order to hunt and flush what game they could find in the king's fields. Game birds were plentiful in these reserved areas close to this castle.

The lithe hounds bounded away. The two men trotted

their horses after them. Jonared carried no bow. He had no desire to kill anything, only take in the beauty of the day and his beloved dogs at their work. The knot in his middle relaxed as the scent of grass combined with horse and fresh air.

The dogs suddenly stopped as if pulled back on one leash. Their ears lifted as they stared to the west.

Jonared's heart tripped and climbed into his throat. He spun his horse around to face the setting sun.

Sir Maton cursed and freed his sword. Only the silence of the dogs allowed Jonared to master his terror and search for the source of their distraction. He rose in his stirrups to better see what horror approached. He and Maton had discussed what they would do in such situations. They would not flee and be attacked blindly from behind as his father had been. They would fight unless they could outrun their foe. Maton would not leave Jonared's side as his father's protector had done. Jonared put his hand on his own sword.

One of the dogs barked in greeting, not alarm.

Two horsemen jogged their steeds into view over a short rise. One of the horses drew and held Jonared's attention. Its red coat rippled as its thick muscles bunched and flowed beneath its gleaming hide. It stood taller than most horses and moved with a lethal combination of grace and strength. A true warhorse. Few still existed in Futhark.

"I've heard of that horse," Maton said. He sheathed

his sword as his own mount began to prance about.

Jonared tightened his hold on his normally calm gelding as it snorted and stomped at the riders. Maton cursed as his mare tossed her head and nickered.

Jonared finally pulled his gaze from the horse to its rider. Stone, damn him. Marshal Bachus rode beside the bastard, his fine mount like a pony compared to the warhorse.

"Good day, your highness," Bachus said.

"And to you," Jonared answered. Stone kept his horse back a few paces. Jonared stared at him, searching for pieces of his father, himself, in the bastard's handsome features. He saw nothing except whatever it was that always raised his hackles around Cage. Today was no different.

Jonared tried to ignore Borak's vile conjectures and his own immature reaction to the man. "How goes your training, Stone?"

Stone looked at Jonared with the cool gaze he viewed the world with. "Fine, your highness."

Jonared ground his teeth when he heard the slight hesitation before his title. Was it his imagination, or did Cage indeed know some rumor about his sire set? "That's a fine animal. Is he trained in the ways of battle?"

The horse flicked its ears toward Jonared as if it knew he spoke of it. Its dark eyes moved like those of a suspicious cat as it watched the dogs and other riders.

"He's a veteran of many fights, Sire."

Jonared's irritation faded a bit. There had been no disrespectful hesitation this time. Discussing horseflesh always lightened his spirits anyway. Long ago almost all nobles had at least one warhorse. The long peace had made such expensive animals rare. It took much time and talent to train such a living weapon. Jonared had never seen one himself.

"It's trained to kill?" Jonared asked.

Cage frowned and patted the horse's proud neck. "Bayard isn't a killer, but he'll protect me."

"I've heard such horses do more than protect their riders. Does he not attack your enemies?"

The warhorse didn't stomp or prance as some horses might, but its muscles quivered beneath its smooth hide. It stood ready to spring into battle like a drawn arrow.

"Most horses will jump over or shy around a man. Bayard will run over an enemy and crush him into the ground. He responds to knee pressure alone and needs no rein to guide him. He knows how to dodge a sword or lance without my commands. He'll barrel over another horse and even use his teeth on man or beast. And he'll let no man ride him except his chosen master. Besides that, he's a tractable mount."

Jonared was impressed and envious. "And he chose you?"

"Obviously, your highness."

The damn hesitation again. He'd ignore it no more. "Walk with me, Marshal Stone."

Jonared dismounted and motioned for Maton to

stay where he was. Stone swung from his saddle, his gaze wary as he looked at Jonared. Something in the man's eyes brought Jonared back to himself. Despite Stone's arrogance, he was subject to the king. As soon as the bastard took a few steps from his horse, the hounds bounded to his side. Toothy grins exposed their sharp teeth as they danced exuberant circles around him.

"Traitors," Jonared muttered. Years ago his father had told him to trust his dogs. If a man's hound distrusted someone, then best not turn one's back. Jonared sighed. Everyone liked Stone except him. They'd gotten off to a bad beginning. Jonared admitted his own reasons were enviousness and perhaps a bit of defensiveness because Stone had been right about his intentions toward his sister. He was the king. He had a responsibility to act as one.

"I understand your stepmother and Sir Berton are to wed in two days' time."

"I wasn't aware of the exact day they'd chosen," Stone said as he stroked the head of one of the dogs.

"I thought to do the honors myself." The idea had just come to him.

Stone stopped and stared at him, his expression cautious. "Lady Anadalune will be appreciative, your highness."

"Will you attend?"

"I will."

"You do Futhark a great service, Marshal Stone. It's

quite the bravest thing do be done by a man, I think." As he said the words, Jonared felt again his envy for Stone. He longed to be as courageous and daring. How he wished to be a warrior king like his ancestors who had united Futhark under one ruler.

"Brave, sire?" Stone smiled.

Jonared was taken aback by Stone's perfect male beauty when his expression was one of amusement rather than hostility. He'd never thought to notice such a thing in a man, but there it was. Otherworldly perfection. It seemed the more time Stone spent with the Keepers, the more his elven heritage shone through. And it did shine. No wonder he won over all who knew him.

"King Jonared, bravery doesn't drive me forward in this duty. I go because you and the Exarch have convinced me there's no other choice. I do what I must."

"But you don't quiver with fear when you look at those mountains." He pointed at the black crags. His throat tightened as he looked at them.

Cage Stone stared at the ebon slopes. "There is evil there to freeze my heart, your highness, but it doesn't hunt me."

Jonared looked at him. "Hunt you? What do you mean?"

"You're quick to see me as courageous, Sire, yet see not your own valiant behavior. The evil intellect behind that Gate targeted your father and likely you in turn."

Jonared wondered if the man made sport of him, but

Stone continued before he could call him on it.

"How many in your kingdom know how your father died? They sit in your banquet hall and see their king presiding as he ever has. They know a world of peace and prosperity. Not so long ago my greatest concern was the price of gowns for my sister and mother. They know not, as I didn't, of the monster lurking at their backs. You put on a bold face and strive to hold the horror from them. I think it's easier to fight than to sit and smile as you must, your highness. I would surely slay the first lord who whined of his taxes."

Jonared saw the sincerity in the bastard's odd light-colored eyes. Emotion prevented him from answering. That this man actually found him worthy of praise filled him with a silly pride.

"Being valiant isn't an absence of fear, Sire. It's going on with your duties and your life when dread shadows your every breath. It's standing when your every sense tells you to flee."

"Your words comfort me, Marshal Stone," Jonared said. His next words died on his lips as Cage stiffened, and his hand flew to the sword strapped across his back.

"To horse!" Stone ordered Jonared.

Jonared stared at Stone as the Marshal sprinted toward his warhorse. The bastard leaped from several paces away into his saddle. The great beast turned and faced the mountains, half rearing with excitement. The hounds suddenly howled, a riveting mixture of hate and fear.

"Your highness!" Sir Maton shouted. He led Jonared's horse to his side.

Jonared needed no more urging. He pulled himself into the saddle despite the terror weakening his limbs.

"Ride, Sir Maton," Stone shouted.

Sir Maton leaned over and slapped the rump of Jonared's horse. The animal sprang willingly away from the bedlam of the hounds. Perhaps it also sensed whatever approached.

He hung tight to his saddle, but Jonared peered over his shoulder at intervals. Despite his fright, morbid curiosity drove him to view the newest wave of death to come from the Gate. He saw nothing but the two Marshals.

Both men sat their horses facing the west. The warhorse stood still as a statue beneath Stone while Bachus's mount danced about. Both men held their bare blades at the ready. The hounds kept up their eerie howls.

"Ride, your highness," Sir Maton screamed above the baying of the dogs and the pounding of hooves.

Jonared rode, but he continued to glance behind them. The shadow of the mountain seemed to reach toward the Marshals. He looked up at the sky. Would demons come from there as they had for his father? Or perhaps more gordragons would pound across the plain.

Castle guards rushed from one of the gates built into the lower levels. Sir Maton shouted orders at them as he herded the king's horse into the dark entrance.

Jonared looked back one last time before the large oak

doors swung closed. Little more than dark silhouettes, the two Marshals faced the west.

Sabell concentrated on the delicate thread of hematite. She wrapped it around the previous thread she'd made until the two formed an intricate braid. Only when she fused the ends together did she take a deep breath and relax.

"Excellent," Tamarin cried. She leaned over the marble table holding the hematite and looked at it closely. She didn't touch it, as the metal would be too hot to handle. "Very smooth and even throughout. I've never seen better. And you're much faster than I ever was."

Sabell swiped the back of her hand across her forehead. The dampness she found gave testament to the energy she used to work her magic. She wanted nothing more than to sit down and prop her feet up. A cup of honey-sweetened tea would be a fantasy come true.

"Come and take a close look," Tamarin said.

Sabell leaned back against the wall. The cool dampness seeped through her cotton blouse, chilling her hot skin. Not even the unrivaled architecture of the Keepers' fortress could keep the moisture and dankness from the deepest underground level. But it was here Sabell needed to practice, in a dark similar to the tunnels beyond the Gate.

"I'm sorry, lass." Tamarin shuffled across the bare

stone floor and patted Sabell on the arm. The elderly woman's knees always grew stiff when they spent time in the depths. "Time is so short. You've learned so quickly, but the Exarch wants you to be ready in five days."

"Five days!" Sabell squeaked. Her knees buckled, and she might have fallen if Tamarin had not taken her arm. "We can't possibly be ready so soon."

Tamarin smiled, sad and kind. The feeble lamplight hid her wrinkles and revealed her for the beautiful woman she must have been in her youth. "You're ready, Sabelline, and soon your Marshal will be also. A few more days will see all the spells put upon him."

That much was true. She had yet to tattoo spells on Cage's arms and legs. He would need the added strength and speed.

"But I . . ." Sabell stopped. What did she have left to learn? Mistress Tamarin had trained her in the manipulation of the hematite and taught her everything known about the beasts inside the cavern.

"You're already better with the hematite than I was when I reset the seals. You've far surpassed Alvara."

Sabell chewed her lip, thinking there was something more she needed to learn, to practice, to prepare her further. "Were you this frightened, Mistress Tamarin?"

"Let's get out of this dark hole and have some hot tea." Tamarin trundled toward the oak door. It swung open silently to reveal the well-lit hallway.

Sabell waved a hand to extinguish the small lamp

beside the door. How many years ago had she learned that small trick as a first year? And now she was ready to undertake the greatest duty of a Keeper.

"Finished already?" Reseda asked. She leaned against the wall near the narrow stairway. The shadows lent a gaunt appearance to her face. She looked older than her years, older than yesterday. Perhaps the extra duty as Sabell's guard wore on her.

"We've done plenty this day." Tamarin limped past Reseda and started slowly up the steps. "Would you like to join us for tea?"

Sabell hoped that Reseda would refuse. Her former friend's presence would bring no comfort. How could a person change so drastically in a matter of days? Or had Sabell not known her at all?

Reseda fell in beside Sabell and gave her a small, sincere smile. "I would like that."

Sabell stared at Reseda. The coldness was gone from her eyes; her old friend was there once more.

"I'm sorry I've behaved so badly, Sabell. I'm not sure why I've been such a brat. Jealousy that you were selected ahead of me and then you received such a handsome Marshal."

"And you're not jealous any longer?" Sabell wanted her friend back, but hurt encouraged her caution. Reseda had been so hateful at a time when Sabell needed her.

Reseda smiled in a shy manner quite unlike herself. "Still wonder what it's like to share quarters with that Marshal of yours, but the more I think about that cave boa the less I wish I'd been selected ahead of you."

Reseda sounded sincere, but her nastiest behavior had occurred after the boa attack. Sabell sighed. She needed her friend. She wrapped an arm around Reseda's shoulders and pulled her tight to her side. "Being my guard might be as dangerous as being me."

"Come along you two," Tamarin called from the top of the stairs. "I need my cinnamon tea."

They hurried up the steps together. Sabell inhaled deeply of the dry fresh air of the ground floor. After the dark confines of the lower level, the ground floor seemed a different world. A good world where the sun shone warmly through the fine glass windows and lit the corridors with natural brightness.

"Let's have our tea in the garden," Reseda suggested, rubbing her arms. "I need to chase away the chill."

"Excellent idea," Tamarin said. "You two run along and pull a bench into the sun. It's hanging low already. I'll order the tea from the kitchen."

Sabell and Reseda didn't argue. They hurried to the nearest door that led outside. The last rays of the sun bent over the hills, creating long shadows. Reseda walked briskly ahead of Sabell on the pebbled path that led around to the back of the fortress. Sabell took her time, enjoying the bright fall blossoms of the mums and the delicate scent of warm earth. Her earlier lustful thoughts toward Cage had cooled somewhat, but the beauty around her brought his image forward once more.

She rounded a corner, and the sprawling main garden spread before her. The crags hiding Kingdom's Gate loomed beyond the carefully cut lawns surrounding the bountiful gardens. Not even the bright and varied hues could prevent chills from crawling up her arms.

"This is my favorite spot," Reseda called. She stood a good distance from Sabell, gesturing toward a small round table made of a stone carved in the shape of a mushroom. Two curved benches framed the table while a red maple rained an occasional leaf upon it. Had that table always sat so far from the fortress?

Sabell started forward but then stopped and stared at the thick shadow under the maple tree. Despite the late hour, it was too dark beneath the boughs. She lifted her gaze to Reseda. Sabell's heart froze when their stares met.

"There you are," Tamarin said from somewhere behind Sabell. "They'll bring the tea shortly. Did you have to go so far?"

Neither of the other Keepers answered. Sabell stared into her friend's eyes in shock. Shock at the vicious hatred. Then the odor hit her.

Rising from the deep shadows under the tree was a miscreation only hell could have imagined. Worse than its appearance was its stench.

The thing took a step toward Sabell. The movement stirred up its horrid odor of rot and decay. Its empty eye sockets stared at her while its mouth hung open in a gruesome parody of a large grin.

"Stars protect us," Tamarin muttered as she bravely moved up beside Sabell. "Run, child."

The monstrosity moved forward another step. It appeared to be a naked corpse of a man in an advanced state of decomposition, except it was taller than any living person. Its skin hung in loose flaps as if no muscles worked beneath its grayish skin. Nails as long as a buzzard's talons sprouted from its fingers.

"What is it?" Sabell asked around her tight dry throat. She pulled Tamarin back a step as the thing moved toward them with a steady heavy tread.

"A gromf," Tamarin answered in a voice less steady than before. "A wound caused by it is fatal. The victim slowly rots while still living until she turns into a gromf herself. The last one was seen hundreds of years ago."

"And it's come for me." Sabell wasn't even armed, and her guard laughed maniacally from behind the beast as she urged it forward.

"What have you done, Reseda?" Sabell screamed even as she wished with all her soul for her Marshal to find her. If he could. A great fear took her heart then as she realized if she was betrayed, perhaps Cage was also.

"Guardians preserve us."

Chapter Nineteen

"Ride from here, Stone," Bachus ordered. His voice was as steady as his hand holding his sword.

Cage ignored him. His new sword felt light and warm in his hand as he stared at the approaching nightmare. The stench of the long dead preceded it and sent the dogs into greater distress.

The brave hounds stood in quivering outrage slightly behind Bayard. The horse stood like a rock; his only concession to the walking corpse was to snort and shake his head as if to rid his flared nostrils of the putrid odor.

"Only one," Cage said.

"So it seems. Now go. You're too valuable to risk, and the king is safe within his walls. It might even abandon its chase."

Cage always kept Bayard's reins tied together in a loose knot so that he had both hands free in battle without worrying about his horse tripping. He checked the knot.

"Don't let it touch you or your horse," Bachus warned when Cage didn't leave.

Mistress Tamarin had described this particular monstrosity and the slow, horrid death it brought its victims. The name she used didn't sound quite right to him, but he knew no other. A gromf.

Cage used his knees to direct Bayard away from Bachus and walk in a slow arc to the creature's left. Bachus followed suit, working his way to the gromf's other side.

The demon stopped and swung its fearsome eyeless gaze from one rider to the other. It lifted its head and snuffled loudly. Empty gaping holes marked the spot where its nose might have once been. Gobs of thick, gray mucus leaked from the holes as it attempted to scent its prey. After a few ponderous swings of its head, it fixed its soulless gaze on Cage.

"How do we kill it, Bachus?" Cage called. Tamarin had no information on it other than its name and appearance.

"I know not," Bachus answered in a cold, hard tone. "Little is known of this hellspawn."

"Then I say we hack it to pieces." Did it understand human speech? Had it once been a man?

Bachus's reply was not with words. He spurred his

horse forward and charged the gromf's back. The creature surprised Cage with a sudden display of speed and grace as it turned to meet the Marshal's charge.

Bayard sprang forward almost as soon as Cage thought it. Cage roared a great shout that had cowed many a robber and bandit. He didn't expect to scare such a hell-born fiend, only turn its attention from Bachus.

The gromf spun toward him and left its back exposed to Bachus. The seasoned warrior swung his sword with cold precision. The well-honed blade took off one of the flabby-fleshed arms near the shoulder. Cage saw the limb splatter to the ground as he directed Bayard wide to avoid the reach of the beast.

The two Marshals ended up on the opposite sides of the gromf once more. If the amputation of its arm caused it any discomfort it gave no indication. Thick, black fluid oozed from the wound and somehow increased the horrid stench.

Without speaking another word the warriors worked in perfect concert to distract and attack the would-be assassin. Cage took off its remaining hand on the next pass, and Bachus removed the rest of the arm a short time later. After that, they dismounted and sliced the creature as it spun uselessly from one blade to the other. When Bachus made a particularly risky maneuver to put his sword in the gromf's chest, Cage used the opening to take its head. Still, it didn't fall.

The two men backed away as the monster staggered

on its undead legs, first in one direction and then another. The pieces of its body lying about the field twitched as if some evil magic still existed inside them.

Cage and Bachus looked around at the results of their swordwork. The dogs stopped howling and stood in silent trembling emotion near the horses. He sensed their fear and the loyalty that kept them here between their master and the monster. Another sound reached his senses.

"Riders coming," he said.

Bachus looked away from the gromf toward the king's castle. "Do you think they waited to see which way the battle would go before coming to help?"

"They would have been in the way."

They quietly stared at the bumbling carcass that refused to fall as the riders approached.

"Think we could burn it?" Bachus wondered.

Cage frowned. "Maybe we should consult the Keepers."

Bachus nodded. Again he and Cage split apart so the gromf was between them. They carefully avoided the head and arms lying in the trampled grass. Cage's sword was longer, so he attacked first and took one leg of the monster off at the knee. It tumbled sideways as Cage leaped out of the way. As it fell, Bachus glided forward and took off its other leg.

The king's soldiers slowed their approach with a wise caution. Their swords were drawn, but the hands wielding them gripped them too tightly. Cage scented the men's fear, a warranted emotion. Many were young, and surely none of them had seen such a thing before.

A few held torches against the deepening twilight.

"Stay back," Bachus ordered as if the soldiers were his to command. "Light more torches and one of you ride to the Keepers' fortress and tell the Exarch what has happened."

Cage smiled, his humor grim. The men hurried to obey Bachus. What man would argue with a warrior that had slain such a nightmare?

A sudden tightness around Cage's neck brought an involuntary gasp to his lips. It took him a breathless moment to realize it was the tattoo around his neck that choked him. Sabelline?

It felt like he'd been punched in the stomach. She needed him. Cage sprinted to Bayard, ignoring Bachus's shout.

The warhorse sensed his need and leaped forward before Cage settled into the saddle. The battle cry he urged his horse on with contained all his fear and rage. Bayard's great muscles strained as he stretched out to full speed. They leaped over a wall that separated the king's field from the Keepers' grounds as if it were a blade of grass.

Cage rode with one hand wrapped in Bayard's mane and his sword clasped in the other. The closer he came to the fortress the more his fear and anger grew. The warhorse responded with more speed as they tore through the fine lawns and flower beds. He smelled smoke and directed Bayard toward it. Cage thought of the cold loneliness in Bachus's eyes and knew his own would be the same if he was too late.

Sabell backed away, pulling Tamarin along with her. She didn't want to turn her back on the demon in case it wasn't the slow, ponderous monster it appeared. She looked about for anything to use as a weapon. A wrought-iron trellis caught her attention.

"Tamarin!" Sabell pointed to the trellis, incapable of more words. Fear almost immobilized her muscles while her mind raced wildly. Fortunately she didn't need to move to work her magic.

The iron was old and stubborn with rust and a long expanse of years since anything other than the weather had worked on it. Though still tired from her practice on the hematite, Sabell called forth a surge of power beyond any she'd used before. Even as her working flowed toward the fancifully wrought trellis, Tamarin's magic passed by Sabell's shoulder.

The gromf shuffled closer, its necrotic stench threatening Sabell's concentration.

Tamarin's magic bent the trellis toward the path as she weakened the bottom poles. "Twist it around its legs."

The hoarse, breathless voice worried Sabell. Tamarin

was an old woman, not meant to meet such horrors. There was nothing to be done for it. They had to stop it. When they backed up another step, its pace quickened as Sabell had feared. As an assassin it must be able to move quickly. Its sluggish pace must be a diversion from its real abilities.

The iron resisted and then surrendered with a low screech. Sweat rolled down Sabell's temples as she helped Tamarin melt the bottom enough for it to fall completely across the path.

At the last moment, the dark-leafed ivy held the trellis off the ground. The weight of the iron and the strength of the vines struggled for a long moment while Sabell feared the gromf would pass it before it fell. Finally the heavy metal working crashed upon the pebbled path in front of the monster.

The gromf neither flinched nor hesitated at the iron lying flat on the ground. Reseda laughed from the shadows beyond the foul creature she'd called forth.

Hearing the mad guffaws of the woman she'd thought her friend gave Sabell the strength she needed.

The gromf put a decomposed foot on top of the fallen ironwork. Sabell thrust all she knew of her power toward the old metal. It obeyed as if newly forged. Both ends lifted as Sabell softened the middle. Working as quickly as she could, she tugged the ends toward each other. Jagged parts of the ironwork tore into the rotted gray flesh of the gromf. It took another step despite the damage. Sabell worked the iron with growing despair, lifting and twisting the metal. Nothing in her experience of using her magic rivaled the way she manipulated the iron. She forced it to follow her commands as it protested with screeches and groans.

Sabell slid back another step, keeping herself between the gromf and Tamarin. The demon's vacant eyes stared at her in the twilight. Her heel bumped into something soft. Tamarin! Dead or a faint? She'd fallen so quietly, without even a cry to distract Sabelline. Having Tamarin at her back had given her courage, but now fear overwhelmed her concentration. Her magic failed her as the beast lifted its foot away from the tangle of iron.

Sabell dared to look away from the gromf and step across Tamarin's limp form. She knelt with trembling legs and felt the light rise of the Keeper's chest. Not that it mattered. She wouldn't be able to pull the unconscious woman to safety before the demon was upon them. Perhaps she could save herself, but no force in the world could make her leave the dear old woman to such a horrid fate.

Sabell looked up, wondering if she could burn the thing. Her skills with flame were limited to lighting and extinguishing lamps and candles. Could she make even such a small flame in her exhausted state? She must try. She looked up, barely able to breathe with the foul air preceding the monster.

The gromf stood barely four arm spans away, its flabby

arms reaching toward her. It lunged but was pulled back. Pulled back by the iron trap entangling one of its legs.

Hope flared in Sabell's chest and strengthened her body. Sabell grabbed Tamarin beneath her arms and dragged her back a pace. The gromf lunged again, its otherworldly strength dragging the massive trellis forward a pace. Sabell tugged her mentor back some more. The gromf hopped forward. Sweat soaked her blouse and Tamarin's also.

"You won't escape it like that," Reseda crackled. She stepped out to the side of the gromf into a bed of hardy yellow marigolds. The traitor raised her hands and snapped them at Sabell.

Sabell flung herself on top of Tamarin as the flash of heat shot over her head. A whoosh and sudden brightness behind her told Sabell what Reseda had done. Her former friend was highly skilled in the throwing of fire. Sabell knew before she looked that her retreat would be cut off.

"I could likely finish you myself, but this is so much more entertaining. After the gromf has its way with you, I'll enjoy helping the other Keepers put you out of your misery. I won't be able to call them until you and Tamarin turn enough so you can't speak. Do you think it will be very painful? It must be horrible knowing what's happening to you."

"They'll burn you for this," Sabell screamed at her. She wished she could do it herself, but she was exhausted. It would be hours before she could work a spell.

Reseda laughed with manic pleasure. "They'll never know I had anything to do with it. I'll discover you and run for help. I'll be so heartbroken by the horror and the loss of my best friend."

Where was help? How could the entire fortress be deaf to the battle outside its doors? Reseda had planned her attack well. Few windows opened on this side of the structure, and most Keepers would be finishing their studies and preparing for dinner. The thick walls would block the noise of their desperate struggle.

Sabell opened her mouth to scream in the useless hope someone might hear. Her weak effort caught in her throat as a roar of primal rage bellowed from beyond the flames. Though it should have deepened her fears, her spirits lifted. A thundering followed the last echoes of the war cry. She pulled Tamarin close to her as the ground quaked beneath her trembling knees.

Sabell glanced over her shoulder. A dark beast burst through the wall of fire. Sparks and pebbles flew from beneath its hooves as it slid to a stop on the pathway. A vision from an ancient painting leaped from the saddle before the last sparks settled.

Reseda's scream of rage overlapped Sabell's cry of joy as Cage sprang in front of her, the growing conflagration behind her reflected from the blade of his sword.

In a strange, guttural language, Reseda shouted a command to the demon. The gromf turned its dead gaze from Sabell to Cage.

Sabell's heart stuttered as she realized Cage had put himself within reach of the gromf by placing himself in front of her. Heat from the magical fire behind her seared her foot, but she couldn't attend it now. Not with Cage standing so close to death.

"Cage!"

He didn't turn. He stepped closer to the gromf! It extended its fat fingers and the terrible talons on the ends of the digits.

Sabell ducked her head and wept, unable to watch her Marshal die.

Cage wanted to check on Sabelline. Poor Keeper Tamarin looked dead. Sabell was as pale as death herself. When she looked at him with such hope, he'd almost turned from the demon to comfort her.

The gromf reached for him. Foul dead tissue hung in wet strings from its long, sharp, blackened claws. What force of creation conceived such a horrid creature?

Despite the gromf's unnatural speed, Cage had no trouble dodging its sweeping arm. He swung the perfectly weighted sword and sliced the limb from its rotting body. He noticed the tangle of metal trapping the gromf. She'd saved herself.

The monster hopped forward on its free leg and closed

the distance by a small pace. The thing didn't give up. Cage took off its other arm before it could reach for him. The creature wasn't an effective assassin. Why send it?

He moved to his right so he would have a clear swing at its head when something hot slammed into him.

Pain crushed against Cage's chest. The fiery bolt of power had thrown him on top of Sabell and Tamarin. Sabell's trembling, cold hand touched his shoulder, and the burning agony in his chest lessened.

Cage cursed his own carelessness. A gromf alone provided little danger to a Marshal, but when combined with the skills of a malicious Keeper, the two would be deadly.

He pushed Sabell's hand from his shoulder. That she spent her strength to heal him only deepened his self-recrimination. He struggled to his feet only to have another flaming attack fly toward his head. Cage dove on top of the Keepers once more. Tamarin grunted. She lived.

Cage searched his belt for a dagger. He only had one small blade from his life before. It would have to do. He jumped to his feet and spun to face Reseda. He threw the knife as he turned.

More fire seared his shoulder as he dropped to the ground beside Bayard. The well-trained mount didn't move as Cage rolled against its deadly hooves.

Reseda screamed, rage and pain, but not enough pain. His small knife hadn't made a lethal wound. Cage gathered himself to rise and charge. The fire and the gromf were squeezing them into a deadly trap. Reseda might turn her flames on Sabell and Tamarin next if he didn't press her.

Bayard snorted a warning, and then another horse leaped through the fire. Bachus spurred his mount onward around the gromf as if to trample Reseda. But his horse was not war trained. It turned aside at the last moment and only brushed against the traitor with its shoulder. Reseda stumbled sideways. Her feet tripped over the metal trapping the gromf. Reseda flailed her arms about and screamed. Not rage this time but terror.

Cage watched in horrible immobility as Reseda fell against the back of the gromf. She knocked the beast forward and sprawled on top of it. Sabell made a small anguished sound behind him. He couldn't look away as the gromf twisted its head an impossible distance and opened its gaping mouth further. Reseda tried to lift herself off its back, but the gromf's black pointed teeth closed on her cheek and neck.

He didn't want Sabell to see any more. Cage sheathed his sword and scrambled to her side. He lifted her into his arms. Her body settled against him with an alarming limpness, but there was no time. He lifted her onto Bayard's back and hurried to pick up the still-unconscious Tamarin. He forced her into Sabell's arms. With some encouragement, Sabell stiffened her back and wrapped the old woman tight against her.

Bayard protested with a shake of his head but stood

firm. Cage took the warhorse's bridle and turned him to face the flames.

"No, Cage," Sabell protested, her voice hoarse and weak.

"Hold tight." Cage ran toward the flames. Bayard faithful and stout of heart, followed without hesitation as they sprinted through the fiery wall.

Jonared stood on top of the lower guard walk. Torches flickered four hundred paces away in the middle of the back lawn. Dark shapes moved in and out of the feeble illumination. The glint of armor marked his men, but many of the distant shapes were female. The Keepers had arrived. Finally.

One of the hounds whined at his feet. He patted it in an absent manner, but the dog's presence lent him some comfort. Not enough to squelch his fear, but he could stand here and trust the dogs to warn him.

"Your highness, there's nothing for us to do here." Sir Maton didn't turn his own stark gaze from the field. "I'd prefer we go inside."

"It's safe enough," Jonared snapped. He should apologize, for he certainly wasn't angry with his protector.

"I don't have the skills of Cage Stone, Sire. I won't know if a demon approaches," Maton insisted in his dogged way. Stone's manners were catching to everyone.

"The dogs will let us know." Jonared would not retreat further. A shiver crawled up his spine. The smell of the dead lingered in his nostrils as if it would never leave.

"I'm thankful for their keen senses." Maton frowned at the two tall hounds that sat on each side of their master. "I don't doubt their courage either, but not even they knew of the fell creatures before Stone."

Did Maton doubt Jonared's courage as he did himself? Stone's earlier words no longer gave him comfort. He had hated running from the assassin and hated himself for the relief he experienced when he didn't have to stay and face the demon.

Maton offered no more protests and left Jonared to his grim thoughts and self-doubts.

The spectacle was too distant to distinguish the shouts as orders were given. The only report sent since their retreat was from one eager young guard. The youth could barely stand still to speak. His wide eyes were filled with horror and excitement.

"Our messenger should have returned from the Keepers by now," Jonared muttered. The young guard had also reported the two Marshals had rushed to the fortress as soon as the guardsmen arrived.

"I'm sure the Exarch will come herself, your majesty, when she's able."

Sir Maton's words gave no comfort. Only one thing would prevent the Exarch from rushing to his side. The attack today mirrored too closely the day of his father's death. He could only guess another assassin had gone for Sabelline. She wasn't only his childhood friend; she was the most important person in the entire kingdom. Her Marshal had been protecting the king when she needed him most. Was there no end to his guilt?

"I think they're gathering wood, as we guessed," Sir Maton said.

Jonared peered through the gloom to the torchlight. Men carried long, thin logs and threw them into a pile. He guessed the demon carcass lay there. Was it dead? Could something so vile have been alive at all?

He and Maton had hurried to this walkway in time to see the beast go after the Marshals. Their swift swords had cut it to pieces, though it fought on long after it had taken mortal wounds.

"I wonder how such a creature intended to catch you, my king. It was surely too slow to assail you while you were mounted."

He wondered the same himself. "I'm sure the Keepers will be able to tell us how the thing intended to make corpses of us. Who knows what might have happened if we'd had no warning. Perhaps it meant to sneak up on us and have surprise on its side."

Maton frowned into the night but made no answer.

They watched until the guards had a large blaze going. As the flames grew, Jonared counted no less than six Keepers and Marshals moving among his men. They'd better stay until nothing but ash remained of the demon.

Jonared wanted answers. He could wait no longer. "Come, Sir Maton. We'll take the king's corridor to the fortress."

Sabell pulled the rough blanket closer to her. It smelled of horse, but she didn't care. Not even the thick wool warmed her. She didn't expect to ever be warm again.

Cage glanced her way as he worked a rough brush over his horse, Bayard. The warhorse stomped his feet and pranced with delight. The animal acted as if ready to go for a run, delighted to have his master close.

"Take this, Mistress." An old stable master leaned over her where she sat on a badly balanced wooden bench. He shoved a dark metal cup in front of her face.

She wrapped grateful hands around its steaming warmth and tried to give the kind man a smile of thanks. She knew her voice wouldn't work. She held the mug close to her face so the steam would rise and melt the frost of her thoughts.

She tried one small sip, though it seared her tongue. Common black tea with a trace of mint. A simple but strong brew.

Cage's low voice woke her from the emotional void she kept sinking into since leaving the garden. Her Marshal would not let her out of his sight, and no one could tend his horse but himself. So he'd brought her to the stable and ignored the Exarch's command to leave her in the care of her fellow Keepers.

Sabell wanted to stay at his side, or, better still, to stand behind him so he would be between her and whatever nightmare came next. There was no end to it. No tomorrow to rest and enjoy a day of peace and recovery. No peace.

"Give him a full share and a half of oats in the morning. I'll move him to a pasture stall tomorrow. Let no one approach him tonight. His blood is still hot with battle."

The old stable master mumbled quick agreement. Who would argue with Cage in his present state? The horse wasn't the only one still heated from the fight.

"Let me take this, Mistress," Cage said in a different tone as he knelt in front of Sabell. She hadn't heard him approach. He gently unwrapped her fingers from the cooling mug and set it beside her on the dirt floor.

Sabell hugged the blanket to her as Cage assisted her in rising from the bench. He wrapped one strong arm around her shoulders and supported her tight against his side.

Sabell had thought herself strong. She'd raised her sister after her mother died, left home and family to join the Keepers. Even faced the cave boa without losing her stalwart way. Tonight nothing remained of her strength of spirit. It hung in tattered shreds about her heart and mind, her will crushed beneath the betrayal and hopelessness.

"Watch your step." Cage tightened his arm around her shoulders as they came to the wide steps that led to the kitchen entrance. The deep calm of his voice beckoned her to lean on him more, give over all control to him.

Why had they thought they could do this, defeat this endless well of evil? One of their own plotted against them. Her friend. A racking shudder shook her entire body as she recalled Reseda's scream. Screams that could have been hers and Tamarin's.

"Here now. There you are." A large woman in a bright white apron bustled toward them as soon as they stepped into the glow and warmth of the kitchen. "Sit you both down, Marshal Cage. I already have tea brewing and some wine warming on the hearth."

Sabell sagged further. The idea of sitting in this bright fragrant place pierced her dull thoughts.

"Thank you, but no, Marci," Cage said, keeping a firm hold on Sabell. "Something sent to Mistress Sabelline's quarters would suit."

"Right away, lad. Take the young lass up, and I'll be along myself."

Cage led her to the servants' steep stairway. She balked at the foot of the endless ascent. She squeaked when Cage swung her up into his arms. She melted against his chest, listening to the steady beat of his heart, content to let him carry her like a child. The emotionless daze overtook her again, so she started with surprise when he pushed open the door to her rooms. A brief glimpse of two Marshals and a Keeper flashed by as Cage stalked across the outer room.

"I'll help her now."

Sabell reluctantly lifted her head away from Cage's comforting chest. Mistress Pinxter waited in front of the bathing room entrance. The tattoo expert had aged since Sabell saw her last. Would any of them survive this disaster?

Cage slowly lowered her to her feet, but his arm remained around her as if he feared she might topple over if he let go.

"I have a bath waiting for her." Pinxter's voice was so kind, so worried.

Sabell's frozen emotions stirred. She fought them back.

"Go now," Cage said, taking his arm from her. "I'll be right here."

"I want you to come with me," Sabell whispered, all her tortured throat would allow. Was it smoke or screaming that made it so?

"Nothing will get to you." Cage pushed her gently toward the bathing room. "I promise to be right here."

Pinxter stepped forward and led Sabell like a blind child into the bathing room. Sabell looked back once over her shoulder. Cage frowned at her, but he was there as promised.

Pinxter wasted no time in stripping Sabell of the stained garments. Bits of leaves and dirt strove with charred patches to ruin the plain dress. Some part of her regretted the waste, but the thought came and went like a miniature moon moth flitting about a candle.

The water was hot, too hot, but her body and heart ached too much to protest. Inside everything was still frozen. Pinxter undid the thick bun of Sabell's hair, gently soothing it down her back. As the water wet the ends of her hair, the odors of burning and rot that clung to her heightened. Her throat seized first, and then the cramping spread to her middle.

Mistress Pinxter helped her hold her head over the side of the tub. She emptied the meager contents of her stomach on the floor. The illness released the tight hold she had on her tears. Violent sobs tore apart the last of her control.

CHAPTER TWENTY

Lantana coughed as the wind shifted and the thin smoke still rising from the smoldering greenery drifted her way. Harmon put a gentle hand beneath her elbow and directed her a few steps to the right.

She breathed easier, but those short steps brought her closer to what had once been Reseda.

The garden was grimly silent except for the young woman. Lantana herself had chosen Reseda to join their honored order. The thing in front of her bore little resemblance to that bright girl from years ago.

"Please, Exarch," Reseda panted. She stretched a horrid hand toward Lantana. Already the young Keeper's flesh sagged and grayed. Her once-bright eyes sat deep in her skull and her mouth hung open, exposing her teeth as her skin drooped away from it. Her pleading was becoming more difficult to understand.

"You ask mercy of me?" It took all Lantana's will to act so cold and unaffected. "You're a traitor not only to your sister Keepers but to all of Futhark. You plotted to kill the king and your friend Sabelline. I assume the deaths of King Jerson and Mistress Alvara also were your doing."

A liquid rattle sounded in Reseda's chest, giving her whimpers an animal-like sound. Lantana wondered if the traitor would lose her ability to speak before they could learn anything from her. She dared to push Reseda, hoping the pain of the transformation from human to gromf would be motivation enough.

"Look beside you, Reseda. See what you're becoming." Lantana pointed to the destroyed gromf. The Marshals had hacked it to pieces and would burn it as soon as they learned what they could from the girl.

Reseda already sat flat on her behind. Twisting her head to look at the gromf almost sent her sprawling on her back. The wounds around her neck and face where the gromf had scratched or bitten her swelled and spilled yellow pus down her shoulders and breasts. Lantana could smell the putrefaction even at her safe distance.

Broken sobs burst from Reseda's gaping mouth. She turned her bleak, deadening eyes back to Lantana. "Please kill me."

Lantana took a moment to interpret the garbled

words. "Tell me why I should ease your way. Tell me how you summoned the demons to attack. How did you mark your victims?"

Harmon put a hand on Lantana's shoulder, lending her strength as if sensing her weakening resolve at the cruel, lingering death taking the girl bit by bit.

Reseda tried to swallow and then made a sound like a cough. When she raised a hand to her throat and clawed at it, small strips of skin peeled off.

Behind Lantana, Harmon made a sound that might have been anything. She didn't think she could watch much more. Her stomach roiled and twisted. "How, Reseda?"

Reseda's stare was empty, soulless, her words virtually incomprehensible. "I dreamed, and it came to me. It asked me, and I told. It spoke to me."

"It? What spoke to you?"

Reseda's head dropped forward and swung slowly side to side.

"Why, Reseda? Why betray everyone?"

Reseda lifted her head again, and now a dark light gleamed in her sunken eyes. Her open mouth completed her ghoulish appearance. "So that Futhark might be free from your control, witch. You and your puppet king. So people can have free will to live as they wish."

The words, slurred and distorted, were spoken in a powerful voice as if the last effort of a dying soul. Lantana stepped back. Soon Reseda would have the strength of the gromf.

"I give you the mercy you would have denied all, Reseda. You, poor child, have been deceived by these voices in your dreams. The evil you wish to release upon us would take not only the freedom of the people but their lives as well. I fear you'll find nothing but damnation on the other side of death."

Lantana stepped back and gave the order. Harmon took charge. Lantana watched, as she felt she must. Her punishment for bringing the girl among them. Only when the Marshals had covered the two gromfs with wood and oil did she retreat to stand with the other Keepers. She stood vigil until the flames burned low to make sure all the remains were incinerated.

Harmon returned to her side. "It is done, Exarch."

Lantana nodded, glad for his steady presence. "Let's see to the living."

Cage ran his hand through his still-damp hair. A weary hand. A bright fire flickered in the Exarch's large fireplace, but the cold he felt could not be warmed by flames.

Sabell sipped from a goblet of warm wine. She and Tamarin occupied two of the numerous chairs sitting near the hearth.

Cage wanted nothing more than to carry her to her

bed and stand watch over her all night. She had shaken off most of her earlier despair, but her face remained pale with either fatigue or remembered fear and trauma.

The Exarch and the king stood side by side behind the massive desk as they spoke in low voices. Cage didn't bother trying to make out their words. He was too tired to care.

Sir Maton stood inside the door, and Marshal Harmon stood beside the room's only window behind the Exarch's desk.

Keeper Tamarin patted Sabell on the arm in silent comfort. She was one tough old Keeper.

Cage's mood lightened for a brief moment watching the two Keepers together. One old and long finished with her mission, one ready to set out on hers, had worked together and saved themselves from a terrible death. If Reseda's plan had succeeded, not only would Sabell be dead and unable to renew the seals, but with Tamarin gone, no one would have been left to train the next metalworker.

A brief knock on the door announced Bachus's brisk entry. On another day, Cage might have been amused by Maton's quick reach for his sword. Not today. Today no place seemed safe.

"The burnings are done, Exarch," Bachus announced. The odor of smoke swirled into the room with him. He hadn't bathed like the rest of them.

"Thank you, Marshal." The Exarch gestured toward

the fireplace. "Please join us. As a witness to today's near catastrophe, you might have insight to offer."

Bachus nodded and strode over to stand beside the large hearth. The king and the Exarch took seats side by side so that they faced Sabell and Tamarin.

Cage thought the king looked nearly as pale as Sabell, but his mouth was set with grim determination. The king's questions of his own courage puzzled Cage but also raised his opinion of him. Jonared wasn't the spoiled child Cage first took him to be. Still, Cage didn't quite trust him with Kristall's well-being.

The Exarch sat up straight and spoke in a firm tone. "Despite the horror of the day, some good has come of it. We've found our traitor, though her treason brings us great pain."

Cage noticed the slight shudder pass across Sabell's shoulders. Tamarin sighed loudly.

"Unfortunately, we were unable to discover the means by which Reseda summoned the demons and passed information to them. Reseda was second choice behind you, Sabelline, to take on this mission. Think of the disaster if she'd undertaken it and betrayed us in the cavern by completely destroying the seals."

"Will Mistress Sabelline be safe now that Reseda is dead?" It was the only question that mattered to Cage.

"I don't know. How did she point these monsters to her victims? Did she mark the king and Sabelline in some manner to attract the assassins? Sabelline tells me she spoke commands to the gromf, and it obeyed her. Do these fell beasts have a language of their own? How dire for us if they're more intelligent and organized than we've always thought. What I fear most is some great dark force that directs their movements from the shadows. That being will know the identity of its targets without further assistance from Reseda. And as to all that, I'm not sure the king was the intended victim today, but rather you, Marshal Stone."

"The beast did go for you first, Stone," Bachus said.

"You think more will be coming for us?" Out of the corner of his eye Cage saw Sabell flinch.

"I do," Lantana answered without hesitation. "It troubles me that we're seeing things outside the Gate that have never walked in the light of day. You'll have things to add to your lesson books, Mistress Tamarin."

"I'd rather have missed the education," Mistress Tamarin said.

"How was such a creature to kill us?" Bachus asked. "It fell easily to our swords."

"Your swords are exceptional, Marshal," Tamarin said. "The gromf appears slow but is capable of great speeds for short distances. Lesser warriors might not have fared so well. Certainly, Sabelline and I could not have outrun it."

"But its smell warned us well ahead of time. Even an unarmed man would have had time to put some distance between it and him," Bachus pointed out.

"I think the gromf can hide its putrid odor until it's

ready to attack. Perhaps the one you met in the fields was lying in wait for your return to the fortress. It hid in ambush, but you were delayed by the king so it came looking for you. The one in the garden was well hidden. Had Sabelline followed Reseda a bit closer, she would have walked right into its arms without knowing it was there."

"How did they get past the Keepers at the Gate?" Harmon asked.

"I can only guess at some sorcery that hides them while they pass by our watchers," Tamarin said with a weary shake of her head.

No one said anything for a while. Cage wondered how many more attacks they could survive. A good deal of timing and luck had saved them today, along with Sabell's clever use of magic. But what about next time?

"We should leave now," Sabelline said in a voice so soft it might have been a whisper.

Cage stared at her. This woman, a stranger for the most part, filled him with such pride. He was humbled by her courage after what she had faced already. Still, she rose to her duty.

The Exarch leaned toward Sabell, her expression gentle and sad. "I fear you're correct, dear. Tamarin tells me you're ready and you've proved you have the heart and the stomach to do what needs to be done. You have the best Marshal this fortress has ever seen."

Cage wondered if the words were to encourage Sabell or convince the Exarch herself. The venture had seemed so far in the future and his training so arduous, Cage had mostly thought of it as an abstract study of tactics. Now the time was come, he felt ignorant and unprepared.

"Cage isn't ready," Bachus said without looking at him.

All gazes swung to Cage. He shrugged. Perhaps the Marshal knew him better than most people.

"In what way?" Lantana frowned at Cage as if he'd spoken of his doubts.

"His spells are not complete. His arms and legs aren't tattooed yet. And he should have a few days to accustom himself to his new abilities."

"This is true," Harmon said. "He needs the spells and time to adjust to them."

Harmon was one of the most heavily inked Marshals. Black lines curled and tangled about his hands and arms. Fanciful lines even marked his jaw and along his hairline. Cage had seen the heavy designs beneath Harmon's shirt. A few days ago, the idea of such marking on his own body would have repulsed him, but now he thought only of survival and success.

"We'll work together on the tattoos," the Exarch said. "As long as Sabell completes each spell, she'll control the power."

"I don't think he needs the full treatment. He's already better than all of us," Bachus said.

For a few moments the Exarch and the other Marshals discussed the most advantageous spells to give

Cage. He said nothing as they discussed him as they would the training of a wild stallion.

Sabell set her wine goblet on the table and folded her hands on her lap. Perhaps only Cage could see the fine trembling of her fingers. She needed rest.

"Can the spells be completed tomorrow?" Cage interrupted.

They stopped talking and stared at him. The Exarch nodded her head slowly. "Yes, but there's danger in taking so many at a time."

"The spells on your legs and arms will distort your coordination for a time. You could injure yourself before you learn to move with the added speed and strength. Even without Mistress Sabelline's magic, the fortress will affect you," Harmon warned.

"Do them all tomorrow." Cage turned to the king, who had been as silent as Sabelline throughout the discussion. "Your majesty, I thank you again for wedding my mother and Sir Berton the following day."

King Jonared smiled tightly. "I will see to all the arrangements."

"Lad, you might not even be able to walk the next day if you receive all the enhancements tomorrow. Even the lightly powered magic of the fortress will give you much to learn," Bachus said.

Sabell turned and looked at Cage. Steely determination lay behind the haunted fatigue in her green eyes.

"I'll be able to walk, Marshal. I'll dance with my

mother at her wedding."

The king gave another tight smile, but no one else looked amused.

"We can't turn to folly because we hurry from fear," the Exarch said.

Tamarin struggled to her feet. Bachus stepped forward and lent her a hand. She swayed a bit but found her balance. "I must retire for the night. I'll see you two for your final lesson two hours after sunrise tomorrow. Before the tattooing."

Tamarin started for the door before turning back to Lantana. "Let them go, Lantana. Do as the boy suggests. He's handled everything we've thrown at him up until now. He can do it. He and Sabell have the fire of the young. Let them fight their war." She shuffled to the door, which Sir Maton opened for her.

Silence filled the room except for the crackling of the dry logs on the fire. Cage waited.

Finally Lantana sighed. "Three days from now, you'll depart."

Jonared lingered until Cage and Sabelline took their leave. He trusted Harmon and Maton to keep the words spoken in this room from others. Maton already knew anyway.

"What is it, Jonared? I can't give you any more assurances than I have already. Our fates rest in the hands of those two now. We've done all we could."

"'Tis not that, Lantana." Jonared hesitated. His earlier conversation with Borak seemed days ago rather than mere hours.

"Speak your mind, Sire."

He stared at the old woman. He'd known her since childhood and trusted her more than any other. Jonared wasn't sure he could have gotten by those first days after his father's murder without her calm guidance. Together they'd worked out the plan to draw the half elf to them. It all came down to putting his trust in her or Borak.

"I had a meeting with Duke Borak Rosmer this morning."

"Your ambitious cousin from the north?"

"Yes. You met him after my crowning."

"I know him. He speaks openly against the Keepers and magic of all kinds."

"I didn't know you were aware of this."

"The Keepers have many ears among the populace, Jonared. Our families, for example, apprise us of the world outside these walls. Our people often visit their homes. One of the Keepers was attacked on her last visit to her father's village."

"I hadn't heard."

"No reason for you to know. There are groups of people who follow the duke's beliefs. Usually they satisfy

353

themselves with jeering and name-calling. Occasionally one turns to violence."

"Is your woman all right?"

"She'll recover. She's had a Marshal assigned to her since."

"Why didn't she protect herself with her magic?"

Lantana smiled. "You know we're bound by the laws set down by your ancestors and the first of my kind to never use our magic against the people of Futhark."

"It leaves you unprotected."

"Nonsense. We have our Marshals, and we have you. The king protects us."

Her blind trust in him moved Jonared to frown. "I'm afraid Borak may plan to do more than speak against you. He's also speaking against me."

Lantana's mouth dropped open. "He thinks to challenge your throne?"

"He claims you've enthralled me with magic, and I'm your puppet."

"And people listen to these outlandish claims?"

"He says you poisoned my mother and called the demons to slay my father so as to put a callow youth in place as king."

Lantana's face darkened. Harmon swore softly.

"I fear, Lantana, that people will believe him if word of these demon attacks gets past the castle guard. I can imagine his accusations if even one creature escapes you and attacks in the city."

"Guardians above," Lantana cursed. "We don't need this worry now."

"I think Borak meant to drive a wedge of distrust between you and me," Jonared continued. "He doesn't know what work you really do so he couldn't know how ludicrous his speculations were."

"Do you think he would try an armed takeover of Sulbreth, your majesty?" Harmon asked.

"I think not, but tomorrow I shall speak with Sir Merlin. He'll spy out such plans."

Lantana nodded thoughtfully. "Good. I've noticed Sir Merlin has ended his self-imposed exile. He'll make a good advisor. None can speak against him. His presence will dispel Borak's claims about our influence with you."

Jonared leaned back in his chair, almost afraid to speak of the rest, but he wanted to put his mind to ease. "The thing about my mother, do you think she might have been poisoned?"

Lantana frowned. "She died quickly of a sudden high fever. There are herbs that can cause such a thing. Our best healers worked to her last breath and couldn't save her. We feared for you and your father for weeks, afraid you would show signs of the same illness. But why would anyone do such a thing?"

"Borak claims she was poisoned to make room for my father to take a lover."

"He did take a lover, but it was over a year later."

"Did you know her?" Jonared didn't breathe as he

waited.

Lantana's frown deepened, and she shook her head. "No one did. Few knew he even had a lover until she disappeared. She was never found. The king grieved again for many months until he turned all of his heart to you. Why do you ask these things now?"

Jonared plunged ahead. "Borak says his lover was not a human at all but a creature you chose."

"Not a human?"

"Cage Stone's mother."

Lantana and Harmon stared at him, their eyes wide and mouths open. Then Lantana snapped her mouth shut, and a shrewd look appeared in her eyes. "I've never seen anything of Thrum in Cage, but I never would have thought of Jerson."

"You think he speaks the truth? You knew?"

"Of course I didn't know," Lantana snapped. "I only debate the possibility it might be the truth."

Jonared reached for the wine. He'd expected Lantana to scoff at the idea. He couldn't comprehend Stone being of his blood. His brother!

"How would Borak know such a thing, were it true?" Harmon asked.

"The duke was much about in those days," Lantana said. "He often visited Jerson. I think he hoped to put one of his own sons on the throne until Jonared was born. He might have been plotting against Jerson as he is against Jonared."

"Stone?" Jonared shook his head.

"If it were true, he would be your younger brother."

Jonared stared at Lantana. Stone, irritating and arrogant, but brave and honorable. His brother. A brother likely going to his death within days.

"Now, you must make sure you are on this side of the seals when you work the spells."

"If we're not?" Cage thought Tamarin looked little better after a night's rest. Sabell was less pale and grimly determined.

Tamarin shook her head. "I can't say for sure, but I believe you would be trapped there with the fell beasts you've sealed away."

Cage ran his finger along the thick line marking the correct route through the caverns. "You say it goes uphill from here?"

"You'll spend no less than three days walking uphill."

It made no sense. "The cavern must run under the sea."

"It slopes sharply downward for the first two days' walk with a mix of worn, uneven stairs and long slopes. Another long day or day and a half of flat passages. There you'll find the glowing worms upon the walls and few demons. Rest and take your time to recover before starting up the last stretch."

Again Cage studied the drawings. Many different hands had added parts to the map as features became known. The first markings must have been hundreds of years old.

"Perhaps the climb upward isn't as steep as the downhill." It was the only thing that would make sense, though the map showed they were near the same.

"On the way home, most of the demons will have already come out on this side. Somehow they know when the seals are reset and know they can't go back to the hell they come from. Still, take all caution. Remember I lost my Jules on the way back."

They all stared silently at the map for a while. Tamarin had no more to tell them, but Cage still felt unprepared. He stroked the hilt of one of his new knives in his new belt.

"Now, children, one more thing." Tamarin stood and put her hands on her hips. "I expect a full accounting when you return. Don't forget a thing. Every little beastie you see, down to the smallest beetle. Every crook and turn in the path, every drip of water down the walls. We'll write it all down together, and you two will train the next couple to go."

"We will," Sabelline promised around a misty smile.

"As you order, Mistress," Cage said, appreciating the kind lady's attempt to pretend she expected them to return.

They left together, finding the ever-present Bachus and Mistress Cicely in the hall waiting for them. Cage didn't know the Keeper well, but she often looked at him with a strange expression that made him uneasy.

"I need to speak with the Exarch," Cage said.

"Is something wrong?" Sabelline asked.

"No. I have some questions for her."

They walked with their escort to the Exarch's office, where Harmon let them enter immediately.

"Is something amiss?" Lantana asked.

"What do you know of The Edge, Mistress Exarch?" Cage could see he surprised her.

Lantana raised an eyebrow. "Perhaps you should tell me first what you know of it."

Aware the others stared at him as if he'd grown two heads, Cage frowned at Lantana. But he answered her. "I know men can't approach it, but I can."

"You can?" Lantana's wary look changed to surprise.

"It's a spell, isn't it?"

Lantana smiled as if he'd pleased her. "I've always believed so."

"Why do you think it's there?"

"I suspect your ancestors placed it there so people wouldn't venture too close to The Edge and fall off. I believe it's a horrifically long fall to the sea below."

"It is a long fall, but I don't think the spell was placed for such altruistic reasons."

"What do you mean?"

"You say my ancestors left Futhark, but where did they go and how did they get there?"

"Nobody knows."

Cage saw he had them all intrigued now. "Like me, they would not have been afraid of The Edge. I think there's a way down somewhere along the boundaries of Futhark. They put the spell there so they couldn't be followed."

"That's a great deal of speculation."

"How else would my mother have come to Futhark and then left again? How would she have left you this sword for me?"

Lantana shook her head with a rueful smile. "You've figured out the sword? I never saw who left it. It appeared in my study one day with a poorly written note to give it to the one who could wield it. He'd arrive within twenty years."

Cage fell silent. He'd only guessed his mother left the sword. Left him a sword and took her love away from him.

"I wish I could examine The Edge, but I can't overcome the spell any more than any other," Lantana said. "I tried when I was younger, as have many Keepers before me. Tell me what you see."

"Futhark sits high above the sea. The water looks blue on days the sun glistens upon it. Birds fly low over the waves and great fish, bigger than horses, jump and dive over the waters. The bottom of the cliff is littered with fallen rocks, and the waves smash into them without abating." Cage realized he would likely never see it

360

again. "It's beautiful."

"Can I ask what prompted you to bring this to me today?"

Cage eased down into one of the chairs. "I've gone over this many times with Mistress Tamarin. She's explained how the tunnel slopes down and then climbs again. I think it's possible it's very near the surface where the seals are set."

"In the middle of the sea?" Harmon scoffed.

"How do you know it's the middle of the sea? No one has ever gone to The Edge and looked to the west. Perhaps there's an island like to Futhark at the other end of that tunnel."

Cage watched the disbelief turn to speculation on all their faces. They were intelligent people.

"But how does this help us?" Bachus asked. "Even if it's true?"

"It means there's something beyond the seals. The Keepers have blindly followed the instructions of the elves without considering there might be another way."

"How would we discover it if there was?" Lantana asked.

"I want to climb the mountain above Kingdom's Gate and look over The Edge," Cage said. He saw the denial in Lantana's eyes before she spoke. "Listen, I'm the only one who can look, and I'll be gone in a few days. Let me see what I can discover. You'll never have another chance."

The Exarch considered, but doubt was still in her eyes.

Bachus stepped forward. "I'll go with him, Mistress. I'll keep an eye on him."

"How will you do so, Marshal? You can't approach The Edge any more than the rest of us."

"I think I can," Bachus insisted. "The spell works on fear to freeze a man so he can't walk another step. I don't think I have any fear left in me."

Lantana nodded slowly. "All right. You can try it, but you must be careful. Time is short."

"We'll leave now if Sabelline can stay with you," Cage said. He hadn't let her out of his sight since last night.

"She'll be properly surrounded, I assure you." Lantana gave a few orders to Harmon. "Wait for your escort to the mountain. I believe I know the best place for you to climb. Marshal Bachus, you may find you have more emotion left than you think when you approach The Edge."

Bachus answered with a wintery smile.

Cage hoped for the Marshal's sake that Lantana was correct.

CHApTER TWENTY-ONE

CAGE OFFERED BACHUS A HAND UP
over the last rocky outcropping. They both were covered
with a sheen of sweat. The climb was more difficult than
he'd expected.

They carefully walked up the steep slope toward The
Edge. A cool breeze blew in from the sea at this height.
Cage sniffed. He loved the salty tang of the stiff and
steady wind.

A few tufts of sad, browned grass were the only
things growing on the dead mountaintop. It was as if
the evil living beneath had seeped its foul humors up
through the rock to kill anything that might take root.
Even the rocks Cage had touched on the way up had
seemed devoid of life. How could that be?

The spell touched him lightly. At the same time, he

heard Bachus draw in a sharp breath behind him. Cage didn't turn. Bachus hesitated only a moment before following.

As they neared The Edge, the magic grew stronger. Bachus began to pant, but he came onward.

Cage slowed. Often the ground was unstable near the cliffs. He stepped forward with one foot and tested his weight upon it. Firm. He went five more steps before he decided to test it no further.

He leaned forward despite Bachus's gasp and looked over The Edge. He saw no path or gentle slope that might provide a way down. Disappointment filled him until he looked further. To the south, the waves broke against large boulders four drays distant from the cliff. The base of the cliff was littered with the usual boulders, but there was also a long stretch of white sand. The waves that hit washed in slow ripples onto the smooth, sandy field. Could not a boat make a landing there?

"It is beautiful," Bachus said. The brave Marshal stood at Cage's side.

"Do you see a way down?" Cage asked. The land curved out enough to hide the near part of the sandy area. Perhaps there was a trail there.

"I don't. There's no way to make our way along the top here either."

Cage sighed in disappointment. Why did he care so much to learn the methods his mother used to make her escape from her responsibilities?

"I'll see if I can find a way down there after you leave," Bachus said. "When you get back, we'll explore it together."

Cage smiled. "Best if you don't wait for me, Bachus."

"Don't speak so. If anyone can bring Sabelline back, it's you."

"You think your training is that good?" Cage teased as he stared out to sea. He tried to imagine the twists and turns of the cavern. Where would it end? The sea stretched beyond his sight.

"My training will be part of it, Cage. But you have the reflexes and instincts of your race. They'll serve you well."

"Where would you estimate the tunnel ends, Bachus?"

The older Marshal joined him in staring over the water. Bachus had studied the same maps in preparation of his aborted journey.

"I see something," Bachus said with an unaracteristic excitement in his gruff voice. He pointed to the northwest.

Cage looked and saw it. A shadow or something. He squinted and concentrated, not even blinking. It was there.

Sabell found her first smile since the attack of the gromf. She didn't look up from her work, readying her needles, but listened with growing amusement.

Bachus and Cage took turns describing their adventure standing on The Edge.

Sabell had never even been close to the cliffs that marked the boundaries of Futhark. Her father's lands were far inland, and the mountains surrounding Sulbreth made The Edge mostly inaccessible.

"You saw an island?" the Exarch asked again.

"A dark shadow on the waters. It's too distant to see clearly," Cage said as he pulled his shirt over his head.

"I wish I'd gone along," Marshal Harmon said.

Mistress Pinxter handed Sabell more bottles of black ink. She shook her head and rolled her eyes. Her workroom seemed quite small with so many crowded into it.

Still, the stern Marshals acting the part of young boys was worth the vexation to Sabelline. The mood around the fortress had been so grim since yesterday.

"You really walked to The Edge, Bachus?" Harmon asked.

"He did," Cage answered. "I've never met anyone who could before."

"What can it mean?" Bachus asked. "Do these demons live on this island and wait until the seals weaken enough for them to pass to Futhark? What draws them here from their home?"

"Lie you down, Marshal Cage," Pinxter instructed. "On your stomach, please."

Cage obeyed. Muscles rippled across his shoulders

and tapered down to his narrow waist. A thin scar stood out white on his ribs. A knife wound? An arrow?

Lantana took up her place on the other side of Cage while she answered Bachus. "If our histories are correct, the elves believed the demons were drawn by the evil nature of men. They set the seals to keep them out, but the magic would fade against the continued onslaught of malicious behavior on Futhark."

Cage turned his head to look at Lantana. "If that is true, does it mean it is an especially wicked time in Futhark? The seals have been weakened more than usual because of extensive corruption and greed?"

"It's a sound theory."

Pinxter stood beside Sabell, and Cicely joined Lantana. They all had their own sets of needles and ink. Soon they were marking Cage's beautiful skin.

Sabell forced her mind from the desecration of his perfection. She must do this to him for them, both of them.

The time passed quickly as they discussed the island and the sand area Cage described. Bachus spoke of his plan to explore the area for a possible path to the bottom of the cliffs.

"I hope I can walk The Edge again by myself," Bachus said. "I admit to blind terror until I actually saw the sea."

The Exarch smiled but didn't look at Bachus. Sabell understood. If Bachus could feel terror perhaps he'd healed a bit. Truly, he was more animated today than at any time since Alvara's death.

"You must try," Cage said. "If Mistress Sabelline and I fail, you might be able to find a way off Futhark. My mother's people are out there somewhere. I know it. The sea calls to me in some way."

The possibility of failure sobered the rousing discussion. The Keepers worked in silence to complete the spells. When they had finished with Cage's upper body, he removed his pants and covered himself with a small cloth so they might start on his legs. No one laughed as his hands fumbled with the laces on his pants. The spells on his hands and wrists were the most extensive.

Someone brought bread, cheese, and mugs of water. Each Keeper took a break, and Cage ate while they worked.

Bachus produced a long, thin stick the length of a good knife and gave it to Cage. He played it through his fingers and in a short while distracted Sabell with his antics.

Cage twirled the stick through his fingers with a speed to lose the eye. Soon all the Marshals and Keepers stared at his hands. It looked like magic.

"I'd say he's adjusting quickly," Harmon said dryly.

Sabell fed a trickle of magic to him, and the stick flew faster, little more than a blur. Bachus mumbled appreciation.

"Back to work," Pinxter ordered, though she'd been as entranced as the rest of them.

The sun had long set by the time Sabell ignited the last spell. Cage sat up on the table and looked doubtfully at his bare legs. Thick lines twined around and up his legs to his buttocks. He put one foot on the floor and slowly lowered his other.

He looked at his feet and then at Sabelline. She could only nod in encouragement. He took a step. And fell.

Cage's quick hands caught himself before he landed on his face. Sabell reached to help him up, but Bachus stayed her hand.

Cage pushed himself to his knees slowly, his meager covering falling away and exposing his lean flanks.

"All of you, out of my workshop," Pinxter ordered. "I'll be all night putting things to rights without half the fortress getting in my way."

The Exarch obeyed as quickly as the others, leaving Sabell and Pinxter alone with Cage.

Sabell collected his pants. "Sit down."

Cage listened to her. His lips were pressed tight together, but his body quivered otherwise. Had it been too much? All those spells in one day—could his heart take such a change?

"Let me do it," Sabell said when he tried to take the pants from her. She avoided looking at his private area as she worked the clothing over his feet and up his legs. He took over and lay back so he could lift his hips and pull them up to his waist.

It took him five tries to get to his feet even with

Sabell's help. He took a step and fell again. Over an hour he worked until he could walk without falling. She healed his bruises and lent her shoulder to lean on.

Cage worked in silence, expressing neither regret nor wonder at the spells. Pinxter went for more food when Cage could walk about the room on his own. By the time she returned, he was jogging.

Sabell pulled herself onto the bench and watched him while she ate. She wasn't really hungry but knew she needed to keep herself strong.

Pinxter urged Cage to rest, but he kept at it. He leaped over the chairs and then the tables. He handled his knives and his swords. Sweat rolled down his brow and glistened on his bare chest.

Sabell didn't ask him to stop. She recognized the unyielding determination in his eyes. It lay as hard on her own heart. One more day.

Kristall bit her lip when Cage entered the king's parlor. She'd hoped to see him for a few moments privately before the wedding. The sight of him shocked, so perhaps it was better this way. She would have time to cover her dismay.

Cage wore new black pants and a loose gray shirt that matched his eyes. Even his boots were new and quite as midnight-colored as everything else.

Cage stopped and hugged her mother in a public display of affection entirely out of character for him. He gifted Anadalune with one of his brilliant smiles. Kristall's heart lifted at his expression.

Anadalune shone with her own joy. Her rose-colored gown clung to her youthful figure as she looped her arm around Cage's. They walked to Kristall, and she received her own hug. Something about Cage's complete disregard for appearances frightened her.

She held tight to him and thought he seemed taller and stronger than ever. The fresh scent of the outdoors that always hovered about Cage came to her and awoke childhood memories. Her protector, playmate, teacher. Why had they ever come to Sulbreth?

Cage released her and stepped back. "You look fit, sister."

Kristall tried to smile but then noticed the dark line about his neck. She took a step back and dropped her gaze to his wrist. Black designs scrolled on the skin visible near his cuff. Even his fingers were twined with the vile drawings.

"What is this?" she hissed. "What have they done to you?"

Cage's smile melted into a hard frown. "It's nothing."

"Nothing?" Kristall shook off his hand when he reached for her. This close, she noted what she hadn't before. His eyes were even different. A line, thin as a thread, traced around the base of his beautiful eyelashes. Had it been so last time they saw him? Cage had always had beautiful eyes, but the markings gave him an ethereal appearance.

"What have they done to you?" Kristall demanded, her voice rising.

Something in Cage's eyes hardened, but she also saw a hint of despair. "They've only done what they must."

"No. They've put a spell on you so that you don't even understand their chicanery. That's why they keep you from us. You don't even see their schemes, but they know we will."

"Kristall, please don't," Anadalune said.

Aware she was crying, Kristall backed farther away from Cage and her mother. He'd done this for them. Given away his freedom, his soul, become such a slave he didn't realize he was enthralled.

"Lady Kristall."

Kristall couldn't throw off the hand of the king when he placed it on her shoulder. Even in her distraught state, she couldn't offend the king. She had forgotten he was in the room, standing with Sir Berton and Sir Maton.

"It's not as you think. Come now. Don't destroy this moment for your mother. Later I will give you what comfort I can and also some answers."

Kristall let King Jonared lead her to the end of the hall where Sir Berton waited. She swiped at her eyes, embarrassed by the spectacle she'd made, but willing to do worse if it would save her brother.

She took a deep breath and stood beside her mother. Sir Berton looked handsome in a sky-blue tunic that matched the azure color of his eyes. Despite her distress, she was very happy for her mother and Berton.

The king himself spoke the sacred commands of matrimony. Cage, as Anadalune's closest male relative, gave her care over to Sir Berton. Jonared then ordered them to be true to each other in joy and sorrow, wealth and poverty, and until the death of one.

The obvious love shared by the couple pushed aside Kristall's fears and anger for a short time. Sir Maton summoned servants who brought wine and a luncheon of roast duckling and warm pastries. Kristall ate little and noted her brother ate even less.

Cage stood to offer a toast. "Some children are blessed with parents who love and protect them. Other children are born unwanted and uncared for."

Kristall saw her mother smile, but tears stood in the corners of her eyes.

Cage gave one of his full smiles. Kristall fought to keep her own mouth from curving. She would not be distracted.

"My birth mother gave me away as if I were a stray puppy. But in doing so, she gave me the greatest gift of all. The woman who took me in, though she had every reason to send me away, loved me. Loved me as her son. She gave me a sister and allowed me to be a brother to her precious child. Her love shaped me into the man I've become. When still a small child, another person took charge of parts of my education. He taught me to fight and act as a man of honor. I love him as my father. Most bastard children dream of their real father taking their dishonored mother to wife or at least acknowledging them as their own. My dream was for the mother of my heart and the man who acted as my father to wed and make us a real family. Today is my dream. It is all I've ever hoped for in this life. May the God of all things bless you, and from this day forward, at your leave, I would name you mother and father."

Everyone raised their goblets—even she had wine— to Cage's toast. Kristall wondered if any of them could swallow around the lumps in their throats.

The anger swelled in her again. Now that the opportunity had come to live as a complete family, Cage was to be taken away from them. His dream had come true, but he wasn't to be part of it.

Not long after Cage's toast, the mood of the celebration darkened. Everyone knew Cage would leave soon. Was this the last time she was to see him? Why? Where was he going?

Cage stood up again. The look in his eyes froze the arguments ready to spill from her mouth. "I must go. There's much I have to do."

Berton and Anadalune stood also. Berton and Cage clasped hands, but it turned into a fierce hug.

"Take care of my mother."

"I shall."

"I want you to take Bayard with you to Durnhold when you go. I've changed my mind about keeping him with me. He'll let you handle him."

"I'll watch out for the hellion and keep him fit for your return."

A brief look of anguish crossed Cage's face before he covered it with a small smile. "I need not tell you of the bandits in that area."

"They won't be there long." Berton's voice roughened, a terrible thing to hear in such a rugged man. "I've always thought of you as my son. No father could be prouder or more confident that you'll do this job and return to us."

Cage nodded.

Anadalune wrapped her arms around Cage's waist and wept softly into his shoulder. He held her just as firmly. They spoke quietly so that Kristall could not hear their words. She started to rise and go to them, but Jonared leaned toward her and put a restraining hand on her arm.

The stern look in his eyes surprised her. Jonared spoke in the voice of the king though he whispered. "Your brother has committed his life to a great cause. It's dangerous beyond your childish imaginings. Don't make it more difficult for him than you must. Give him your love and blessing so that he might turn to its warmth on a dark night. This I command you as your king. Be strong for his sake."

Kristall stood when the king was done, confused by such treatment from the normally kind man. Cage came around the table to her, a wariness in his eyes that gave her an ache in her chest. She threw herself into his arms.

Cage grunted, but caught her easily. "You always used to do that when I went on a job and when I returned."

"And I shall do it again when you return this time."

"I'll expect it."

Kristall tried to think of all the things she wanted to say to him, but she couldn't find a starting place.

"Buy yourself some new clothes before you leave for Durnhold," Cage said.

Kristall nodded against his chest, her tongue coming loose at last. "Do you remember when the tutor Mother hired tried to kiss me?"

Cage snorted, still holding her close. "I remember that son of a bitch."

She lifted her head from his chest and looked into his gray eyes. He'd never lied to her, not even when she was a little girl following everywhere on his heels.

"Who will chase away the demons while you're gone?"

Cage swallowed. "I'm going to lock all the demons away, little Krissie. They won't ever bother you again."

A sob broke from her lips despite the king's command when he used the name he'd called her in her toddling years. She swallowed back the next sob. Be strong for him. "I shall count on it."

Cage stepped out of her arms and touched her face. "You can always count on me, little sister."

He strode out without looking back. His steps seemed less graceful than usual. Perhaps he was as blinded by tears as she was.

Jonared couldn't speak for a while after Stone left the room. The women cried in quiet grief. Sir Berton's expression was so pained, he might as well have been crying also.

Jonared glanced at Sir Maton. His protector stared at the women with sadness and sympathy. Jonared was king. Why must he feel so helpless all the time?

"What can you tell us, your highness?" Sir Berton asked. "I've seen the look of a man devoid of hope before. Why does my son wear it?"

"I can only tell you of some things, but whatever I say must not leave this room. I would have your pledge on this."

They all readily agreed.

Jonared bid them sit once more. "I'm sure you've heard somewhat of the rumors surrounding my father's death."

"Nothing we would lend credence to, your highness," Anadalune said in a voice still rough with tears.

"I wish that were so. The most closely held secret of my kingdom is the existence of those monsters you dismiss so easily as children's tales. They are real. The Keepers and their Marshals exist to keep them at bay. Every twenty years or so, a special magical spell must be worked to strengthen the wards that keep the monsters away from Futhark. This is one such year. It's always a dangerous duty, but something is wrong this time. The demons have erupted from their lair with unheard of frequency and attacked far from their den. My father was a victim. There have been numerous other attacks since then."

"Why has no one heard of this or seen the beasts?" Sir Berton asked, a skeptical frown upon his brow.

"We strive to keep it from the populace. There would be disastrous panic if these hellspawn attacked the city."

"My son is to undertake this dangerous mission you speak of?" Anadalune asked.

"He and a special Keeper trained to work the magic. He has been undergoing rigorous lessons, both physical and of the secret knowledge of the Keepers."

Jonared paused, unsure what else he should reveal.

"You speak of this magic and demons as if we should just accept such nonsense, your highness." Lady Kristall hesitated before his title in just the way her brother usually did. The worshipful look she often wore in his presence was gone. She glared at him with cool arrogance. The dampness in her eyes added to her fierce expression.

Except Stone wasn't her brother but his. Perhaps.

"Don't think to question me on this, Lady Kristall. The world is full of things you have never seen and are incapable of understanding." Jonared regretted speaking to her so harshly, but he would be damned if he'd accept the same arrogance from her as he did from Cage Stone.

"I'm sure that she didn't mean to question the truth of your words, your majesty," Lady Anadalune said with enough quiet dignity to make him feel like a bully. "As you say, this is all beyond her experience. Why did it have to be Cage? I've known of the Marshals since I was a child. Surely there was one who could undertake this dangerous task instead of my son. My father told me once the Marshals were unmatched in skill with blades."

"This is true. But not one of the Marshals could defeat Cage Stone. With the magical enhancements given to him, his physical abilities will increase tenfold."

"Enhancements?" Sir Berton asked.

"The tattooing you saw on Stone improves his physical abilities, from his eyesight to his strength and speed."

They plied him with many questions for a long while. Some he answered, some he could not or would not.

"So your tournament was a ruse to find a great swordsman?" Lady Kristall asked, her tone still hostile despite his reprimand.

"Somewhat. I also discovered my own protector, Sir Maton. But his work with the blade is not the only reason. I doubt I need to tell you that Stone is special in other ways."

They all fell silent. All of them looked hostile now. He should have let Lantana do this. "His elven blood gives him extra senses. He feels the demons coming, has warning. He senses magic. Who knows what else? Perhaps you do."

They volunteered nothing. Jonared sighed and continued. "A Keeper with the ability to foresee said one of elven heritage would come to help us in this dire time and that he would be a fighter. We used the tournament to draw him to Sulbreth. We didn't know if he would come, but the Exarch noticed him the day he signed the list."

"So you baited your trap, and your innocent, unsuspecting prey walked in," Kristall said with narrowed eyes.

"A very valuable bait," Jonared said, but no one smiled.

"A bait he had to give his life to receive," Sir Berton said. "If Cage had won the tournament and not agreed to be Marshal, would he have received Durnhold, your majesty?"

"He would never have refused, Sir Berton, and it's important you know why. Stone did refuse at first, and neither my pleading nor appeals to his duty to Futhark swayed him."

"What changed his mind, then?" Kristall asked.

Jonared knew it would wound them again, but they had to hear it. "His love for you convinced him he must see this through. You see, if the Keepers and I fail in our quest to reseal the prison, the demons will spill into Sulbreth. They'll destroy and kill. The taking of human life seems the only thing they desire, so when they finish with Sulbreth, they'll move into the countryside."

"And Durnhold is the closest manor to Sulbreth," Sir Berton finished for him. The warrior looked furious. "A clever trap for him, your highness. My lady wife warned me the deviousness of your court was beyond match, but I didn't realize you were the master."

"Save your anger, Berton. I feel no guilt for manipulating Stone into this. He is one man, a small sacrifice for all of Futhark."

"So my brother goes to his death?" The fight drained from Kristall's beautiful eyes.

"Not so, lady." Jonared berated himself for using such a word as sacrifice. "Yes, he goes to great danger, but others have gone before and returned to us."

"But never when things are as bad as they are this year? Isn't that what you said?" Anadalune asked.

"True. But we've never had a Marshal like Cage Stone before. He's a special man. If it can be done, he will do it."

Kristall stood up, her eyes dry and hard. She seemed suddenly shed of all her girlhood and now a woman. She lifted her chin, so like Cage Jonared was sure the elf was her brother, not his.

"Cage will return. He'll close this gateway to hell. You shall see. My brother always wins." She didn't ask his leave but spun and stalked out.

Jonared stared at her back, thinking she held herself with a pride equal to a queen. His queen.

Chapter Twenty-Two

"HE'S A MOST HANDSOME MARSHAL," Leesa said, filling the long silence.

"He is," Sabell agreed. The uncomfortable quiet settled on them again.

"I can not bear to let you go when I've only just gotten you back," her father said.

Sabell took her father's hand. They sat at the small table in the Exarch's own private dining room. The feast on the table was mostly untouched, the wine untasted, and the meats cooled in their juices.

For a brief bitter moment, Sabell wanted to point out to her father that all the time together they'd lost was because of his stubbornness. But looking at his stark expression, she forgave him, though she doubted he had forgiven himself.

"When shall you leave?" Leesa asked.

"I don't know for sure but soon," Sabelline lied. She wasn't to speak of it even to her own family. No one knew besides the few people who'd been present in the Exarch's study when it had been decided.

Cage had one lesson to learn to work his spells. Later today she would work with him, adding her magic to increase his abilities. The Exarch herself was seeing to preparing their packs and supplies. All in secrecy. Who could know if Reseda was the only spy?

"Surely someone else could do this thing," Merlin said.

"I must do it, Father. I've been training for years, and there's no one else."

Silence.

"Cage will protect you," Leesa said, more question than confidence in her words.

"He's exceptional," Sabell said. She hoped things were going better for Cage as he bid his family farewell. "No one could protect me better."

"Why don't they send a hundred swordsmen with you?" her father asked.

"We're trying to sneak by our enemies. If all goes well, Cage won't even have to draw his sword." Sabell turned to Leesa. "Tell me about the king's court. Have you caught the eye of every single man in Sulbreth?"

Leesa smiled, an unusual shyness in the curve of her lips. "Only one has my eye."

Their father snorted, but there was a fond humor in

the sound. "Of course, she selects one out of reach."

"Who?" Sabell asked, the happiness in her sister's eyes delighting her as well.

"Sir Maton Reves."

"The king's protector? He's very brave. And pretty."

"Pretty!" Leesa cried with false outrage.

They all laughed.

Sir Merlin entertained them with humorous descriptions of Leesa's attempt to gain the attention of Sir Maton. "I've no doubt the poor man will succumb in the end. Seldom has any male been hunted with such single-minded intensity."

"Perhaps when my mission is finished, the poor man won't be so busy protecting his king." Sabell cursed herself as soon as she said the words. It brought everyone's thoughts back to the reason for this meeting. This farewell dinner. The long silence again.

"I wish to have your blessing, Father."

Her father took her hands in his. "I've withheld my support from you for years, dear one. Not because you did anything wrong, but because I was angry that I lost you. Never during that time did my love waver. It does not now."

Leesa added her hands on top of theirs.

Their father's voice trembled as he continued. "You have my blessing and all my love and faith with you. I would come with you if they would allow me. A father should protect his daughters."

"You have. I was the happiest child to ever play on the green lawns of Futhark. Now the responsibility has passed to another the same as if I had married."

"I know. Every father knows when he has daughters, he'll lose them to a husband one day. I only wanted more time. And I wanted to know my girls would be safe when I gave their hands to another."

"He's a good man."

"A man I don't know at all."

Sabell had nothing to say to that. There was no time for her father to get to know Cage.

"You know his family," Leesa said. "They're good people."

Sir Merlin nodded.

The silence returned, but it seemed not so sad and hopeless. Sabell was glad they had some of that, though she had little for herself. They kept their hands clasped together for a long while. A knock on the door startled them.

Marshal Mezzin had been standing watch outside. "My pardons, Mistress, but I must remind you of the time."

Sabell nodded and rose from the table. They all shared a long hug. Leesa cried silent tears, and her father's arms shook with his restrained emotions. She couldn't have survived if he'd cried also. She held her own tears at bay and didn't look back as she walked out the door. She didn't have the courage.

She hoped her sister captured Sir Maton and gave

their father lots of grandchildren. Perhaps then he would move past the sorrow of losing his eldest child.

Sweat beaded on Sabell's brow as she directed a thread of magic toward the spells she'd drawn on Cage. He danced and spun in the middle of the pit. Other Marshals surrounded him as they followed Bachus's directions for their attacks.

Sweat also gleamed on Cage's bare torso as the afternoon sun warmed the training yard. Though they had worked for hours, the moisture on Cage's skin was the only sign of his exertion. He breathed easily and moved as gracefully and quickly as he had at the start of the exercise.

Sabell kept her attention on her Marshal, but she noticed the comings and goings of many Keepers and Marshals. The Exarch and Harmon stood a few paces away, having joined the audience over an hour ago.

"Halt," Bachus ordered.

The Marshals lowered their wooden swords and sagged with either exhaustion or relief. Except for Cage. He frowned at Bachus. "What?"

Bachus didn't answer. He dismissed the other Marshals. Sabell stopped the flow of magic to Cage as the Exarch and Harmon strode forward.

"Your quick command of your talents combined

with the magic is quite impressive," Harmon said, giving a rare compliment.

Cage frowned and looked at Bachus.

Bachus shrugged. "The spells have helped him in a limited manner. There was little strangeness for him to overcome. If he'd had time to train, he might have reached his current level without the spells."

The Exarch nodded, no surprise on her face. "He's as ready as we can make him."

"I'm not sure we helped him much," Bachus said. "I wish we had more time."

"We'll make it or not. A few more days of training won't make a difference," Cage said. "Every hour we wait makes it more likely another assassin will come for Mistress Sabelline."

"I don't want to wait," Sabell said. She knew she would lose her courage if she had to face anything as terrifying as the gromf again. Once beyond the Gate, she would have no choice but to continue. Another betrayal, another demon, and she might not be able to take that first step into the darkness.

"Tomorrow," Lantana said. "One hour before sunrise. Bachus, select three Keepers and their Marshals to escort us. Instruct them to tell no one. Marshal Stone, I need to speak with you privately. After the evening meal, we'll all meet one last time in my office."

"Bachus?" Cage asked as he retrieved his shirt.

"I'll stay tight at her side," Bachus said. "Come,

Mistress Sabelline, inside please."

Sabelline didn't argue. Without Cage by her side, the outside frightened her. The world frightened her.

Jonared took a seat beside Cage across from the Exarch. The bastard gave a respectful nod to his king. An odd pain punched Jonared in the chest. He'd hated this man only days ago.

"Cage, we know you've held many things back from us," the Exarch started.

"I've given you everything you've asked, Mistress," Cage interrupted. "What more do you want of me?"

Lantana's lips curved into a tight smile. "I wish to study you, learn what thoughts circle about in secret through your head. I want to understand how you sense things the rest of us do not."

Cage looked away for a moment and then back to her. "Perhaps if you'd come to me honestly and told me of your need, your problems, I might have trusted you enough to share such things with you. Instead you used tricks and playacting to test me and pull me into your scheme."

"Surely you've learned to trust us by now," Jonared said. "You've fought the demons."

"I trust your intentions, your highness, Mistress Exarch."

Lantana again gave her tight smile. "You still question our competency."

Cage frowned. "I think you make a gallant effort, but I still think you're half blind."

"I agree," Lantana said. "Why won't you help us? You know things, things that might help us."

"Perhaps you should trust me to tell you anything I know that might assist you."

"He did suggest I keep the dogs by my side," Jonared said. It felt strange to defend Cage. "And told us to watch for a traitor."

"You could tell us more," Lantana insisted.

"What would you have me say, Mistress? Do you want to know the song the stones of this fortress sing? Shall I tell you how my sword hums a tune of death to me? Shall I tell you how your dogs love the Marshals? How the wildness of the sea calls to me? Or would you rather hear how the stench of this city sickens me, the noise that keeps me from sleep, the pain of the trees that stand between you and the evil of Kingdom's Gate?"

Jonared stared at Cage. The bastard's voice had never changed in volume, but the rawness grew with each question. The pain of a man alone in his oddities.

"I'm sorry, Cage. I would sit all day for the change of many moons to have you tell me of such things." Lantana shook her head. "I'm so afraid to lose you and too afraid not to send you."

"You've convinced me I must go, Mistress. I won't

turn back now even if you wish it."

Lantana smiled again, sad this time. "I shall miss your defiance. But I actually had another reason for asking you here with the king present."

Cage looked at Jonared. The man's gray eyes were fierce with the emotions already stirred up. It was only going to get worse.

"What do you remember of your mother, Cage?" Lantana asked, calling the bastard's attention back to her.

Cage shrugged. "I remember what she looked like, her voice, her scent, some things she told me."

"Such as?"

"Personal things."

Jonared found himself leaning forward, a tenseness invading his every muscle. "Did she say nothing of your father?"

Cage looked at him, the familiar wariness in his eyes. "Nothing. I never met him until after she left me with Lady Anadalune."

"Where did you live until that time?" Lantana pressed.

"We lived alone in the wood somewhere, I think."

"Why did she take you to Lady Anadalune?"

Cage's face darkened. "A question I've asked myself many nights, Mistress. What kind of mother abandons her small child to strangers? To a father who hated the boy from the first and who would never claim him?"

"Did your mother ever actually tell Lady Anadalune

you were Lord Thrum's child?" Jonared asked.

Cage glared at him. "I wasn't privy to all their conversations. My mother took me to the Thrum holding and spoke with Lady Anadalune. She told me to stay with the lady and walked away, never to return."

The anguish beneath the anger, the hurt of a child, surprised Jonared. Cage's fierce allegiance to his stepmother made such sense now. Suddenly the warrior before Jonared seemed only a man. A man with his own ghosts and fears. A fear that he was so flawed his own mother could not love him.

"What is the point of all these questions, Mistress?"

Lantana looked at Jonared. He gave her a nod to continue.

"A short time after King Jonared's mother died, his father took a lover. A few days ago, someone told the king that the lover bore a child. A boy child. You."

The bastard stared at the Exarch and then turned to Jonared. He didn't laugh in disbelief as Jonared had expected. "Is it possible, your highness?"

"Do you think it is, Stone?"

"I never looked on Thrum as my father, and he often claimed to have no memory of my mother. She was a beautiful woman, not easy to forget."

"None of us ever saw Jerson's lover."

"Why did he set her aside?" Cage asked, shaking his head. "Because she carried me?"

Jonared's heart went out to the other man. Stone's

shoulders slumped. He dropped his proud gaze to the floor.

"He never did," Jonared said. "She left him, broke his heart. He never looked at another woman after that as far as I know."

"Do you believe this, your highness?" Cage looked at Jonared.

Something in the tilt of his head, the starkness and loneliness in his gray eyes reminded Jonared of the man he saw in his own mirrored glass each morning. "I do. You are no brother to Lady Kristall. You are my brother."

Jonared wasn't sure what type of reaction he expected from Stone, but he couldn't have imagined it would be despair.

His bastard brother turned to Lantana. "Why do you tell me these things on the eve of my departure? You've taken my freedom, changed my soul, and likely are sending me to my death. Why did you have to take my family away also?"

Lantana looked as shocked as Jonared felt. Had he thought Stone would be thrilled to be of royal blood? To have a brother? A brother who had hated him and made no secret of it.

Stone stood up and trudged wearily toward the door. He paused with his back to them. "I trust, your majesty, you'll still honor the tournament prize to Lady Anadalune and Kristall, though I can no longer claim them as kin. Please do not tell them of this, or their honor might dictate they refuse Durnhold. Also, it comforts me to think someone would grieve at my passing."

The door closed softly behind him. Jonared stared at it, thinking he should chase the man down. And say what?

"What have we done?" Lantana whispered.

"We've caused great injury to satisfy our own curiosity," Jonared snapped at her. His anger was for not only her but himself.

A brother. Why couldn't he have known him sooner? They could have hunted together. Cage could have taught him much of weapons. They might have courted the ladies together, drunk wine, raced their horses.

Jonared dropped his face into his hands. He'd found a brother, and tomorrow he would send him into hell.

Bayard nickered like a young, eager colt as Cage held out the apple pieces for him. The warhorse lipped the fruit off his hand with barely a touch of his velvety muzzle.

"It amazes me, sir," the stable master said with a shake of his gray head. "He's like a lamb with you, but he's a vicious hellspawn with the rest of us."

"It's his training, master," Cage said. He rubbed behind the horse's ears as much for his own comfort as the animal's. Would they ever ride to battle again? Or even better, ride in peace?

"You go with Berton now, you old nag. He'll find a nice pasture for you and perhaps a few fine fillies to keep you happy while I'm gone. Don't kill anyone either."

Why did he feel like he was saying farewell to his last true friend? Because he was. His family was no longer his family if the king and the Exarch spoke true. Their surmises rang with sincerity. Damn them. He wanted no king's blood in his veins. Why had they ever come to Sulbreth and the cursed tournament?

Though she made no sound, Cage was aware of Sabell's presence. They were on their way to the last meeting with the Exarch to plan tomorrow and receive last bits of advice and encouragement. Cage wanted only to go, to leave behind the confusion and hurt. Better to be fighting for his life against foes he could see than battling the emotional pain of the past day.

Cage patted the mighty horse one last time and led Sabell from the stable. The sun was long past setting, but he could still sense the sinister ridges that glared at him from the direction of the Gate.

He appreciated that she didn't question him about his private meeting with the Exarch. Strangely, Cage thought he could trust her with the secrets of his birth. But why burden her? He saw her own sorrow and suspected her farewell to her family had been as gut-wrenching as his own. Of course, hers had really been her family.

He couldn't imagine growing up in the splendor of

the king's palace. Or having an older brother rather than a younger sister. Would King Jerson have accepted his bastard son? Given him love and a place at his side?

He couldn't think of not having Kristall skipping at his heels and throwing endless questions at him. Or not having Sir Berton to teach him of honor and loyalty. Or Anadalune showing him unconditional love. But they hadn't really been his to love. His mother had not only abandoned him but left him to live a lie. He no longer cared if he ever returned to Futhark.

Sabell walked at Cage's side, wondering at his strange mood. What had happened at his meeting with the Exarch earlier? She had thought they had grown closer, learning to trust and rely on each other. But since returning to their quarters to bathe after his meeting, Cage had been cool and remote. Similar to how he'd been when first they met.

The farewell to his horse reminded her again how different he was from other men. The great beast had acted as if it understood him, at least his mood.

As they entered the Exarch's office, Cage looked ready to face a gromf.

"Please come in and take a seat," Lantana said with a wary look at Cage.

Sabell sank into one of the chairs facing her leader, but Cage chose to stand behind her. Lantana frowned at him but said nothing. Mistress Cicely was present, surprising Sabelline. Harmon was the only other person in the room.

"I'm sure you're both feeling the sorrow of bidding your loved ones farewell." Lantana sighed. "I wish I had the magic to lift this from you so you could put it aside and think only of your journey ahead. Such is not my power. I can only counsel you to believe with all your heart that you will return to them."

Lantana gestured to Harmon. He carried a small flat package to her.

"What I give you now is a relic from the time before humans ruled Futhark. It has been mentioned in every history from the known time of the Keepers. I believe it was constructed by your race the same as your sword, Cage Stone."

Sabell frowned. So much had happened, she'd barely taken note of Cage's new sword and the speculations about its origins.

"This item is kept safe by the Exarch until such time as it is needed. Each time a Keeper and a Marshal enter Kingdom's Gate, they use this wondrous item. It has a magic about it that is beyond our understanding. The Keepers keep this device a close secret lest someone try to steal it."

Sabell leaned forward. Hope surged. A powerful

weapon, no doubt.

Lantana unfolded the thing on her desk. Sabell watched, holding her breath to see what was inside with the black cloth arranged so carefully over it.

Lantana smiled and held up a section of the cloth. It shimmered in the lamp's glow but appeared to be as black as the deepest dungeon.

Cage stepped past Sabell's chair and picked up a corner of the black material. "It's very thin."

"Yes." Lantana refolded it. "It won't take up much space in your pack. Despite that, it provides insulation from the cold and damp of the tunnel."

"And that is its magic?" Cage asked.

Sabell's heart plunged. This was the wondrous artifact? A large piece of black cloth?

"It's not its greatest wonder. In the dark of the cavern, it will hide you. No demon can see it or you. It will not only cover you, but your scent and most quiet sounds such as your breathing."

Cage touched it again. "It does all that?"

"I know you sleep less than most men, Marshal Stone, but even you must rest sometime. Nothing can find you when you're beneath this unless it trips over you. And one more thing." Lantana paused as if to dazzle them with another great wonder. "You can see through it."

Sabell understood the usefulness of such a thing, but it wasn't nearly as exciting as Lantana thought it. She wanted her bed, a last night of sleep on a soft warm mattress of down.

"It's big enough to cover you both at the same time if you sleep close together. You will also need to share your body warmth in the deeper parts of the tunnel." Lantana handed the cloth to Cage. "I don't know your current sleeping arrangements, but the two of you must learn to share a small space for safety and warmth. You have only tonight to get the feel of sleeping under the blind, as we call it."

Cage ran his hand over the blind with a soft touch as if it were fragile as well as precious.

"Now, you must try and sleep. We will rise early and reach the Gate at first light."

Cage offered Sabell a hand to rise, making her wonder if her exhaustion was so obvious. As they walked toward their room, Cage graced her with a smile unlike any she'd ever seen from him. He looked like a boy planning to invade the pantry.

"What?" Sabell couldn't help but smile in return, glad to see his earlier mood lightened.

"We've been ordered to go to bed together, Mistress. It's been a long time since I slept with a woman."

"Well, Cicely?" Lantana waited until Sabelline and

Cage took their leave before she turned to the Keeper.

Cicely shook her head. "It's so vague. I see nothing specific for either of them."

"You saw something," Lantana insisted. She regretted her impatience, but the last few days had reminded her she was an old woman.

Cicely folded her hands in her lap, her knuckles white. "There was something, but I don't understand it."

The tension in the girl and her expression sent a spasm of fear through Lantana's heart. "Speak up."

Cicely swallowed once, and then her words came with slow hesitation. "It was more a sense of . . . Cage has the strangest aura."

Sighing with her frustration, Lantana leaned back and waited.

"Cage has such a strong life force when you see him in person. I think that's why I could never see his face before in my foretellings. He shines."

"He needs to," Lantana said, trying to sound encouraging. Cicely couldn't call up foretellings at will, but she often caught images of the future when around someone. The greater the emotional stress on someone, the greater her chance to see something about them.

"I'm not sure what it means for resetting the seals, Exarch."

Lantana's breath caught and held. Cicely had never seemed so troubled in the telling of her visions, not even when she read someone's death.

"Tell me, dear. What did you see?"

Cicely shook her head. "I saw nothing. I only know that Cage and Sabelline will not return through Kingdom's Gate."

CHAPTER TWENTY-THREE

SABELL STARED AT HERSELF IN THE mirrored glass. Her hair was piled on top of her head in preparation for her bath. Her plain, common brown hair. Her green eyes were her best feature, but they were set in a regular face. She touched her skin, wondering if it was soft compared to other women's.

She let her robe fall away and examined her body in the cloudy glass. She had never attracted the attention of men, driven them to lust.

Cage's playful invitation to sleep together had only been that. A jest. He'd held her before when nightmares woke her. But there had been nothing of lust in that, not for either of them.

Sabell sank into the warm water. How long until she would have another hot bath? Never? She worked the hard bar of vanilla-scented soap into a rich lather between her hands before rubbing it across her breasts. Yes, her skin was smooth and soft.

No sounds came from the outer room, but she knew Cage was there. She trusted him to be there, between her and whatever might threaten her. She trusted him to do his best to see her through her mission, but what else was there between them?

She lifted one of her legs and began to lather it. The man she would sleep with, spend every moment with for the next few weeks, was mostly a stranger. They had trained together, studied together, taken their meals together, and fought demons side by side. But they weren't really friends. They didn't know each other. They shared no confidences, no casual conversations even.

She soaped the other leg. Was it her fault? She'd never wanted a Marshal, never cared for the type of man who loved his sword and the thrill of battle. Had she kept herself from becoming more personally involved with him? Or was it Cage who held himself aloof?

Her arms seemed too heavy to lift, but she lathered them each in turn. Cage had made no attempt to befriend anyone. Bachus, a man with no heart, was probably the person in the fortress who knew Cage best. What did that mean? Cage was most comfortable with a man who had no feelings? Did an elf feel things as a human did? Did Cage even think of himself as an elf?

Sabell scrubbed her private areas and her stomach.

Lantana lamented Cage's secrecy often. What did go through his mind? Sometimes he only seemed to be with her in body, his soul somewhere else.

The water had lost most of its warmth when she finally stood up. A soft cloth awaited her. Did Cage also?

As Sabell pulled her robe on, she came to a decision. She wouldn't go into the Gate with a stranger.

Cage stroked the blind. It was familiar to him on the same instinctual level as his new sword. He shook it out and spread it on Sabell's bed.

Other nights, Sabell's bad dreams had brought him to her side, but he'd never intentionally started the night sleeping with her. He heard occasional splashes from the bath chamber. He'd taken a quick cold soak in the Marshals' barracks while Bachus guarded Sabell.

Cage touched the spell markings around his neck. The burning lust he'd experienced when the spell first ignited had sputtered out beneath the wash of emotions since that day. Not that he didn't continue to see Sabelline as a desirable woman, but he didn't feel as if he would expire if they didn't take a tumble this very moment.

Cage sat on the edge of the bed and tugged off his boots. He set them beside his sword. Sleeping with Sabell presented a problem for him if not for her. She maintained a cool distance from him most of the time. He sensed her trust in his skills as Marshal, but she allowed no further attachment to grow.

Cage berated himself for wanting more. Was it only because of the unwanted truth the Exarch and King had forced upon him today? He was without family or friends now. He was so angry. So . . . alone.

Sabell made another sound. Was she going to spend the entire night in her bath? She should if she wished. They might both be dead tomorrow or the next day or the next. She should find comfort and enjoyment where she could.

Should he? The warmth of a welcoming woman's body would comfort him. But Sabell was the only one available. She wasn't meant for giving comfort to desperate soldiers. She was a fine lady. And how much would it complicate their journey if he made love to her this night? Was she experienced with men? He knew some of the Keepers and Marshals shared more than training and lessons.

She wasn't his to take in such a manner. Why would she welcome him? He was a bastard, a half-breed, and a stranger. If they had met in the world outside the Keeper's fortress, Sabelline's family would never have let him meet her. She wouldn't have wanted to, him with his bastard blood. Unless he was known as the king's bastard brother. That would have opened doors for him. Why had his mother denied him his father? Cage stood up and walked to the fireplace. He stoked the flames, adding another log.

He forced himself to look ahead, not back. He wouldn't spend his last night in Futhark, perhaps the last night of his life, feeling sorry for himself and cursing the mother who hadn't loved him.

At first Sabell thought he wasn't in the room. Then she saw him crouching by the fireplace, the flames reflecting in his light eyes. He rose and walked toward her.

What she saw in his eyes sent her heart to thumping. Did she want this? He stopped one small step in front of her. She looked at him, his perfect face, his slim, muscular body, his intense clear eyes, and most of all, his desire for her. Her own answered.

"Can we talk?" Why did she whisper?

He led her to the bed. The blind shimmered as Cage pushed it aside and sat on the edge of her down mattress. She sat beside him, curling one leg up on the bed so she could turn and face him. She carefully tucked her robe around her legs, trying to think of where to start.

"How was your time with your father and sister?"

She almost lied and said it was fine. "Sad. Heartbreaking."

Cage took her hand, his touch gentle and warm.

"My father wouldn't speak to me or let my sister visit me when I joined the Keepers. I didn't ask him for permission. One time when we were visiting the king, I walked out of the castle and into the fortress. I hid my magical skills from my family, so they never expected such a thing. We hadn't seen each other for years until King Jonared called him back to Sulbreth."

"It must have been lonely for you."

"Very. And now it's too late. We wasted all those years."

"I'm sure he always loved you."

"I doubted it many times, but you're right."

"And does it give you comfort now, to know he loves and worries for you?"

Sabell smiled. "It does. Is that selfish of me, to be comforted by his sorrow?"

Cage smiled back. "Probably."

"How was your mother's wedding?"

"Wonderful. Sad. Heartbreaking."

They laughed softly together.

"I could tell when I saw you earlier it didn't go so well."

Cage's smile wilted. "It was more than that."

"Your meeting with the Exarch? I thought she was making a last hour effort to squeeze some secrets out of you."

Cage's mouth quirked in a half smile. "She was. Mostly she asked about my mother."

"Lady Anadalune?"

"My blood mother."

"Why?"

Cage shrugged, his gaze wandering toward the fireplace. "Nothing of consequence."

Sabell put her hand under his chin and turned his head back to her. "Something. Tell me."

Cage shook his head and pressed his lips together. "I hardly know myself."

"What happened to your birth mother?"

Again he shrugged, as if it was of no importance, but she wasn't fooled.

"Did she die?"

"No. She left."

"Left?" She'd heard Cage and Bachus speaking of the beach they'd seen below The Edge, but she didn't think that was what Cage spoke of with the look of a lost child in his eyes.

"Left me. Gave me to Anadalune and walked away. I watched her go. She never looked back."

Sabell couldn't say anything. The pain in his voice was the confusion and despair of a small boy.

"Anadalune and Berton were the best parents I could have asked for and Kristall a wonderful sister. But why would my mother leave me like that? Why didn't she love me?" His voice broke on the last words.

Sabell moved toward him, and then his arms were around her. Suddenly all the tears she'd held back for the sake of her family flowed from her eyes. For her, for them, for Cage and his family.

Her tears were silent as she buried her face in his

shoulder. His arms tightened as he rocked her in a slow rhythm. When she lifted her head, she found his mouth near to hers. It was only natural to fit her lips to his, so easy to kiss him.

And kiss him. Thoughts of Futhark, demons, and dark tunnels fell away. Somehow she was on her back and his hard body was pressing against her. Still he kissed her, his lips a powerful magic.

He stopped and lifted his head. His eyes glittered with reflected firelight as he looked down at her. "Should we do this, Sabelline?"

"I want to."

He smiled, but the sadness lurked still. "No more than I, but that doesn't mean we should."

She ran her hands through his silky hair and then down to his shoulders. "Why not?"

"Why do you want to, Sabell? You're a fine lady."

"No. I'm a Keeper, and you're my Marshal."

Cage rolled to her side and pulled the blind over them. "That is our relationship."

"Is that all we are?" Sabell missed his warm body on top of her.

"No." The words were low and fierce. "We're a weapon, honed and sharpened like the finest blade. We're going to make it, Mistress. I promise. We'll return to our families."

The strength of his vow filled her with hope. "Yes, we will."

Cage took her hand and put it on his chest. "If we do this tonight, become lovers, it will be for comfort and forgetfulness. You'll regret it when you return."

He was wrong. She would never meet another man like him, but his honorable intentions held her tongue.

"You promise? We'll return?"

"I do."

"Hold me."

Cage pulled the blind over their heads. He settled on his side and pulled her tight against him. She still wore her robe, and he had his pants on, but their bodies combined to make a warm, cozy nest. His shoulder wasn't a soft pillow, but somehow her head fit it well.

The dread and excitement of the morrow should have kept her awake, but her eyes grew heavy. She drifted softly into sleep, where she dreamed of blue waves rolling gently onto a stretch of white sand.

Cage knew when Sabell fell asleep. He relaxed the hold he kept on his superb senses. She smelled of sweet vanilla. He could hear her heart, feel her soft breath as it brushed across his chest, feel the softness of her curves against his length.

He grimaced at the discomfort of unabated lust. Damn his honor, but he couldn't take her when she was lonely and scared. He guessed she wasn't greatly experienced. Her kisses were not those of a woman who'd romanced many men, though thoroughly arousing. Damn.

Though still tempted to wake her, Cage knew she needed her rest. As did he. The blind was comfortable and warm. It would prove useful on their journey.

Cage turned his mind from that and cleared it of all the sorrow of the day's farewells. He drifted into a light sleep and sought the beauty he'd seen with Bachus. The blue waves. The white sand. The song of the sea.

Jonared shivered in the predawn dampness. When he and his father had hunted together, he had loved this time of day. Now he feared the gray light and what it might hide. The quiet seemed more ominous than peaceful.

"Here they come," Sir Maton said softly.

Cage Stone and Sabelline walked out onto the green lawn with the Exarch and Marshal Harmon trailing along behind. If his brother—it was so strange to think of Cage so—and Sabelline dreaded the journey ahead, they hid it well. Sabell looked more confident and determined than she had since the duty came to her.

Jonared stepped forward to meet her. Memories of many childhood afternoons spent together flitted across his thoughts. She was his friend, and now his needs must send her into horrible danger and perhaps to her death.

Somehow she smiled at him as she took his offered hands. "Thank you for coming, your highness."

Jonared pulled her closer and leaned forward to kiss her cheek. "It is mine to thank you, Sabell. I would choose another for this if I could."

Sabell's smile lingered, but a sadness touched her eyes. "My fate was chosen by a power even greater than you, my king. Give me your blessing, and you'll have done all you can."

Jonared dredged up a smile, but his heart was heavy. "Blessed be your duty, Mistress. May the one true God guide your steps and add His grace to your journey."

Sabell bowed her head and moved past so he was left to face Cage Stone. Stone was dressed as Sabell had been in tight-fitting black pants and shirt. His odd sword hung on his back, and a variety of fell-looking weapons were strapped around his waist and across his chest with blackened leather harnesses. Even his boots were black.

"You'll watch out for her?" Jonared asked.

"With all I have."

Cage's words reminded Jonared somewhat of a wedding vow. The partnership between Keeper and Marshal was complex and secret.

"I would give you my blessing too, Cage." Jonared thought it might be the first time he'd called his brother by his given name. A brother. And now he must send

412

him to danger also. How could a king be so impotent?

"I would have your promise instead, your highness."

Jonared nodded. How could he deny Cage anything? "What would you ask?"

"I once feared your intentions toward my . . . toward Lady Kristall."

Jonared could only nod. His intentions had been suspect.

"I now must ask you to protect her and trust your honor to do so. Now that she is an heiress to a wealthy holding, I fear the crows will descend in the form of greedy suitors. Sir Berton will protect her well, but it's not the same as fear of my retribution. They no longer need worry about that, so I ask you ensure they must worry about you."

Jonared offered his hand. "They shall. Perhaps they'll fear me in a different way than they did you, but I pledge my word that only the most honorable of men shall even see her face. Most men fear the king's wrath. At least, I thought so until I met you."

Cage smiled. How could they smile at a time like this? "Do younger siblings ever respect their older brothers as they should? Lady Kristall has never feared me for even a moment."

Jonared blinked against a sudden burst of emotion. He had to stop them. This was his brother!

Cage reached out and took Jonared's hand. As he shook it, he squeezed almost painfully. "Thank you, my king."

Before Jonared could speak, Cage spun away and joined Sabell and the Exarch. Lantana had convinced Jonared it would be a foolish risk for him to see them all the way to the Gate. But it was too soon to say farewell!

A number of Marshals and Keepers stood patiently and alertly in the dim light. Marshal Bachus helped Cage secure a large black pack on his back and still keep his sword free. Another Marshal helped Sabelline heft a smaller pack. Then there was no reason for them to linger.

The group started off across the lawn, the escorting Marshals and Keepers surrounding the precious pair. Cage Stone didn't look back, but Sabell turned and waved once. Then the mists and shadows swallowed them.

Sabell's confident spirits lagged as they walked beneath the oaks. It was so quiet she could hear the brush of clothing against skin as they walked. The previous night had passed quickly. She'd thought she wouldn't sleep at all, but she had. Her dreams had been peaceful and beautiful, though she remembered them not at all. Cage had woken her early so she could break her fast and take her time dressing. The hot tea and warm biscuits were the last fresh food she'd likely have for a while.

Sabell adjusted her pack. It was heavy already, but in a few days she'd likely wish for the weight of more food. Cage looked over at her, a question in his eyes. She shook her head. When had she learned to read his expressions so well?

They passed from under the trees. Here the dark tarried in the shadows of the crags in front of them. Someone called a soft salute. One of the Marshals standing watch.

They all paused while Marshal Harmon spoke to a Keeper and her Marshal. When they started forward again, Sabell's heart fluttered with growing trepidation. She was actually going into Kingdom's Gate!

She fought to keep her steps strong and steady as they passed the spot where the cage boa had attacked her. Cage's hand touched her elbow with a light, brief brush. Her resolve firmed. They had first fought together against a foe on this spot. He'd saved her then. She trusted him. Trusted his promise. The Gate loomed in front of her.

Jonared leaned on the cold, stone railing. This high balcony faced Kingdom's Gate, though the cavern was hidden by distance and early morning mists. Low clouds promising rain later in the day hugged the eastern horizon and depressed the spirit of the day even more. If that was possible.

"My lady," Sir Maton greeted someone.

He caught her scent, meadow flowers he thought, and knew who it was without turning. "Good morning, Lady Kristall."

Jonared stared across the lawns. Were they at the Gate yet? Did some foul monster await them there? Where did Sabell and Cage find the courage to cross the threshold? Could they succeed? Survive?

Kristall leaned on the railing with him. Her arm brushed his for a moment. Her presence reminded him of the burden of his promise.

"Did they leave today, your highness?"

"Yes."

"Did you see them off?"

"I did," Jonared answered, speaking as quietly as she did.

The silence stretched, hanging between them as heavy as the moist air. Even the birds were silent this dreaded morn.

"My brother is the most fiercesome fighter."

"In all my kingdom," Jonared agreed, but to himself he said, "my brother."

"He can slay anything that might . . ."

"If anyone can, it would be your brother," Jonared said when her words ended in a choked sound.

"Will they, or even can they make it?"

Jonared couldn't answer. He wouldn't lie to this woman entrusted to him by his brother. Instead he put his arm around her delicate shoulders and pulled her tight against his side. There was nothing of lust or flirtation in the gesture.

Together they watched the day arrive and thought of the two who walked in the dark. Jonared was sure Kristall worried most about the man she thought of as her brother. As king, Jonared tried to push aside personal dread for Cage and Sabell and consider only the thousands of his people who would suffer if the two failed.

Cage could smell the fear of the Keepers and Marshals escorting them. The Exarch's fear was different. Her anxiety was deeper than the prospect of a demon springing from the shadows. She was frightened of failure. Their failure.

He touched Sabell when they passed the tortured ground where they had slain the cave boa. Her hesitation was so slight no one noticed but him. She should have married the king. Sabell was so strong, more than he. What a queen she would have been!

The malicious air that surrounded the cavern pulled Cage from his pleasant thoughts. He put them away for now and perhaps forever.

No solid presence of evil lurked nearby. The dark maw of the cave itself resembled some heinous beast. And they intended to walk right down into its gullet.

Lantana wished for wise words of hope and fortitude. Sabell and Cage faced her, their black attire blending into the dark rocks behind them in a disconcerting way. She would find the strong words, but she actually wished to hug them and cry some tears.

"I have every faith in the two of you. Remember subterfuge is your hope. Worry not about the beasts that pass you by and come our way. We'll deal with them, and your return passage will be safer."

Sabell nodded, but Cage raised an eyebrow.

Lantana lifted her chin and wondered how she would live with herself after this day. Cicely had said they wouldn't return through the Gate, but Lantana would send them anyway and hope they reset the seals before they died. She looked them in the eye as she bid them to go to their deaths.

"Go now with all our hopes and blessings. There's no one I would trust more with the existence of Futhark." She kissed Sabell on the cheek, but Cage stepped back so that she only took his hand.

Bachus and Cage grasped each other by the wrists in the manner of swordsmen but said no words. Cage took the lead and strode with soundless steps to Kingdom's Gate.

Sabell looked over her shoulder, not at anyone but at

the sky. The first drops of a light rain pinged down on the gravel. Cage pulled a short, wide sword from his harness and stepped into the dark. In the space of a blink, Sabell followed him. They were gone. Gone into the dark and the hell that waited for them.

THE CLOCKWORK MAN

WILLIAM JABLONSKY

Karl Gruber wasn't an ordinary German clockmaker. And it wasn't an ordinary night in 1893 when his unique creation, a sweet spirit name Ernst, came into the world. Fashioned of cogs and wheels and nickel, this inanimate object had no beating heart. He ticked . . . like a clock. Yet somehow Karl gave his fantastic man the gift of life.

On the amazing pages of a diary, Ernst records the events of his time-keeping existence. With mortal sensitivity, he lives with enthusiasm and passion, feeling, thinking . . . even loving. This piece of clockwork is alive. Some might call him a piece of work with his shimmering blue eyes. Within his mechanical soul is a sterling personality that far exceeds the average human being.

Then a dire series of events puts this automated man out of action for over one hundred years, plunging him into a dormant state of despair. He wakes in the twenty-first century, facing a dangerous, unfamiliar civilization. Ernst has a new purpose. He cannot stand by and watch as innocent people are intimidated, endangered, and harmed. The Clockwork Man does not comprehend apathy. Apathy is a human frailty.

As long as Ernst can rewind, he will live in the shadows of the city, shunning materialistic society and avoiding the capture that threatens to reduce him to a museum-quality piece of machinery. Another urban legend has been born . . .

ISBN# 978-160542099-8

Mass Market Paperback/Science Fiction

US $7.95 / CDN $8.95

SEPTEMBER 2010

May Earth Rise

HOLLY TAYLOR

The Y Dawnus are known as the Gifted. These irreplaceable members of High King Arthur's early medieval society live in a mysterious land in 500 A.D. The Dreamers, the Dewin, the Druids, and the Bards, these chosen ones are his talented pillars. Without them his empire cannot survive. When they are taken captive by the Coranians in a battle for Kymru, the fate of the world hangs in the balance.

In this Fourth Book of the Dreamer's Cycle, cruel deprivation and a full-scale conflict bring the Y Dawnus to the brink of annihilation. Confronting his mortal enemy, Havgan the Warleader, Arthur and his forces must fight a formidable opponent backed by menacing powers that threaten to end their magical, elite kingdom.

Loyal to King Arthur, Gwydion, the Dreamer of Kymru, must contemplate the loss of Rhiannon, former heir to the Ardewin. She alone is the love of his soul. If he fails, he will never see her again. A daring escapade against the Coranians threatens to separate them forever.

In a treacherous realm where captives are collared and sacrificed, where ruthless territorial boundaries are drawn and enforced, where death by poisoning and torture are the norm, the highest morals are at stake in love and in hate. Only the strongest survive in the pursuit of freedom. And only the deepest passion will drive away the evil that lurks in a mystical land of fragile kingdoms, powerful warleaders, and ancient magic.

ISBN# 978-193383657-7

Trade Paperback/Fantasy

US $15.95 / CDN $17.95

NOVEMBER 2009

www.dreamers-cycle.com

Garden of the Moon

Elizabeth Sinclair

In the year 1850, Sara Wade is a single woman living with her parents.

But Sara isn't just any woman. Sara has an extraordinary gift: She speaks with ghosts.

Ashamed of her daughter's "affliction," Patricia Wade sends Sara away to live alone at Harrogate Plantation, bequeathed to Sara by her adored grandmother. Set among towering, ancient oak trees and a garden so lush and beautiful it rivals Eden itself, Harrogate represents a haven for Sara—a place to escape where she won't be scrutinized and reprimanded for every move she makes.

But Harrogate holds more than Sara's freedom. Within Harrogate's borders abide two ghosts: one who is determined to win her heart, and another who will stop at nothing to ensure that never happens.

Destiny awaits in the Garden of the Moon.

ISBN# 978-193383698-0

Mass Market Paperback/Paranormal Romance

US $7.95 / CDN $8.95

DECEMBER 2009

www.elizabethsinclair.com

The Piaras Legacy

Scott Gamboe

Long ago, so the legends say, the Necromancer Volnor invaded the continent of Pelacia. His legions of undead soldiers ravaged the land unchecked, until the three nations united and pushed their evil foes back into the Desert of Malator.

But that was centuries ago, and few people still believe the tale. Other, more worldly matters occupy their time, such as recent attacks by renegade Kobolds. But Elac, an Elf who makes his way as a merchant, is too concerned with his business affairs to become involved in international politics. Until a marauding band of Kobolds attacks Elac's caravan and he finds himself running for his life.

Befriended by an Elven warrior named Rilen, he travels to Unity, the seat of power on the Pelacian continent. There he is joined by a diverse group of companions, and he sets out on an epic quest to solve the riddle of his heritage and save the land from the growing evil that threatens to engulf it.

ISBN# 978-193383625-6

Trade Paperback/Fantasy

US $15.95 / CDN $17.95

Available Now

www.scottgamboe.net

R. GARLAND GRAY

FAERY FAITH SERIES

PREDESTINED

ISBN# 978-193281552-8

Mass Market Paperback / Romantic Fantasy

US $6.99 / CDN $9.99

AVAILABLE NOW

Rights Sold: Thai

FEY BORN

ISBN# 978-193281582-5

Mass Market Paperback / Romantic Fantasy

US $6.99 / CDN $9.99

AVAILABLE NOW

WHITE FELLS

ISBN# 978-193383619-5

Mass Market Paperback / Romantic Fantasy

US $7.95 / CDN $9.95

AVAILABLE NOW

www.rgarlandgray.com

Be in the know on the latest
Medallion Press news by becoming a
Medallion Press Insider!

<u>As an Insider you'll receive:</u>

• Our FREE expanded monthly newsletter,
giving you more insight into Medallion Press

• Advanced press releases and breaking news

• Greater access to all your favorite
Medallion authors

Joining is easy. Just visit our Web site at
<u>www.medallionpress.com</u> and click on the
Medallion Press Insider tab.

m e d a l l i o n p r e s s . c o m

Want to know what's going on with
your favorite author or what new releases
are coming from Medallion Press?

Now you can receive breaking news,
updates, and more from Medallion Press
straight to your cell phone, e-mail, instant
messenger, or Facebook!

twitter

Sign up now at www.twitter.com/MedallionPress
to stay on top of all the happenings in and
around Medallion Press.

For more information
about other great titles from
Medallion Press, visit

medallionpress.com